S R Condor is an award-winning
as *RSVP* (about a garden party fr
toxic masculinity and hairdressing
is compelled by a terrible childh
Squad is a Cliffstaple Mystery and

The author lives in Whitsta[illegible]
rescue tabby cat.

Find out more at srcondor.com.

Also by S R Condor

Chris On A Bike

CHRIS
AND THE
VICE SQUAD

A CLIFFSTAPLE MYSTERY

S R Condor

FYNLEY

Published in 2025 by Fynley Publishing

ISBN 978-1-7393285-2-8 (paperback)
Also available as an ebook

Page design and typesetting by SilverWood Books
www.silverwoodbooks.co.uk

To all those who answered my question:
'Is a squirrel funnier than a badger?'

Prologue

The woman lowered herself down over the rock and picked her way through the seaweed-carpeted waves towards the shore. The rough stones beneath her feet gave way to fine sand, so she slipped off her trainers and carried them, feeling the wet grains ooze between her toes. Her drenched shirt clung to her arms and shoulders, a refreshing antidote to the heat of the afternoon sun.

Behind her, the rotten spars of a long-abandoned jetty rose out of the water like a dinosaur's ribcage, and beyond that was the wreck, shifting as each new surge lifted it and then dumped it back on the seabed. There was a crack of splintering wood and the ship's figurehead detached from the prow and crashed into the water.

Ahead on the beach she could see rows of dunes fringed with tufts of wild grass. A scream made her flinch as a gull swooped overhead, its wings causing a rush of air that stirred the damp lock of hair that had fallen over her eyes. Then the sky was filled with a cacophony of herring gulls and terns manoeuvring and jockeying like extras from a Hitchcock movie.

'Hi! Wait a minute! I got caught up in all this kelp,' a wheezy voice behind her rasped. 'We're all safe. I counted them out and I've counted them back.'

She pressed forwards. 'Can you get a signal?' the owner of the voice asked. 'Only I've cracked my specs and can't see a damned thing.'

A figure emerged from the dunes no more than twenty metres to the woman's right. He was completely naked. Another figure appeared, then another – six… nine… no, at least a dozen men and women of all ages, all naked and all waving and pointing in astonishment.

Natives. Chris hoped they were friendly.

Part One

One

Eric's face was puce with exertion, the vein on his temple pulsing like an overstuffed chipolata. 'See? You've gotta keep rubbing it. A slow, circular motion is best – like this. That's right. Now start to pick up the pace. Good. Good.'

'I'm worried about using too much oil,' said Chris nervously.

'You can't use too much. Keep applying the Danish until it brings it out in all its glory.'

Christine Heron was finding it difficult to share Eric's passion for the beauty of wood, but as he was kindly helping her polish a plank of walnut, it felt churlish to titter at his terminology. Eric, however, was oblivious to any such childishness. He was capable of having earnest conversations about tongue and groove, studs and counter-sunk screws without even a hint of a smile crossing his pasty, liver-spotted features. Chris wondered whether this was true of all occupations and serious hobbies, that habituation bred immunity to innuendo. Did firemen never giggle about 'getting the hose out' and could sailors always keep a straight face when 'shining the porthole'?

'Don't let it drip down the side. Mop it up before it stains,' Eric added with gravitas.

Thankfully, Chris was rescued from this *Carry On* by a cry of 'Tea's up!' and she joined the shambling procession towards an awning where a large table groaned under the weight of beverages, cake and tins of cheap biscuits.

As she sipped on a mug of lukewarm stewed tea and nibbled on a tasteless sugary coconut cookie, Chris surveyed her fellow woodworkers, who were huddled together like penguins seeking protection from the March wind. They were all members of Chisellers' Cabin, sited in one corner of the Cliffstaple Community Garden, where volunteers enthusiastically raised cabbages, carrots and artichokes and then tried to offload them at premium prices on unwary passers-by. The Cabin was a workshop, akin to a large garden shed, that contained four two-person workbenches. Racks of hand drills, screwdrivers, saws and hammers decorated the walls. In pride of place was a mounted sign with letters burnt into the wooden surface: 'Don't Forget To Clean Your Tool After Use'.

Outside, there were four more workbenches plus a couple of extravagant pedal-driven devices: foot-powered lathes that would not have looked out of place in one of the Spanish Inquisition's top-rated torture dungeons. Power tools were frowned upon at the Cabin; this was a facility for the promotion of traditional skills, to prevent the extinction of hand-planing, inlaying and whittling in the computer-drawn, machine-made, flat-packed modern world. The real purpose of Chisellers' Cabin (and many like it throughout the country) was to combat social isolation, particularly amongst older men. The practicality and creativity of woodworking in a supportive group was a positive contribution to their wellbeing. They could feel valued as productive members of society and get a handmade bird box into the bargain.

Chris, of course, was not an older man; she was a sixty-year-old woman. When it came to social isolation, she was happy to plead guilty as charged, but that was largely by choice rather than circumstance. As for mental health, her self-evaluation said 'surprisingly sane'. Sure, she shared her house with a mannequin named Grayson as well as her cats, Aitken and Waterman, but that wasn't mad, just good old-fashioned British eccentricity. She had once, very briefly, dated a guy who kept a life-sized cardboard cut-out of Danny DeVito in his bedroom. Chris was certainly less eccentric than that.

'It's OK, Mum,' her daughter had reassured her in their weekly Zoom call between Cliffstaple and Melbourne. 'I think your various weirdnesses are in perfect harmony, and Mason and Jason think that having an off-the-wall gran is the coolest thing ever!' The less positive view of ex-husband Simon was that Chris was 'bat-shit crazy', but as he was in the running for the 'Most Mind-Crushingly Dull Person in Britain' award, she took his view of her sanity with a catering-sized pinch of salt.

Chris was not the only female Cabin member, and she gave a wave to Libby and Paulette, who were sitting on the far side of the refreshments table, perched uncomfortably on a tree trunk that had been fashioned into a rustic bench. Libby and Paulette were in their forties and, Chris assumed, a couple – well, they had matching dungarees. They were currently teasing Eric about the quality of the biscuits and, going by the increasingly heated nature of the debate, Eric was falling for their trolling hook, line and sinker. Eric ran the Cabin with the kind of humourless but competent efficiency typical of someone who had retired from a middle-management career and couldn't cope without having *something* to be in charge of. To his credit, he was a patient teacher, and in the last few weeks Chris had learnt how to hold a saw properly, how to adjust the blade depth of a wood plane and, less usefully, how to make a dovetail joint.

'You've been going to the discount supermarket again, haven't you, Eric?' accused Libby, waving an oaty biscuit in his face.

'These aren't proper Hobnobs, are they? They're fake!' added Paulette, joining in the fun.

'I think they're very tasty,' protested Eric, 'and if I'm going to keep subs at £3 a session, economies have to be made.'

'That's as maybe, Eric, but you wouldn't scrimp on tools or timber, would you? Quality over quantity, don't you agree, Chris?' said Libby, trying to recruit another collaborator.

Chris's instinct was always to side with the underdog, however deserving they were of their status. 'We're not short of choice. There's that delicious-looking cake, for example,' she said, pointing to a large block of dark fruitcake so dense it seemed to be sucking in daylight.

'That's my wife's Dundee cake, an old family recipe. Shall I cut you a slice, Christine?' said Eric, reaching for a carving knife.

Chris shook her head sorrowfully. 'Nut allergy,' she said, storing the lie to ensure future consistency. 'One bite and I'd swell up like a flatulent manatee. What about you, Martin?'

Martin, a dishevelled man of indeterminate age, but probably mid-fifties, didn't respond to Chris's effort to include him in the discussion. He sat hunched, head down, his ragged white-man's dreadlocks hiding his face. With a Crocodile Dundee-esque knife he was sharpening a pencil so furiously that within minutes only a stub would remain.

'You'll be lucky to get an answer out of Martin,' observed Eric rather unkindly. 'Reckon he's taken a vow of silence. Probably become one of them Baptist monks.'

'If he wants to be silent, that's… cool. Too many folk think they have to speak when they have nothing to… say,' said Felix, an angular guy with a voice like Bob Marley gargling gravel that, for some as yet undiagnosed reason, sent a delicious tremor down Chris's spine. He was perched on a stool perusing *What Lathe?* magazine.

'It's good cake,' observed Jethro. Chris liked Jethro; he was an amiable, accident-prone chap who could have been any age between eighty and a hundred and twenty. 'Too many cherries though.' And, as if to demonstrate his point, he extracted a glacé cherry from his slab of cake and flicked it so it rebounded off Eric's elbow and landed in Martin's lap. Martin brushed the intruding cherry away and continued to hone his pencil to a lethal point.

Chris glanced round at the group. This did not constitute the entire membership of Chisellers' Cabin, but they were the ones that Chris had taken the effort to get to know over the last four weeks. There were other regulars. Sharing a bench a little away from the table were three men in their sixties with grey hair and glasses who were indistinguishable from each other in looks and personality. Chris had established that at least one of them was called Dave, but she wasn't sure which.

It was surreal company that Chris was keeping for three hours every Thursday morning, but where else could a girl get one-to-one woodwork tuition for the equivalent of a pound an hour? These were not people she intended to add to her admittedly short list of friends; these were purely practical relationships, so she could learn a new skill. Chris was from a generation when girls were taught domestic science whilst boys were given an array of lethal weaponry and taught woodwork and metalwork instead. Chris had not once felt the urge in the last forty-plus years to make rough puff pastry from scratch – life was too short for that – but the ability to mend a wobbly chair, build a boot rack or fix a sticky door? That was proper knowledge.

Not that most of the members of Chisellers' Cabin appeared to be that interested in the practical application of their art. Sure, Libby and Paulette were crafting a magnificent bench seat with hand-spindled support rods, and Martin was intent on constructing something that might have been a life-size replica of a Galapagoan giant tortoise out of willow branches, but the older men seemed happy to spend their twilight years manufacturing wooden toys. You couldn't enter the Cabin without tripping over a duck on wheels, a wooden steamship or an over-ambitious doll's house. If Mason and Jason were any guide, Chris doubted these lovingly fashioned gifts would be received with as much enthusiasm as a new smartphone, games console or hand-crafted bank transfer.

If any of her fellow Cabin-dwellers had asked Chris why she was there, sawing, planing and treating a walnut plank, she had an enigmatic response prepared: 'It's Charles Dickens's fault!' Unfortunately, no one had.

Two

If we track back through our lives, thought Chris as she set to work with the saw, there are always crossroads at which decisions that seemed minuscule at the time went on to have effects more far-reaching than we could possibly have imagined – what chaos theory termed 'the butterfly effect'. Incidentally, *Chaos Theory* was going to be the title of her autobiography.

Twelve months ago she'd decided to go for a bike ride rather than spend a more profitable hour proofreading 'Time and Tide: The Projected Effect of Climate Change on Water Sports'. The subsequent close encounter with a speeding ice cream van had left her with an artificial hip and a reputation for crime-fighting.

And then, just six weeks ago, her apparently innocuous decision to venture back into her Pit of Despair had turned out to be another crossroads moment with unexpected consequences. Daughter Chloe had long been encouraging Chris to pursue other interests, to widen her circle of friends. Her blog, *Chris on a Bike – Mapping the Hidden Pathways of Kent*, had pretty much kept her engaged, off the streets and out of harm's way. However, the hidden pathways had by now reached saturation point or were so hidden or inaccessible that Chris was struggling to generate fresh content. Perhaps she should go back to painting again. She had dabbled with art the previous summer and she was sure that somewhere within the chaotic depths of the Pit of Despair there was a set of Japanese pastels and an unwatched DVD of *Capturing English Landscapes for Beginners*.

The Pit of Despair was Chris's affectionate name for her spare room, aka Chloe's old bedroom, in which she stored her life's detritus.

By 'store' Chris really meant 'throw in haphazardly and forget'. She didn't find the Japanese pastels or the DVD, but she did rediscover a cardboard box filled with *The Collected Works of Charles Dickens*, bound in faux red leather with gold trim. These had belonged to her parents, a legacy from clearing their house ten years ago, after her mother's death, the point at which Chris had become a fifty-year-old orphan. The rest of the house contents had been distributed to charity shops or the council recycling centre, with the exception of three china Alsatians, one of which lived in Melbourne with Chloe, one that sat on her mantelpiece and a third that had been smashed into a million pieces by a hyperactive cat chasing a ping-pong ball. As the Dickens books still carried the smell of her childhood home and were unsmashable, she had kept them. For the past ten years they had lain in two cardboard boxes that had previously held twenty-four bottles of a rather cheeky white Rioja.

Chris now decided that Charles Dickens should, once more, be brought into the light. The books' redemption came thanks to a suspiciously damp-looking patch behind the bookshelves in the living room. A normal, non-crazy person would have had the patch investigated by a skilled tradesperson and rectified. Chris preferred to hide it and hope it would somehow disappear. That out-of-sight tactic had served her very well to date.

The books filled the middle shelf and obscured the damp patch rather neatly. Quite how any Victorian had managed to write so much given the average life expectancy back then was beyond her. Charles probably had someone else change his duvet cover for a start. To Chris's mind (and, as a freelance proofreader, she felt she had some expertise in the matter), Dickens was unsurpassed in his use of language, his vivid characterisations and his razor-sharp portrayal of the human condition. Of course, she had no intention of actually reading the books. Nobody read faux-leather-bound hardback books, did they? They were purely decorative, virtue-signalling interior design. They said to visitors: 'Here lives an intelligent, cultured woman who, at any time, could reach for classic literature from her well-stocked shelves.' Chris had read *Great Expectations* at school and the first ten pages of *Hard Times* and that had been enough to tell her that there was no great work of English fiction that wasn't better consumed as an eight-part TV adaptation.

Two weeks after Charles Dickens had taken his rightful place on the sitting room wall, Chris was sitting on the sofa, bookended by Aitken and Waterman, watching *Britain's Funniest Animals* on TV. This was not for entertainment but for education. Much as Chris loved her cats, they had yet to provide her with an alternative income stream by performing any charming, wacky or hilarious stunts. They couldn't play the piano or meow the national anthem, and neither of them resembled Hitler, so Chris thought that watching the programme together might give them a few tips. About halfway through a not terribly funny clip featuring a cockatoo with stress-related issues, there was an ominous creak from the corner of the room followed by the sound of thunder as the thirty-six volumes of novels, short stories and sketches fell to the ground in a flurry of paper, faux leather, splintered wood and plaster dust. Aitken and Waterman leapt a full metre into the air, circled the room twice and hurtled through the door to safety. If Chris had had her phone camera readied, she would finally have captured footage worthy of submitting to *Britain's Funniest Animals*.

Chris then made two mistakes. The first was to phone ex-husband Simon to ask if he had the number of a local handyman. His immediate response was to hare round to check the damage himself. As she explained to Simon (through the letterbox), although they had been relatively amicably divorced thirty years ago, this did not give him carte blanche to revel in his ex-wife's every disaster and misadventure. Her second mistake was to contact a local tradesman whose main skill seemed to be the ability to suck in his breath through his teeth to make that awful 'this'll cost ya' sound. As he muttered something about 'horsehair plaster' and 'subsiding brickwork', Chris's mind was picturing a *Children in Need* totaliser, racking up unfeasible costs. Her saviour came in the unlikely form of her neighbour and buddy Next-Door Nick. Over a couple of glasses of Sauvignon Blanc, Next-Door Nick opined that the hole in the wall was nothing that 'a bit of filler' couldn't sort, and as for the shelf, which now lay in three pieces, that was something Chris could easily 'knock up' herself. 'I've got an old wooden kitchen work surface you can have,' he added helpfully.

And why wouldn't Chris take the home renovation advice of a former sociology lecturer over that of a qualified tradesman? It was also Nick who had pointed her in the direction of Chisellers' Cabin. Apparently, he had a mate (definitely not him) who had semi-retired and had been feeling depressed (still definitely not him) and had found the practical companionship of the Cabin had got him through a difficult stage in his life (absolutely not him).

So that was the backstory, why she was standing at a workbench in a garden oasis in the centre of the seaside town of Cliffstaple with people she had known for just four weeks.

The first rule of the Cabin's health and safety guidance was: 'Concentrate on the job'. If Chris had been concentrating rather than reminiscing about the previous year, she'd have spotted the knot in the wood that caused her saw to jolt and jump and slice into her hand. She stared in stunned silence as the scratch above her thumb started to widen. It wasn't painful, but she started to feel giddy at the sight of blood – particularly as it was her own blood. This is embarrassing, thought Chris. I've had a hip replacement operation and three broken ribs, and, admittedly thirty-one years ago now, I've endured fourteen hours of labour. I can't possibly faint over a teensy-weensy saw cut.

From somewhere she heard Eric's voice shout, 'Medic!'

As Chris's legs wobbled, Martin was there, holding her injured hand by the wrist and gently applying a clean handkerchief to the wound. 'It's OK,' he said in a reassuringly soft voice. 'It's not too deep, barely worth stitches.'

From the Cabin's first aid kit Martin extracted a sterile pad and a gauze bandage and skilfully wrapped Chris's hand. She tested it by clenching her fist – it was tight enough to staunch the blood flow but still had flexibility so that her bike riding wouldn't be affected.

'I'm used to battle scars,' she joked once she had recovered her composure.

'We all have them,' replied Martin. 'Some are deeper than others.'

Eric appeared, accident report form at the ready, disappointed that a good crisis had already been averted. 'If that mishap has been dealt with, can I suggest we all convene at the tea point?'

*

Eric stood and rapped a battered silver teapot with a Phillips screwdriver. 'If I may interrupt your refreshments, I've got a Chisellers' announcement!'

'You're pregnant?' said Jethro, expertly flicking a glacé cherry so that it ricocheted off the teapot with a ping.

'You're upgrading the biscuits?' said Libby hopefully.

Eric was unamused. 'If you could rein in the levity for five minutes. I've been thinking…'

Paulette and Felix spontaneously applauded.

'… that when I set up the Cabin five years ago…'

Chris fancied she heard a snort of derision from Martin, but when she turned in his direction he had his head down, his hands busy sharpening his pencil.

Eric was oblivious to any signs of rebellion and pushed his glasses further up the bridge of his nose. '… my concept was that fraternity is more powerful than individualism.'

Jethro looked as though he was about to make a questioning intervention, but Libby patted him on the arm and, grinning, he returned his attention to his slice of Dundee cake.

'I am proud of what I have achieved, what we have all achieved in that time. I have seen your woodworking skills improve, your confidence increase, and we've seen some truly impressive builds.'

'But…' anticipated Libby.

'But we've all become increasingly isolated, wrapped up in our individual projects. I fear that the spirit of strength through collectivism is declining.'

'That sounds a bit communist, Eric,' Paulette said, her tongue firmly wedged in her cheek. 'I'm not sure how that will be received at Cliffstaple Golf Club.'

'Nothing communist about working together. It's what embodies the British spirit,' Eric replied.

'Oh for God's sake, get to the... point, Eric, man! My varnish will have congealed by the time you've... finished!' growled Felix, causing another spinal tremor in Chris. That man could have made the shipping forecast sound sexy.

'So I was thinking' – Eric glared – 'that we should come up with a joint project, something we can all work on together, something that will say to the Cliffstaple community: "This is what can be achieved with teamwork."'

Chris shifted uncomfortably on her stool. This teamwork idea sounded too much like enforced jollity for her tastes. Proofreading was like sheep farming, a necessarily solitary profession.

'I was thinking we could build something for the Festival of Fish or Cliffstaple Harbour Day,' Eric continued.

'A giant wooden winkle.'

'Thank you, Jethro. Any thoughts, Martin?' said Eric, refusing to rise to the bait.

There was an awkward silence, which seemed to grow deafening as the seconds ticked by.

'So, what's that you're working on, Martin?'

'Just a project, something personal,' Martin muttered and he headed back towards the workshop area.

Chris was tempted to follow him so she could thank him properly for having tended to her wound, but his body language suggested that he didn't desire company.

'What *is* that he's building?' said Paulette, looking over at Martin, who had recommenced construction in the open area outside the hut.

'It looks like some sort of bivouac, a wicker igloo,' said Eric.

'Bit small for that,' said Libby, 'unless it's for a child.'

'A wicker Wendy house?' Paulette pondered. 'Could be.'

Chris was about to add her giant tortoise theory to the discussion when, thankfully, Felix intervened. 'It's a... coracle.'

'Ooh, I 'ad one of those,' said Jethro. ''Ad to get it lanced.'

'A coracle's a prehistoric boat, a kind of circular one-person canoe,' explained Chris before Jethro had the chance to share any more of his medical history.

'A boat?' exclaimed Eric excitedly. 'That'd be perfect for Harbour Day. Perhaps we could all help Martin with that?'

'I'm pretty sure Martin doesn't want any help,' said Felix. 'Besides, he told me it's nearly ready.'

'It's nice to hear that Martin talks to someone,' said Eric. 'Perhaps we could all build coracles and race them against each other?'

'That's not very collaborative,' remarked Libby.

'And its overly competitive,' added Paulette.

'And if you think I'm going to sea in one of them cora-thingys, you've been sniffing too much wood glue,' said Jethro, rising slowly and shuffling back to the workshop area.

Eric looked visibly crestfallen as the rest of the Cabineers rose from their seats. 'Well, you come up with a better idea, then.'

'Why don't we all think about it?' said Chris, adopting the role of peacemaker. 'Then we can discuss it again next week.'

Paulette and Felix both chorused their agreement, which seemed to placate Eric. Libby, however, was looking suspiciously at the biscuits wrapper. 'Hibnibs? Hibnibs, Eric? I told you these were knock-off Hobnobs!'

Three

Chisellers' Cabin was just a five-minute ride from home on Chris's e-bike, Rod (short for RamRod, its brand name). A further advantage of spending every Thursday morning there was that, once out of the house and away from her laptop, Chris could get a decent ride in and still be back home in time to give two starving cats a late lunch.

After Eric had called the meeting to a close, she unlocked her bike from its mooring alongside a shipping container filled with gardening equipment, a stash of rusty paint tins and pieces of wood that would come in handy – one day. From here she could cycle straight down to the seafront. It was still early spring, so the mad influx of visitors that used the Easter holidays as a starting gun had not yet materialised and children were still securely caged behind school gates.

A sea breeze brought a blush to Chris's cheeks and encouraged her to keep her pace going. She couldn't go top speed along the seafront, the perils of disobedient dogs and inattentive, phone-obsessed, buggy-propelling mothers were too great, but she could still give her muscles a good workout. At the Hotel Parador on the seafront, half a dozen people were braving the spring chill and sipping coffees at outside tables. Someone waved as Chris passed, but she wasn't sure if it was directed at her. She had responded too many times to waves, smiles and cheery 'Hellos' that had actually been intended for someone else, and had once nearly hugged a complete stranger who had approached her with arms outstretched before realising, at the last minute, that the object of their affection was a playful labradoodle. Since then, Chris had opted to always give a non-committal nod unless she was absolutely sure she knew the person. Besides, in her cycling getup of yellow helmet, blue shades and black thermal snood she was practically unidentifiable, and that anonymity suited her very well indeed.

Past the hotel and the path cleared, allowing her to pick up the pace. On her left was the lifeguard station, a small wooden shack on stilts. A seagull came in to land on the roof, to join another. Chris remembered seeing on a wildlife documentary that albatrosses mated for life. She had barely managed seven years with Simon. She wondered whether albatrosses still enjoyed each other's company after decades on the wing or did they, like she and Simon had, simply run out of things to talk about? She couldn't imagine seagulls exhibiting the same loyalty as albatrosses; they were just into stealing chips from unwary holidaymakers and harassing innocent e-bike riders.

As she whizzed past, Chris caught a peripheral glimpse of two yellow-and-red-clad lifeguards standing on the balcony gazing out to sea. There was something about the stance of the lifeguard on the left that caused Chris to do a double-take, but they were out of sight within seconds.

There was a pleasingly straight track ahead, which, without the obstacles of traffic or walkers, was a good opportunity to test her lung function and, more importantly, her muscular flexibility. Chris had adapted perfectly to her titanium replacement hip, but over the winter her other, organic hip had started aching, perhaps in envy of its hi-tech counterpart.

Chris reached her optimum speed, head down, maximising the aerodynamic profile of her yellow cycling helmet. Her mind drifted back to that conversation at Chisellers' Cabin: Eric's Challenge. Something they could build together for Harbour Day. Some kind of boat? Chris's only-child instinct told her to back off. Communal projects were like surprise parties, school reunions and chef's specials – to be avoided at all costs. But, then again, she liked a challenge.

She swung round a bend, leaning into the turn, Rod's tyres

gripping the concrete. She glanced up, squinting into the sunlight, to see, in the middle of the path… a bum. To be more accurate, it was the figure of a man with his back towards her, bent over, his hands touching the ground. But in that moment all of Chris's attention was focused on the briefness of the man's electric-blue running shorts, which left little room for the imagination – or, indeed, anything else. They were the kind of shorts last seen on a 1980s footballer and she was closing in on them at 28kph. Within seconds, Rod's front wheel would find an alternative parking slot between two satin-clad buttocks.

Chris slammed on the disc brakes as firmly as she dared. The back of the bike lurched sideways in a manoeuvre that six months ago would have catapulted her from the saddle and back into the Trauma and Orthopaedics Unit at Kent Coast Hospital. Practice made perfect and she'd learnt how to handle the extra weight of an e-bike in conjunction with the ruthless efficiency of disc brakes. She threw her weight in the opposite direction, and the low step-through frame enabled her to neatly hop off the bike barely a metre from the endangered arse.

The owner of the electric-blue running shorts showed barely a flicker of surprise when he stood, turned and stood nose to nose with Chris. His toothy grin suggested he was completely unaware of how close his posterior had come to being cleaved by a rubber tyre.

'Fun run?' he said.

She looked down at his feet to discover that he had been bent over writing 'CFR 1K' on the path in thick chalk letters.

Chris studied the man. He was in his late forties and had the slender frame of someone who had never accidentally eaten an entire chocolate Swiss roll in a single sitting. His satin running shorts might have looked obscene from the back but from the front they looked positively pornographic – like assorted root vegetables in a cheap carrier bag. Chris assiduously maintained eye contact from that point on.

'Fun run?' she asked, gesturing to her bicycle, as if that answered his question.

'Saturday week,' said Satin Shorts. 'All ages welcome,' he added rather unnecessarily.

'Good God, no!' Chris exclaimed, also rather unnecessarily.

For Chris, 'fun run' was the perfect example of an oxymoron. The words didn't belong together. She couldn't see the point of running. She'd tried it once and all she got was shin splints, chilblains and jogger's crotch. Chris could swim (badly) and had been known to hit a tennis ball into a low orbit, but cycling was her exercise of choice – at least with that you got somewhere quickly.

Satin Shorts persisted. 'You can register on the website,' he said, pointing to a poster pinned to the side of a beach hut which read: 'Cliffstaple Charity 5k Fun Run'.

'CFR 1K' now had a meaning – it was a waypoint for the runners. 'Tempting offer, but I think I'll pass, thank you,' said Chris, remounting her bicycle.

She had to rethink her route. She couldn't risk re-encountering those shorts on the return journey, so instead she decided to visit her unofficially adopted donkey, Tiny Barney.

Chris turned right and sped away, back across a side road and then up a gradually ascending path that skirted the town and led into a series of country roads crisscrossed by farm tracks. She had formed a bond with Tiny Barney (Chris's name for him, as she had no knowledge of any other) after discovering him while researching a new cycle route for her blog. He resided alone in a field adjacent to Hermon Hill Farm. She'd had a soft spot for donkeys ever since her parents had sponsored one at a West Country animal sanctuary (Barney the First) for her eighteenth birthday. After her parents' deaths, Chris had carried on the sponsorship until she realised she had been supporting the same retired donkey for forty years. Her only evidence of his existence was a yearly photograph and a chatty update; unless Barney the First had record-breaking longevity, the sanctuary must have been sneakily substituting donkeys. Chris was impressed by the sanctuary's chutzpah and maintained the standing order. Besides, £10 a month was a small price to pay for showing that she did *something* for charity.

Hermon Hill Farm must have farmed something originally: cherries or chickens or cobnuts. Other similar ex-farms in this area of North Kent had been converted into luxury family homes, conference venues, celebrity drying-out clinics and, in a couple of cases, likely secret lairs for Bond villains.

As the apparently sole occupant, Tiny Barney had a spacious field with a view of a pretty copse on the other side on the lane. A weathered sign identified it as a private wood, Hermon's Copse. Chris could think of nothing in the world she wanted more than her own wood – it was the only reason she continued to waste £2 a week on a lottery ticket. When she was a girl she used to make dens in her local park, under the branches of a weeping willow or within the cover of a mature rhododendron bush. She would sit there for hours, devising complex and meticulously scribed rules for a club of which she was the only member. But a whole private wood? Just imagine the sort of den she could construct there!

To Chris's dismay, there was no sign of a small tan-coloured donkey with a dark mane and a white nose. She stepped up onto the lowest rung of the rickety wooden fence to get a better view. No, no sign. The field wasn't empty though. Even worse, Tiny Barney's rightful place in the field had been supplanted by two llamas – or were they alpacas? Chris wasn't sure of the difference. These were white and stocky with short legs – like her first boyfriend in his favourite mohair jumper. She pulled out her phone and took a photo.

The as yet unidentified beasts noticed Chris's interest and approached with steady, unafraid steps. Chris got down from the fence and took two paces back. She loved all animals – well, except for crocodiles and slugs – but there was something about the attitude of these two that made her wary. They had a cocky strut that suggested they had already evicted Tiny Barney from his field and, if she didn't like that, they'd sort her out too.

As she turned to remount her bike, Chris realised that not only had Tiny Barney disappeared but so had Hermon's Copse. The frail wire fencing that was no more than a symbolic effort to deter intruders had been replaced by a white hoarding at least three metres high – an intimidating, insurmountable barrier. Chris followed the hoarding down to where the lane met and continued parallel with the main road between Cliffstaple and the neighbouring city of Becketon.

Thirty metres along the road, there was a letterbox-sized slot cut into the hoarding, presumably to provide a viewing point for the curious public. Standing on tiptoes, Chris looked through it, but her view was obscured by the side of a green portable toilet. She averted her eyes in case it was currently in use – she might not have had much of a reputation to protect, but being outed as a voyeur of construction workers' latrine usage could have pushed things too far.

Ten metres further on, she encountered two huge sheet-metal gates, heavily padlocked. Alongside the gates was a display board with an artist's impression of a Shangri-La housing estate in which attractive young families rode bicycles, pushed baby buggies, flew kites and generally embraced their privilege. The picture was accompanied by a sign: 'Coming Soon: Hermon Village – an exciting new development of affordable detached residences from Danny Figg Homes'. It was accompanied by the company logo with the tagline: 'We give a Figg about homes for your future!'

Under the sign, daubed in thick green paint, were three pieces of graffito: 'FIGHT FOR OUR NATURE!'; 'PROTECT HERMON COPSE!!'; and, more directly, with an additional exclamation mark, 'FIGG OFF!!!' There was also a stencilled tag in the same green paint that seemed to read: 'CrEW'. Chris shook her head. None of this made any sense, but she took a few pictures on her phone in any case.

The disappearance of Tiny Barney coupled with the annexing of Hermon Copse had sucked any sense of joy from this cycle ride. Chris turned Rod round and headed for home.

*

Outside 15, Sea View, a familiar figure was manoeuvring the recycling bin. Not for the first time, Chris wondered whether Next-Door Nick's bin obsession was actually a front. He seemed to be there every time she left the house and every time she returned. Perhaps, rather than the mild-mannered semi-retired sociology lecturer he claimed to be, he was actually a sleeper agent operating deep undercover as he collected information on domestic activities in a North Kent coastal town to feed back to his Chinese paymasters. Sleeper agent or not, Chris was happy to have Nick as her long-standing neighbour. He was genial, quiet and available to step in and feed her cats at a moment's notice.

'Afternoon, Chris. Good ride?'

'What's the difference between an alpaca and a llama?'

'That's not the conversation opener I was expecting. Aren't they the same thing?'

'I don't think so,' said Chris. 'Here, I took a photo.'

Nick took Chris's phone and shrugged. 'Have you looked online?'

'What? CompareTheLlama.com?'

Nick grinned. 'Sure, or you could ask the Sea View WhatsApp group.'

Chris shuddered. Nick had been trying to recruit her to the road's WhatsApp group for the last two years. She wasn't an unfriendly neighbour – she was happy to smile and say hello when passing – but having a string of messages about unwanted furniture, broadband outages, erratic bin collections and illegally parked cars littering her lovely new smartphone was not to be encouraged. Besides, she was pretty sure that the contents of her recycling bin were already the subject of local gossip, so it was safer to keep her head down.

'You see, Nick, that's the problem with modern life – there's no mystery any more. What's the fun in just answering questions with the press of a button when it's the search for truth that's most rewarding?'

Nick paused thoughtfully, as though his neighbour had just imparted a fundamental nugget of wisdom.

'Besides,' Chris continued, 'if I'd already googled the answer to the llama/alpaca conundrum, I wouldn't have had an excuse to stop and chat to you, Nick.'

Nick blushed in response, which caused Chris to hastily unlock her front door and slip into the house.

*

'So, Mum, how's it going with… what are they called again? The Vice Squad?' asked Chloe.

Chris grinned at her daughter's image on her laptop screen. It flickered slightly, but as it was being beamed from ten thousand miles away, this was still a miracle of technology. A far better use of science than pseudo-ruminant identification.

'Vice Squad? I might have to pinch that! Just one more session and my shelf will be finished and Chisellers' Cabin will be but a passing shed in the night.'

'You're not going to stick at it? I thought it was a good chance to make new friends?'

'Friends? Oh no, they're… err… mostly weird. They're all obsessed with either woodgrain or tools, and now they're proposing a joint nautical project. If I get roped into that, I'll never escape.'

'A joint project? That sounds like it could be fun. Give them a chance. Please.'

'And besides, with all the woodwork-related innuendo, it's only a matter of time before I say something inappropriate. It's not like I need any more friends. I've got plenty.'

'Like who?'

'You and Dan and Mason and Jason and Aitken and Waterman… and Nick and Zeta.'

'And Grayson?'

Chris glanced up at Grayson, who was sitting at the other side of the kitchen table dressed in his usual dark suit and white T-shirt. He now sported a pair of black Ray-Bans, which made him look like he'd stepped off the set of *Reservoir Dogs*.

'And when did you last see Zeta?' Chloe continued.

'I don't know – couple of months ago.'

'So, "plenty of friends" is actually four close relatives who live on the other side of the planet, two cats, your next-door neighbour, a shop mannequin and a police officer you haven't seen in weeks.'

Chris felt it was time to change the subject. 'So where are my square-jawed son-in-law and my impossibly photogenic grandsons?'

'Out on the ocean. He's borrowed a dinghy from a mate and is teaching them to sail.'

'Is that safe?'

'Of course. They're all excellent swimmers and will be fully life-jacketed.'

'I mean, it's Australia and… well, I've seen *Jaws 1*, *2* and *3D*.'

'There were three *Jaws* films?' asked Chloe.

'Four. And seven *Police Academy* movies.'

'Is that relevant?'

'It won me a tie-break in the Duke of Clarence pub quiz last year.'

'I'll pass on your advice to Dan and the boys – assuming they successfully evade any marauding great whites. Anyway, Mum, why don't you give Zeta a call tomorrow? Mum? Mum!'

Chris's mind had temporarily left the Zoom conversation and travelled back over that day. Two hungry cats… two seagulls on the lifeguards' hut… two llamas/alpacas in a field… the animals went in two by two…

'MUM!' shouted Chloe. 'Are you still with me?'

Chris opened her eyes and thumped the table so fiercely that her mug of tea leapt in the air and deposited its contents in Grayson's lap. 'EUREKA! I've just had a brilliant idea.'

Four

The container ship crawled across the horizon en route to either London Gateway or Tilbury Docks.

'No action?' asked Wilf.

Zeta panned the sea, from the forest of gently turning wind turbines to the edge of the Isle of Lepus, just three or four kilometres away. She refocused the binoculars on the island's strip of white sand, which looked tempting from that distance. The beach at Cliffstaple was a mixture of shingle and razor-sharp shards of discarded oyster shells – pretty, but not conducive to stretching out on and taking in some rays.

'Action?' she replied, lowering the binoculars and passing them back to her fellow lifeguard.

'Nobody in peril on the sea?'

'Nope. Lovely and quiet out there.'

'And no zombie invasion on Leper's Island?'

Zeta wasn't sure whether to correct Wilf, to explain that 'lepus' was Latin for 'hare'. She suspected the mistake was deliberate, another of Wilf's traps, the sort that born-and-bred Cliffstaplians often set for comparative newbies like her.

'No, even the undead are keeping a low profile today.'

'Shame. 'Spose we may as well shut up shop then.'

Zeta remained motionless, staring out to sea like Penelope awaiting Odysseus's return. 'You want people to be in danger?'

Wilf put his hands on the balustrade of the lifeguards' hut and stretched his hamstrings in a primitive preening gesture. 'If nobody gets into difficulties, what's the point of us lifeguards? We'd be unemployed.'

'Well, I'm a volunteer and don't need potential drownings to make myself feel valued.'

'Yeah, but you're a special police constable an' all, aren't you?' Wilf continued, untroubled by the dubious morality of his stance. 'If there's no crime, what are you going to do with your spare time? Take up knitting?'

Zeta was tempted to bite at this casual sexism, but she detected the cheeky glint in Wilf's eye just in time to stop herself. She suspected it was a glint that would make him popular with many of the female beachgoers over the coming summer.

'Besides,' said Wilf, 'I've got old Ted's record to break.'

Zeta zipped up her red-and-yellow jacket over her red one-piece swimming costume, pulled on an old pair of khaki shorts and grabbed her backpack from a hook inside the hut's door. She wasn't going to ask, wasn't going to fall into Wilf's trap. He was only twenty, six years younger than her, but he had an abundance of self-confidence that seemed to place him in an entirely separate generation. Or perhaps, Zeta pondered, it was she who was twenty-six going on sixty.

Wilf grabbed his own backpack and locked up the lifeguards' hut.

'What record?' she asked. Damn.

Wilf grinned widely; the smile of victory. 'Last summer. He rescued seven people – four on lilos, two on tractor inner tubes and a female vicar on an inflatable porpoise. This year, I intend to capture Ted's crown.'

'Ooh, that sounds like a challenge.'

'You wouldn't believe the sort of unseaworthy vessels that are launched over a great British summer. I guess "Britannia Rules the Waves" gets taken a bit too literally.'

*

Zeta unchained her racing bicycle from the side of the hut. She left her helmet hanging over the drop handlebars so as to enjoy the way the spring air caused her baby dreadlocks to fly out in her wake. Safety-first cyclist Chris would have disapproved of such recklessness in her friend.

Zeta had spotted Chris earlier that day, speeding past the hut. Or rather, she'd recognised Rod, her bicycle. Cyclists in fluorescent yellow jackets and cycling shades were fairly ubiquitous, but there weren't many bright orange e-bikes with red-trim wheels and 'RamRod' on the frame in Cliffstaple (or indeed anywhere). She'd been meaning to catch up with Chris, to phone her, suggest they meet for coffee or lunch and a laugh. Somehow life sped by faster than an orange e-bike and days became weeks became months. Her special constable duties were averaging a day a week; add a half-day for voluntary lifeguarding, a full in-box of work for her online marketing consultancy and a demanding keep-fit regime, and there simply wasn't time for something as trivial as a social life.

She glided across the high street, effectively dismounting as she reached her front door – an anonymous green door to the side of an upmarket estate agent's. She hoisted her bicycle up onto her shoulders and negotiated the narrow stairway that led to her upstairs flat. The spare bedroom had for the past year acted as a de facto office. She'd intended getting another lodger, someone to share costs, but she'd gradually absorbed all the available space. The flat itself was sparsely furnished – functionality rather than frippery. It didn't really feel like home to Zeta, but then nowhere did. She wasn't ready to settle down into domesticity and sometimes doubted she ever would be.

Priorities. First, send off the invoice to Lunge and Parry, solicitors and conveyancers, for their swanky new website that would persuade the casual browser that they were a fluffy, family-friendly, socially responsible firm and not two overweight, chain-vaping ambulance-chasers operating out of a scruffy trading estate on the outskirts of Cliffstaple. Done.

Next, update her own website to include a couple of glowing reviews from satisfied customers. She wasn't sure whether anyone looked at her site – most of her business seemed to come in by word of mouth – but appearances were important. Done.

Next, consult the diary to find a slot to catch up with Chris. *Hi Chris! How's it rolling? Ages since we caught up. Fancy lunch? I can do the day after tomorrow, or the 30th or...*

Zeta was mid-text when an email alert appeared on her computer screen. It was from Sgt Spurgeon, North Kent Constabulary. Curious.

FAO SC Jama, the email began. No *Dear Zeta* or even *Hi!* Sgt Spurgeon's management style may have lacked warmth, but Zeta had grown to appreciate that under his intimidating physique lay a man who was not exactly a pussycat but not the unneutered feral tomcat he tried to present to the world.

Thursday 09:00 Briefing Ops Room. Operation Dryad. Attendance requested if poss. Spurgeon

A week's notice for a briefing? That was strangely efficient for North Kent Police. Curiouser and curiouser.

Zeta had been the chosen one at the station, inspector's pet. But since she had turned down the opportunity to become a full-time proper copper, she'd sensed a backlash. Suddenly she was at the bottom of the roster when it came to interesting assignments. Now it was all pub-chucking-out-time patrols and crowd-management duties. The only time she had value was for corporate videos, when they needed a handy black face to wheel out in front of the camera to demonstrate North Kent Police's commitment to diversity. But this? Whatever Operation Dryad was, it sounded right up her Strasse.

She returned to her unfinished text and deleted it. It would be better to wait until she knew what the demands of Dryad were before agreeing any dates with Chris. She'd text her next Thursday evening instead.

Five

'An ark?' Eric was incredulous.

'Yes, Eric, an ark. As in Noah, Great Flood, the animals went in two by two.' Chris resisted the urge to break into song. With her voice, that was always a mistake – she even mimed at karaoke.

Eric paused, poured himself another mug of tea and looked round at the assembled woodworkers as though he was Solomon about to give judgement.

'Nice idea. I was thinking about some sort of kiddies' toy too. An ark would fit the bill. Perhaps we could carve some little wooden animals. Dave's very good with giraffes.'

'No, not a toy, Eric,' said Paulette. 'Why not a proper sailable ark? Or at least something we can float in the harbour.'

'I think it's a brilliant idea, Chris,' agreed Libby.

'But an ark?' Eric was unconvinced. 'I gave you guys a week to come up with ideas. Someone must have a more practical suggestion.'

'Perfect for Cliffstaple Harbour Day,' added Paulette.

'Nautical but nice!' Jethro had started on his second slice of the Victoria sponge made by Eric's wife.

'But an ark?' said Eric, who seemed to be stuck on repeat.

'You said you wanted a… boat,' rumbled Felix, who had moved on from *What Lathe?* magazine to *You and Your Chisel Monthly*.

'But an ark?' reiterated Eric for the third time. 'Aren't they rather big?'

'Oh, it would be a scale model,' said Chris, trying to give the impression that this was a carefully considered plan and not just an idle thought that had occurred to her during a Cliffstaple to Melbourne video call.

'How big was Noah's effort?' asked Jethro.

Libby tapped into her phone for the answer. 'According to the Bible, his ark… was three hundred cubits in length.'

'What's a… cubit?' asked Felix.

Libby consulted her phone again. 'About half a metre.'

'What's a metre?' asked Jethro.

'One hundred and fifty bleedin' metres?' exclaimed Eric, ignoring Jethro's ignorance of the metric system. 'It'd never fit in the hut!'

'I did say a scale model,' muttered Chris defensively. She was beginning to think that her first instinct – to give Chisellers' Cabin a big swerve – had been prudent after all. It was only Chloe's insistence that had made her progress the idea.

Paulette's eyes were closed as she conducted mental acrobatics. 'One to forty-seven.'

'Sorry?' Eric still looked dumbfounded.

'Scale. That gives us a length of 3.2 metres. About ten and a half feet,' she added for Jethro's benefit.

Felix was sufficiently engaged to put down his magazine. 'It's a lot of material, but I reckon we could beg, borrow and… steal.'

'Good,' said Libby. 'Those in favour of the ark…?'

All of the members present, except for Eric, raised their hands. Even, to Chris's surprise, the Three Daves, who she'd forgotten were even there, let alone paying attention to the conversation.

Eric stood, affronted. 'Only the chair can propose a vote.'

'So propose one then,' Felix demanded.

'I'll need to consult with Martin first. He is our unofficial vice-chair.'

'Where is Martin?' asked Libby.

The group glanced around and then at each other, as though Martin might be masquerading as one of the present company.

Jethro even searched under the table, in case he was hidden beneath the Victoria sponge.

'Dunno,' said Eric. 'Haven't seen him since, let's see… last Thursday.'

'He's not been at any of the other… sessions?' asked Felix.

Eric shook his head. 'Come to think of it, no, he hasn't.'

'Perhaps he's on holiday,' suggested Libby.

'Never known him to take a holiday. Not in five years,' said Eric.

'Or working from home?' added Paulette.

'I'll check out his workbench,' said Felix, standing.

'You'll need the cupboard keys.' Eric threw a bunch of keys to Felix, who caught them effortlessly in his huge hand.

'I'll join you,' said Chris.

This was an opportunity to let the group discuss her idea without her being there. In the past, it had come as a surprise that people sometimes talked about her behind her back – she'd assumed she was far too dull. But a series of circumstances the previous summer had thrust her into the limelight and, for a (thankfully brief) period, she had been, quite literally, the talk of the town. Besides, this was also a chance to enjoy Felix's company. His speech was slow and considered, so much so that Chris had to resist the temptation to finish his sentences for him, but his voice…! That voice! One moment as rough as a bag of nails, the next like golden syrup being drizzled off a wet spoon.

Furthermore, if she was going to keep her half-promise to Chloe to make more of an effort to bond with the group beyond her own project's 'shelf-life', then Felix would be a good person to start with. He seemed to be at the saner end of the scale, his passion for eclectic woodworking journals notwithstanding.

'I'll check his locker. See if he's left his…' Felix gave one of his trademark pauses, as though inviting Chris to guess what would come next.

'… wallet?' Chris suggested, then silently cursed herself for interjecting.

'… tools,' said Felix.

Technically, nobody had ownership of any of the workbenches, and the allocation was on a first come, first served basis, but the unwritten law of Chisellers' Cabin seemed to dictate that Eric and Martin were exceptions to that rule. Martin's bench was just inside the door on the left, as far from Eric's as was possible within the confines of the hut.

Felix knelt, unlocked a cupboard door under the workbench and took out a slim wooden case with a gold clasp.

'Do you know Martin well?' Chris asked.

'Not sure anyone knows… Martin,' Felix purred. 'I've been coming here a year and I've hardly had a…'

Chris waited patiently for the denouement.

'… conversation with him. Man's passionate about his craft, though, and I respect that.'

'Eric was suggesting that Martin is his second-in-command?'

'He wouldn't say that in his presence. I heard those two have a bit of… history.'

'History?' Despite her best intentions, Chris couldn't resist a bit of gossip.

'That's what Libby told me. Some say the Cabin was Martin's idea, but Eric made sure it was his name on the… paperwork.'

'Ooh, a woodworking coup d'état? Eric seizing control must have put Martin's nose out of joint.'

'I guess. Libby said things got pretty… heated.'

Felix opened the case to reveal a set of chisels arranged in size order and nestling in individual velvet-lined grooves. They were lovingly polished and sharpened and had a beauty that went beyond their practical use.

'All present and correct. These are Martin's babies. He wouldn't leave them here if he was working from…'

This time the pause was too much for Chris.

'... home?'

Fortunately, Felix didn't take offence at having his sentence completed. He simply nodded slowly, returned the chisel case to the cupboard and relocked the door. He then inspected a rack of saws, again ordered by size and each with a handmade guard protecting the teeth.

'Could he be visiting family?' Chris asked.

Felix shook his head. 'No idea. He's never mentioned any... family.'

This alone was strange as, apart from wood, second-hand tools and the disappearance of independent shops from Cliffstaple High Street, 'family' was the number one topic of discussion at the Cabin. Barely an hour passed without photo galleries of grandchildren and great-grandchildren being passed around for the attention and approval of the company. Chris could appreciate Martin's taciturnity on the subject as she had been similarly secretive. It wasn't that she feared the competition – she was confident that Mason and Jason could out-gorgeous any of their rivals – it was just that it was her family and she didn't need the superficial approbation of strangers to appreciate their value.

Felix stood back from the bench. 'Everything's here. All his tools, his sharpening stones, his clamps, his aprons, his... overalls. Nothing's missing.'

Chris stood back as well and studied the scene. Perhaps she could conjure up in her mind's eye how Martin's workbench had looked the previous week. A few years ago she'd proofread a paper on 'Mind Palaces', a memory technique that increasingly compensated for her natural forgetfulness. She visited the area of her memory palace where she'd stored visual memories of Chisellers' Cabin; for this she'd chosen the dressing table in a spare bedroom. This was not a well-maintained area – it was as poorly organised as the real 15, Sea View – and the memory was jumbled, disordered. In her mind she opened the workshop doors and examined the racks, the workbenches, the cupboards. Then, there it was, the fundamental difference between Martin's workstation of this week and last. It was so blindingly obvious that it shouldn't have needed any tricks of mental agility.

'Where's his coracle?' she asked.

*

'You don't think he's taken it for a test sail?' said Libby, looking anxious.

'A test row. You don't sail a coracle,' interjected Paulette, to Libby's annoyance.

'Technically, a test paddle,' interjected Eric, to both Paulette and Libby's annoyance.

Chris and Felix had reported back the findings of their reconnaissance mission to Martin's bench. The group seemed to be split into four camps: the Concerned (Libby, Paulette, Felix and Chris); the Unconcerned (Eric); the Non-Communicative (the Daves); and the Oblivious (Jethro).

'So you think we should call the police?'

'Oh, come now, Libby,' Eric chuckled. 'Don't you think you're being over-dramatic? Martin's either taken his coracle home to finish or he's given up on it altogether. It didn't look very seaworthy to me.'

'That's what I'm worried about.'

'Can't you phone him?' said Paulette.

'Don't have his number,' said Eric.

'You could send him an…'

The group waited anxiously on Felix.

'… email.'

'Don't have an email address.'

'So how do you get in touch?' asked Chris.

'At the cabin. He's always here, isn't he? Except today, of course,' Eric added unnecessarily. 'Pound to a penny he'll be back right as rain next week. And he'll be really excited when he hears about our plans for the ark.'

'The ark?' said Jethro, his mouth full of Victoria sponge. 'I thought we were waiting for Martin's vote.'

'Yes, but in Martin's absence, as chair I can exercise my right to use his proxy vote as per the Chisellers' Cabin constitution.'

'Oh,' said Jethro. 'Is Martin not around then?'

'NO!' chorused the rest of the group.

'He's missing,' explained Paulette.

'Can I have his workbench then?'

The group's collective concern for Martin's wellbeing was not sustained. When she'd calmed down, Libby agreed that she'd been silly to get so het up. Martin probably had a cold, or had gone to visit an aged relative or had discovered something better to do with his time. The missing coracle wasn't significant either, as, if Martin had finished building it, why wouldn't he take it home with him? They poured themselves more tea, cut more cake and discussed how they were going to design, source materials for and construct a 1:47 scale model of Noah's ark within four months.

Chris sat quietly, listening to the increasingly animated discussion. It was good that the others weren't unduly worried by Martin's absence, but, even so, something was nagging away at her. The missing coracle, Eric's ambivalence, and then, what was it that Martin had said about some scars being deeper than others? Something was not right.

Six

Chris had escaped the Cabin and been back at home for three hours. Long enough to feed two cats, load the washing machine and do some hard graft on 'Hare Today, Gone Tomorrow? A Wildlife Conservation Strategy'.

Libby and Paulette had kindly transported her finished shelf to 15, Sea View. Now it was sitting proudly in her sitting room, leaning against the wall on which it would be installed, one day, if she ever got round to it. She feared the worst, as she'd already spotted Aitken and Waterman eyeing up its immaculately polished walnut veneer as a potential new scratching post.

'I'll just finish this chapter and then I'll go and watch some crap TV,' she said to Grayson, who was sitting at the far side of the table, apparently naked except for a pair of sunglasses. 'Tomorrow you'll have your clothes back, freshly laundered.'

She was just setting her aged washing machine for an extra turbo spin cycle, even though this would generate a quake that risked shaking the fillings out of her teeth, when there was a knock on the front door, followed by a ring on the bell, followed by another knock. This signified that she had a visitor, a not particularly welcome visitor who tended to call round uninvited about every three months.

'Simon! What a lovely… Oh my giddy aunt.'

As she'd suspected, it was her ex-husband, Simon, but whereas he normally wore the uniform of a dull middle-aged man (supermarket jeans and checked shirt), this evening he had come as

Satin Shorts' twin brother, in a white singlet, skimpy shorts (bright red) and expensive-looking running shoes.

'For frick's sake, you'd better come in off the doorstep – you've taken twenty grand off the value of my house in the last five seconds,' she said, ushering him into the house and propelling him, at arm's length, into the kitchen.

Simon nodded at Chris's hand, no longer bandaged but with a visible scar. 'What have you done to yourself this time?'

'This? You should see the other guy.'

'Don't I get offered a coffee?' Simon asked as the washing machine reached its gear-shrieking crescendo.

'WHAT'S THAT?' yelled Chris.

'A COFFEE. I SAID, "DON'T I GET OFFERED A"' – the washing machine, spin cycle completed, came to a sudden, silent stop – '"COFFEE?"'

'No need to shout,' responded Chris. 'And the answer is no. What do you want?'

Simon sat down at the table and, reaching behind him, removed a backpack. It was perhaps the smallest backpack Chris had ever seen, more like a removable hunch. As he searched inside it, his eyes drifted upwards and alighted on Grayson.

'Your dummy...'

'His name is Grayson.'

'He's naked.'

'He's not. He's wearing Ray-Bans.'

'Where are the rest of his clothes?'

'A little accident with a mug of extra-strong builder's tea. His outfit's in the washing machine.'

'Do you think it's decent?'

'Decent?'

'Having a naked male mannequin in your kitchen. What would the neighbours say?'

'Have you seen the way you're dressed? You look like an extra from a *Jane Fonda Workout* video.'

'At least I'm wearing clothes.'

'That's debatable. Anyway, Grayson would never go commando in polite company. He's wearing pants.'

Simon stood and peered over the edge of the table to confirm that Grayson was indeed wearing underpants – brown Y-fronts with an orange trim.

'Satisfied?'

'Those pants…'

'What about them?'

'Are they mine?'

'Of course not,' said Chris, switching on the espresso machine as a distraction. 'I bought them last year. In a jumble sale.'

'Really? A jumble sale?'

'Absolutely. They had a special on men's underpants. Buy one, get one free.'

'Sorry?'

'BOGOF, Simon. Bog off.'

They were indeed Simon's pants, now approaching their thirty-second birthday. Chris had discovered them in the bottom of the airing cupboard a couple of years after their divorce had been finalised. She'd kept them, not out of any sentimental reason and certainly not for warped fetishist purposes, but because she never threw anything away if it could be put to an alternative use. So it was that Simon's nylon-mix Y-fronts had spent three decades in Chris's duster bucket. They doubled as a perfect substitute chamois leather for cleaning windows – absorbent and apparently indestructible. She had dressed Grayson in them just this morning, for the sake of decency.

Simon wasn't impressed. 'I still think it's, well, inappropriate.'

'It's OK, he's safe. I had a cheeky peek,' said Chris, filling two coffee cups. 'Down there, he's completely smooth – like a doll. He's androgynous. Something else you've got in common,' she added, sotto voce, as she placed Simon's cup in front of him.

Simon either missed Chris's jibe or chose to ignore it. He withdrew a sheet of paper.

'What's this? Are we renewing our divorce vows?' asked Chris eagerly.

'It's a sponsorship form. I'm doing a fun run on behalf of the Cliffstaple and Bottisham Walruses.'

Chris groaned audibly. The Cliffstaple and Bottisham Walruses were the most self-righteous of all the local community groups – somewhere between a Rotary club and a satanic Masonic lodge. They were at the front of every parade, at every news photo opportunity, and always had the largest stall at the Cliffstaple Festival of Fish. Chris reckoned that to qualify as a Walrus you had to be over fifty, drive a Lexus, use a Marks and Spencer's store card and have an inflated sense of your own importance.

'Can't you do a Just Giving page like a normal human being?' said Chris, extracting a pen from the drawer of the kitchen table. 'And are you sure you're physically up to it, Simon? You're not in the best shape.'

'I've been training. Every evening for the last two months.'

Chris perused the form.

'It's 5k,' Simon added.

'I was thinking more in the region of £2.50.'

'No, the distance. Five thousand metres. I reckon I can manage that.'

Chris looked at the list of previous sponsors, which ran to three sides of A4. Never be the first name on a sponsorship form – that was one of her mottos. You needed to establish what the accepted level of charitable spirit was. Most people had donated £5 or £10.

'How about £5 per thousand metres?' said Chris, filling in the next vacant line. 'That way, I save money if you die before completing the course.'

Before handing back the form, she turned to the first page. One donation at the top of the list stood out. It was for £250.

'Wow, someone's flush!' she exclaimed. The signature next to the donation was a scrawl that seemed to read 'Danny Figg'.

'Is that *the* Danny Figg? As in Danny Figg Homes?'

'Yes. You know him?'

'Never heard of him until a week ago.'

'Never heard of Danny Figg?' Simon was incredulous. 'He's one of Cliffstaple's leading businessmen and a very generous supporter of the Walruses.'

Chris took her phone out and opened her photos folder. 'Have you seen what's happening at Hermon's Copse? They're paving paradise and putting up a... development of affordable detached residences.'

'Bit slow off the mark, aren't you, Chris? They've been discussing that in public meetings and on *North Kent Today* for the last year. There was even a special pull-out feature in the *Cliffstaple Gazette and Shopper*.'

'Yeah, well,' said Chris, examining the bottom of her coffee cup, 'I try and avoid local media. Once you've been the headlines yourself, it loses its allure.'

'And you're always moaning about homelessness and housing shortages, so you should welcome guys like Mr Figg who do something positive.'

'But not by building on woodland.'

'Private woodland,' Simon countered. 'I'd have thought that'd be something else you disapproved of.'

Chris thrust her photo of the artist's impression of the new estate in Simon's face. 'And look at it! A vanilla hellhole of baby buggies and kite-flying.'

Simon got up to leave, folding his sponsorship form and repositioning his micro backpack. 'I think it looks terrific. Jan and I have got our eye on one of the eco-bungalows.'

'It's not right,' Chris muttered. 'Blocking off Tiny Barney's view. Someone ought to do something about it.'

Simon sat back down at the table abruptly. 'Not you, Chris. Don't even think about going all activist again. Think of Chloe, the cats, your plastic, Y-front-wearing friend here – don't start supergluing yourself to the Becketon Road.'

Chris had a brief history of strictly lawful public protest. In her view it was lawful to chain yourself to a tree when they were going to chop down two dozen mature planes during nesting season. And it was lawful to pour contaminated river water through a council office's letterbox. However, Chris's days of activism were a quarter of a century behind her. Direct intervention was a young woman's game, particularly when the alternative was a comfy sofa, a laptop, a mug of tea and a pack of fig rolls.

'Don't worry, I'm not planning on joining this lot.' She showed Simon the photo of the CrEW logo.

'What's that? A Banksy?'

'Wish it was. It'd have more aesthetic merit than the rest of Hermon Village. Anyway, don't fret, I'm going to be too busy building an ark.'

Simon shook his head. 'I'm not even going to ask.'

*

Chris hung Grayson's damp clothes on her makeshift washing line, which was strung between a drainpipe at the back of her house and the edge of her ramshackle garden shed. It hung at throat level, which was a garrotting hazard, but fortunately it was loose enough to negate any danger of decapitation. One of these days she'd get round to installing a rotary washing line – or perhaps she'd give up doing laundry, full stop. She honestly couldn't recall when she'd last used her iron.

How had she managed to completely miss public discussion about the Hermon's Copse development? She'd been keeping her head down, immersed in her work, and she'd obviously taken this to extremes. Zeta would be able to give her the lowdown, the inside track. Another good reason to get back in touch.

Seven

North Kent Police Station occupied a seven-storey 1960s office block in the least sought-after part of Becketon, sandwiched between the ring road and an eight-screen multiplex. The station existed in a state of limbo between demolishment and being declared an outstanding example of Brutalism by some misguided town planner. Its uncertain future, and the perpetual need for budgetary restraint, meant that the building was decaying.

On the sign outside, the 'e' from 'Kent' was missing, encouraging the local online community to Photoshop alternative versions. Strangely, each time the missing 'e' was replaced, it was stolen again. Presumably there was a lucrative local black market in giant 'e's. Inside, the paint was peeling, the dysfunctional air conditioning was more likely to spread airborne disease than comfort, and the inadequate number of electrical points meant that the floors were a health and safety nightmare, crisscrossed by wires secured by masking tape. Its residents loved it.

There was an unsaid collective understanding that, for all the building's failings, it was better the devil you knew. And with dividing walls and individual offices still prevailing, there was no risk of open-plan areas or the curse of hot-desking. Who needed ergonomic furniture and focused spaces when you had a snack-dispensing machine, a dartboard and a corridor that doubled as a perfect office cricket pitch?

The large meeting room, still bearing its nostalgia-evoking nicotine colour scheme, was already filling up when Zeta entered alongside James, the only other special who had been awarded the honour of an invitation. It was either this or, according to the duty roster, checking out complaints about anti-social parking. Zeta had become a special to fight crime and keep the peace, not to be a pepper-spray-wielding traffic warden.

Sgt Spurgeon and PC Atherton were already seated in the front row, their combined girth taking up the space of four chairs. In the rows behind were dotted a significant percentage of the station's uniformed force. Zeta and James found a spot at the back, as far away from direct eye contact as possible. There was a hubbub like a jostled beehive – hushed conversations and expectation.

After five minutes, as the buzz was reaching a crescendo, the doors swung open and three people entered the room. Zeta recognised the first two: a woman in her early forties with a severe pageboy haircut and an immaculately tailored suit, and a slightly younger man with a floppy blond fringe, chinos and an arrogant strut. They were CID. A scandal had necessitated a purge of the department nine months previously and CID, from DI Dunn downwards, had been dispersed to the four winds, or at least as far as Dover. Zeta hadn't had any dealings with their replacements and had only seen them in passing, sat at a separate canteen table or squeezed into the single functioning lift. Her colleagues in uniform referred to them as 'the Fairy Liquid Mob', as they were now 'New, Improved and Squeaky Clean'.

The third arrival, a slim woman of about fifty with red hair pulled back into a ponytail and furtive eyes behind square glasses, took a chair apart from her colleagues and scanned the waiting audience.

The suited woman placed a laptop on the rostrum, plugged in the lead connecting it to the projector and attached a USB. The wall-mounted screen behind her was illuminated with a heading: 'Operation Dryad – Strictly Confidential'. Her audience cooed like Victorians watching a magic lantern display for the first time.

'For those of you who don't know me, my name is DI Ash Turing and my colleague is DS Caspar Beech.'

'Ash and Beech?' whispered James in Zeta's ear. 'And they used to call us Woodentops!'

'And this is...' DI Turing glanced across to the woman in the square glasses, but she gave a slight shake of her head. It was an almost imperceptible gesture, but one that did not escape Zeta's notice.

'What I mean is... everything in this briefing is for your eyes only. Nothing can be shared outside the room – not with your colleagues, your family or your friends.'

'Not on social media,' added DS Beech, flopping his fringe from right to left.

'And definitely not to your media contacts. Yes, we know all about those. Any leaks will be investigated and addressed with the utmost severity.'

Such a statement would usually have been greeted with a sarcastic chorus of 'Ooh!' by uniform, but there was gravitas in DI Turing's manner.

'Next slide, please.'

DS Beech, who was on laptop duty, pressed a key. On the screen appeared the face of a middle-aged man. It was not a handsome face, thought Zeta. It was a face that you wouldn't argue with; one you might cross the road or even continents to avoid. It was a face that would have 'Educated at the University of Hard Knocks' on its Facebook profile. Late fifties, bald and with dark eyes that stared out unflinchingly from the screen.

'Wouldn't want to tip 'is pint over! Looks like a right thug,' piped up PC Atherton, his distinctively high-pitched voice cutting through the background murmuring.

'This is the victim, Mr Daniel Figg.' DI Turing looked directly at PC Atherton, unaware that the constable was unlikely to recognise his own faux pas. 'He is a prominent businessman, an upstanding member of the Cliffstaple community and a personal friend of the chief superintendent. A month ago he received what we assess to be a credible death threat.'

Figg. Why did that name seem familiar? Zeta delved into her memory banks but, surprisingly, came up with an empty balance sheet. That alone worried her. At the grand old age of twenty-six, were her mental faculties waning? She'd read that the brain stopped generating new cells around that age, so was hers decluttering, chucking out old knowledge to make space for the new?

She was so distracted that she nearly missed the next slide, a photo of a handwritten envelope addressed 'To Danny Figg', and the contents, a sheet of paper with, in letters cut out from a magazine: 'You're next!'

'Doesn't seem particularly threatening,' observed Sgt Spurgeon, shifting in his chair and pushing his hand down the rear of his trousers to free the cloth that had been sucked between his buttocks.

DI Turing gave an involuntary grimace. 'What is significant is the method of delivery. This note was left at his office at the Hermon Copse development attached to a dead squirrel.'

'What kind of squirrel?' chirped PC Atherton.

'Sorry?'

'Red or grey?'

'What does it matter what colour it was? It was a dead squirrel!' exclaimed DS Beech.

'Well, grey squirrels are an invasive species from North America and, in this country, the red squirrel population is largely restricted to—'

'That's impressive squirrel knowledge,' whispered Zeta.

'He watches nature documentaries in the gym while he's pumping iron,' explained James.

The next slide answered PC Atherton's question. It was a photo, and even the slowest members of the audience could deduce that a) it was a squirrel, and b) it was dead. Squished, in fact.

'Ah, a grey one,' he trilled. 'That figures.'

There was a ripple of applause from PC Atherton's colleagues and a couple of them patted him on the back in congratulation.

'Though it's got a patch of red on its tail, which is really interesting considering—'

'If we can move on from rodents?' suggested DI Turing. 'At the scene of the crime we also found a number of examples of this tag.'

The next slide revealed a stencilled logo in green paint that seemed to read 'CrEW'.

'And we have reason to believe that this is the work of a band of…' DI Turing paused for maximum dramatic effect. '… eco-terrorists.'

The collective 'Ooh!' from the audience was definitely not a sarcastic one. Organised crime was far more invigorating than the disorganised variety.

DS Beech stepped forward to take on the next stage of the briefing. 'There is very limited intel about this group, but we are certain that they are local, to within a twenty-kilometre radius of Becketon.'

Before James could stop her, Zeta had spontaneously raised her hand. 'What about Discord, Telegram, et cetera?'

DS Beech nodded in approval or perhaps in relief that there was at least one intelligent officer in the room. 'Good question. Unusually, we have been unable to find any trace of them online, on social media or on other communication channels. This leads us to believe they are planning an escalation of activities.'

At this point, he instinctively glanced across to the bespectacled woman. She gave no reaction, keeping her gaze fixed on the uniformed officers.

'We think this is a small cell, no more than four or five members. And there's one particular gentleman that we're very keen to monitor.'

DS Beech pressed a key and the screen revealed a mugshot of a man in his late twenties: white, pale, gaunt and with lank, light brown dreadlocks that were decorated with beads and feathers. The quality of the photograph suggested it was about thirty years old, but even at such low resolution Zeta fancied that the man's brown eyes showed a strange combination of sadness and steely determination.

DI Turing now stepped forward. This was obviously a carefully choreographed double-act with DS Beech. 'This is Martin Tobias Livingstone. He was an Environment Agency officer before he went rogue and began cultivating a reputation as one of the county's most disruptive activists. He was a prime suspect in thirty-seven cases involving trespass, vandalism, obstruction and sabotage. Eventually, he was successfully prosecuted over his occupation of Wycken Woods on the Isle of Lepus and was sentenced to eighteen months imprisonment, of which he served eleven months.'

Sgt Spurgeon raised his arm and DI Turing looked at him quizzically.

'Sergeant Spurgeon, ma'am. I worked on that case, but it was years ago. I was a beat copper fresh out of Hendon. Racked up some very handy overtime on Wycken Woods – they spent months trying to get him out of them trees. Every time we thought we'd got him cornered, he'd pop up on the other side of the woods. He's got to be past that sort of thing by now. He's probably wearing a chunky-knit cardigan and dishing out Werther's Originals.'

Zeta smiled to herself. This was Sgt Spurgeon's favourite tactic with CID: play dumb and lull his counterparts into complacency.

'And a death threat doesn't seem his style – he was a pain-in-the-arse crusty but pretty harmless. Why do you figure him for this?'

DI Turing nodded as if in recognition of Spurgeon's challenge. 'Before my time, of course, but perhaps you can remember the media's nickname for Mr Livingstone?'

Sgt Spurgeon shifted in his chair again, pulling at the seat of his trousers and causing DI Turing to look away momentarily. 'Let's think. It was "Nutter" or "Nut-Job" or summat like that.'

'Nutkin,' said DI Turing, with the smile of a woman who was about to declare checkmate.

'Yeah that's it – Nutkin!'

'As in Squirrel Nutkin.' And with perfect timing the slide featuring the photo of the dead squirrel reappeared on the screen.

The audience cooed in appreciation of the audacity of leaving a squished rodent as a calling card.

'So where does uniform come in?' asked Sgt Spurgeon.

'Since calling this meeting, matters have moved on. We've had Mr Livingstone under surveillance, but a week ago he disappeared.'

'He clocked you and did a runner?'

'Possibly,' said DI Turing, and again, Zeta spotted a micro glance in the direction of the anonymous bespectacled woman, 'but unlikely. Let's just say tracing him has become a matter of urgency.'

'So this is where we need your assistance,' said DS Beech. 'Keep an eye out for Livingstone and any sign of this CrEW lot. But be low-key about it.'

'Gather intelligence – discreetly,' added DI Turing as she closed the laptop and cradled it under her arm, signifying that the briefing was at an end. 'But note two things. No word of this outside this room, and do not directly approach the suspect. We have reason to believe he is dangerous.'

The hubbub rose in the room as all the officers turned to their neighbours to discuss this exciting development. Turing whispered something in Sgt Spurgeon's ear, then she and Beech swept out of the room. Zeta looked towards the chair on which the bespectacled woman had been sitting. It was empty. Somehow her departure had evaded even Zeta's notice.

*

'So what do you think about this CrEW stuff?' asked James as he and Zeta settled at a table at the far end of what passed for the staff canteen.

Zeta prodded her lunch. Her lunch resisted. Thrice-cooked chips were a good thing, but the same could not be said for a thrice-microwaved jacket potato. This might have been launched over the boundary from nearby Becketon Cricket Club. She looked around to make sure there was no possibility of them being overheard – she took DI Turing's warning seriously.

'An eco-terrorist cell? In Becketon? Can't see it myself. I mean, they might write a snotty letter to the local paper or deliver a petition to the council, but death threats?'

James had made the more sensible lunch choice of a cheese and pickle roll. It didn't look particularly appetising, but at least it couldn't double up as a lethal weapon. 'Well, I'm up for it, Strawbs.'

'Strawbs' was James's affectionate nickname for Zeta – Zeta 'Strawberry' Jama.

'Better than monitoring double-parking outside the primary school. Those yummy-mummies can be proper vicious.'

'And besides,' continued Zeta, 'this Martin Livingstone guy's been dormant for, what, nearly thirty years?'

'That's the thing with treehuggers. They're fundamentalists. You never know what they're capable of. Besides, I heard the chief super put a rocket up CID's arse to get this sorted pronto.'

Zeta shushed James, having spotted the approach of Sgt Spurgeon.

'If I may have a quick word with SC Jama?' he said. 'In private?'

James took the hint and his cheese and pickle roll to a distant table.

'What's up, Sarge?' asked Zeta.

'CID have got a task, and I think you're the woman for the job.'

'Me?'

'Yes.' Sgt Spurgeon leant in and whispered, 'You're going undercover.'

Eight

Chris fished the teabag out of her mug and stared at her phone. *Extraordinary meeting at the Cabin 09:30 sharp!!* read the text.

Extraordinary. Not just the message or the unforgivable use of double exclamation marks but the fact that Eric had texted her. Her first concern was not about any meeting but how Eric had got hold of her number. She guarded her personal information obsessively – to the point of paranoia, her daughter had suggested. All addressed envelopes and labels from deliveries were stripped and promptly shredded, unidentified calls went unanswered and spam emails were first removed to a separate folder before being deleted.

Health and safety. That was it. On her first morning at Chisellers' Cabin she had filled out a form confirming that she had received the necessary safety briefing and providing emergency contact details: name, address, email, phone number and next of kin. She'd written 'Grayson Heron' for her next of kin as Chloe was too distant to be relevant and Aitken and Waterman would be no help in an emergency. But to be texted about a meeting? Surely this contravened all manner of data-protection regulations. What was so important that they couldn't have been told yesterday? This had better be a significant crisis – a sinkhole swallowing the Cabin whole or the pedal-driven lathes rising up to overthrow their human masters – or she would be having serious words with Eric.

She gulped down the dregs of the tea and put her Misplaced Apostrophe's mug in the sink. There was a perfectly serviceable dishwasher, but it was too much effort to open the door, pull out the rack, place the mug, push the rack back in and close the door. She would spend the five-minute cycle ride to the Cabin compiling her Top Ten list of 'Labour-Saving Devices That Aren't'.

Chris needed to have her road sense dialled up to eleven as commuter traffic, late for the first conference call of the morning, paid scant regard to trivia such as indicator use or protocol at mini-roundabouts. She turned right off the rat-run, down the cycle path on Fiddler's Walk and through the iron gates into Cliffstaple Community Garden. Fortunately (or unfortunately, depending upon how the meeting went), the community garden was free of sinkholes and the lathes stood idle and non-sentient. There was already a gathering around the refreshments table under the blue and white striped awning – Libby, Paulette, Felix, Jethro and two out of the three Daves.

'Good of you to join us, Christine,' said Eric as she chained Rod to the railings.

Coming from anyone else, she would have assumed this was sarcasm due to her being five minutes late, but Eric seemed incapable of such subtlety. He held a metal teapot aloft and rapped its side with a Phillips screwdriver.

'I call this extraordinary meeting…' The freshly made tea spattered from the spout onto his naked forearm. '… bugger!'

Paulette and Libby tittered.

'Get on with it, man. We don't need all that… flimflam,' heckled Felix, and he yawned as though he had been dragged from his bed at an ungodly hour.

'Thank you all for gathering at such short notice. I have been giving serious thought to what I am now calling "our special project".'

'I'm only here for the cake,' muttered Jethro.

'And I've decided that… um… Chris's idea of a scale representation of Noah's Ark is admirable.'

'But?' anticipated Felix.

'Not viable.'

'You were all for it yesterday,' said Libby.

'Superficially, I was, but overnight I reconsidered. It puts too much demand on labour and raw materials. My idea of a toy ark with carved animals is the more sensible and achievable option. Me, Paulette and Felix will concentrate on the ark itself and the rest of you can carve Noah and all the animals.'

Chris couldn't exactly translate the chuntering from round the table, but it seemed to be general disgruntlement. She, on the other hand, was delighted with this development. She had absolutely no desire to spend a morning a week whittling a menagerie of giraffes, rhinoceroses, elephants or even tiny donkeys. Eric's volte-face gave her the perfect opportunity to divorce herself from the group with dignity. Besides, she had some new prospectuses from the University of North Kent to get her teeth into and a particularly tricky academic treatise, 'A Blast from the Past: How War Statues Reframe Historical Narratives', which at first glance looked suspiciously as though it had been written by an AI program.

Paulette took a folded sheet of paper out of her backpack and spread it across the table, holding down the corners with unused mugs. 'I've already drawn up the plan.'

They all crowded round the plan. It certainly looked professional, with projections, dimensions and even an estimate of materials needed.

Felix whistled through his teeth. 'You must have been up all night drawing this. It's... magnificent!'

The only person who was less than impressed was Eric. 'Yes, well, perhaps we can use that as a template for the toy ark. Just change the scaling.'

'But...' started Libby.

'I've made my decision. And Martin, if he were here, would agree.' Eric gazed upwards, as if seeking divine approval. 'That concludes the business of the extraordinary meeting.'

'That's it? You called us all in at half nine on a Friday morning just to tell us you were cancelling the... project?' shouted Felix with the outrage of a man who had been deprived of half an hour's sleep.

'I've got a potential new Chiseller coming in to meet me at ten,' Eric said defensively.

'Ooh, we've got a visitor coming too!' said Libby, nudging Paulette. 'Is this newbie anyone we know?'

'No, she's a young girl' – which, on Eric's compass, was any woman under the age of fifty – 'so, best behaviour, everyone. We could do with some, um, fresh blood,' and he involuntarily ran his tongue over his upper lip.

Chris shifted uneasily on her log stool. She was pretty sure that Eric was a harmless old duffer, but he was beginning to sound like a sex-starved vampire.

*

Chris, Libby, Paulette and Felix were gathered around Libby and Paulette's carved seat, which was sitting on one of the outdoor benches.

Chris was there because, now that her shelf was complete, she thought she might as well pitch in on someone else's project for the rest of the morning. The other three seemed to be holding a council of war.

'So much for democracy,' said Felix, wielding an awl like a Shark from *West Side Story*. 'Perhaps we should take over this operation. Rise up and overthrow the… autocracy.'

'Eric seems pretty sure of Martin's views. But in my experience, they don't agree on anything,' said Libby.

'Perhaps we can have another vote when Martin reappears,' suggested Chris, though her inner voice said that today would be au revoir to the Cabin and all its petty small-town politics.

Paulette used a chisel to channel out a delicate Celtic swirl on the armrest of the seat. 'We suspected Eric would backtrack. That's why we have a Plan B.'

Eric's voice invaded their space. Not his usual voice but with a tone that reminded Chris of her late mother's telephone manner. 'We pride ourselves on our policy of inclusiveness. We even have women at the Cabin! Let me introduce you to a few of our intrepid Chisellers. Gang, this is Lena.'

Chris looked round with a smile to welcome the new arrival and found herself staring into the familiar dark brown eyes of her friend Zeta Jama.

Zeta, to her credit, judged the situation in a nanosecond – only the finest poker player or expert spy-catcher could have detected the slightest raising of her eyebrow, the merest twitch of her mouth.

'As you can see, Paulette, Libby, Felix and, um, Christine are working on a lovely ash bench. Even better, we've all agreed to work on an exciting collaborative project, haven't we, people?'

Chris fancied that Paulette's grip on her chisel tightened.

*

Eric was buzzing. The rest of the Cabin were happy to discuss more important issues, such as whether it was worth resharpening saws or the scandalous effect of shrinkflation on Wagon Wheel biscuits. 'Young Lena seemed fascinated by everything we do here. The history of the Cabin, who the members are, what we're working on. I'm pretty sure I've recruited another member to our happy band of brothers. And sisters, of course.'

Chris kept her counsel. She wasn't sure what Lena/Zeta was up to, but she was one hundred per cent sure that she wasn't remotely interested in whittling a wildebeest.

'So the large ark idea is effectively sunk?'

'I'm afraid so, Libby. It was a nice idea but—'

'Excuse me? We're looking for Eric Tarlton? We're from BBC Kent's *Look Lively* news programme.'

The interrupters were a woman and man in their mid-twenties. The woman was tall and broad, like the most formidable netball player from Chris's schooldays, with agricultural shoulders that could lever an ox cart out of a ditch. Attractive, but in a decidedly scary way. The man had long, lank hair and a figure that suggested he enjoyed pepperoni pizza and *Call of Duty* more than salad niçoise and cycling. On his substantial shoulder was perched an impressively small broadcast-quality video camera and in his left hand was a grey boom microphone that looked like an obese ferret.

Eric smoothed down what remained of his hair and straightened a non-existent tie. '*Look Lively*? I wasn't expecting—'

'We heard that you're constructing an ark for Harbour Day? Thought it could be a good item for tonight's show.'

'That's Plan B,' whispered Libby in Chris's ear. 'My god-daughter Alice. I had a feeling Eric might try to worm his way out of things, so I arranged some additional support. Who'd have thought that twenty-four years of birthday book tokens would generate such a rapid response?'

*

Chris's own experience with broadcast media and the *Look Lively* programme had already resulted in unwanted fame, bordering on notoriety. She had no wish to repeat the experience, so she retreated to the workshop, where there'd be some tins to label or saws to rack that would keep her away from the scope of the camera lens.

She found an ideal distraction – an old Golden Virginia tobacco tin containing assorted drill bits that was just begging to be reorganised according to size. Less than twenty minutes had passed before she heard Eric's telephone-manner voice approaching. He was guiding the camera crew towards the workshop.

This sent Chris into a flurry of poor decision-making. A normal person would have simply carried on with their current activity or perhaps smiled for the camera. A more outgoing person might even have faced the lens and given a cheery endorsement of the Cabin for the viewers at home. Given the range of choices available, Chris decided to hide.

Well, not exactly hide – that would have looked weird. Instead, she felt that the retrieving of a strategically discarded hammer at that key moment would fit the purpose. She dropped a claw hammer, side-footed it under the furthest workbench and followed it to sanctuary.

The sub-workbench environment was surprisingly cosy. Above her she could hear Eric continuing his guided tour: 'As you can see, there are six further workbenches, which means we can work in all weathers.'

'So whose bench is whose?' said a young female voice, presumably Alice's.

'We don't claim ownership of any particular bench, but I tend to work from this one. As you can see, I'm working on this inlaid jewellery box. Perhaps I can get it into a better light so that your cameraman—'

'And this bench?' asked Alice.

'That's Martin's, though he's away from the Cabin at the moment.'

'This has been so interesting, Eric, and you've been so informative.' Chris could imagine that Alice was actually patting Eric's hand. 'If you don't mind leaving us to do a bit more filming and the wrapping up?'

Chris was trapped. She gave it five minutes and then, holding the hammer handle between her teeth, she conducted a nine-point turn that allowed her to face the body of the workshop, albeit from a hamster's perspective. She had presumed that the coast was clear, but she was wrong. She now had a close-up view of Alice's robust ankles.

Chris held her breath, which wasn't easy with a hammer-filled mouth. Alice and her cameraman were talking in hushed tones. Chris strained to hear their conversation, but it was obscured by distant banging, sawing and the whirring of the pedal-driven lathes.

After a couple more minutes the ankles departed and Chris could safely crawl from her impromptu hidey-hole. The *Look Lively* team were gone and her anonymity had been preserved.

*

Eric was chuffed. His chest was thrust out like a bantam hen that had just won *Chicken Love Island* and Chris imagined that if she'd strewn seed on the ground he'd have pecked at it.

'That's just what we need to raise the profile of the Cabin. Alice and Connor were happy they'd got enough material to run a feature on tonight's programme. They thought the ark was a great example of community spirit and they plan to link it to an ongoing feature they're running on Harbour Day and Cliffstaple's nautical heritage.'

'So you've changed your… mind,' observed Felix.

'Not changed,' Eric said. 'I've reviewed the situation, weighed the evidence and decided to be ambitious.'

'Chalk one up for Plan B,' said Paulette under her breath. 'Never underestimate the influence that a young woman with access to TV coverage can have on a self-important old man.'

'So that's agreed?' said Libby. 'We can start sourcing materials?'

'And funding,' said Eric, visibly energised, like an unbeliever who had just seen the light. 'I'll write to the Harbour Day Committee to inform them of our plans.'

Chris was crestfallen. The ark was her idea – how could she back away now? She looked around the group and could see positivity coursing through them. Libby, Paulette and Felix were poring over the plans; Eric was recounting his triumphant media liaison with two-thirds of the Daves; and, for some reason, Jethro was standing on his tree-trunk stool and saluting by holding a Bourbon biscuit to his temple.

'Aren't we forgetting Martin?'

'Who?' said Eric.

'Martin. Doesn't he have a veto?'

Eric pondered this for no more than a second. 'Martin will be supportive of the ark when he comes back. If he comes back.'

Nine

Chris looked at the clock on her kitchen wall. It read three minutes past six. That meant it was two minutes to – she set all her clocks five minutes fast to ensure she was never late. All except the one on the oven, which had reverted to 00:00 after a power cut six months previously and she hadn't got round to figuring out how to reset it.

Two minutes to six. Just enough time to give Aitken and Waterman their tea – poached salmon slices in gravy tonight. She'd already unlocked the garden gate to save her expected visitor the inconvenience of scaling the wall.

Nothing had been arranged, no arrangements agreed, no communication whatsoever, but Chris just knew.

As the clock's hand flicked round to five minutes past six, a shadow moved across the kitchen window. This was followed by a sharp knock on the door, the knock that she'd been expecting since that morning's events. She opened the kitchen door and Zeta skulked in.

'I've got a perfectly serviceable front door, you know. The doorbell even works – or it does if you karate chop it on the left-hand side and then quickly push the button three times in succession.'

'Old habits die hard, I guess,' replied Zeta.

'Coffee? Tea?'

'Peppermint tea, if you've got it.'

Zeta lowered her hoodie, took a seat at the table and leant down to scratch Aitken's ear. Waterman looked at their visitor with the kind of disinterest-come-contempt that only a cat could muster. Chris never ceased to marvel at how two cats could live together, eat together, sleep together and wash their bums together and yet have such distinct personalities.

'Isn't this the point at which I should say something like "Hello stranger" or "Long time, no see" or "We must stop meeting like this"?'

'Sorry, but I've been overwhelmed by all the emails, texts and calls I haven't received from you.'

'Touché.' Chris placed the tea in front of Zeta along with her battered biscuit tin commemorating the marriage of Prince Charles and Lady Diana Spencer. 'So what are you up to? Still a special, I hear.'

With a triumphant appearance at the Police Bravery Awards and a ringing commendation from the chief constable on her CV, Zeta had seemingly been on a fast track to a stellar career within the force. But it appeared as if Zeta had other ideas and she had yet to make the transition from voluntary to permanent.

'Sorry, I should've been in touch,' said Zeta, perusing the open tin before extracting a custard cream that Chris couldn't even remember buying, 'but I've been so busy that life kinda overtook me. Consultancy work's been flying in and I've taken on a new voluntary role—'

A nagging, flickering light bulb in a corner of Chris's brain shone brighter. That bike ride along the seafront, about two minutes before her near collision with Satin Shorts; two figures looking out to sea. 'You're a fricking lifeguard!'

'A beach safety operative, I'll have you know.'

'Why?'

'I'm a good swimmer.'

Chris nodded in response. She had personal experience of her friend's swimming prowess. In fact, had it not been for that prowess, Chris wouldn't be alive and sipping on her delicious Colombian double espresso. 'Not surprised you've got no time to drop in on your old muckers if you're a copper, a lifeguard and a' – she selected Zeta's business card from the pinboard by her fridge – 'digital solutions consultant.'

Zeta was too busy pondering the etiquette of rejecting a custard cream that, on the evidence of her first bite, was two years past its best-before date to offer a response. Chris was also pondering the existence of Zeta's biscuit. She never bought custard creams – didn't like them. She decided to catalogue this in her 'Unsolved Mysteries' folder, alongside why she kept putting the roasting fork back in the same kitchen drawer that it consistently jammed from the inside.

'And on top of that, you're adding woodworking as another string to your sitar? It's not surprising you've no time for anything else, Zeta. Or are you self-identifying as Lena now?'

Aitken leapt onto the table and clattered clumsily into the biscuit tin, which provided Zeta with a welcome, if temporary, diversion.

'Never know when you might need woodworking skills,' Zeta said, deflecting.

'Stop deflecting. You're trying to tell me you want to spend a morning a week in the company of superannuated walnut fetishists?'

'Well, you do.'

Which, even Chris was forced to admit, was a fair point.

'If you're seriously interested in joining Chisellers' Cabin, then I'm… I'm… Bob the frickin' Builder.'

'Can we just change the subject? We've not seen each other for, what, three months?'

'No. Answer the question.'

'I can't.'

'Can't or won't?'

'They're not mutually exclusive, so both.'

Chris sighed. She knew Zeta well enough to recognise that she was in 'immovable object' mode. Either they'd continue this pointless repartee for a further twenty minutes or she could give ground, at least for the time being.

'Want to stay to dinner?'

Zeta grinned broadly. 'A table at Maison Heron? I'm honoured. What's on the menu?'

Chris opened the fridge and examined the contents of the salad drawer. It wasn't pretty. A couple of carrots that were developing a facial hair problem, three tomatoes that were squishy enough to throw at politicians, and a courgette that resembled a body part of Shrek that even Pixar wouldn't dare animate. 'Um… ratatouille?'

*

The onions and garlic were caramelising nicely and Zeta had shared a cracking anecdote about a client of hers who had discovered that their steel erection business was getting some very dodgy hits off Google Search. That was the secret of their friendship, thought Chris. They could give each other space, but when they met up they instantly clicked into place. As for the age difference, Chris had long felt that she was still twenty-six but trapped in an older body. She suspected that, for Zeta, the reverse might be true.

The kitchen clock read six thirty-two. 'Do you mind if I switch on *Look Lively*?' said Chris, reaching for the TV remote control. 'There was a camera crew at the Cabin today.'

She noted that Zeta neither showed surprise at this revelation nor asked why the *Look Lively* team had been there.

Chris hit the 'on' button and the 'mute' button simultaneously. It would be a good fifteen minutes of proper local news before they got to the feelgood feature at the end of the programme – assuming that the Cabin hadn't been gazumped by a skateboarding duck. But to her surprise, the familiar face of ace reporter Alice appeared immediately, with the community garden and the workshop as her backdrop. She hit the volume.

'Among the cherry tomatoes in this hidden corner of Cliffstaple, a major investigation is building.'

On the screen, Alice commenced her walkabout in typical roving reporter style. Behind her, Eric was waving to the camera, one of the community gardeners was strolling past with a trug of spring greens and Felix was testing the sharpness of a hand lathe with his thumb.

'We've heard from a reliable source that the police are searching for a notorious eco-terrorist who is believed to have been using a local woodworking group as cover for a campaign of intimidation and sabotage.'

Alice's roving had now taken her to the interior of the workshop.

'North Kent Constabulary are unwilling to reveal the name of their suspect but advise the public to stay alert and report any suspicious behaviour.'

At this point the camera operator panned down to show the area under one of the workbenches and the TV screen was briefly filled with Chris's overall-clad posterior.

'But as for the members of Chisellers' Cabin? For now they're keeping tight-lipped.'

The camera cut away from Alice to a shot of Chris emerging from under the workbench with a claw hammer gripped between her clenched teeth.

'This is Alice Buttler for *Look Lively*, reporting from Cliffstaple.'

Chris turned the TV off.

'Bugger,' said both Chris and Zeta, simultaneously but for entirely different reasons.

*

A second surprise was that the mouldy veg ratatouille was not just edible, it was approaching deliciousness. Chris waited until they'd both finished before relaunching her interrogation.

'So Alice wasn't interested in community ark-building after all? I presume that's also why Lena was glad-handing Eric this morning, was it?'

'If I say "No comment" again, will you give up?'

'Probably. It's not my problem. I barely know Martin – he seems like a decent enough cove and is good at stemming blood, but that's about it.'

Zeta semi-flinched. The *Look Lively* feature hadn't mentioned any names. 'Martin?'

'I don't know – I just presumed it was him they were referring to. Bit hippyish, hasn't been seen for a week. Put two and two together, I guess.'

'A potential eco-terrorist?'

'How should I know what an eco-terrorist looks like? He wasn't wearing a "Save the Planet – Eat the Rich" T-shirt, if that's what you're implying.'

'Cards on the table time – in confidence?'

'OK.'

'Cross your heart? If it leaked that I'd shared case info, I wouldn't just be out on my ear – CID would throw the book at me too. And as for you, let's just say that you'd need a bigger workbench to hide under.'

'And hope to die. I may be many things – grammar pedant, kamikaze cyclist, ratatouille chef de cuisine – but a blabberer I am not.'

Zeta paused, looked around the kitchen and lowered her voice, even though the only other witnesses were Aitken and Grayson (the latter now, thankfully, respectably attired). 'CID asked me to do a bit of undercover snooping, see if I could dig out some more intel about this Martin Livingstone. I really can't tell you any more, but it involves a credible death threat.'

'A death threat?'

Zeta nodded. 'Attached to a dead squirrel.'

Chris snorted so hard that a spatter of snot escaped her nose, fortuitously avoiding the open biscuit tin. 'A death threat? From Martin? You've got to be kidding! I've never met a gentler soul. His abiding passions are a finely sharpened pencil and a hand-crafted coracle.'

Zeta pricked up her ears. 'A coracle?'

Ten

The clouds of white blackthorn blossom embracing the track distracted Chris, and she had to duck to avoid a low-hanging branch. She felt the nostalgic sting of nettles teasing her bare legs. The path was narrow and proud with new growth; if she met someone coming the other way, one of them would be forced to lean into the vegetation. On her left, a gathering of dunnocks was having a family argument, and when she stood up on Rod's pedals to peer over the hedge into the fields on her right, a herd of cows were busy predicting the weather by either standing up or lying down. Much as she loved 15, Sea View, with its creature comforts and comfortable creatures, Chris decided she was truly at her happiest when in the saddle.

She had called in at the Cabin that morning, but it was in turmoil following the previous night's *Look Lively* report. Everyone was shocked and confused at being the focus of a police investigation. Well, everyone except Jethro, who was simply confused. There was a name that was left unsaid but must have been uppermost in everyone's minds: Martin. It didn't take a Stephen Hawking to put a police search for an eco-terrorist and Martin's disappearance together and draw the obvious conclusion.

Chris was there long enough to refocus everybody's attention onto the ark build. If anything could stop the Chisellers from imploding, it was the delegation of tasks concerning the planning, funding and resourcing of a completely pointless project. Eric nominated himself as lead designer and director of stakeholder relations, Paulette and Libby put their hands up for project management and publicity, and

Felix volunteered for the procurement and resourcing brief. Chris threw her hat in on the resourcing brief too; she'd had a cunning idea about where she could secure materials and even cold, hard cash.

As she slowed down to weave her way through a narrow opening that marked a border between fields, Chris's cycle-sense detected another cyclist behind her, and so, as the path widened again, she pulled over to let them pass by safely. No one appeared. Strange. This was the second time this had happened, or rather hadn't happened, since she'd set out from the Cabin. Like any good cyclist, she was always aware of her fellow travellers. She routinely hurled abuse at TV dramas that portrayed drivers following other cars across deserted landscapes for miles without being spotted. Chris shrugged and remounted. Perhaps they'd taken another route or perhaps she'd imagined it. No matter; she was nearly at her destination.

First stop: Tiny Barney's field. Chris leant Rod against the fence and climbed up to perch on the top. It swayed under her weight and she was sure she heard a creak. Whether that was a consequence of the fence's poor condition or her rediscovery of chip butties with extra mayo was up for debate.

At first sight, the field was completely empty. Even the alpacas (a minute of internet research had confirmed their species) were absent. Then, on the very far side of the field by a large shed, was that… Tiny Barney? She screwed up her eyes as if that would magically give them a zoom function. Whatever it was, it certainly wasn't an alpaca and it looked donkey-shaped but somehow sadder – it moved slowly and seemed hunched.

Chris's mantra was usually to follow the dual paths of 'leave well alone' and 'mind your own bleedin' business', but the one thing she couldn't walk away from was an animal in distress. She looked left and right as though crossing a busy road and then hopped down into the field.

The ground wasn't as even as it looked from atop the fence. As she landed, her left foot disappeared into an animal burrow or maybe a hoof impression concealed by the scrubby grass – a fast track to a broken ankle. Suitably sobered by this lucky escape, she picked her way carefully across the field as though negotiating a Lego-strewn carpet in bare feet.

By the time she'd crossed the halfway point, Chris was able to safely come to two conclusions: firstly, that the mystery animal was indeed a donkey, and secondly, that it wasn't Tiny Barney. This was a full-size donkey of advanced years and, far from being a victim of maltreatment, he was happily eating from a trough at the side of what was, on closer inspection, a large chicken coop.

'Sorry to disturb you, mate. I thought you were someone else.' Was it proper etiquette to formally introduce oneself to a donkey? 'I'm Chris, by the way,' she added, to be polite.

The donkey looked up from the trough as if to suggest that at his venerable age he didn't need small talk or having his lunch interrupted. On that, he and Chris were in firm agreement.

She patted him on his shoulder. 'I'll leave you in peace to enjoy your food. If you see Tiny Barney, can you say hi from me?'

'Mmmmmm.'

The sound came from behind her. It sounded like a connoisseur had taken a sip of a particularly fine Beaujolais.

'Mmmmmm.'

She turned slowly to find she was face to face with a brace of alpacas.

Chris was pretty sure that alpacas weren't dangerous, but then again neither were cows and that didn't stop the occasional farmer from getting trampled to death. And up close, this close, they seemed less cuddly and more unpredictable.

The nearest alpaca raised its head so that it was nearly level with Chris's and bared its teeth.

'Mmmmmm.'

Never look a gift alpaca in the mouth, she thought rather randomly, but she had nowhere else to look. Strangely, the beast seemed to have only a lower set of teeth, decorated with grass stains, which it displayed in a grimace like an entrant in a gurning competition. When Chris should have been considering her fight or flight options, she was transported back to that Christmas when she was six or seven and her grandmother had laughed so loudly at the *Morecambe and Wise Christmas Show* that her top set of dentures had shot across the room and landed in a bowl of eggnog.

She was hemmed in. She tried to back away, but she had the chicken coop to her left and the donkey to her right. The alpacas kept on with their remorseless approach.

Chris waved her arms – 'Shoo! Shoo! Gangway!' – but that had no effect.

'Idiot,' she admonished herself, 'they're alpacas – South American. They must speak Spanish. Um... Vamos! Arriba! Arriba!'

The lead alpaca gave Chris a look of utter contempt, as though her butchering of its native language was the final insult. It made a throaty grunt and then threw its head forward.

Chris smelt the spitball before she felt it hit her shoulder. It reeked of decaying vegetation and gastric juices and... Even her powers as a wordsmith failed in the face of its unique pungency. She had changed plenty of nappies and cleaned many a stinky litter tray, but this was beyond the pale.

Fight or flight?

Being duffed up by a pair of alpacas might be an embarrassing way to meet your maker, but for Chris it would be entirely on brand. On the other hand, although she almost certainly couldn't outrun them, flight did seem to be the better of the two unattractive options. Perhaps the element of surprise would give her a head start.

'Ready, steady—'

'Pepsi! Shirlie! What have you found there?' The voice was female and posh. But not posh-posh. Not lacy cuffs, Liberty scarf, Glyndebourne picnic posh. Well-educated but down-to-earth posh.

The newly identified alpacas dutifully turned and trotted away, revealing the owner of the voice. She was a handsome, unmade-up woman of about forty, in countryside chic: brown hair tied back, plaid shirt, jeans tucked into green Wellington boots. Scruffy but impeccably scruffy. By her side an aged collie stood dutifully to attention.

'Can I help you?' she said.

'Hope I'm not trespassing.'

'I'm afraid you are.'

'Oh, sorry. I was looking for a donkey. Thank you for rescuing me.' Chris could hear that her own voice sounded surprisingly quaky. Perhaps her close encounter with Pepsi and Shirlie had shaken her up more that she realised.

'Oh, alpacas aren't aggressive. Not unless they've got BLS.' The woman's voice had softened, apparently in cognisance of Chris's wobbliness.

'BLS?' Chris immediately checked her rudimentary knowledge of K-pop bands and winners of *Britain's Got Talent.*

'Berserk llama syndrome. But these girls have a clean bill of health.' The woman took a rag from her pocket and wiped the vibrant green globule of spit from Chris's yellow cycling jacket. 'Come on, let's get you cleaned up.'

*

As Liz ('Elizabeth Fyffe-Hermon – three "f"s, like the bananas') busied herself sponging off alpaca sputum and making tea, Chris Heron ('one "r", like the wading bird') took in her surroundings. Hermon, Heron… for the sake of an 'm' they could have been distant relations, but Chris was pretty sure her lineage – sewage treatment and Kent coal mining – put paid to any chance of a family connection, however distant.

Hermon Hill Farm's kitchen was quite unlike the farmhouse kitchens beloved by daytime property renovation programmes. It had no decorative wheatsheaves, no marble-topped kitchen islands holding bowls of photogenic fresh fruit, no racks of copper-bottomed pans and no shelves of terracotta storage jars. There was plenty of exposed brickwork, but that was only where the damp plaster had fallen off the walls.

The kitchen did have a large Aga, but that was merely a stand for a microwave and boxes of dogfood. In the corner was a smelly old dog bed, which was promptly occupied by a smelly old dog (Ernie, the aged collie). The main feature was a large kitchen table stacked with paperwork and an open laptop. Somewhere distant, a pack of farm dogs (perhaps Ernie's great-grandchildren) unleashed a volley of barking.

'I've never known them to spit before. I think the girls must have thought you were threatening Don.' Liz hung the damp cycling jacket over the back of the door and placed two mugs of tea on the table.

'Don? Ah, Don the donkey?'

'Yah. They're good buddies, the three of them.'

'I see. From a distance I thought he was Tiny Barney.'

'Tiny Barney?'

'The little donkey. I've been a bit worried about him – I thought the alpacas had evicted him.'

Liz threw back her head and gave a throaty laugh. 'Oh, you mean Lance. I sold him. He's gone to stud.'

'Stud?' Chris was somewhat befuddled. 'How does that work?'

'How does a stud work? No offence, Chris, but you look a bit long in the tooth to need the birds and the bees explaining to you.'

'I was just trying to figure out… Do they have to put him on a box or does he get winched up?' Chris conjured up a disturbing mental image of Barney the tiny donkey atop a stepladder, trying to balance whilst performing his insemination duties.

Liz looked equally befuddled. 'I'd hope they'd be pairing him with a comparable miniature donkey.'

'Miniature? He's meant to be small?'

Liz's laugh turned into a snort. 'Lance – or to give him his full name, Lancelot Wonderment the Third – is a pedigree miniature donkey.'

Over the years Chris had discovered two things: one, that spontaneous stupidity was a great catalyst for sparking instant friendship, and two, that there was something curious in the waters of the area that caused complete strangers to open up about intimate details of their lives.

Lance was getting his oats in more ways than one, and as a result, Liz now had the funds for another pair of alpacas and a down payment on the turning of the old milking shed into a farm shop. Liz Fyffe-Hermon with three 'f's was the fifth generation to run Hermon Hill Farm. 'And probably the last,' she predicted moodily. Times were hard, farming was increasingly uneconomical and overheads were driving her and many of her fellow smallholders into penury. She'd tried pick-your-own soft fruits and yoga retreats and was now experimenting with alpaca experience holidays, but this was not enough to keep the voracious bank manager at bay. The proposed farm shop with attached petting zoo was her final gambit.

There was a burning question in Chris's mind, but it was one that could bring this embryonic friendship to an abrupt halt. Better to give discretion its due and file the question away for a more appropriate time.

When Chris revealed that, as well as an alpaca-botherer, she was a freelance proofreader, Liz's eyes lit up. She took a hardback A4 notebook from underneath the laptop.

'What do you think?' Liz said, opening the notebook and thrusting it under Chris's nose. Evidently, Liz liked to scribble her ideas in long hand, a practice of which Chris wholeheartedly approved.

It was an ad for the planned farm shop in Liz's flowery copperplate handwriting. Chris usually politely refused all requests for ad hoc (and therefore unpaid) proofreading, but as she had trespassed on Liz's property, hassled Don the donkey and enraged Pepsi and Shirlie, she felt that this was fair compensation.

Hermon Hill Farm Shop – your first call for fresh Kentish produce.

What followed was a list of the kind of earthly delights that would be on offer: artisanal cheeses, home-baked breads, free-range eggs from happy chickens, hand-carved ham (presumably from less happy pigs). Chris tried not to bristle at the overuse of 'artisanal', and she had never understood why something hand-carved would necessarily be tastier than something machine-sliced. Still, now was not the time for nit-picking. She spotted a spelling mistake and a misplaced apostrophe, which served as payment for Liz's kindness to strangers.

Despite all of the farm's trials and tribulations, Liz stayed positive and smiley – at least until Chris, bolstered by two mugs of tea and a chocolate digestive, took that burning question out of deep storage.

'What's the deal with Hermon Copse? I presume that was yours too?'

'It was. I sold it eighteen months ago. Didn't want to, but I got an offer I couldn't refuse. Silly money for a private wood that you can't touch. Or so I thought.'

'So, Hermon Village?'

'Mr Figg, the property developer, told me he was interested in turning Hermon Copse into a nature reserve – and I believed him. How he got planning permission for that monstrosity is beyond me. Some brown envelopes exchanging hands with the local council, I reckon.'

'But that's outrageous!' exclaimed Chris, outraged.

'Yep, but what can you do? And the money from the sale gave the farm a twelve-month stay of execution, so I can't claim the moral high ground. In my defence, Figg wanted to buy the whole farm, but I held out. At least for the time being.'

Chris detected that she'd touched a nerve and that it would be inappropriate to pursue the subject with such a new acquaintance. It certainly wouldn't be appropriate to reveal that her next task was to dangle a begging bowl before the self-same property developer.

Thankfully, any awkwardness was broken by a ripe fart from the dog bed by the Aga (at least, Chris hoped that was the source rather than Liz). She couldn't help but wince as the gas cloud reached her nostrils – its pungency almost rivalled that alpaca vomit. Perhaps Ernie had been trained to let rip when guests had outstayed their welcome. Could Aitken and Waterman be trained to do likewise whenever Simon dropped by for a visit?

'Mustn't keep you.' Chris grabbed her jacket from the door. 'Thank you for the tea and forgiveness.'

'My pleasure.' And Liz sounded as though it had been.

Chris often felt she was poor company, but perhaps when you were surrounded by dumb animals and debt, any human company, even that of a trespassing, donkey-stalking cyclist, was welcome.

'If you see Tiny Barney – sorry, Lancelot Wonderment the Third – send him my love.'

'Will do. Though I guess love is the one thing he isn't short of.'

Eleven

Police work was boring. Well, a good ninety-five per cent of it was.

The TV cop dramas that Zeta had watched avidly in her youth would have had you believe it was all car chases and forensic breakthroughs and confrontations with shouty superintendents. The reality was endless inputting, pointless patrols and internal memos that tweaked operating procedure but then demanded you attend six further courses to prove you understood that procedure – by which time the procedure had been tweaked again.

Crimes in the Becketon area were low level and predictable: drug-related, drunkenness, shoplifting, car crime, outraging public decency (Cliffstaple FC's car park was a popular dogging location). Nothing to stir the blood of an experienced investigator or even a special constable. The eighty/twenty rule applied here too – eighty per cent of offences were committed by twenty known individuals, so the routine was to pick them up, dust them down and start all over again. CID hoovered up all the sexy cases, and uniform (the drones) were left with the detritus. So when something new crossed the threshold of North Kent Constabulary, something mysterious, something newsworthy, everybody wanted a piece of the action. This was why, on the fourth floor, there were six police officers gathered around a single computer screen.

'This'd better be good.'

The officers looked round as the door crashed open and DI Ash Turing strode in with DS Caspar Beech in her wake. Zeta noted that DI Turing was again wearing an immaculately tailored suit but, crucially, a different one. She doubted that most of her colleagues in uniform could afford more than five pairs of underpants (assuming they turned them inside out at the weekend), so this was a blatant statement of sartorial superiority. A smart suit was not to Zeta's taste – it suggested that the wearer was happier stuck in an office rather than out crime-fighting on the streets of Becketon.

'On second thoughts, this'd better be earth-shatteringly awesome.'

'Make space for the detectives,' said Sgt Spurgeon, nudging a couple of his junior colleagues but notably not offering up his own generously upholstered chair. 'Thank you for joining us. Detective Inspector, Detective Sergeant, I think you'll find this rather interesting.'

'It'll certainly be a novelty to receive intel first-hand rather than on the evening news,' said DS Beech, taking the seat next to his boss.

'I can assure you that nobody on my team said anything to *Look Lively*,' said Sgt Spurgeon, affronted.

'Yeah, sure. Your lot are leakier than a colander that's run out of Tena pants,' replied DS Beech.

PC Atherton tensed in response to this jibe, his muscles straining his shirt material. Fortunately, his senior officer was a wise old bird and knew how to calm turbulent waters.

'We in uniform have as little as possible to do with that programme. Not since they ran that feature on "Kent's Porkiest PCs".' Sgt Spurgeon paused for comic effect. 'We were upset that we only came third.'

'Entertaining as this interdepartmental dick-waving is, some of us have important work to attend to?' suggested DI Turing.

'Thank you,' replied Sgt Spurgeon. 'If you please, SC Jama?'

Beech and a few of the PCs looked surprised at the idea of a special constable leading a briefing, let alone a briefing to CID, but DI Turing merely nodded in agreement.

Zeta stood in front of an enlarged street map of Cliffstaple. Despite her confident exterior, her insides were churning. This was uncharted territory. She took a pin and placed it on the map.

'This is Martin Livingstone's home on Gable Terrace, which I understand has been under surveillance.'

'Day and night,' confirmed DS Beech.

'Yet somehow the squirrel escaped the trap,' said DI Turing, glaring at her junior officer.

'Now, intelligence has determined that the suspect had recently constructed a coracle – a single-seater boat,' Zeta quickly added as a couple of hands started to rise.

'Intel that SC Jama gathered from the community woodworking group. DI Turing's suggestion that we put in an undercover investigator worked a treat,' said Sgt Spurgeon, currying favour.

DI Turing gave a self-satisfied nod in response.

'The nearest launching point for that coracle would be Skinner's Beach. Here.' Zeta placed another pin on the map.

'The quickest route from home to beach is what? Straight down the high street?' noted DI Turing.

'Where there are three CCTV cameras. Here, here and here. At high-tide times on the days after the last sighting of Livingstone he was not picked up on any of them.'

'So?'

'My theory was that he deliberately avoided the CCTV by cutting down the various smugglers' alleys.'

'And?' Ash and Beech were leaning forward in their seats, fully engaged.

Sgt Spurgeon levered himself out of his chair with an exaggerated groan. 'So, on my instruction, constables Atherton and Passwater checked properties on the route. This property here' – he leant across Zeta to stick another pin on the street plan – 'at 4, Totter's Alley, has a motion-sensitive camera doorbell. Crank up the computer, Constable Passwater.'

The audience switched their attention to the computer screen and, at the click of a mouse button, three seconds of dark, grainy footage played. A hunched figure with a domed back passed through the camera's range from right to left.

'Donatello, I reckon. Or maybe Raphael,' said Sgt Spurgeon.

'Who are…?' started DS Beech, but he was interrupted by his DI.

'I believe the sergeant is making a *Teenage Mutant Ninja Turtles* joke. Very droll. That is our suspect carrying his coracle on his back and heading in the direction of the sea. Date and time?'

'A week ago. 04:55,' Zeta answered.

'Good work, SC Jama.'

Zeta couldn't help but notice that Sgt Spurgeon beamed at CID's recognition of his protégée's thorough policework. Perhaps she had been wrong about her career path. Perhaps this was where she truly belonged.

'So, what conclusions do we draw from this?' asked DI Turing, as though setting an exam question for the officers.

'Perhaps he was testing the coracle for seaworthiness and found out it wasn't. With the tides round here, he'll probably wash up in Norway in a couple of weeks' time,' said PC Atherton.

'In the dark? Seems rather unlikely, don't you think?' said DI Turing, and PC Atherton humbly muttered his agreement.

Zeta made a mental note to brief her fellow lifeguard, Wilf. An eco-warrior in a coracle trumped a vicar on a porpoise.

PC Passwater, a rookie fresh out of training, shot up her hand. 'I reckon he's topped himself – he looks the type.'

Zeta heard Sgt Spurgeon groan and he put his hand to his head. This Q&A was not showing his charges in their most positive light. Of course, that was assuming that there was any light bright enough to bleach out their collective shortcomings.

'Oh sure, if he looks the type, that must be the answer,' said DI Turing.

PC Passwater nodded enthusiastically, her inexperience failing to detect incoming sarcasm.

'In a depressed state, Mr Livingstone forewent more straightforward means of self-dispatch and instead spent weeks carefully constructing a primeval boat to facilitate his sad demise. Any other brilliant suggestions?'

'He could've been doing a runner,' suggested DS Beech, 'or rather a paddler. If he knew we were onto him for threatening Mr Figg.'

'Possible, but I'm not sure an escape attempt on the North Sea would have made as much progress as, say, the six-twenty from Cliffstaple Station to Victoria,' noted his superior.

Figg. Figg. There was that name again. Where had she heard it before? Zeta surreptitiously took her phone out of her pocket and checked all her personal email boxes. Nothing. She uttered a silent curse, admonishing herself for her efficiency in clearing the spam and deleted email folders.

'He could've been off on 'oliday. P'raps he fancied a cruise,' piped up an unidentified voice from the crowd before he was sensibly shushed by his colleagues.

Sgt Spurgeon sighed the sigh of a man who had decided, reluctantly, to put this meeting out of its misery. He raised his right index finger.

'Yes?' said DI Turing with a crocodile smile.

'You think we've got a Canoe Guy.'

'Thank you, Sergeant. If you could explain to your less enlightened colleagues?'

Sgt Spurgeon raised himself from his chair like a sumo wrestler at the start of a bout. 'DI Turing believes that Martin Livingstone has faked his own death with the intention of assuming a new identity.'

DI Turing nodded. 'Very good. Motive?'

'Usually it's either for money – if he's got life insurance – or to escape debt.'

'Or?'

'Or DS Beech is right. He knew he was in the frame for the threats against Mr Figg.'

'Excellent. I knew I could rely on your experience to sort the wheat from the chaff, Sergeant Spurgeon.' DI Turing beamed, her tone blurring the lines between high praise and patronage.

The other officers all turned to each other and exchanged congratulations as though this was a conclusion they'd reached through collaborative effort rather than one they'd been led to by the nose. All the officers except one, that is. Zeta was still head down, absorbed in her phone.

Figg. The first two pages of Google Search were dominated by references to Danny Figg Homes and Daniel Figg himself, with various links to his homepage and then media references, press releases, features in local and some national media, Wikipedia, X, LinkedIn, Facebook, Instagram. His bald, unphotogenic features loomed out from the top of her screen. Then, on pages three and four, references to lesser Figgs started to seep in, plus the occasional fig recipe. Zeta made a mental note to try that 'easy fig tarte tatin' recipe should she ever get round to inviting Chris over for dinner.

Finally, on lowly page five, she found what had been nagging at her, a Companies House listing: 'T Figg Debt Recovery Solutions – Director: Tony Figg; Secretary: Daisy Figg'. Tony Figg had emailed her the previous year seeking her expertise for website development and search engine optimisation, and, boy, did he need it. A pang of Chris-inspired social conscience had caused her to delete his email from her in-box and, until now, her memory. The Facebook page had a photo and there was no doubting the family connection with Danny Figg – they were like two peas in a pod.

'So, we're all agreed on a plan of action.' DI Turing's voice filtered back into Zeta's consciousness. 'If Livingstone's gone into hiding, we need to go public. Spurgeon, can you alert the coastguard and liaise with all local fishermen and pleasure sailors – he must have landed somewhere.'

'Will do,' said Sgt Spurgeon. 'If he's on the water, we'll find him – even if he's halfway to Bergen.'

DI Turing nodded. 'DS Beech, arrange a press conference. That should satisfy the chief super.'

Something wasn't right. Involuntarily, Zeta shook her head – a gesture that didn't escape the weasel eyes of DS Beech.

'It seems we have a doubter, Detective Inspector.'

'Something you wish to share with us, SC Jama?'

All faces turned towards Zeta.

'Sorry, ma'am, it's just that this is all assuming that Mr Livingstone's behind the death threat. What if he isn't?'

'You have an alternative suspect?'

'Um, no, but… Daniel Figg's got a brother, for a start.'

'So?'

'He's in debt recovery. Perhaps he's got form.'

'That's rather a brutal stereotype. Anything more, Special Constable?'

'Isn't that the first rule of investigation? Look at the family?'

It was difficult to read the look in DI Turing's eyes, but it certainly involved a heady cocktail of astonishment and anger. Sgt Spurgeon leapt (metaphorically, of course) to intervene.

'You must excuse SC Jama. She is inexperienced and over-zealous. I'm sure she wasn't doubting your ability. Were you, SC Jama?'

Although she wasn't feeling contrite, Zeta acted the part. She looked down at her shoes and mumbled, 'No. Sorry.'

DI Turing laughed, which was a disturbing sound, something between a cackle and a gargle. 'No matter. I seem to remember that I was prone to a bit of bolshiness when I was starting out – and look at me now!'

All of the officers present broke into relieved laughter, as if this were the funniest anecdote of the year.

'But no, SC Jama' – and Turing emphasised the 's' – 'the first rule of investigation in the real world is to concentrate resources. Livingstone is our most viable suspect for the death threat, but if you need any more convincing…'

On cue, DS Beech took a USB out of his top pocket and inserted it into the desktop computer.

'… this footage is from the Becketon City Council planning meeting about the Hermon Village development, from last September.'

The screen showed an angry confrontation. Residents were standing, pointing and shouting at the committee of councillors, and police were moving in to disperse the mob.

DI Turing leant over, pressed the mouse button to pause the film and, with an expensive-looking fountain pen, pointed at a gesticulating figure at the bottom left of the screen.

'That is Martin Livingstone.'

Twelve

Chris was shrink-wrapped in a moral dilemma.

Back on the path side of the fence, safe from further alpaca harassment and reunited with Rod, Chris opened her backpack and withdrew a white envelope. Inside was a polite, formal letter addressed to Mr Daniel Figg, c/o Danny Figg Homes, that she'd written over breakfast that morning. It sought his financial support for the Chisellers' Cabin Ark-Building Project. If he was prepared to sponsor Simon's crappy fun run for the Walruses then surely he would cough up a few quid for a properly worthy cause.

She'd already battled with her conscience once when writing it. In begging for money, was she de facto endorsing Figg's destruction of Hermon Copse? But what could she realistically do – boycott Hermon Village? She was hardly likely to buy one of those 'affordable detached residences'; she didn't own a baby buggy or a kite for a start. She had concluded that, in taking money away from Figg, she might be mitigating some of the planned environmental carnage. It was warped logic but sufficient to get the letter written and sealed in the envelope. Her encounter with Liz Fyffe-Hermon had caused her conscience to perch on her shoulder again and whisper in her ear.

Chris looked at the envelope. If she tore it into pieces and threw it into the nearest bin, nobody would know. It would be a small gesture of solidarity. Then again, this letter wasn't for her; she didn't really give a damn whether the ark was built or not. The letter was for Eric, for Felix, for Libby and Paulette, for Jethro, for the Daves and for Martin, if he ever turned up again. And the likelihood was that Danny Figg himself would not be around at the development, so she could safely drop off the letter. Assuming there was no reply (and she reckoned that Danny Figg probably got hundreds of similar entreaties), then her conscience would be doubly clear. She would have done her duty to her Cabin mates but at the same time would not have metaphorically jumped into bed with a low-life copse-destroying property developer.

If any passer-by had observed Chris over the previous ten minutes, standing astride her bicycle, having a heated debate with the invisible angel and devil on each shoulder, they wouldn't have given her a second glance. This was standard behaviour for North Kent.

*

As she approached the gates guarding the Hermon Village development, another option sprang to mind. If the gates were closed, she could use that viewing slot as a letterbox. The envelope would flutter down behind the Portaloo, to be trampled into the earth and into oblivion by a thousand mud-caked industrial boots. Job done.

Lady Luck sneered at Chris's optimism. Not only were the gates unlocked, they were slightly ajar.

She pushed the left gate far enough so that she could poke her head around it. The site was empty. Perhaps it was lunchbreak and the entire workforce had decamped to a greasy spoon in Becketon. She wheeled Rod through the gap and shut the gate behind her.

Chris momentarily closed her eyes and located an unused section of her memory palace. You never knew when you might glean important information, and something told her this was one of those times. She reopened her eyes and concentrated on her surroundings. To her left were three green temporary toilets standing in a line. Beyond them was a large Portakabin on which, in fresh, vibrant emerald paint was daubed: 'Hands Off Our Trees' with the same CrEW tag as the graffiti on the fence outside. To her right were three pieces of heavy machinery, all currently idle: a large orange JCB with pronged digger bucket, an industrial woodchipper that looked as though it could swallow trees whole, and an enormous downward-pointing drill that resembled the Mole from *Thunderbirds*.

'Hello? Hello?' Chris cautiously ventured further into the building site that had laid waste to the meadowland that had previously bordered Hermon Copse. Ahead, the treeline waited patiently, a woodland on death row without even the promise of a last meal.

'Anyone around?'

Silence, except for the faint whisper from the wind in the doomed trees. A plea for help.

The only sign of any construction was directly ahead of her, a three-metre-high cube made from rough wooden panelling. Chris recognised this as the sort of fencing that was usually erected in preparation for laying foundations.

'Hello?'

Someone had helpfully built some wooden steps up to the top of the panelling, which was obviously an invitation to look in, as tempting as a button with a 'Do Not Press' sign. Chris did another quick scan, scaled the steps and peered over the edge. It was an empty hole – as holes invariably were – and was seemingly waiting for something, presumably concrete, to fill it. She could see that the bottom of the hole was ten metres down and there, in the far corner, was a further hole, like a giant burrow. Chris leant over a bit further, but she couldn't see the bottom of the hole within the hole. Perhaps it was a secret entrance into Wonderland?

On tiptoe, she levered herself up onto the edge of the wooden panelling to get a better angle. Suddenly she felt her feet leave the safety of the steps. Her head and shoulders lurched forward and her fingers dug into the wood, searching for grip. Her entire body tipped and her hands lost their purchase, her nails tearing desperately at the planks.

The dark bottom of the hole seemed to rush towards her. The smell of damp earth filled her nostrils. Chris closed her eyes and prepared for impact.

There were hands grasping her tightly. One on her left shoulder, the other on the waistband of her shorts. Pulling her back? Or pushing her forwards? Which came first, the chicken or the egg; the grip or the overbalance?

The hands pulled Chris up and backwards. She saw blue sky again as her feet hit the reassuring solidity of the ground and she exhaled with relief. Relief that was short-lived as she was physically spun round to confront a puce-faced Incredible Hulk in a yellow hard hat. Her mother would have described him as being 'as wide as today and tomorrow'.

'You!' the Hulk snarled, face in her face. Pepsi and Shirlie's alpaca breath was fragrant by comparison. 'You're one of them, ain't you?'

It was impossible to answer this question without knowing who 'them' were. Chris didn't want to instinctively disassociate herself from 'them' only to discover they were a really cool bunch with excellent taste in music and a well-stocked wine fridge.

'"Them"?'

'Them!' The hard-hat Hulk pointed to the Portakabin. 'Look what they've done to me office!' he wailed.

The Hulk released his hold, which was even more alarming as it freed his muscular arms and bucket hands, capable of unlimited destruction.

Chris recovered her breath and gave her best sales rep smile. 'I represent Chisellers' Cabin. I've come about an ark.'

*

It was not a conscious effort, but in this time of need Chris had unwittingly dredged up the tactic of Verbal Confusion. This had been a chapter heading in *Self-Defence for Cowards*, a self-published guide that had been a week's worth of proofreading the previous winter.

The chapter explained that if a beered-up stranger demanded 'What are you looking at?', the correct answer was not 'Nothing' or 'Your fat face, you knuckle-dragging troglodyte' but something surreal along the lines of 'Badgers are rubbish at Pictionary' or 'Pineapples are the bounciest fruit.' This could befuddle and disarm the aggressor, buying time for escape.

'I represent Chisellers' Cabin. I've come about an ark' had the same effect.

The Hulk's brow furrowed and he took two paces back. ''Ave you got a death wish? You nearly fell in that 'ole.'

Chris didn't reply with 'Only because you pushed me', as that would only have reopened hostilities and, on reflection, she couldn't be absolutely sure about the sequence of events. Perhaps the Hulk had actually saved her life.

'Thanks,' she muttered. 'I'm looking for Mr Daniel Figg. It's regarding a community project.'

'You've found 'im.' And, as though a sack of ready-mix concrete had been lifted from his chest, Danny Figg relaxed and smiled. The Incredible Hulk turned back into Dr Bruce Banner – well, if Dr Bruce Banner had been a bald halitosis sufferer.

'Sorry about that, love. Thought you were one of them eco-terrorists. Been drivin' me nutty.'

'I'm not an eco-terrorist, I'm a proofreader,' said Chris, as though the two states could never co-exist.

From somewhere behind his back, Danny Figg magically produced a matching yellow hard hat. 'Never, ever, enter a buildin' site without wearin' an 'ard 'at. 'Ealth an' Safety would 'ave me balls on toast.'

Chris swapped her yellow cycling helmet for the yellow hard hat – it didn't seem like an upgrade.

'That's better,' he said. 'Protect yer pretty bonce from fallin' bricks.'

As there was no overhead building work in progress, Chris was unsure whence any falling bricks might originate unless they were dropped by a particularly strong seagull. Still, as it was a long time since anyone had called her bonce pretty, she wasn't going to debate the point.

''Ow d'ya get in anyway?' he said, as though Chris might have tunnelled under the hoardings or paraglided in.

'Through the gate? I did call out, but nobody seemed to be around.'

'All the lads are on other jobs till I sort out a couple of issues. Was the gate left unlocked?'

'Yes.'

Danny Figg muttered a curse that was hardly befitting of a respected local businessman and leading supporter of the Cliffstaple and Bottisham Walruses. 'Look, you go and make yourself comfy in me office,' he said, pointing to the graffitied Portakabin, 'and I'll go and lock up.'

Danny Figg marched off, leaving Chris to ponder the wisdom of allowing herself to be locked in a building site with a heavily built property developer with anger-management issues. 'Beware of strange men,' she'd advised Chloe when she was growing up. Perhaps, occasionally, she should take her own advice.

Thirteen

The office was smarter on the inside than the out, though that was hardly an achievement.

There was a low coffee table bordered by sofas of the type that were almost impossible to get out of when you had one titanium hip and another that had started making a strange clicking noise. A variety of expensively produced brochures were fanned out on the tabletop: 'Danny Figg Homes', 'Danny Figg Eco-Bungalows', 'Danny Figg Affordable Living Solutions'.

The walls were festooned with framed photographs intended to endorse the company's credibility: smiley Danny Figg at the opening of various developments; Danny shaking hands with the mayor, the local MP, the chief constable; a minor royal, foot on spade, planting a tree beside a beaming Danny.

The next section in the gallery was designed to present Danny Figg as the ordinary guy made good. A family photo, from the late sixties or early seventies, judging by the outrageous size of their shirt collars, that showed a proud couple with two young children. Danny and, presumably, his brother, in school uniform and satchels. The same two boys, older, leaner and muscular, in a boxing ring. A proud Danny helping his aged mother cut the ribbon on a show home.

The display was interrupted by an open key cabinet attached to the wall. Underneath, a table sported a surprisingly expensive coffee machine, one that far outranked Chris's own humble espresso maker. This beauty was the sort that featured in the 'As if you could afford this...' sections of Sunday supplements, a mass of chrome, vents and pipes. Alongside, as if reminding visitors of their host's humble beginnings, was a cheap plastic kettle, a box of teabags and a canister of white sugar stained brown by irresponsible teaspoon use.

On the opposite wall was a small fridge and yet more framed photographs. These were mainly news clippings, the usual corporate puff pieces, but in amongst them, surprisingly, were more controversial stories: 'Furore as Council Approve New Homes Planning'; 'Police Capture Wycken Woods Protestor'; 'Locals Say Green Pleas Ignored'.

Clever. Very clever. Chris could appreciate the psychology that had gone into the display. This was Danny Figg 'warts and all'. How could you fail to trust someone who explicitly admitted criticism?

To counter this was a section of certificates and awards: 'Best New Development'; 'Greenest British Bungalows'; 'Top Family-Friendly Employer'. The sort of trophies offered in exchange for buying a table and an overpriced chicken dinner with warm champagne at a meaningless evening of awards presented by a comedian who had appeared twice on *Mock the Week*.

If the entrance area of the office was the friendly, approachable Danny Figg, the far end was the businessman. A large solid oak desk virtually filled the width of the Portakabin. It was like a ship-in-a-bottle puzzle as to how it had been accommodated. Perhaps the office had been built around the desk.

The desk itself held all the expected symbols of authority. A large computer screen, a pen holder, a blotter and a nameplate, in case you were unsure whose office you'd stumbled into. A jumble of fluorescent jackets and branded hard hats had been carelessly thrown into the corner beside it.

As a whole it was genius. Carefully crafted chaos. A humble Portakabin which was a practical casebook on consumer psychology. A web for luring the unwary, who would only escape after having committed to a purchase that would lock them into a lifetime of mortgage payment anxiety.

The door behind Chris opened – quietly. She pretended she hadn't heard it and continued to browse the gallery.

‘That’s me and T there. In the ring together.’ Danny was so close behind her, she could feel his voice on the back of her neck.

‘Your brother?’

‘Twin brother. Happy days, eh? We can’t turn the clock back though, can we?’ he said wistfully.

‘No, I’m afraid not.’

‘So, what’s all this about an ark then?’

Danny swept past Chris and removed his safety helmet and jacket. Underneath, all was pinstripe and gold. The suit jacket stretched to cover a white shirt that was open one button too far, but what really caught Chris’s attention was the bling. It was like looking into a pirate’s treasure chest. A chunky gold chain hung round his neck and his fingers were so festooned with signet rings it looked like he was wearing golden knuckledusters. Pride of place was his wristwatch, huge and solid gold. With that weight, Chris reckoned he would get a pretty good arm workout just from… no, that was a mental image that she didn’t want to have living rent-free in her brain.

Danny Figg took his seat in a large black leather office chair behind the desk and beckoned her to take one of the two chairs on the facing side. Chris smiled to herself as she noted that the visitors’ chairs were lower than their host’s.

‘I’ve got a letter that explains it.’ Chris put down her cup of extremely good coffee, took the envelope from her backpack and reached across the desk.

Danny Figg recoiled as if he’d been offered kryptonite. ‘Whoah! Put that away!’

‘It’s just a letter explaining—’

‘Don’t care what it’s explaining, love. I don’t accept no envelopes from strangers ever. That’s ’ow me first missus got me. Bled me dry. Just read it out loud.’

Chris did as she was instructed.

‘Dear Mr Figg,’

Danny Figg gave a nod of approval of the formal address.

'The Chisellers' Cabin is a community venture based in Cliffstaple. It is an inclusive group preserving traditional craft skills. We are embarking on a special project for Harbour Day, a working scale model of Noah's Ark, but we need help with materials and funding.

'As you are North Kent's leading builder of advanced housing solutions, we were hoping that you could support our own humble construction effort.'

Chris had felt physically sick writing this, on account of both the sentiment and the abuse of the English language.

'We should be grateful for any help you can provide.

'Yours, on behalf of Chisellers' Cabin,

'Chris Heron'

Chris tried to hand the letter to Danny Figg, but he shook his head, so she returned it to her backpack.

After a couple of minutes' thought, he leant back in his chair.

'Yeah, I like it. If you fink about it, Noah's Ark was the first eco-home, wasn't it? Mind you, I bet old Noah didn't have a top-of-the-range fitted kitchen, a home cinema and parking space for three family cars.'

Danny Figg took a large bunch of keys from his pocket, unlocked the top drawer of his desk and took out a cheque book.

'Sold. Must say, you've got a good patter there, Chris. If you ever fancy moving into property sales, give me a bell. So, 'ow much do you want?'

Chris hadn't expected to get into the site, let alone be faced with a blank cheque. She couldn't even recall the last time she had seen a cheque book. How much to ask for? He had pledged £250 for Simon's fun run and getting one up on her ex-husband was a particularly strong motivation, even after thirty-plus years.

'Umm, £500?'

'Done. Who should I make it payable to? You?'

'No, err, I don't know.' She didn't know whether Chisellers' Cabin had a bank account. 'Can I get back to you on that?'

'I'll leave it blank, then you can fill it in yourself.' He tore the cheque off and pushed it across the desk.

'This says £1,000.'

'Yeah. Five 'undred for your community group and five 'undred for you. Probably best to keep that nearly-fallin'-in-the-'ole incident to ourselves, eh? If 'Ealth and Safety 'eard that you'd been able to roam around the site unsupervised, it could get a bit awkward.'

'I can't accept this,' said Chris, embarrassed.

Danny Figg took a sip of coffee from a tiny espresso cup that, in his huge hands, looked like it was from a doll's tea service. 'Look, p'raps I feel a bit guilty that I scared you back then.'

'I wasn't scared,' said Chris, lying. She'd nearly soiled her cycling shorts.

'Even so. I've been through a lot lately, so I get a bit jittery 'bout the unexpected. First I an 'ole in the ground that puts a spanner in the works and on top of that I get a death threat. Me! A bleedin' death threat!'

'Have you told the police?'

'Course I have – though fat lot of good it will do. That's why I sort out my own problems. Then, to cap it off, I get that daft CrEW lot defacing my office.'

'I assume they're worried about the trees.' Chris pictured that giant woodchipper sucking up ancient oak trees like a toddler eating spaghetti. 'Even Liz assumed that Hermon's Copse was protected.'

'Who?'

'Elizabeth Fyffe-Hermon. Your neighbour.'

'Banana Betty? She still got a chip on 'er shoulder?'

'No. We were having a chat about miniature donkeys and it came up in conversation.'

'Listen, Liz "Fyffe with three effs" got a bloody good deal. She gets to play Dr Doolittle and I provide affordable 'omes for families. If that's not a win-win, I don't know what is.'

Chris felt she was in danger of losing the goodwill she'd built, and now she'd got the cheque in her bag she didn't feel inclined to return it. 'Sorry, I just thought that—'

Danny Figg stood up and took a framed certificate from the wall behind him. 'See? The North Kent Sustainable 'Omes Award. Got that three years running. Don't you worry, love. You leave caring for the trees an' all that to Danny Figg.'

Chris stood up. 'I'd better go and deposit this generous cheque. Thank you, Mr Figg.'

'Will do. You're welcome to visit anytime – just make an appointment, eh? Oh, and stay away from me 'ole!'

As Danny Figg unlocked the gates, he magically produced another glossy brochure. 'Nice to 'ave met you, Miss 'Eron. As a further gesture of goodwill, I'm prepared to offer you a special five per cent early-bird discount on my latest build.'

It wasn't until she had safely passed through the gates that Chris stopped to look at the brochure. 'Cliffstaple Heights Assisted Living Apartments'. The cheeky bastard.

Fourteen

She'd done it again.

Zeta stared forlornly at the baked potato sitting on her plate. Snooker-ball hard with a mop-head of Cheddar cheese. It looked like Boris Johnson after a sunbed.

The canteen was incapable of producing an edible jacket spud. Zeta knew this, but she kept ordering it. Four times running now. To keep doing the same thing in the expectation of a different outcome was a sign of insanity, wasn't it?

She sighed, pushed the untouched plate to one side and took a small black leather notebook from an inside pocket. She opened it towards the back rather than the front. The front was filled with her father's meticulous but indecipherable handwriting. It was precious – untouchable. The back was where she made her own private notes about investigations in homage to the memory of her father, a high-ranking police officer in Somalia. She had been just two years old when he disappeared (or was disappeared), and she had no memory of him, only a faded passport-sized black-and-white photo.

Zeta looked at the mugshot on her phone. DI Turing had insisted that they all carry a copy so they could be constantly on the lookout. Martin Livingstone didn't look like Public Enemy Number One; he looked gentle, kind, even. Anyone can do anything, she reminded herself.

'Penny for your thoughts, Strawbs?'

Zeta's concentration was broken by the arrival of James, who parked himself and something that resembled a spaghetti bolognese fresh out of the tumble dryer on the far side of the canteen table.

She swiftly tucked her phone back inside her jacket pocket. 'Just making some notes about this morning's CID briefing, before they slip my mind.' Not that anything would slip Zeta's mind. When she needed to remember something, it stuck.

'At least you've got something interesting to write about. I spent the morning giving a talk about online fraud at the Becketon Golden Years Recreation Centre.'

'That's important. Cybercrime is rampant and the over-sixties are particularly vulnerable.'

'Yeah, but they were expecting a Tony Bennett tribute act. You've never seen a more disappointed audience. One of them threw a Mr Kipling French Fancy at me.'

'Not sure you missed much.'

'Neither did the French Fancy flinger,' said James, brushing fondant icing from his tunic.

'Anyway, it was standard stuff – stupid observations from the usual suspects.'

'Standard stuff? My partner-in-arms leading a briefing to CID and putting a flea in the ear of the DI?'

'Ah, you heard about that.'

'The whole station heard about it.'

'Who from?' It was less than an hour since the confidential briefing had finished.

'PC Passwater. Got a mouth like the tannoy at St Pancras Station. You're a legend – again.'

'A legend? That means I'll be back on pub clear-out duty.'

'Safer gig than social clubs for seniors.'

Zeta stared at her notebook for a minute. 'Can I pick your brains?'

'Sure,' said James through a mouth full of spaghetti. 'What's bugging you?'

'Hypothetically, if someone's gone missing, what's your first course of action?'

'Track last movements, speak to family and friends, possible witnesses.'

'And then?'

'Check phone and bank account activity. Look for any cash withdrawals.'

Zeta nodded. 'And if, after a week, all those options have drawn a blank?'

An earnest expression crossed James's face. 'This is still hypothetical, right?'

'I think they're all jumping to conclusions and missing something.'

'Missing what?'

'I don't know.'

James sighed deeply. 'All right, so I'm guessing this morning's top-secret briefing was about that eco-hippy geezer? The squirrel murderer of Becketon.'

'Eco-hippy's got a name – Martin Livingstone.'

'Eco-hippy's easier to remember. He's getting on a bit, isn't he?'

Zeta checked her notebook. 'Fifty-eight.'

In two forkfuls, James cleared his plate of bolognese. 'That's your answer – he's probably wandered off somewhere. They all do at that age.'

'That age? Sergeant Spurgeon's in his fifties too.'

'There you go then.' James belched. 'That spag bol was rank, by the way. You not eating your spud?'

Zeta pushed her plate across the table. If James could subdue the jacket potato from hell, then good luck to him.

'Accident then. Your chap's probably dead. You know better than anyone what the riptides are like round here.'

Zeta nodded. It was a more logical conclusion than the current theory of a carefully crafted ruse to fake his own death and assume an alternate identity. She pictured that mugshot again. Those eyes. They weren't cunning. They were haunted, hunted.

'There is another possibility though.'

'What's that?' James was head down, stabbing at the potato with his knife in a frenzied attack.

'Foul play.'

'Kidnap? Can't imagine you'd get much of a ransom for a crusty.'

'Or worse?' said Zeta.

'Murder?' James scoffed. 'Without a body? Jeez, Strawbs, just cos you've got one homicide on your CV doesn't make Becketon the corpse capital of the UK.'

'Only a thought,' said Zeta.

James pushed the plate away, the jacket potato having claimed a second victim. 'You're not planning to go off-piste again? You came within a gnat's pube of getting chucked out last time and you're the best mate I've got round here.'

Zeta stood and smiled. 'Course not. This is all hypothetical. Right, James?'

Fifteen

Once the hangover from her sixtieth birthday bash the previous year had worn off (and that had taken a good couple of weeks), Chris had resolved that now she was officially in her dotage and qualified for free prescriptions, she would do only one remarkable thing each day. One remarkable thing would prove that life was still worth living, but any more would be just too damned tiring.

As she had already been assaulted by alpacas and had stared fully into the abyss (well, a ten-metre-deep hole) and it wasn't even teatime, that was plenty for one day. Actually, it gave her an extra credit in her Remarkable Things account, which meant that she could, if she so chose, spend tomorrow under her duvet.

Her last task for today was to stop by the Cabin and hand Eric the £1,000 cheque and then home to catch up on some quality cat time.

The main road between Becketon and Cliffstaple was notorious, not so much for the weight of traffic but for its speed. Most car drivers regarded those pathetic 40mph speed limit signs as strictly advisory – pootling was for snowflakes. Chris was loath to use the road in any vehicle less robust than a Chieftain tank, but with that blood-money cheque in her pocket thumping like a tell-tale heart, she couldn't face passing by Hermon Hill Farm on her journey home. She was Judas with her thirty pieces of silver. It would be evident in her face. Liz would see it, as would Don and Pepsi and Shirlie. Chris sniffed her armpit. She needed a shower. She stank of sweat, alpaca vomit and betrayal.

As she prepared to launch herself into the traffic, she saw The Cyclist. A black-clad figure was standing astride a bicycle about fifty metres along the road towards Becketon. This was the third time today: first on leaving the Cabin, then on the approach to Tiny Barney's field and now across the road from the Hermon Village site. Of course, it could be coincidence, her imagination bordering on paranoia. Three completely different cyclists all innocently enjoying the spring weather. It could be. There was only one way to find out.

Chris spotted a gap in the traffic and, setting Rod's battery mode to high, headed for Cliffstaple. After five minutes of furious pedalling, she pulled off the road next to a black Range Rover that was courteously blocking both the pavement and half the road. She made a great show of examining Rod, checking the chain, testing the brakes and using the Range Rover's wing mirror to check behind her. The Cyclist was still there, still fifty metres back. They too had pulled over to the side of the road.

From a distance, all Chris could make out was that The Cyclist was slim and athletic – a ninja on two wheels. She scanned her phone for non-existent messages, planning to give The Cyclist a generous two minutes to pass her and disappear into the distance. One hundred and twenty seconds exactly. Another check in the wing mirror. Frick! Still there.

Who was this? Chris was pretty sure she hadn't done anything to upset anyone that grievously. Proofreading wasn't a profession that created many enemies. There might be lively debates about the Oxford comma (and she was a supporter), but hiring an assassin would be something of an escalation. Another crazy thought – was the mystery cyclist doing Danny Figg's bidding? After all, she had trespassed on his building site and he did have apparent anger-management issues. He had seemed all sweetness and light when she left him, but… She recalled what he'd said: 'I sort out my own problems.' Had she inadvertently seen something she shouldn't have? Was she now a problem?

This was bonkers – she'd only just left the construction site. Property developers didn't have bike-riding mercenaries on standby. Did they?

What to do? Phone the police and say that someone might have put a tail on her ass? Current police response times were in the gutter as it was, and factoring in North Kent Constabulary's assessment of her ('mad as an articulated lorry-load of frogs' had been Sgt Spurgeon's professional opinion), she'd hardly be high on the priority list. Chris tried Zeta's phone, but it went straight to voicemail. She didn't leave a message. What could she say that wouldn't be toe-curlingly embarrassing when left for posterity?

Chris set off again. After ten minutes, she spotted salvation on the left. An elderly gentleman walking his dog. She cruised up, hopped off her bike and walked alongside him.

'Afternoon!' Chris said. 'Morning!' and 'Afternoon!' were the accepted greetings in this part of the world. Why people had to sound surprised that it was either 'morning', 'afternoon' or, occasionally, 'evening' was beyond her understanding.

'Afternoon!' said the dog walker.

'Beautiful dog. Is he some sort of spaniel?' If Chris could give the impression that she'd just met a good friend, then surely that would deter her cyclist stalker.

'*She's* a sprocker,' said the man, looking straight ahead.

'Ooh, a sprocker? That's a cross between...?' Get dog-people to talk about their dogs and the conversation could go on for ever.

'A springer and a cocker spaniel.'

In her peripheral vision, Chris spotted the black-clad cyclist speeding past. Her cunning plan had worked.

'My mate had a cross between a cocker spaniel and a fox terrier. Called it a focker!' Chris couldn't help herself.

The dog walker didn't laugh. 'I've got a wife, you know.'

'A wife? Good for you,' said Chris. 'What's she a cross between?'

'Just saying. In case you've got the wrong idea.'

'The wrong idea?'

'I'm not available.'

He had to be eighty-five, and that was a generous estimate. And he thought that she was trying to pull him. Is that where her relationship window was positioned now? The over-eighties? She'd have to take a vacuum pump and a defibrillator on dates from now on.

'I wasn't trying to… I didn't mean… Have a nice day.' Chris found herself getting flustered and red in the face. She got back on Rod and set off again before Mrs Sprocker turned up in high dudgeon to reclaim her husband.

As she approached the outskirts of Cliffstaple, Chris berated herself for her stupidity. She was seeing danger lurking round every corner. Every traffic camera was tracking her. Every wheelie bin held a lurker. Still, at least she had some good material for her *Chris on a Bike* blog. 'The Wheelie Bin Assassin' had a good ring to it.

Chris was deep in blog-thought as she passed a side-turning, and then The Cyclist was on her tail again, just thirty metres behind and gaining fast. Frick! She switched Rod's battery setting back up to high, bent low over the handlebars, and accelerated down the hill and into Cliffstaple.

Time for Plan B – or was it Plan C? The old part of Cliffstaple town was crisscrossed by narrow alleys. Local guidebooks referred to them as 'smugglers' alleys', but Chris reckoned that was just for the tourists. She couldn't imagine that Victorian town planners were thoughtful enough to design their streets specifically to accommodate the trafficking of illegal contraband. The alleys were difficult to navigate on foot, let alone by bike, and in her thirty years of residence Chris still hadn't developed a reliable mental map of how they connected. In light of which, she was pretty sure her pursuer would find it impossible to follow her.

Rod's battery indicator flashed a warning: one bar left. Chris would have to lose the ninja quickly or she'd be toast.

Without signalling, she swung left off the main road onto Cole Walk and then immediately right along an unnamed overgrown track that ran behind a row of houses. At the end of this she veered left across a residential road, narrowly avoiding a mobility scooter, and then hard right up Hooper's Passage.

The end of Hooper's Passage opened into a residential square with a patch of common garden and a children's playground. Chris cut straight across the grass and, as she passed by the slide, she took a glance behind her. There was no sign of The Cyclist. Thank God she'd lost them! Back home, mug of tea, biscuit tin and cats.

Then, to her left, visible through the bars of the climbing frame... They'd not followed her across the grass but were taking the path round the outside, intending to cut her off before she could re-join the road.

Chris pivoted 180 degrees and headed across the grass and back up Hooper's Passage. There was another alley, squeezed between a Methodist church and a converted fish-canning warehouse, that led out into a car park and then onto the high street. Surely nobody would be reckless enough to bike-jack her in full view of afternoon shoppers.

The alley was narrower than Chris had reckoned on. The ends of Rod's handlebars scraped against the brickwork on both sides, sending up clouds of red dust. If she were to meet anyone coming in the other direction, she'd be trapped. The vertical strip of light indicating the far end of the alley got steadily bigger and then she was out, into the sunlight and into the car park. Beyond that lay the high street and safety.

The final bar on the display blinked out and Rod's battery died. Without battery assistance, Rod became an ordinary bicycle. A twenty-eight-kilogramme bicycle. A lump of lead on two wheels. And when your legs had become accustomed to maximum battery assistance, it was like a broomstick had been thrust between the spokes.

Halfway across the car park, Chris conceded defeat. If this was where she was to meet her fate then at least it would be handy for mourners who wanted to lay a commemorative posy on the anniversary – and if they stayed less than ten minutes, they wouldn't even incur a parking charge. On the other hand, she'd already faced down two angry pseudo-ruminants and an even angrier property developer. A mere youth on a bicycle would make it a hat-trick.

The Cyclist screeched to a halt in front of her, nimbly hopped off their bicycle and took off their helmet. A cascade of auburn curls fell down, framing a freckled retroussé nose. Chris was not one for hyperbole, but her pursuer was beautiful.

'You're her, aren't you?' panted the young woman.

What was it, Personal Pronoun Day? Chris wasn't sure if being 'her' was better than being 'them'. 'Who?' she said. She hadn't met many ninja assassins, but this was not how she'd pictured them. It was like looking at a shampoo ad. Whoever this woman was, she was definitely worth it.

'You're Chris Heron. *The* Chris Heron.'

'I'm *a* Chris Heron,' said Chris cautiously. What had she done to deserve a definite article in addition to the personal pronoun?

'I thought I recognised you from the TV news.'

'Oh frick!' Chris had hoped that the TV recognition phase was well behind her. Since her role in locating a missing professor had made national news, she'd endured six months of 'It's you, isn't it?', to which she normally replied, 'That's a question for my analyst.'

'Look, no offence, but I don't do autographs. Or selfies. Or children's parties.'

'I need your help. You know my father.'

'Sorry?'

'I'm Skye. My dad's Martin. Martin Livingstone.'

Sixteen

Chris liked noses. She wasn't fussy – Roman, Greek, button, hook, they were all good, even those ones that were so upturned you felt you were staring up the nostrils. Her own nose was straight and almost beak-like (she preferred the term 'aquiline'), appropriate for someone named Heron, as schoolfriends had reminded her on a daily basis. The nose was the first thing she noticed when meeting someone. Due to lifelong shyness, she still wasn't too comfortable with eye-to-eye contact. Fixing on the bridge of a person's nose instead was a foolproof trick.

The nose across the kitchen table was adorable. It belonged on a silent movie star. If Chris could have applied a bob haircut and a black-and-white filter to Skye, it would have suited her perfectly.

'Why are you staring at my nose?' asked Skye. 'I haven't got a zit, have I?'

'I wasn't staring, I was pondering,' lied Chris.

'Pondering?'

'Why you would pursue me the length and breadth of the Kent countryside on a bicycle.'

'I told you. I didn't know where you lived, so I waited outside the community garden and followed you from there.'

'That's a bit creepy. I've got a website. You could have sent me a contact request.'

Skye glanced sideways at Grayson as though assessing comparative creepiness. 'I did. Twice.'

Chris was forced to admit that it had been a few weeks since she'd looked at that in-box; she had more than enough work on as it was. She sipped her tea. Inviting a complete stranger into her house was probably foolish, but she was certain that Skye couldn't be a crazed serial killer. Not with that nose.

'Why me then?'

'You solve mysteries.'

'I solved a mystery. Once. Finito.'

A tear appeared in the corner of Skye's eye and trickled down her cheek, bypassing her perfect nose.

'OK then.' Chris sighed in resignation. 'Why don't you start at the beginning again. Something about your father?'

'Yeah. I was worried anyway as he was behaving a bit strangely and I hadn't heard from him for a couple of weeks. Then I saw that news item about the police hunting an eco-terrorist...'

'And you thought it must be your dad?'

'He's not an eco-terrorist. He's got some history of activism – I'm dead proud of him for that – but that's all in the past. He reckons woodcraft has become his passion. "A gentler life," he says.'

'I still don't understand why you thought scaring the crap out of me would help you find him.'

'I remembered that case from last year – the ice cream van and the missing professor. You found him, didn't you? So when I saw you were a member of the same woodworking group...'

'I'm sorry, Skye, I can't help. It's not what I do. '

'But you know Dad?'

'Not really. I've talked to him a few times, mainly about woodgrain and chisel-handling techniques – he's a dab hand at first aid too. He seems a decent guy, but I don't have any insight into his whereabouts.'

Skye's shoulders sagged and she looked down into her mug. Aitken and Waterman, who both seemed to have taken a shine to her – something that even Zeta couldn't claim – wound themselves round her legs in comforting solidarity.

'Look, Skye, you need to talk to the police, not a proofreader.

'I did. I spoke to some detective – DS Beech. He wouldn't listen to me. Got me thrown out of the station for wasting police time.'

'Wouldn't listen to you? But you're Martin's daughter.'

'That's what I said.'

'And?'

'He said I couldn't be. That Martin Livingstone doesn't have any children.'

Now Chris's interest was very definitely piqued.

*

Over the following half hour and powered by a banana (as the contents of the Chas and Di biscuit tin were not vegan-friendly), Skye told her story.

She'd had a happy if unconventional childhood being brought up by her mum, at first in a Druidic community in the Inner Hebrides, which, naturally, was the origin of her name. 'You were lucky not to have been born on Muck,' noted Chris, which induced a smile that crinkled that nose.

After that, they'd commune-hopped before settling down in Blekeness, a strange, isolated area known by locals as the South Kent Desert. Here, Skye's mother, Pippa, had set up her business as a spiritual life coach and wellness mentor.

'You weren't lonely?' asked Chris.

'Far from it. It was like having a dozen aunts and uncles. And about thirty cousins. Many of us still keep in touch.'

'But a bit disruptive?'

'Must admit it was weird going to school for the first time aged thirteen. The good thing about an unconventional upbringing is you have to adapt quickly.'

The one thing that Skye hadn't had in her life was a father.

'You must have asked your mother. If only to find out what his name was.'

'It never occurred to me when I was young. I didn't know any different. Mum told me I was a "cosmic love child". It was only when I hit my teens that I challenged the space-baby story.'

'And what did your mum tell you then?'

'That she didn't know who my father was. That I was the result of a drunken fling at a party but my mum saw me as a miracle. And you don't question miracles.'

It was a good backstory and one that warranted a second cup of tea.

'So how did you find your father?'

'Jake, my boyfriend, bought me a DNA ancestry test for my birthday. He thought that, if I didn't have any family apart from my mum, I should at least know where my roots lay.'

'And it matched you with your dad?' Chris found it hard to imagine that Martin would have willingly committed his DNA to a commercial enterprise.

'No, but it picked up a first cousin on the unknown side of my family. We chatted online and by a process of elimination we figured out that Martin had to be my dad. It was still tricky to track him down as he's completely off-grid – no social media, and he doesn't even have a mobile phone.'

'So how did you find him?'

'I came across an old article from the *Cliffstaple Gazette and Shopper* about the opening of Chisellers' Cabin. It had Dad's name and photo. Turned out he was living less than ten miles from where I was living. What are the chances?'

'Your dad must have been surprised when you got in touch.'

Skye nodded. 'That's an understatement. He didn't know I existed. He was suspicious at first that I might be a scammer, so we organised a comparative DNA test and bingo! A match! I had my dad!'

Chris looked more closely at Skye – into her eyes this time rather than at her nose. On first appearances she seemed a world apart from bedraggled, dreadlocked Martin, but there was something there. She wouldn't say Skye was the dead spit of her father, but those eyes… Now she could see it.

'How did your Mum take it? Was she happy for you?'

'She was furious. Said he wasn't my father, that I knew nothing about him, that he could be a psycho or a pervert. Even tried to ban me from seeing him. I'm twenty-five, for God's sake – she can't ban me from anything. Besides, he's my dad; he'd do anything to protect me.'

'So you got on well?'

'Yeah. It took a little time before we could each let our guard down, but we found we had loads in common. The environment, philosophy, politics, and we're both vegans. I even changed my name, so I'm Skye Livingstone now. A massive improvement on my birth name.'

'What's your mum's name then?'

'It's Pippa Atlantis. Suitably cosmic.'

Chris could understand the name change. Skye Atlantis sounded like an airline.

'If it's only been a couple of weeks, how do you know your father isn't visiting friends or on holiday?'

Skye looked around as though there might be other eavesdroppers in addition to Aitken and Waterman. Chris half expected her to start checking Grayson for concealed listening devices.

'Out of the blue he told me to stop contacting him. That he thought he was being watched.'

'By who?'

'He didn't say, or wouldn't say. He just said that I could be in danger if I got too close. That it had been a big mistake to track him down.'

'To be honest, Skye, that sounds a bit, well…' – Chris was trying hard to find a more compassionate word than 'nutty' – '… screwy.' Which, on reflection, was not much better.

'Exactly. That's why I'm worried that he may have, you know, done something stupid. That's why I need your help.' And the dam broke, flooding both sides of Skye's retroussé nose with a flash-flood of tears.

Chris was not one to be moved by a sob story, but there was something about the young woman on the far side of the table, head hunched, shoulders heaving. That could be Chloe. And although Chris wouldn't be that bothered if ex-husband Simon mysteriously disappeared, she could imagine the impact it would have on a daughter.

Chris knew she was being drawn in against all her best intentions.

'Would it help if I spoke to your mum? Perhaps your dad got in touch with her? Perhaps she has some idea where he might be?'

Skye shook her head vigorously. 'No. She hasn't seen or heard from him in twenty-six years. If she knew I'd told anyone, she'd be livid.'

They sat in silence for a couple of minutes, Aitken and Waterman double-teaming to provide their visitor with cat comfort.

'I'm sorry, Skye. I'm not a private eye. I wouldn't know where to start.'

Skye nodded sorrowfully and rose from the table. 'I understand. I'm sorry for scaring you earlier. I won't stop looking for my dad though.'

Chris conceded to the inevitable. 'OK. In that case, there's someone I'd like you to meet.'

*

Skye had left and Aitken and Waterman had eaten their fill of tender chunks of rabbit in a meaty jelly. Chris took down the framed film poster of *The Spy Who Came to Dinner* from her kitchen wall. Beneath the white-with-a-hint-of-apple paint the notes of her previous investigation (into the disappearance of a professor of forensic science) were still faintly visible, like a half-remembered dream.

She took a packet of whiteboard markers from the kitchen table drawer, selected a green pen and wrote a heading in large letters as high up on the wall as she could reach: 'The Hunt for Martin Livingstone'.

And with a red pen she underlined it. Twice.

Seventeen

The following morning was bright and sunny and an easterly breeze whipped the top of the waves like a Pete's Pantry cappuccino. Although it was still early in the season, the seascape was busy. Kite surfers launched themselves off the peaks, defying gravity, and dinghies twisted and jockeyed to catch the best of the wind. Less pleasingly, a jet ski shattered the peace as it roared, testing the boundaries of its permitted area as identified by yellow buoys.

'Perfect,' said Wilf from his lookout position on the balcony of the lifeguards' hut.

'It's certainly a beautiful day,' agreed Chris, squinting into the sunshine. 'Makes you appreciate living by the sea.'

'No, it's perfect for Wilf, lifesaver extraordinaire. Look at them! So many potential victims.'

'You have to excuse Wilf,' said Zeta. 'He has a rather singular attitude when it comes to his civic duty.'

'Just think, at any moment that jet ski could lose control and plough into those kite surfers. Carnage!'

Although she could only see the back of Wilf's head, Chris imagined that he was salivating at the prospect of nautical disaster. She was beginning to wish she'd arranged to meet Zeta after her shift and at a genteel seaside cafe instead.

*

The lifeguard station was her second stop of the morning. The first had been to the Cabin, to belatedly hand over Danny Figg's donation. As it was not an official Chisellers' day, only Eric and Felix had been there, although Eric made enough noise for a whole workshop of woodworkers. On receiving the cheque, he danced around the community garden, waving it above his head like a morris dancer on ecstasy.

'Manna from heaven,' he wheezed as he completed his second lap. 'This money plus Felix's contribution of unwanted railway sleepers from his friends at Network Rail means there is nothing to stop our ark!'

Chris looked quizzically at Felix, but he winked and raised his finger to his lips in an 'ask me no questions, I'll tell you no lies' gesture.

'I must alert the Chisellers that it's full steam ahead. From today, we're operational six days a week. And you, Chris, must pass on our gratitude to Mr Figg,' said Eric once he had gathered his breath. 'We should invite him to officially launch the ark.'

'I will do, when I get the chance, Eric.'

'I don't know how to thank you.'

Chris saw an opportunity to make an exit. Even though it had been her suggestion, she'd come to realise the construction of an ark was well beyond her limited woodworking abilities.

'No problem. See this as my parting gift.'

'You're leaving us?' Eric looked crestfallen.

'Well, you know what it's like in the heady world of proofreading. Work's piling up and I've got a romantic novel called *Love up the Aisle* about a forbidden tryst between supermarket workers "Bakery" Brad and "Deli" Delia that is simply *screaming* for attention. I just don't think I can spare the time, Eric.'

'I see,' said Eric, leaning back against a workbench. 'Jethro will be devastated though.'

'Jethro?'

'It was a surprise. He's carving a figurehead for the ark and he wanted you to model for it.'

Chris couldn't imagine anything worse. 'Couldn't he ask Paulette? She's got classical features. Or maybe one of the Daves?

Or a gender-neutral figurehead – this is the twenty-first century, after all.'

'No, his heart was set on you. Don't worry, I'll break the news to him.'

Chris sighed deeply. This was emotional blackmail at its finest. Quite why she was becoming a poster girl for the over-eighties was a mystery. 'Tell Jethro I'll do three one-hour sessions. That's it.'

*

There was a rap on the frame of the lifeguard station and Skye's head appeared round the corner. She smiled with relief when she saw Chris. 'Sorry I'm late, but it's crazy out there. Took me ten minutes to get through the crowd.'

Behind her, the entrants for the Cliffstaple Fun Run were strolling down towards the start line. Most were ambling, chatting to friends or taking selfies; a handful were exercising, stretching their hamstrings, and a couple of young women were preparing for the event by having a cheeky vape.

'Zeta, Skye. Skye, Zeta,' said Chris, performing the formal introductions.

'And I'm Wilf, RLSS-qualified lifeguard,' he said, his eyes gleaming as they lit upon the new arrival. 'Can I give you the guided tour of the hut?'

'Don't you have somewhere else to be?' said Zeta. 'Any one of those fun runners outside could fall into the sea at any moment.'

'Someone's got to keep an eye on the water. It's super busy out there. Besides, have you heard about the geezer in the coracle? It's double points if you spot him!'

To Skye's credit, she merely gave a gentle, sad smile in response.

'I'll keep watch,' said Zeta. 'Besides, I passed a group of Japanese exchange students outside the Hotel Parador. They looked in desperate need of some safety advice from a qualified lifeguard.'

Wilf weighed up the odds between one, admittedly beautiful, hut guest and the prospect of a whole bevy of exchange students. He nodded at Chris and bowed gracefully to Skye. He would have held and kissed her hand if Zeta hadn't intervened by directing him out of the door with the sole of her foot.

The three women watched Wilf disappear into the crowd. Skye sat on a bench at one side of the hut and Zeta switched the kettle on.

'I passed those Japanese exchange students too,' observed Chris. 'I don't think a single one was under seventy years old.'

'All part of his education,' said Zeta, grinning broadly. 'So, Chris, if you could give us a bit of space as well?' And she nodded towards the door of the hut.

'But don't you need me to help with Skye's story?'

'I'm sure Skye's quite capable of telling me herself.' Zeta had adopted a more serious tone of voice, assuming her police officer persona.

'I'd like Chris to stay,' Skye said. 'I wouldn't be sitting here without her.'

Zeta weighed up the pros and cons of this. 'OK, I suppose Chris can sit on the balcony so she can hear us and keep an eye on all the activity at the same time.'

'An unofficial lifesaver? Cool!' Chris said. 'I'll shout if Godzilla emerges from the depths.'

In the event, the sea activity was relatively benign. The wind had dropped, so the kite surfers were merely gliding off the waves and the jet ski had taken a break or, hopefully, suffered a terminal malfunction. This made it easy for Chris to divide her attention between the sea, humming sea shanties and eavesdropping on the conversation in the hut.

Skye kicked off with a potted history of how she had discovered her father's identity, which closely matched the account she'd given Chris the day before. Zeta stayed silent until Skye got to the bit about Martin warning his daughter to keep away.

'What was his mood like?'

'Did he seemed frightened?'

'Did your father have any enemies?'

'Did he mention any names?'

Chris pictured Skye shaking her head sadly, unable to give helpful answers to any of these questions. To Skye, her father was a gentle, peaceful and lovable man. She couldn't imagine why anyone would wish him harm.

Zeta followed this up with more questions, ones that, to Chris's mind, pushed the boundaries of a cosy chat.

'Does your father own his house?'

'Does he have an income?'

'Has your father recently taken out life insurance?'

'Do you have a key to his house?'

Chris half rose to her feet, thinking she should intervene. She'd brought Skye along because she needed help, not an interrogation. A throaty engine noise announced the return of the jet ski, so she missed the final five minutes of the conversation.

'Zeta? Are you going to be much longer?' Chris called out.

At that moment there was the sound of the hut door crashing open.

'Those Japanese exchange students…' Wilf sounded angry.

'Oh, hi, Wilf. You took your time,' said Zeta breezily. 'Chris and Skye were just leaving, weren't you, guys?'

Skye and Chris edged their way out between Wilf and the doorframe.

'Thanks for the chat, Skye. Give me a call if you think of anything else.'

Skye smiled broadly. Perhaps her interrogation by Zeta had reassured her that someone in authority was taking her story seriously. 'Will do,' she said, crinkling that nose. And then she was gone.

Zeta lightly grabbed Chris's shoulder. 'Can you hang around outside while I hand over to Wilf?' she whispered. 'I think I've got a plan.'

Eighteen

Leaving Zeta to placate Wilf, Chris wheeled Rod across the promenade and up the steep grassy bank on the other side. She found a good viewpoint between a couple of brightly coloured beach huts, propped her bicycle by the side of one and awaited the appearance of the first of the fun runners.

The Cliffstaple Fun Run traditionally followed the same course, straight along the promenade as far as the pier of the neighbouring town, Heybourne-on-Sea (or what was left of the pier after the great storm of '86). By Chris's rough calculation, there and back was indeed about five kilometres. She was sure that Satin Shorts had measured the course with precision.

From somewhere towards the Parador Hotel, an air horn sounded and within a couple of minutes the runners started to stream past Chris's position. Sure enough, the first to appear were the uber-competitive types who were intent on stripping any semblance of fun out of 'fun run'. Four of them, all men in their late thirties, jostled for position, chests thrust out, determined to lead the pack. As athletes, they may not have been fast enough to represent their nation at the Olympics, but they were as sure as hell going to whop this field of retirees, children and members of the local knitting club.

As the speedsters disappeared into the distance, the main pack of fun runners started to pass by, as varied a collection of ages, outfits and physical prowess as it was possible to imagine. Chris was surprised at how many people she recognised. Perhaps she was more integrated with the local community than she realised. The lady from her local greengrocer's gave her a wave. She was followed by Poppy from Cliffstaple Pharmacy, running in tandem with her boyfriend Gus from the Spokesmen Cycle Shop on the high street. Next came a neighbour whose name Chris could never remember, either Helen or Charlotte, chaperoning her two immaculate, designer-attired children. Then there were Libby and Paulette from Chisellers' Cabin, keeping up a brisk pace, and on their shoulder was Next-Door Nick.

This was a revelation and Chris was rather impressed. Nick had never mentioned a penchant for running in their bi-weekly wine-and-slagging-off-the-neighbours sessions. He exchanged a nod and a few brief words with Paulette and Libby – presumably they knew each other from that time when Nick was 'definitely not' woodworking at the Cabin. Nick increased his pace to a slow, loping run and swerved around someone dressed as a rhinoceros – or possibly a real rhinoceros on a day out from Becketon World of Wildlife.

And, talking of wildlife, next came the Cliffstaple and Bottisham Walruses, at least a dozen of them in specially printed T-shirts, no doubt financed by well-intentioned sponsors. Simon was already looking flushed and sweaty and Chris started calculating what refund she might get for him failing to complete the course.

'Come on, Simon, hon! You're doing us proud!' a voice shrieked in Chris's ear, as though a seagull had just learnt to speak English. 'Keep on running, Walruses!'

Chris didn't need to look round. 'Hello, Jan. Good to hear you again. I think hubby needs all your vocal support. He looks a bit wobbly and there's still more than four kilometres to go.'

'Oh hi, Christine, hon. Didn't see you there,' said Simon's wife. She nodded at Rod the e-bike. 'Still cycling, I see. I'd have thought you'd have given up by now, the way you keep falling off and everything.'

'You know what they say about bike riding, Jan – you've got to get straight back on again. Still, I don't need to teach you anything about bikes, do I?'

'Never seen the point of them,' Jan replied. 'Deathtraps, if you ask me.'

'I didn't,' muttered Chris under her breath. 'I'm surprised you're not out there running too. I thought you and Simon did *everything* together.'

'I draw the line at running, Christine, love. After having four kids, my pelvic floor's in the basement.'

This was a mental image that would sit with Chris for the rest of the day and on every occasion in the future when she took the lift in a department store.

Thankfully, Jan moved on to try to catch up with the Walruses at the Heybourne Pier turning point. The stragglers filtered past, supported by Satin Shorts, who presumably, as organiser, was responsible for ensuring that no runners took a wrong turn and veered off into the sea by mistake. The promenade finally cleared to reveal Zeta standing astride her bicycle and looking at her phone.

'How's Wilf?'

'I calmed him down by giving him Skye's number.'

'You didn't?'

'Not her real number of course – the Irritable Bowel Syndrome Advice Line. I keep it handy for such occasions.'

'So what do you think – about Skye?'

'She's cute.'

'She's also got a boyfriend.'

'I like a challenge.' Zeta grinned.

'Behave. So what now – are you going to debrief me?'

'Yep. Over lunch?'

'OK. Where? The Wavecrest Cafe does a good vegetarian special or you could come back to mine and raid the Chas and Di biscuit tin.'

'I've got somewhere better in mind. Follow me,' said Zeta.

*

With Zeta leading the way, they pushed their bicycles further up the steep grassy slope until they reached the road that ran along the top.

For the first two kilometres the road ran parallel to the promenade, so they could glance down to their left and see runners reaching the halfway point and the faster ones already heading back towards Cliffstaple. Chris spotted Simon, hunched over, catching his breath and being offered water by a rhinoceros and a hippopotamus. She felt a pang of guilt for her cynicism. At least Simon was out there trying, whereas she'd been sniping from the sidelines, or, in this case, a grassy knoll.

Zeta was setting an easy, considerate pace and Chris followed in her slipstream. Heybourne-on-Sea was a town marked as 'up and coming' by estate agents. It offered more value for renters and buyers who were being priced out of Becketon and Cliffstaple. Unfortunately, within the next five years they'd probably be priced out of Heybourne-on-Sea as well. The start of the high street hadn't received the 'up and coming' memo and was stuck in a 1970s bubble.

'Here we are,' said Zeta, pulling over to the side of the road and chaining her bicycle to a lamppost next to a cafe.

Chris looked at the proposed lunch venue. It wasn't the peeling paint on the facade or the grubby net curtains shielding the bottom half of the windows that caused her to feel trepidation, nor even the faded window sticker advertising Cresta Cream Soda; it was the name: Trev's Top-Notch Nosh. Whatever lay inside might well be nosh, but Chris was certain it wouldn't be top notch.

Giving a hefty shove with her shoulder, Zeta barged the sticky door open and entered. The interior of Trev's establishment did little to allay Chris's fears.

'This is a shithole!' she hissed to Zeta.

If there was one thing worse than a cafe without an available table, it was a cafe where all the tables were available. The tables themselves were topped in a blue Formica that Chris hadn't seen in thirty years, and the dark red crusts on the necks of the own-brand ketchup bottles seemed to predate the Formica.

The menu above the counter was another collector's item, its letters pegged onto a sticky board. The menu itself was admirable in its consistency: chips with everything, even the egg mayonnaise salad.

'Let's get out of here while we still can,' Chris urged.

'No, this is perfect,' Zeta replied.

A combover-crested head, presumably belonging to the titular Trev, appeared above a glass frame housing suspicious-looking bread rolls.

'What can I get you, ladies?' he inquired, displaying a mouth that resembled a Victorian graveyard.

'We're lost,' said Chris. 'How do we get to Becketon bus station from here?'

'Ignore my friend,' said Zeta. 'She'll have a tea with milk and one of your delicious-looking cheese and tomato rolls. Just a bottle of water for me, thanks.'

Zeta collected the order and sat at a table facing the front window.

'What are we doing here?' asked Chris.

'Having lunch.'

'Do you want to kill me? Look at this place – even the salmonella comes with chips.'

'Shh,' hushed Zeta. 'Do you want to hear about my chat with Skye Livingstone or not?'

In this battle, Chris's curiosity overcame her fear of food poisoning. She looked down at her mug of tea. A curious oily film shimmered on the surface, the sort that endangered seabirds. Suddenly she wasn't thirsty. 'Go on.'

'CID is working on the basis that Martin Livingstone's faked his own death.'

'Why would he do that?'

'Usually it'd be for financial reasons, but CID's money is on a flight from justice.'

'And you don't agree?'

'Setting up an alternative life takes preparation, organisation. You need to have a new identity, bank accounts, a digital history.

That takes time and there's nothing to suggest that Martin had the inclination or the knowhow.'

'You're sure?'

'That's what I wanted to get out of Skye. As far as she's aware, her dad is anti-tech, doesn't have life insurance and, though not exactly loaded, has no real money problems.'

Chris cautiously lifted the top of her bread roll. There, neatly positioned between a wedge of yellowing cheese and a limp slice of tomato, was a used matchstick. She pushed the plate away to the far edge of the table. 'So what's your theory?'

'I don't know.' Such an admission was a rarity from Zeta. 'But I'm worried for his safety. After all, he was last seen heading to the sea with a coracle on his back.'

'Occam's razor?'

Zeta nodded. 'The most straightforward solution is usually the right one.'

'An accident? There's not much we can do then but wait for him to wash up somewhere. Poor Skye. She'd only just found her father, and then to lose him…'

'But I'm not one hundred per cent convinced about an accident. That part of the coast is shallow for a long way out and the weather was calm the day of Martin's disappearance. Things just aren't adding up,' said Zeta.

'So, if not an accident…?'

'Foul play. If Martin was causing trouble, if he was a thorn in the side of powerful people…'

'Coracle sabotage?' suggested Chris.

'That's assuming he even got as far as launching it.'

A mental image of Danny Figg's distress at his graffitied office loomed into Chris's mind: 'I sort out my own problems.'

'Then that's for the police to investigate,' she said. 'They've got the resources and the expertise.'

'Agreed,' said Zeta. 'That's why we're here.' And she pointed out of the window.

Chris gingerly pulled the net curtain to one side, thanking the stars that she'd remembered to pack the hand sanitiser, and looked across to the far side of the street. 'Happy Endings Funeral Services? You think they've got Martin in their fridge?'

'No, the flat above is the registered address for T Figg Debt Recovery Solutions; Director: Tony Figg, Company Secretary: Daisy Figg.'

'Says who?'

'Companies House.'

'You've completely lost me.'

Zeta took a deep breath, as though she was about to explain to a child where babies came from. 'CID think Martin Livingstone's behind a death threat to Danny Figg.'

'I remember. Dead squirrel and all that.'

'They've got tunnel vision. They're not looking for any other suspects.'

'Such as?'

'His brother, for example.'

'His brother sending him a death threat? Wouldn't that create a rather awkward atmosphere around the dinner table at Christmas?'

Zeta smiled at the thought. 'All I need to do is create doubt. To be able to suggest to CID that Martin's disappearance may not be linked to Danny Figg. Then they will have to go back to square one, to investigate this properly.'

'I think I follow your reasoning. But why am I sitting in Trev's House of Botulism?'

'So we can keep an eye out for Danny's brother Tony. I tried phoning earlier, but there was no answer.'

'And if and when Tony turns up?'

'That's where you come in.'

It was the answer Chris had been dreading.

Nineteen

Chris liked hanging around cafes to kill time while waiting for a train, or to shelter from the rain or to avoid people she knew. They usually had good wi-fi, heating and cake. However, the prospect of spending any more time in Trev's Top-Notch Nosh was pushing her to the limit. She wasn't a snob and she loved a greasy spoon, but in Trev's case the grease was rancid bacon fat and she'd rather not imagine what he'd been doing with the spoon. Her untouched tea was stone cold and… hang on, did that cheese and tomato roll just move by itself? Friendship or not, she was getting out of there.

'I think that's him,' said Zeta, gesturing for Chris to sit back down. 'He's been walking his dog.'

Chris turned and eased back a corner of the net curtain. On the far side of the road was Danny Figg. Well, it would have been Danny Figg if he'd gained three stone, lost a fight with a garden strimmer and been rooting through a skip for his clothing. Apart from that, Tony Figg was the spitting image of his brother.

He was wearing shapeless grey jogging bottoms and a muddied orange hooded top. On the end of a lead was an overweight mastiff wearing a matching orange cravat. Dogs resembling their owners was undoubtedly a fact. What Chris hadn't ascertained was whether people selected dogs that resembled themselves or whether, over time, the owners morphed into facsimiles of their pets. She suspected the latter.

'He's definitely carrying the Figg gene.' Chris recalled the photo in Danny Figg's office of the two brothers in a boxing ring. 'But they've rather grown apart physically. Can we leave now?'

'Leave? We're going in. An audience with Tony Figg – undercover intelligence gathering.'

'You're determined to trash your career, aren't you?'

'No one will know. The story is that I'm seeking his help to recover a bad debt. One of my clients is refusing to pay.'

'And who am I?'

'My mother.'

Chris raised a quizzical eyebrow.

'I was adopted?' Zeta suggested.

'Let's settle for friend and confidant. The closer to the truth we can keep this, the better.'

'Oh, wow, so we're doing this? I never thought you'd agree. This is why I love hanging out with you – you're game for anything!'

And Chris was as surprised as Zeta. She would never have thought she'd participate in such a ridiculous escapade, but in the twelve months she'd known Zeta, they'd done sillier things and lived – just.

*

The front door through which Tony Figg had disappeared ten minutes previously was anonymous. The plastic doorbell had a space for a name but had been left blank. Zeta pushed the bell, but no sound was audible and the button became irretrievably wedged in its hole.

'No answer? Oh dear. What a shame. Guess I'll have to go back home and socialise with my cats instead,' said Chris.

Zeta gently pushed the door and it swung open. The interior of the frame suggested that it had been forced years ago and nobody had bothered to make the necessary repairs.

'Damn,' said Chris.

Zeta led the way up a narrow, dark staircase that creaked ominously underfoot and smelt of damp dog. At the top was a plain white door that wasn't anonymous but rather made it clear that these were indeed the offices of T Figg Debt Recovery Solutions. Zeta rapped on the door, but there was no answer. She rapped again. A dog barked.

'The cheque's in the post,' said a voice on the other side of the door.

'Tony Figg?' said Zeta.

'Tommy Frog? Never 'eard of 'im.'

'Tony Figg. Your name's on the door.'

'Ah, that was the previous occupant. 'Aven't got round to changing the signage, see?' said the disembodied voice. 'So I can't 'elp you with any outstanding financial issues.'

The irony of the owner of a debt recovery company hiding from his creditors was not lost on Chris.

'That's a shame,' Zeta persisted, 'as we wanted to put some business the way of Mr Figg.'

There was a pause and then the sound of the latch being opened. Tony Figg's face appeared round the corner.

'If you're the police, you'll need a warrant.'

'Just potential clients. We were told you were number one for debt recovery in Kent.'

'Number one, eh? If you'd like to phone my PA and make an appointment?'

'I did phone – twice. There was no answer.'

'You'd better come in then. Better beware of the dog, though; she doesn't take too kindly to strangers.'

The offices of T Figg Debt Recovery Solutions could have been twinned with Trev's Top-Notch Nosh opposite. Tony Figg directed them into a room with a desk, two chairs for visitors, a half-eaten pizza and a dog bowl at which the mastiff was currently lunching noisily. Along one wall was a series of filing cabinets whose open drawers spewed confidential client documents. Through a half-open door on the other side of the corridor, Chris could see a dishevelled bed – well, a mattress on the floor – and a stack of emptied takeaway containers. This was apparently a multi-functional premises.

''Scuse the, um, disorganisation,' muttered Tony Figg, directing Chris and Zeta to the chairs, 'but my PA's on holiday and her cover hasn't, um, turned up.'

'No problem,' said Zeta. 'I'm Lena and this is my business associate, Christine. She has a debt that she needs help recovering.'

'I do?' said Chris, surprised at this departure from their agreed cover story.

'She's a proofreader, a first-class one, and one of her clients is refusing to pay.'

'They are?' said Chris, incredulous.

In her career, Chris had only suffered one bad debt. She'd agreed to proofread a debut self-published novel, a thriller entitled *The Cliffstaple Cockle Killer*, in which a serial killer was dispatching his victims by slitting their throats with a sharpened cockle shell. The writing was as risible as the plot. Chris had spent two weeks struggling to give it a semblance of professionalism then sent it back. The author didn't understand the proofreader's role and had expected a rewrite. A rewrite wouldn't have saved *The Cliffstaple Cockle Killer*; it needed napalming.

The client refused to pay and Chris wrote it off, putting it down to experience. She had briefly fantasised about exacting revenge on the author with a range of sharpened seafood shells, but at no point did she consider employing a debt collection agency, let alone one that was based above a budget funeral parlour.

'So we thought some gentle persuasion from your good self could, shall we say, lubricate the payment process?'

Chris was not sure where Zeta had sourced her alternate Lena personality. She was sounding as though she'd walked off the *Peaky Blinders* set. Still, it seemed to be authentic enough to fool Tony Figg.

'You've come to the right place. Daisy!'

Chris and Zeta looked towards the door, expecting the arrival of the company secretary. Instead, the mastiff glanced round and gave a quizzical 'Ruff?'

'Leave that food alone, we're talking business 'ere!'

The mastiff sighed and the company guard dog/secretary trotted out of the room.

'My rate is thirty per cent of all monies recovered, no questions asked. OK?'

'Sounds fair,' said Chris.

'Good. So how much are you owed then?'

Zeta might be an old hand at undercover tactics, but Chris was already out of her comfort zone. Make it worth his while, Chris. '£21,000,' she blurted out.

Tony Figg looked impressed, mentally calculating his commission. 'Twenty-one grand? I never knew proofreading was such a nice earner. So you have a name and address?'

Zeta leant across the table and looked Tony Figg directly in the eyes. 'His name is Livingstone. Martin Livingstone.'

Tony Figg's face didn't betray a flicker of recognition. 'Good. And is this Livingstone geezer local? Travel expenses are on top of my fee.'

'Yes, he's local,' said Zeta. 'You heard of him?'

Tony Figg looked thoughtful and then shook his head. 'Nah, can't say I have. Got an address for him?'

'We can get you it.'

'And I'll need fifty per cent upfront, which is three thousand one hundred and fifty.' Tony Figg looked more like a darts player than a businessman and his mental arithmetic was as impressive. 'Cash, of course.'

Chris was feeling decidedly uncomfortable. She had started the day expecting to introduce Skye and Zeta to each other and be back at home for lunch. Now she was within a hair's breadth of handing over her entire rainy day nest egg to a gangster in an orange hoodie. 'Of course. We'll be in touch when we've got the cash, won't we, Zeta?'

There was a pregnant pause. 'Daisy!' shouted Tony Figg. 'On guard!'

There was the heavy thump of mastiff paws positioning themselves behind the door to the corridor.

'Zeta?' Tony Figg's face darkened and he poked a pudgy finger at the two women. 'You said your name was Lena.'

Zeta tried to effect a carefree laugh. 'Ah yes. Lena, but my friends call me Zeta.'

'Why?'

'It's a nickname?' suggested Chris.

'In that case, I'm sure you won't mind proving it by showing me some ID, will you?'

'Would you believe it?' Zeta chuckled. 'I've left my purse at home. Tell you what, we'll pop back later, shall we?'

'You two are going nowhere,' said Tony Figg, 'until you tell me who sent ya. It was 'im, wasn't it?'

'Nobody sent us here. As we were saying, Christine is owed money…' Zeta said.

Chris glanced around to assess their chances if they were to make a run for it. Tony Figg didn't appear quick, but he could fill a doorway, and there was the company secretary slapping her chops on the other side. They couldn't stand and fight; they didn't even have a sharpened cockle shell between them.

'So 'e thought 'e could put the frighteners on me, did 'e? Flesh and blood? What a joke!'

Flesh and blood? 'You think your brother sent us here?' exclaimed Chris.

'*Think?* I bleedin' know that ungrateful sod's behind it. And look at 'im, Mr Highfalutin, Big Cheese Property Developer. It was me what gave 'im his break, me that financed his first build. "T," he said, "I'll never forget how much I owe you." Hah!'

Strangely, the more passionate Tony Figg became, the more he deflated. It was like watching the Wicked Witch of the West on the receiving end of a bucket of water.

'Just cos I'm in the debt recovery business, everyone thinks I'm the bad egg. Not any more. Go back to Danny with this message.

You tell 'im that T's coming for 'im.' Tony unlocked a drawer in his desk, took out a bright blue USB stick and waved it in Chris and Zeta's faces. 'I've got the evidence, and this time all 'is police and posh council mates aren't going to help 'im. And, yes, this time it's personal. You got that?'

Zeta and Chris nodded dumbly.

'Go on, get out before I do something I regret!'

Not in any mood to query their instructions, Zeta and Chris stood, opened the office door, stepped over the company secretary, who had settled down for a post-lunch nap, and escaped down the stairs and out into the street.

*

Chris bent over to catch her breath and return her heartbeat to a regular rhythm. 'Frick, I thought we were goners there.'

'Shall we steady our nerves with a cuppa?'

Chris glanced across the road at Trev's Top-Notch Nosh. 'I'm shaken but not that shaken. What were you up to in there, Zeta?'

'Me? It was you that ballsed it up by forgetting my cover name.'

'Excuse me for being crap at espionage. I must have missed that lesson in proofreading school. And what was all that with "Martin Livingstone" followed by the Paddington Bear stare?'

'Just testing a theory,' said Zeta.

'Any chance of you sharing that theory with your… what was I again? Oh yes, "business associate"?'

They crossed the road and unlocked their bikes. 'It's a long shot, but if Martin was connected with the intimidation and sabotage of Danny Figg's business, or even if Danny Figg thought Martin was responsible, then he may have taken certain steps.'

'And if you don't want to dirty your own hands but need someone you can trust, then who's better for the job than your own brother?'

'So it's crossed your mind as well?'

'Only as an idle and probably mad thought. And your tactic was to track down this potential hitman and confront him in his own flat?'

Zeta gave an embarrassed grin. 'Yep. Stupid. Didn't think that one through. It was spontaneous.'

'Well, if Tony Figg had done us in, at least we would have been handily placed for the budget funeral parlour downstairs.'

'What do you think about Tony being behind his brother's death threat? There's obviously bad blood,' said Zeta.

'Yeah, but all that "tell 'im I'm coming for 'im" stuff sounded a bit panto. Nobody talks like that in real life, do they?'

'Trying to pretend that him and his brother are mortal enemies? Could be, Chris. See, I told you we're a good team.'

'Yeah, proper Cagney and Lacey, we are.'

'Who?'

'Never mind. But if you could avoid getting your teammate murdered, that would be appreciated. Someone at the police station must have a bit of history on the brothers.'

'Sergeant Spurgeon – but I can't ask, I'm supposed to be back on routine duties. However, I can think of another candidate. Come on, Chris, saddle up. We're going shopping.'

This day had already got out of hand, but where Zeta led, Chris knew she would surely follow. Why was that? Was it curiosity? Fear of upsetting her friend? Or was it that once you'd got the front seat of the rollercoaster, you couldn't get off, no matter how knicker-wettingly scary the ride became?

Chris mounted Rod the e-bike and turned on the ride computer. 'This shopping expedition, Zeta, will it get me killed?'

'Probably not,' replied Zeta comfortingly as she set off in the direction of Heybourne-on-Sea town centre.

Twenty

The Blue Horizon shopping centre was the proudest achievement of Heybourne-on-Sea council. A tragedy of concrete and plate glass, it squatted on the outskirts of the town on what had previously been a cherry orchard. It boasted three storeys and over seventy retail units where shoppers roamed the walkways like zombies in an apocalypse movie. Young mothers chaperoned bored children, newly paired couples prodded scatter cushions, and older couples stopped at one of the six cafes (one of which was, ironically, called Cherries) for their eighth cup of tea.

Chris couldn't see the point in shopping. The internet had made life so much easier, with food, alcohol and life's other essentials delivered to your door – or rather, dumped on your doorstep. And for items missed off the shopping list, the friendly high street beckoned. Once she'd passed fifty, Chris didn't need to window shop; she knew what she liked, she'd defined her style and she didn't feel any urge to examine her cellulite in a changing-room mirror. Besides, the bigger stores were out of reach, re-sited on themed just-out-of-town retail parks practically inaccessible to people without a car.

Blue Horizon had done nothing to disabuse her of these prejudices. It had taken a further half an hour's ride and a vertigo-challenging crossing of the footbridge over the A-road to reach it and Chris felt confident that her first visit would also be her last. If Chris was bewildered by the lights, smells and piped, auto-tuned chart music, Zeta knew exactly where she was going. She led them up two flights of escalators and through a door marked 'Private – Staff Only'. Just inside the door on the right was another door, this one with the imposing sign: 'Security – Do Not Enter'. Zeta entered. Chris followed.

After the neon lighting of the shopping complex, the darkness caused Chris to blink to readjust her vision. It was a small room dominated by a wall of CCTV screens that showed live feeds from all areas, from the car park to the soft-play area. In front of the screens was a bank of buttons and levers and two high-backed chairs.

'She's going to pick the red one,' said a young male voice.

'I'll go for black then. Tenner on it?' said a familiar older male voice.

'Done.'

'Can anyone play?' asked Zeta.

'Only if you've brought cake.'

One of the chairs swivelled to reveal the former PC Barry Conway. 'Ah, you've brought the lovely Chris. That's even better than cake!' And he stood to embrace both women.

It had been six months since Chris had seen Barry, but she knew him to be a good man – and a brave man as well.

The second chair swivelled and a tall, lean, good-looking man stood.

'And this is my latest trainee, Manjit,' said Barry.

Manjit smiled and nodded a greeting.

'Barry's the senior security operative for Blue Horizon. Perfect job for a retired copper,' explained Zeta.

'Chief security operative, I'll have you know.'

'What's with the "red or black"?' asked Chris, nodding at the screen that seemed to be the centre of their attention.

'Just a harmless bit of fun. That lady there has been examining that rail of dresses for the last five minutes. We're predicting what colour she'll choose.'

'And Baz has won the last three in a row, but I reckon I've got him this time. Look! She's picked the red dress,' said Manjit.

Now the screen had the undivided attention of four people. The shopper selected a red dress, examined it, turned towards the pay desk, had second thoughts and replaced it on the rail.

'Ooh, you hit the post there, Manjit, lad!' Barry cheered.

A shaft of light flooded the room as the door behind them opened and a middle-aged woman entered. 'Come on, Manjit, we were supposed to be on electricals five minutes ago.'

'Sorry, Pat, just about to fleece a tenner off Baz. This woman's definitely going for the red frock.'

Pat squeezed between the two men and scrutinised the screen. 'Nah, she's a browser not a buyer.'

'Tenner on it?' said Barry.

'OK. You're on,' said Pat.

The ladieswear shopper was blissfully unaware that she now had a rapt audience of five viewers as she circled the clothes rack twice before selecting a black dress and heading out of camera shot.

'You done it again!' exclaimed Manjit. 'You lucky bugger, Barry.'

'Come on, Manjit, let's patrol electricals before we lose all our money to that hustler,' said Pat, slapping a ten pound note on the control panel and shepherding her colleague out of the door.

'Double or quits later?' shouted Barry as his colleagues left, slamming the door behind them.

'So, to what do I owe the pleasure of this surprise visit?'

Zeta placed her hands on the back of Barry's chair and Chris took the one recently vacated by Manjit.

'Danny and Tony Figg?'

'The DTs? What about them?'

'Your intel?'

'Danny's a big cheese now. Property development, chair of the Rotary club, rumoured to be worshipful master of Becketon Freemason's lodge.'

'And Tony?'

'They're twins, not identical but pretty close. Haven't heard of T in years.'

'"T"?'

'Yeah, everyone called Tony "T" or "Big T" or "Terrible T", depending on their opinion of him. Back in the day, he ran security for local pubs and clubs, but he's probably snuffed it by now.'

'Oh, he was very much alive when we saw him this morning – scarily so. Do you know anything about their history?' said Zeta.

'When they were young, they were a bit naughty. Drink, soft drugs, a bit handy with their fists, but nothing serious. We jokingly called them "the Becketon Krays", but they weren't in that league of nastiness. After that, clean as a whistle. Danny was rumoured to be a bit dodgy, but show me a successful businessman who isn't.'

'And T?' asked Chris.

'As far as I know, a model citizen. I certainly never had cause to feel his collar.'

'What was their relationship like? When we met Tony, he wasn't showing a deep sense of brotherly love.'

'Ah, now that's a story that's going to require tea and biscuits. Pop the kettle on, Zeta, love, and I'll make us a brew.'

*

Armed with tea and Jaffa Cakes, Barry began.

'Like I said, they were handy with their fists, so a social worker directed them to a local boxing gym to help them redirect their youthful aggression.'

'Danny's got a picture of them in a boxing ring on his office wall,' said Chris.

Barry nodded. 'They were good amateur boxers, won a couple of junior titles, but, of course, there was no money in it, and the one thing the brothers loved was cash.'

'And now one's a multi-millionaire whilst the other's stony broke by the looks of it,' observed Zeta.

Barry shovelled three Jaffa Cakes into his mouth at the same time and somehow managed to continue. 'They started doing some illegal bouts upstairs in pubs after closing, but it was still pin money. Then they got an offer they couldn't refuse.'

'To do what? Something illegal?' said Zeta.

'To fight each other. Brothers, twins even, that was box office. Twenty grand, winner takes all.'

'Twenty grand would have been a fortune back then. Who would pay that sort of money?'

'A local bookmaker stumped up the purse. Sure, you could charge people to watch, but running an illegal book was where the profit was.'

'Did you hear what happened at the fight?' Chris was getting engrossed in Barry's story.

'Hear about it? I saw it. I was there!'

'Undercover?' asked Zeta.

'Still as pious as ever, I see, SC Jama. No, I bought me own ticket.'

'To an illegal fight?'

'Between the Figg twins? I'd have traded in my own mother to be there. Besides, half of North Kent nick had a bet on it, so I had to look after our investment.'

'So who won?' asked Chris, who was also on her third Jaffa Cake, but at least she was eating them one at a time.

'I'm getting to that,' said Barry. He turned one of the flexible lamps on the control panel to shine directly on his face, to add to the suspense. 'Picture this: Saturday night, quarter to midnight, at the Hare and Hogshead on the Becketon Estate. Two hundred punters packed into the upstairs room, thick with ciggie smoke, boxing ring in the centre. Ten three-minute rounds.

'Now, T was the better boxer of the two, but the clever money said Danny had that "win at all costs" edge. First round was cagy, sizing each other up, but T caught his brother with a couple of hard, straight jabs. Then round two, he got him with a beautiful left hook and dumped Danny on his arse for an eight count. We all thought that T would finish it off in the next round.'

'But...' said Zeta.

'T came out of his corner for round three with no energy, like he was punch drunk, and Danny started to get on top. Round four, T was running on empty, but his brother wasn't going to let up. It was brutal.'

'Didn't the referee step in to stop the fight?'

'Chris, love, this was the Hare and Hogshead, not Madison Square Garden. We had to watch two more rounds of carnage before T collapsed in a heap. A few of the lads carried him to a car and drove him to Kent Coast Hospital. It was three weeks before he was discharged and rumour was that from that point on the brothers never spoke to each other again.'

'Not surprised, if T had been hospitalised by his brother.'

'It wasn't just that, Chris. Why did T just run out of gas like that? There was lots of talk about his water bottle being spiked, but nothing was ever proven.'

'Spiked? By Danny?'

'Assume so. Like I said, he had a "win at all costs" reputation even when he was a youngster.'

'So Tony might still want revenge?' said Chris.

Barry shrugged. 'Wouldn't you?'

Zeta kissed Barry on the cheek. 'Thanks, Barry, you're a marvel.'

'Anytime, Zeta.' Barry then looked at Chris and pointed at his cheek. 'Don't I get a thank you kiss from you too?'

Chris kissed the tips of her fingers to blow Barry a kiss but stopped mid-gesture. On the screen behind Barry's head, a woman was deciding whether to buy a black or red dress.

'Barry, either it's Groundhog Day or that footage is on a loop.'

Barry smiled innocently. 'Oh yes, so it is.'

'So you already knew she'd picked the black dress before making those bets with Manjit and Pat.'

'Betting's a mug's game.' Barry grinned. 'They've got to learn that somehow.'

*

'What do you think?' asked Chris once they were safely outside the frenetic consumerism of Blue Horizon.

'That we've found the number one suspect for the Danny Figg death threat.'

'It's a hell of a chip that Tony's got on his shoulder.'

Zeta nodded. 'For all those years? That's bearing a grudge to the extreme.'

'Not really. His brother did cheat, beat him to a pulp and put him in intensive care,' said Chris. 'I've got a friend I haven't spoken to for fifteen years since a fractious "jam or cream first?" scone argument.'

'Why now though? Has the Hermon Village development set him off for some reason?'

'And what's the connection with this CrEW lot? I can't see Tony Figg as an eco-terrorist,' said Chris.

'That's if CrEW even exists as a real group. Perhaps it's a charade, a clever distraction technique.'

'I don't like to make snap judgements about people, Zeta, but Tony Figg devising a clever distraction technique? That's even more unlikely than him being a clandestine eco-terrorist.'

Zeta nodded in thoughtful agreement.

'So what next?' Chris asked.

'You go home, and I figure out how to get this new intel into the investigation.'

'But it doesn't help Skye, does it? It doesn't help us get any closer to finding out what happened to her father.'

'If I can close off one line of investigation, maybe another will open.'

'Maybe?'

'This isn't over, Chris. Not by a long way.'

Twenty-One

Achieving the perfect temperature of an early-morning bath was an art rather than a science. It had to be so hot that it was only just bearable. Cycling in and around Heybourne-on-Sea may have been battery-assisted, but it had still put a strain on Chris's just-out-of-hibernation muscles, something only an extra-hot bath could remedy.

She tested the surface with her toes. Like Goldilocks and the first bowl of porridge, it was too hot. Exactly eleven seconds of cold water, that was good. Toes in, right foot in, left foot in, lower legs… Ah, that was hot… Thighs… Was it too hot?… Hover the bum above the surface for ten seconds, then… plunge. Frick! Frick! Frick! Chris hadn't felt as much nether-region discomfort since she'd bought that tea tree oil shower gel.

It took a further thirty seconds of endurance for her body to adapt – an exquisite balance between pain and bliss. A bath was a metaphor for life: nothing good came without pain, but there was only a brief period of contentment before everything became lukewarm and, ultimately, cold.

She checked the door was safely bolted against cat incursion. The magnetic effect a bathtub had on inquisitive cats was something those science boffins had yet to figure out.

Chris closed her eyes and thought about yesterday. About Zeta's questioning of Skye, the nerve-jangling encounter with Tony Figg, and Barry's tale from the past. There was still a loose thread that was annoying her, something that didn't fit the pattern. She needed a second opinion.

At 8 a.m. precisely, Chris leant out of the bath and pressed the mousepad on her laptop, which was sitting on the closed lid of the loo.

'Hi, Mum! It's OK, the coast is clear,' said Chloe. 'Dan's in the garden helping the boys practise tying sailing knots. They've trussed him up tighter than a Christmas turkey.'

Chris pressed the 'start video' icon and Chloe grinned. 'Though you could video call after you've had your bath and then you wouldn't have to worry about accidental overexposure.'

'Multi-tasking,' her mother explained. 'Life's too short to take individual actions. So my favourite grandchildren enjoyed their yachting trip then?'

'They've become obsessed. I guess bloody single-mindedness runs in the family.'

'I'd have thought you'd be into it too, growing up by the sea.'

'No, thanks. The sea's for looking at and flying over. Boats are not in my comfort zone. Talking of which, how's your ark going? Everything OK at the Cabin?'

'Nothing exciting to report.'

'You're not going to end up circumnavigating the globe, are you?' said Chloe.

'It's going to be moored to the quayside. Like I said, nothing that exciting. To tell you the truth, I'm thinking of giving it a miss. Now that they've started the build, there's not much I can contribute.'

Chloe put on her serious telling-off face – one that could intimidate her mother, even from ten thousand miles distant. 'You promised me you'd spend more time on this hobby, Mum. And socialise properly. You promised.'

'I've been busy proofreading *Love up the Aisle*. It's a steamy, retail-based potboiler, and I have seen Zeta, so I don't break *all* my promises.'

'Did you send her my love like I asked?'

Chris hadn't. In the hunt for Martin Livingstone, things had been too hectic for pleasantries. 'Of course I did, and she sends hers in return.' Which, of course, she hadn't. 'Can I ask you a hypothetical question?'

'Go on,' said Chloe, suspiciously.

'If you suddenly found out that Simon wasn't your real father, would you want to track your birth father down?'

'You're telling me that Dad isn't… um… Dad?'

'No, of course he is. Unfortunately. But say, hypothetically, he didn't exist. That I'd had a one-night stand thirty-odd years ago and you were the result.'

'Did you?'

'No, of course not. I mean, before I met your father I had a couple…'

'I do so love our wholesome mother–daughter chats,' said Chloe wearily.

'And then you searched for and tracked down your birth father.'

'Hypothetically.'

'Yes. But – and this is important – I forbade you from meeting up with him. Would you think that strange?'

There was a silence. For a moment Chris thought that the Cliffstaple–Melbourne connection had frozen, but then Chloe bowed her head and sighed.

'This isn't anything to do with a missing environmental activist, is it?'

Chris knew that her daughter was a sensitive and perceptive woman, but this was bordering on psychic.

'What made you ask such a crazy question?' She tried a bluff.

'I follow the *Look Lively* page on Facebook. I like to keep in touch with the old place…'

Uh-oh. Chris was still learning about twenty-first-century communication. You didn't even need to go viral to have global reach.

'… and I'd recognise my mother's backside anywhere.'

Chris wasn't sure if that was a compliment or not. 'Ah, yes, I knew there was something I'd forgotten to mention,' she said sheepishly.

'Promise me you're not off on another hare-brained escapade? You're the only mother I've got and I'd like you to keep intact.'

'Message received,' said Chris (which wasn't specifically a promise not to).

'And if it's not too much trouble, I'd like to find out what you've been up to directly rather than via social media newsfeeds.'

'Will do. Sorry, Chloe. About my hypothetical question…?'

Her daughter sighed deeply again. 'I'd expect you to be cautious, concerned, even, but to ban your adult daughter from contacting her birth father? Yes, that would be weird, even for you.'

Chloe's answer confirmed Chris's nagging doubt about Skye's story – the reaction of her mother, Pippa. Holy moly! Was this mother's instinct kicking in? What would she have done in the same situation? Sure, she'd have checked him out online, surreptitiously followed him on social media, bought a pair of high-powered binoculars with night-vision capability, issued Chloe with all the usual dire warnings about stranger danger, but she wouldn't have gone as far as forbidding her from meeting her birth father.

'Thanks, Chloe. As usual, you're right. Perhaps I need to talk to someone about finding my inner peace.'

'And outer peace, Mum. And outer. Keep in touch and don't do anything daft. I'd better go and untie my husband.' And Chloe blew her mother her usual raspberry kiss to end the call.

*

That settled it. Zeta had her police channels to work through, but that didn't mean Chris had to sit there twiddling her thumbs. Chris finished the last mouthful of marmalade and Marmite on toast (a combo that strangely worked), took a whiteboard pen from the kitchen table drawer and on the wall drew a blue line from Skye's name and wrote *Pippa Atlantis* – not a name that was easy to forget. Under Pippa's name she wrote two notes in green pen: 'Hostile about Martin?' and 'One-night stand?' Could Skye investigating the past have had any bearing on the whereabouts of her father in the present?

A Google search brought an immediate result. Top of the page: 'Pippa Atlantis – Holistic Wellbeing Solutions' and an address in Blekeness. The website was well designed and featured a biography of Pippa and soft-focus photographs of her looking earnest, caring and new age. She was undoubtedly Skye's mother – the same bone structure and, dammit, even her nose. The full-length shots had her sitting in a cross-legged yoga pose and, in another, lighting an incense stick. Pippa even made a kaftan look good.

'Reconnect With Your Inner Child' implored one of the headings. Chris had no difficulty connecting with her inner child; it was the external adult that was the problem.

'Realign Your Chi' suggested another. Chris having just had a bath had checked and she was happy that her chi was aligned – or at least as aligned as could be expected for a sixty-year-old woman.

Below was a list of the services tackled by Pippa's holistic wellbeing therapy:

- *Issues with alcohol dependence or unhealthy diet?*
- *Problems with commitment and sustaining relationships?*
- *Confidence crises and underachievement?*
- *Do you find the modern world bewildering?*

Four out of four, thought Chris. Maybe I really do need some holistic wellbeing. This could be a win-win: investigate Skye's background and get a shot of cosmic therapy into the bargain. She pressed the button marked 'Appointments'.

Apparently, the good people of Blekeness and its surrounds were happy with their wellbeing and their chis were clearly perfectly aligned as there were plenty of available slots. Chris clicked on a tab for one o'clock that afternoon, filled in her name and address details and paid the discounted £30 for the introductory session. Only then did she consider the weightier problem of how to get to such a remote location. According to the travel planner, it would take five and a half hours by public transport, involving three trains, two buses and a thirty-five-minute walk. By car, however, it was only one and a quarter hours.

Zeta and I aren't conjoined twins, thought Chris. She's got her line of investigation, why shouldn't I have mine? She texted Next-Door Nick: *Morning. Got any plans for the day?*

Twenty-Two

The drive to Blekeness had taken longer than the hour and fifteen minutes promised by the travel planner; nearer to an hour and forty-five. This was partly due to a provocatively named 'traffic-calming system' outside Becketon but also to Nick's insistence on driving exactly eight miles an hour under the speed limit. His pootling usually caused Chris to dig her nails into the car's upholstery in frustration, but not today. She had plenty of time to make her appointment with Pippa and it was good to appreciate the passing landscape at a slower speed. Chris found herself humming Iggy Pop's 'The Passenger' as she gazed out of the car window.

Blekeness was technically a desert, a barren coastal landscape populated by dunes of shingle, tufted grasses and patches of wildflowers. As the houses and shops of the nearest town were left behind, the road became a single track with the occasional passing place for oncoming traffic.

To their left, the sea appeared. Technically the English Channel, but a quieter, more serene version, and, today, a sheet of turquoise. A couple of anglers cast their lines and then settled into their folding chairs. It was the sort of warm spring day when it didn't matter if the fish weren't biting.

To their right, a pub, the Captain's Fancy, tatty with sea-wind-battered paint and displaying a welcoming chalkboard offering the finest fish and chips in Blekeness. From the look of the area, probably the only fish and chips in Blekeness. After that there was the occasional house, all of them single storey, some no more than a cabin, each with a small white picket fence and collections of wildflowers. No house numbers here, only names: Campion Cottage, The Vista, Azure House. Chris could understand the attraction – perfect isolation. She bet the residents weren't WhatsApping each other about bin collections.

'I thought we could go for a walk first. There's a bird sanctuary about half a mile on from the car park. Then lunch at that pub we just passed,' said Nick.

'Ah.'

'What do you mean, "Ah"?'

'I have an appointment. If you see a house called Varuna, give me a shout.'

'So this isn't a date – I'm a free Uber?'

'I should only be an hour. We can grab lunch afterwards, OK? And look, there's a lighthouse that's open to the public. That'll keep you amused.'

Chris should have felt more guilty about exploiting Nick's generosity than she did. Perhaps she should address that in her forthcoming introductory wellbeing session.

In total, Blekeness had only about twenty residences. She asked Nick to drop her off so she could continue her exploration alone and on foot. Every house gave off an aura of creativity and, as she wandered, Chris tried to deduce who lived in each one. The first had to be a writer, given the large picture window framing an open laptop and a ginger cat. The next needed no deduction as a board outside advertised seascapes for sale. The third also presumably belonged to an artist. Instead of wildflowers and seashells, its front garden was dominated by a sculpture made from flotsam: fishing nets, Crocs, a child's kite, lager cans and driftwood. Chris couldn't figure out what it was supposed to represent, but if it kept that rubbish off the beach, it got her vote of approval.

The next house had a pentacle detail in the window, a bunch of dried seaweed over the doorway, and pebbles, painted black and white, arranged into a yin and yang symbol. A wooden nameplate read 'Varuna'. Chris knocked on the door.

*

Pippa Atlantis looked tall. She may have been only a couple of centimetres taller than Chris, but the uprightness of her posture made her seem statuesque in comparison. Her loose-fitting cream linen pyjamas gave the impression that she got out of bed looking awesome.

'Chris Heron? Bang on time. Punctuality is a positive function of both respect and inner confidence. Welcome to Varuna.'

The house seemed smaller on the inside, an illusion created by the interior design. The walls of the room that Chris was ushered into were covered in hangings of eastern origin, all deep golds, reds and browns – beautiful but with the side effect of absorbing any daylight that sneaked in through the slats of the shutters. A couch was covered by a throw of a similar pattern. Before the fireplace stood a large ceramic statue of Ganesha, the Hindu elephant god. As a whole, the room looked like a tourist giftshop rather than the temple of eastern mysticism that had been intended.

Chris coughed and felt her eyes water as a spiral of incense smoke from a burner at Ganesha's feet hit her nostrils. It smelt of cinnamon, sandalwood and a bottle bank on Boxing Day.

'Would you like tea?'

The incense had reached the back of Chris's throat. She could murder a cup of builder's. She nodded.

'Macha, kabusecha or tamaryokucha?' asked Pippa.

'Oh, um, the middle one. Kabuki? Milk, no sugar, thanks,' said Chris, taking potluck.

Pippa disappeared to rustle up whatever Chris had inadvertently ordered, so Chris took the opportunity to have a nose around. There was a tall bookshelf that was filled with glossy hardback books: *The Way of the East*; *Sri Lanka Uncovered*; *101 Buddhist Temples to See Before You Reincarnate*. In front of the books the shelves were crammed with small china pots, carved ebony figurines and handwoven wicker somethings – the sort of items that could be purchased for a song, didn't take up much luggage room and were a bugger to dust.

Chris located a vacant space in her memory palace to store all this new information. On the far wall was a large framed print of a tiger and a number of smaller frames. There were also certificates – the only thing that Pippa's place of work had in common with Danny Figg's. Pippa's certificates were qualifications in her chosen field. Apparently, Sedona University had awarded her a doctorate in Spiritual Enlightenment and a master's in Psychic Metaphysics, perhaps better options than the 2:2 in English Literature and Politics that Chris had spent three years getting.

On a cabinet lining the walls stood a number of framed photos. Chris was immediately drawn to the one that showed a group shot of a dozen people in a wild landscape, including a young Pippa cradling a baby in her arms.

'That's Skye, in case you were wondering,' said Pippa from behind her.

'I thought it must be,' said Chris, turning round.

Pippa was standing with a tray that held a red patterned teapot and two tiny Japanese teacups.

'Oh, you know the Hebrides?'

'Only from the television.' Chris quickly turned her face back to the wall to hide any nervous twitch. She'd nearly blown her cover in the first conversation. Some spy she'd make.

Pippa sat on the floor, effortlessly adopting the lotus position, and gestured for Chris to follow suit. 'Tea then talk is my mantra.'

Chris gulped. She wasn't sure if she could sit cross-legged since the hip replacement and she was even less sure that she'd be able to get back up again.

Pippa arranged the cups, making small, ritualised movements. She unfolded a cloth, wiped the rim of the first cup, poured a stream of hot lime-green liquid into it and placed the cup before Chris. Chris looked at the cup with dismay. She'd had green tea before, but that had been via a tea bag and had at least looked drinkable. This looked like a urine sample after an overdose of asparagus.

'Kabusecha isn't taken with milk. And this is a vegan house,' said Pippa, gesturing for Chris to take the first drink.

As a proofreader, Chris rarely struggled for words, but the taste of the tea was challenging her professionalism. The best tasting notes she could come up with were: hedge trimmings stewed in sea water and seasoned with roasted rabbit droppings.

'Delicious, isn't it?' said Pippa, taking a draught from her cup. 'I'm planning a pop-up Japanese tea-house for the summer season.'

'You could call it "World of Infusion",' suggested Chris, wondering if she could craftily toss the remaining contents of her cup into the indoor bamboo.

Pippa rose without a creak and sat on the couch, indicating that Chris should take the seat beside her. Chris did so, but only after having rolled over onto all fours.

'So, Chris' – Pippa's voice was like a gentle breeze and her breath smelt of marigolds – 'for our introductory session we'll just touch upon the root of your concerns and then, together, plan a path to a brighter future. What brings you here?'

Chris was tempted to say 'a pissed-off neighbour in a Fiat 500', but Pippa didn't seemed the type to enjoy a quip. 'I'm having difficulty in my relationship with my daughter.'

Pippa opened a drawer in a lacquered Chinese cabinet and selected a walnut-sized crystal which she placed on Chris's opened palm. 'I'm seeing auras of frustration, dishonesty and negativity. Tell me more. What is your daughter's name?'

'Zoe,' said Chris, who was not good at making up lies on the spot. 'I'm concerned because her father is back in her life and it's forcing us apart.'

As a tactic, it was a subtle as a sledgehammer. Come up with a story that had parallels to Skye's and see if that tricked her mother into revealing more.

'And her father is not a good man?'

'He cheated on me, lied, gambled away all our savings and used to cut his toenails in the bedroom and leave the clippings on the carpet.' As a charge sheet, it was damning. In real life, Simon was guilty of none of these; he was just a bit boring, nothing worse.

'I see,' said Pippa in a neutral tone. Not 'Tell me about it!' or 'You think your daughter's father is bad, wait till you hear about mine', just 'I see.'

'So what should I do? Should I ban Zoe from seeing him?' This was really pushing the line, but nothing ventured…

Pippa betrayed not a flicker of a reaction. Not a shift in stance, nor the blinking of an eye nor the twitch of a lip. If Chris's story held any resonance with Pippa's own situation, then she was keeping it firmly under wraps.

'The answer…'

'Yes?'

'… will be found within yourself, Chris.'

'Oh. Where exactly?'

'I recommend a programme of psychic cleansing. This will purge your negativity, re-engage your spirituality and light the way to truth and purpose. Here, let me teach you a breathing exercise.'

Pippa took Chris's hands and pulled her to the centre of the floor.

'I want you to close your eyes and take breaths deep into your lungs.'

Chris did as she was instructed. The influx of oxygen made her almost giddy.

'Now breathe in through your left nostril and out from your right. In… out… in… out.'

Chris felt something stir in the depths of her right nostril. Would it be bad karma if she inadvertently fired out a bogey?

'That's good. Now swap nostrils. In from your right and out from your left. In… out… in… out.'

Now something was stirring in her left nostril as well.

Pippa's voice was soothing, almost hypnotic. 'Place both hands on the top of your head and place the sole of your left foot against your right knee.'

This was even worse. Now there was the danger of accidental emission from both ends. Chris cursed herself for having eaten a veggie chilli the previous night. Those kidney beans were simply asking for trouble.

From somewhere in another room, Chris heard the merciful *Ding!* of a timer.

'And relax,' said Pippa. 'Alas, the sands of time have run their course for today, but if you'd like me to help, I suggest a two-hour session once a week for twenty weeks.'

Chris did some mental arithmetic. 'That's thirty times two times twenty… £1,200?'

'£2,400. Psychic cleansing is £60 an hour. Not inexpensive, I understand, but how can you put a price on karmic harmony?'

Chris could put a price on karmic harmony; it was the same as a bottle of Rioja from her local off-licence. 'I shall have to address my bank manager's inner negativity first. I'll be in touch. Thank you for the tea.'

'The House of Varuna is always open to the seeker of wisdom and the teapot is always full. Choose the right path, Chris,' said Pippa as she closed the door.

*

Nick was sitting on a bench outside the lighthouse with his eyes closed, drinking in the sun.

'So how did your therapy session go?'

'You followed me?'

'Of course. I'm not going to let my favourite neighbour disappear without having some idea where she's gone.'

Chris felt another twinge that could have been guilt for taking Nick for granted but was more likely her knee muscle still furious about that cross-legged pose. 'I'm not sure. I was threatened with more tea.'

'Do you want me to drive you home now?'

'No, Nick, I want to treat you to the finest fish and chips in Blekeness and then we'll check out that bird sanctuary.'

Twenty-Three

'Can I have a word, Sarge? In private?'

Zeta had Sgt Spurgeon's mark. He was crass, provocative and slovenly. His trousers were low-slung, his sense of humour lavatorial, and he could empty an entire box of custard doughnuts. He was also clever and caring and trustworthy. But if you ever suggested as much to him, then you'd be in deep trouble.

She had been trying for a couple of weeks to engineer the opportunity for a discreet one-to-one with her sergeant, but in the frenetic surroundings of North Kent Police Station, discretion was not just a virtue, it was practically impossible. Zeta had been otherwise engaged too. A day-long training course on the Judicious Use of Pepper Spray took a sizeable chunk out of her monthly operational hours. Then there had been the Becketon Easter Parade; two hundred pre-schoolers sugar-rushing on chocolate eggs had been a unique crowd-control challenge.

'Not a problem, I hope, SC Jama? I've only got twenty minutes before the inspector's weekly update.'

'Room 701?' suggested Zeta.

Sgt Spurgeon raised a quizzical eyebrow and nodded.

Room 701 was not secret as such, more forgotten. A solitary office on a floor that was otherwise dedicated to the maintenance requirements of the building, housing the computer servers, electric circuit boards and facilities storage. During the last building audit, Room 701 had been either overlooked or deliberately omitted. Which meant it would never be decorated or recarpeted or have the radiators bled. For the select few who knew of its existence, Room 701 was Shangri-La.

'Everything's gone quiet on the Figg death threat, Sarge. Have you got any inside knowledge?'

'You've 701'ed me for an update on the case, SC Jama? It's hardly top secret.'

'Indulge me, Sarge. I've hardly been in the station and, well, have you ever tried to get chundered Easter egg chocolate out of a uniform?'

'More than once,' admitted Sgt Spurgeon. 'Go on, take a seat on the least rickety chair and I'll take the sofa.'

Zeta sat primly on a chair which wobbled precariously and took her favoured black leather notebook out of her pocket in readiness.

'You chose a good time to be out of the station, SC Jama. The last two weeks have been bedlam. Going public on Livingstone caused all of the crazies to come out of the woodwork. We've had psychics, conspiracy theorists, bloggers, geo-locators, kite surfers, drone enthusiasts and your common-or-garden cranks. All with a theory, all needing to be logged.'

'Any sightings?'

'It's like *Where's Wally?* Three hundred and seventy-two at the last count, including one of him having a coffee with Lord Lucan outside the Hotel Parador and another of him riding Shergar along the Cliffstaple to Becketon cycle path. No, don't write "Shergar" in that notebook, Jama; google it later. Just take it from me, it's Nutsville out there.'

'So nothing confirmed?'

'Zilch. Nothing on Livingstone or that CrEW mob. And now, having opened Pandora's bleedin' box, CID want to wind the investigation down. As usual, it's uniform who are left to clear up the shit.' Sgt Spurgeon looked like a man at breaking point.

'After only two weeks?'

'Exactly. Rumour is that Figg's had a word in the chief constable's ear at a lodge meet. All the media attention is bad PR and he doesn't want it on his doorstep. According to DI Turing, Livingstone got carried away with the death threat so has hotfooted it out of town and Figg doesn't want to press charges anyway. It's a victimless crime.'

'Except for the squirrel,' said Zeta. 'You don't think he went down with his coracle then?'

Sgt Spurgeon shook his head. 'It's possible, but I think we'd have found him or his boat by now. I reckon Livingstone will sneak back home in a couple of weeks and we'll give him a rap on the knuckles and make him sit on the naughty step for a while.'

'What about Danny Figg's brother? Has anyone followed that up?'

'Not that again! You don't let anything drop, do you, SC Jama?'

'It's the difference between viewing Martin Livingstone as a suspect or a victim.'

'Cards on the table time – what's your real interest in this case?'

Zeta drew a breath. She was about to place an awful lot of trust in her sergeant. 'I made a promise to Martin Livingstone's daughter.'

'He hasn't got a daughter.'

'I've spoken to her. I'm sure she's the real deal.'

Sgt Spurgeon buried his head in his hands again. 'Zeta, you're still young and green. Just cos someone tells you they're a blood relative doesn't make them so.'

Zeta drew a second breath as she was about to commit herself deeper. 'And there's bad blood between Danny and Tony Figg that goes back years.'

Sgt Spurgeon looked at his watch and stood. 'I'm frightened to ask, but how does a new kid on the block come by this knowledge?'

'From Barry.'

Sgt Spurgeon leant back and laughed so loudly that Zeta was worried it would send people scurrying up to the seventh floor to investigate. 'Barry Conway? He's so full of sh… stories. You've dragged me up here on the back of one of his yarns?'

'Not just that. We went round to see Tony Figg too. Undercover.'

Sgt Spurgeon abruptly stopped laughing and sat down again. '"We"? You and ex-constable Barry Conway conducted an unofficial undercover investigation? Could my day get any worse?'

'No, Sarge, not Barry. I took Chris Heron with me.'

'My day just got worse. You undertook an unofficial undercover investigation with the Crazy Bike Woman of Cliffstaple?' Sgt Spurgeon prowled the length of Room 701. 'One day, Jama, you going off-piste is going to bring us all down.'

'Sarge, I'm really sorry. I just...'

'But what is the correct course of action? What would you recommend? Report you to the DI? Put you on a disciplinary?'

'I know you think I've let you down, but...'

'What I should do is lock you in here and throw away the key. That way we'd all be safe from your impulsiveness.'

'I'll write it up as an official report and submit it to DI Turing. I'll make it clear that I had no instruction from any senior officer to justify my actions,' said Zeta.

Sgt Spurgeon paused his prowling. 'Like buggery you will, Jama. You really think I'd throw my best SC to those plainclothes wolves?'

'What should we do?' said Zeta.

Sgt Spurgeon thought for a minute, chewing on the calloused skin on his thumb. 'The thing is, Jama, your instincts are usually spot on. Promise me you'll park all this "unofficial investigation" malarkey, and I'll get Constable Atherton to pay Tony Figg an official visit.'

'Athers will need a reason to knock him up, won't he, Sarge? Otherwise it might look suspicious.'

'Constable Atherton is an experienced officer. He'll think of something. Perhaps we've had a complaint that Mr Figg was playing his Celine Dion albums at maximum volume.'

Zeta smiled. 'I can't see him as a big fan.'

'Or maybe his neighbours have reported anti-social cooking smells.'

'Judging from the number of takeaway boxes in his office, I don't think Tony does much fancy cooking.'

'More Heston Services on the M4 than Heston Blumenthal, eh, SC Jama?' Sgt Spurgeon chuckled bodily at his own joke.

'Heston who, Sarge?'

'No matter,' said Sgt Spurgeon, deflated that his rapier wit had gone unappreciated. 'As long as we're agreed that Tony Figg is no longer your problem.'

Zeta nodded.

'Good. I'll give you some deskbound work that'll keep you out of mischief.' Sgt Spurgeon opened the door of Room 701. 'Now I've got to run. I'm five minutes late already for the inspector's riveting weekly update and by now someone will have nabbed all the pink wafers.'

*

Meanwhile, the Crazy Bike Woman of Cliffstaple was back at Chisellers' Cabin. It had only been a couple of weeks, but the scene had changed dramatically since the TV publicity. The number of volunteers had doubled and she struggled to recognise anyone.

Centre stage under a makeshift awning outside the workshop, the ark was beginning to take shape. Skeletal ribs were already in place and, like an army of worker ants, overall-clad woodworkers were busily ferrying wooden slats and measuring, sawing and hammering them into place. Inside, Eric and Paulette were poring over a plan spread out over a workbench and weighed down on each corner by a claw hammer.

'You've changed my design! You can't simply move the centre of gravity.' Paulette sounded angry.

'It gives us more space. Otherwise there's no room for the animals,' Eric replied defensively.

'Hope I'm not interrupting,' said Chris, interrupting. 'I can't believe how much progress you've made.'

'Christine!' exclaimed Eric. 'We thought you'd abandoned us.'

'Been busy on… stuff. The ark's bigger than I thought – are you going to be able to get it out of the community garden?'

Eric tapped the side of his nose. 'Fail to plan, plan to fail. It'll fit through the rear gates, and Felix has got a contact with a crane and trailer. Sorted.'

'It's good to see you've got extra hands. Let me know if there's any menial help you need this morning. I'm a whizz at putting the kettle on.'

'You've got a more important task today, Chris,' said Paulette, taking her arm and escorting her to the far side of the garden, away from all the hammering and sawing. 'Jethro needs his muse for the figurehead.'

Paulette checked that they were safely out of earshot and sat down on a bench, dragging Chris alongside her. 'Have you heard any more about Martin? I'm sick with worry.'

'No, but the police are on the case,' said Chris.

'The police?' Paulette snorted. 'They don't care. They think he's an eco-terrorist. They're not interested in his safety.'

'And you don't? I heard he has previous for that sort of thing.'

'Take it from me, that's ancient history. Martin's just a quiet, kind guy, and now' – a tear appeared in Paulette's eye – 'with all this attention, I'm worried it's made him do something silly.'

'All I can tell you, Paulette, is I know someone who is on the investigation and she's the best. If anyone can find Martin safe and well, she's the one to do it.'

Paulette nodded, at least temporarily comforted by Chris's words, and brushed away her tear, embarrassed about the display of emotion. At the far side of the garden they encountered Jethro, moodily staring at a large block of balsa wood.

'Here you are, Jethro. Your model's arrived,' said Paulette.

Jethro beamed. 'Ah, Chris. If you could sit opposite me. I printed off a few examples.' He delved into a tatty Tesco carrier bag and withdrew some sheets of A4 paper. 'I like the first two – what do you think?'

Chris examined the sheets, which were photos printed from a Google images search. A dozen ships' figureheads, all female, all topless. She handed the sheets back. 'If you think I'm getting my waps out in a community garden, you've got another think coming, Jethro.'

'But it's traditional,' Jethro protested.

'I don't give a damn about tradition. These girls are staying undercover.' Chris could hear Paulette stifling a titter.

'Have it your way,' Jethro grumbled. 'I suppose I can use my imagination.'

'Jethro,' said Chris in her sternest voice, 'I'm not having you imagine me in any state of undress. Either it's head and shoulders or you can find yourself another muse.'

Chris adopted a suitably dramatic profile and Jethro spent the following hour frenziedly chipping chunks off the block. As she ducked to avoid another fragment of balsa wood shrapnel, she felt her phone vibrate in her pocket. It was a call from Skye.

'Hi, Skye. Sorry, still no news—'

'I've just been round to my dad's house, 29, Gable Terrace. Can you get here? He's been burgled.'

Twenty-Four

Abandoning Jethro to his block of balsa wood, Chris ran to the bike rack and unlocked Rod. She considered phoning Zeta, but that would take valuable minutes, so she settled for a text instead: *Break-in at Martin's. 29, Gable Terrace. Meeting Skye there. Chris xx* On reflection, a phone call would have been quicker than Chris's single-fingered, correct-punctuation texting.

Gable Terrace was a similar distance from the sea as Sea View but on the other side of the high street, no more than five minutes away on Rod. Instead of turning right out of the community garden, Chris swung left.

At the end of the path, where it met the main road, a black Range Rover was parked half on the pavement, so Chris had to squeeze between the front of the car and the wall of the path. She glared angrily at the occupants, but the couple in the front seats were too busy swapping saliva to notice the impact of their anti-social parking behaviour.

Gable Terrace, like many of the residential streets in Cliffstaple, was an eclectic mix of housing styles. Some 1950s semi-detached houses with their now-far-too-small integrated garages; a couple of imposing late-Victorian detached villas; a block of modern purpose-built flats; and, towards the top end of the street, two rows of two-up two-down fishermen's houses – Gable Cottages, the original terrace. When Chris had first moved to Cliffstaple thirty years ago, they were the sort of properties you couldn't give away, impractical for modern life. Since the gentrification of Cliffstaple and particularly the advent of Airbnb, their value had rocketed. Alas, most were now holiday lets; very few were still lived in on a full-time basis.

Skye was on the pavement outside Number 29.

'Is it definitely a break-in?' asked Chris as she stepped off her bike. This was not as dumb a question as it sounded for she had on a couple of occasions arrived home to find her own front door wide open when she had left in too much of a hurry and failed to properly close it behind her.

Skye nodded and pointed to the side of the door. 'They wrenched off the key safe. It's my fault. I insisted that Dad get one installed as he can be a bit dippy at times. The next-door neighbour noticed it and called me. I didn't even know Dad had given them my number.'

'You haven't been in, have you?' asked Chris.

'No, I thought I'd better phone for back-up first,' said Skye.

'And you thought I'd be a better option than, say, the police?'

'I phoned 999, but they didn't seem very enthusiastic. They said they'd send someone round when they could.'

Chris took out her phone and called Zeta. 'Hi, Zeta, did you get my text?'

'Phone 999.'

'I have – or rather Skye has. She said they didn't suggest they'd rush round in a hurry.'

'That sounds par for the course. Domestic burglaries are deprioritised at the moment. Skye will be lucky if she gets anything more than a courtesy call.'

'What do you recommend?'

'Get a locksmith, take a record of what's been nicked and get a crime number for the insurance. That's if Martin ever turns up to make a claim.'

Chris was surprised at her friend's taciturnity. 'Can't you pop round yourself?'

'I'm working today, Chris. I'm not your private police force.'

'Zeta, I didn't—'

'Sorry, Chris, I was out of order there. Between you and me, I've been warned off by Sergeant Spurgeon, so if I sauntered over there, he'd go ballistic. Again. I'm ninety per cent sure it's opportunistic. There are a couple of thieves who work this area and probably they've seen the media coverage so know the house is empty.'

'And if it isn't?'

'If there's a mad axeman in the attic, send me another text,' said Zeta comfortingly.

*

Skye let them both into the house.

'Shh!' Skye whispered. 'Just in case the burglars are still here.'

'If they are, I reckon surprising them is the least sensible thing for us to do. SPIKE! YOU DIDN'T NEED TO BRING ALL FIFTEEN MEMBERS OF THE CLIFFSTAPLE RUGBY TEAM WITH YOU! NO, THEY DON'T ALL NEED BASEBALL BATS!'

The two women listened, but there was no sound from anywhere in the house. No doors opened, no floorboards creaked and, thankfully, there were no grinding, axe-sharpening noises from the attic.

Skye walked into the sitting room. 'Oh no, they've wrecked the place!' she wailed.

Chris followed her in. The room seemed OK. A bit messy but nothing compared to what it sometimes got like at 15, Sea View. She'd have to have a major tidy-up if she ever invited Skye round. Books had been pulled out of the bookcase, a two-drawer filing cabinet had disgorged its contents onto the carpet, and the cushions of the sofa had been tossed onto the floor. Chris caused more havoc looking for her keys at home.

The two women did a quick circuit of the house to check all was clear. It was a lovely small house but one that hadn't had any TLC in a long time. The brown and orange wallpaper had, mercifully, faded since the 1970s and, on the stairway, a couple of the original gas mantles were still in situ. There were, however, some fine examples of the homeowner's woodworking expertise: an inlaid wooden box on the dressing table, a bed linen chest made from reclaimed timber, and a carved freestanding bookshelf on the landing. In every room Skye got more distressed, although to Chris's eyes it was only the sitting room and a few opened drawers in the main bedroom that showed any signs of disturbance.

'It's probably best to take photos of the scene and check what's missing,' said Chris. 'It doesn't sound like North Kent Constabulary will be sending round a forensic team to dust for fingerprints.'

Chris left Skye to make an inventory of the upstairs rooms and returned to the sitting room, where she took in her surroundings, committing them to memory.

The papers spilling out of the filing cabinet were old utility bills and guarantees dating back years. She picked a fat manila envelope out of the lower drawer. It contained photocopied newsletters (titled 'EnviroKent') that had yellowed with age – relics from pre-social-media times. She scanned one at random. It carried updates on protests, legal advice, poems and even a handmade crossword, but nothing that seemed particularly inflammatory and, crucially, no reference to CrEW.

Chris turned her attention to the books and started to replace them on the shelves. There were classics of English literature, including, ironically, a set of Dickens; the seven volumes of Proust in French; and, more impressively, a complete set of Terry Pratchett's Discworld novels. These had been left in a pile at the foot of the bookcase as though they had been opened, shaken and then dumped by someone who had been looking for something. What that something might have been, Chris couldn't even hazard a guess.

In another pile were hardback coffee-table books: *Planet Earth*, *A Beginner's Guide to Joinery*, *Protecting Britain's Hedgerows*, *The Forager's Cookbook*. Next to these were biographies and non-fiction: *A Long Walk to Freedom*, *I Am Malala*, *The Book of Hope* – a collection that some tabloids would have described as a Mountain of Woke. There was nothing out of the ordinary; if Chris had been asked to visualise Martin's home life, this would have fitted it exactly.

Chris had the overwhelming sense that she was intruding. Perhaps it was a flashback to the clearing out of her parents' house after her mother's death. In any case, she needed fresh air so she walked out into the kitchen. The back door was locked, with the key in the lock. Clearly nobody had entered or exited this way.

The garden was no more than a yard. A large wooden bench dominated the space, presumably another example of Martin's handicraft. A passionflower climbed the rear wall of the house – a more impressive specimen than the one she had spent ten years trying to nurture in her own back garden. The potted plants and shrubs were all healthy and cared for. This little space was Martin's sanctuary, his bolthole.

'Are you a friend of Martin's?' Two heads popped up from the other side of the garden fence, a man and a woman in their seventies.

'I hope so. I'm Chris. I'm here with Martin's daughter.'

'Yes, we saw you with Skye outside. We telephoned her when we noticed the damage to the key safe. Is everything all right? We don't like to intrude, but...'

'Did you see who did it?'

They both shook their heads in a coordinated movement. 'No, must have happened sometime last night,' said the man.

'It looks like uninvited guests but not much damage. Skye's just checking whether anything's missing.'

'Bless her. I don't suppose she's heard from her father? He's a lovely man and we're both so worried.'

'Not yet, but I'm sure everything's fine. We're hoping he just needed to take a break. He'd been under a bit of stress lately,' said Chris, trying to be more reassuring than she felt.

'See, Glenys,' said the man to his wife, 'I told you not to fret. That business with the will was just a coincidence.'

'The will?' Chris's ears couldn't have pricked up faster than if she'd been a greyhound responding to the clunk of the opening of the traps.

'Yes. Martin asked us to witness his will recently. Glenys here has got it into her head that this means he's done something, um, silly.'

Chris noted that it was the second time that day that *something silly* had been suggested as a possible explanation for Martin's disappearance.

'Please don't worry yourselves. We're going to get the locks changed and I'm in regular contact with the police. We're all confident that Martin's safe and well,' said Chris, lying again.

By the time Chris returned to the sitting room, Skye was perched on the sofa, writing notes on her phone.

'Anything missing?'

Skye shook her head. 'Nothing, as far as I can tell. Dad doesn't have anything worth stealing – no laptop or smartphone – and nobody would bother with that TV.'

Chris had seen iPads that were bigger than the TV set nestling in the corner of the room.

'Bank cards?'

Skye brandished a card. 'Bedside table. If they were looking for valuables, they didn't try very hard.'

'Perhaps that's it. Someone broke in, quickly realised there'd be slim pickings and left. I saw the neighbours.'

'Glenys and Ken?'

'Yes. They send their best wishes.'

Skye wandered out to the kitchen and filled the kettle. 'They're sweeties. They and Dad are virtually the only permanent residents in this part of the street.'

'They said they'd witnessed your dad's will.'

Skye reappeared with tea in orange and brown mugs that matched the wallpaper. 'They were probably the only people he trusted to do that.'

'You didn't find a copy upstairs then?' asked Chris, and then immediately regretted her ability to plant her foot in her mouth.

'I didn't look. Why would I? Dad's not dead.' Skye sat hunched on the sofa. 'I'd know if he was dead.'

'Sorry, Skye, I didn't mean... Excuse me a sec, I think I've left my phone in the garden.'

*

Chris paced the small garden like a lifer doing circuits of the prison yard. Why had she mentioned the will? Why had she upset a worried daughter? Why did she have the subtlety of an elephant on a pogo stick?

'Are you all right, dear?' called Glenys from the other side of the fence.

Chris realised that her muttering had not been wholly internalised.

Something that Skye had recently said resonated: 'the only people he trusted...'

'I'm fine, thanks, Glenys. You mentioned witnessing Martin's will. You don't remember the name of the solicitors?'

'Oh, Martin wouldn't go near solicitors – he called them bloodsuckers! He'd written his will in the back of a hardback book. He assured us it was legal, that you don't need official forms.'

'You didn't notice the title of the book?'

'Oh no, dear, didn't pay it any attention. A will's private, after all, isn't it? I got the impression the book was just something he had to hand.'

When Chris returned to the sitting room, Skye was still deep in thought and, thankfully, didn't seem to have taken Chris's question about the will to heart. 'The locksmith should be here within the hour. Thanks for coming over, Chris. You don't need to hang around if you're busy.'

Skye picked up the empty mugs and headed for the kitchen. Chris sat on the sofa and stared at the piles of books. Something was out of place. Something didn't fit the pattern.

A Beginner's Guide to Joinery. Martin wasn't a beginner, he was an expert, and there were examples of his woodworking prowess in every room of the house. She picked up the book and turned to the flyleaf at the back. There it was in Martin's own handwriting: 'The Last Will and Testament of Martin Tobias Livingstone'. It had been witnessed barely a week before his disappearance.

The text of the will was brief: 'I leave all my worldly possessions to my daughter, Skye Estella Livingstone.'

Chris shut the book and returned it to the middle of the pile.

Twenty-Five

Zeta was sitting at her desk staring forlornly at her computer when the imposing shadow of Sgt Spurgeon fell across the screen.

'Not disturbing you, am I, SC Jama?'

'From a stocktake of the station's crime-prevention material? All disturbances welcome.'

'And how's that going?'

'For some reason we've got 80,000 "Stranger Danger" posters but only three "Street Safe" leaflets and one inflatable police officer, Barney the Becketon Bobby. Do you want me to print you a spreadsheet, Sarge?'

'Not at the moment. I've got a job for you.'

Zeta's cloud lifted. 'A proper police-type job?'

'Yes. We've had a noise complaint come in from a Jackie DeMort, owner of Happy Endings Funeral Services. Dog barking in the upstairs premises.'

'T Figg Debt Recovery Solutions? That's a happy coincidence.'

'Exactly. PC Atherton's tried to contact the resident a couple of times over the last week but without success. Perhaps if you accompanied him, his luck might change.'

Zeta lowered her voice to a whisper. 'But, Sarge, Tony Figg knows me from my visit with Chris Heron.'

'So when Mr Figg sees you again but this time in uniform, it should be a bit of a surprise for him, shouldn't it? And sometimes surprised people say things they shouldn't.'

*

Whilst Zeta was being assigned her new task, Chris was back in the saddle. The glorious thing about bike riding was the up-close view of how the countryside changed throughout the year. It had been only a month since Chris had last followed this path around the back of Hermon Hill Farm, but the small bird population seemed to have doubled and the blackthorn blossom was now in full abundance. Nature was at its most vibrant.

The small bird population was not the only thing that had doubled. As Chris swung right to join the path that ran parallel to Tiny Barney's field, she could count four alpacas. She pulled over, stepped up onto the fence and waved. Liz, who was tending to her alpacas' needs, returned Chris's wave and trotted over, accompanied by Ernie the collie.

Liz nodded in the direction of the alpacas. 'Pepsi and Shirlie were lonely, so I got them a couple of fellas.'

'George and Andrew?'

'Gosh, yes! How did you guess?' Liz looked genuinely surprised.

'A careless whisper?' suggested Chris.

'I hope that this time next year we'll be hearing the patter of tiny hooves.'

'And how's Tiny Barney the pocket-sized superstud doing?'

'Not living up to expectations apparently. The new owners aren't happy, but that's not my fault, is it? I never gave any guarantees about his libido. Fancy popping in for a cuppa?'

'Can't today, I'm afraid. I'm on a mission. But I do have a favour to ask.'

'Ask away. I still owe you for that proofreading for the farm shop.'

'Can I borrow a couple of alpacas?'

*

Jackie DeMort was the embodiment of a modern funeral director. Far from the lank, austere stereotype of an undertaker, she was… mumsy. More Mrs Doubtfire than Mr Sowerberry. Bright, cheery, some might say cuddly, Jackie was clearly the perfect person to handle the most sensitive matters.

'I don't like to complain, but when you're having discreet conversations with clients who are saying goodbye to their loved ones, hearing agonised yowls from above can somewhat destroy the ambience.'

'I can imagine,' said PC Atherton, doing much better at keeping a straight face than Zeta. 'We'll have a word with the occupant.'

From the pavement, Zeta pushed the broken door open and pointed up the stairs. Atherton knocked twice on the office door of T Figg Debt Recovery Solutions. Daisy barked in response.

'Mr Figg? North Kent Police here. We've had a complaint about noise?' he shouted in his distinctive shrill voice. 'Please could you open the door?'

Daisy barked again.

'Mr Figg? Are you all right?'

'Ruff!'

'What do we do?' said Zeta. 'Try and get a warrant?'

'We're responding to a breach of the peace, aren't we, Jama?' And Atherton leant his huge frame against the door, which, to the sound of splintering wood, gave way as easily as if it had been made of Japanese tissue paper.

There was a thundering of paws on lino and Daisy turned the corner, hurtled towards Atherton and leapt, covering his face with huge, slobbery dog kisses. He cuddled and patted the mastiff in response. 'Good girl! Who's a good girl then?' He grinned at Zeta. 'I had a mastiff when I was a kid. Love 'em. I'd get one now if it wasn't for my "No Pets Allowed" landlord.'

'Hello? Anyone home?'

Zeta and Atherton sniffed the air. It wasn't pleasant.

'Listen, SC Jama, if you'd rather wait downstairs…'

'No. I'm fine,' said Zeta, resolutely.

'Have you ever seen a corpse before?'

'Athers, you really need to work on your chat-up lines.'

To Zeta's relief, the fetid atmosphere was due to Daisy's lack of 'walkies' opportunities rather than any decomposing remains. There were piles of her faeces dotted around every room of the flat, but of her owner there was no sign. Daisy welcomed her guests. Her orange bandana had been replaced by a smarter red dog collar and she escorted the police officers during their search of the premises like a proud homeowner. An open kitchen-cupboard door and kibble strewn across the floor indicated that she had become self-sufficient.

'It looks like Tony's done a runner,' noted Atherton.

'And left his dog behind?'

'Maybe I scared him off, paying him a visit. Or he's behind on his rent and has done a bunk.'

Or Chris and I set that particular hare running, thought Zeta. She leafed through some papers on the desk. 'Perhaps there's a clue here.'

Atherton took the papers out of Zeta's hands and put them back them on the table. 'For that, we'd need a warrant. There's no sign of foul play beyond animal neglect, and whilst I'd like to hammer anyone for abandoning such a cute dog, our hands are tied. I'll leave him a note in case he wants to get in touch about compensation for a new door.'

T Figg Debt Recovery Solutions' company secretary looked up at them with sorrowful eyes and made a throaty warble that sounded like a question.

'What about Daisy? Should we take her to the Dog's Trust?' asked Zeta.

As Atherton paused for thought, Daisy rested her substantial paws on his substantial thighs.

'Tell you what, I'll take her back to the station for safe-keeping until Figg reclaims her or we can find a foster home. You need proper looking after, don't you, my girl?'

'Ruff,' agreed Daisy.

*

After bidding farewell to Liz, Chris continued towards the main road and paused at the junction. To her left, concealed behind the hoarding, was the Hermon Village development, but what caught her attention wasn't the noise from the building site, it was the lack of it. She cycled round to the entrance. The main gates were padlocked shut.

Happily, the green Portaloo was no longer obscuring the line of sight through the viewing slot. The site was deserted and, apart from the addition of a cement mixer, little progress had been made in the three weeks since her last visit. Curious. Danny Figg had mentioned that the hole that Chris had nearly fallen into had put a spanner in the works. Perhaps Figg's hole was deeper and the spanner bigger than he'd anticipated. Nothing to see here – thankfully – thought Chris as she mounted Rod and headed for home.

Back at Sea View, Nick was, for once, not rearranging his bins but carefully manicuring a rose bush.

'Have you converted?' he asked as Chris dismounted Rod.

'To what? Hydro-electricity?'

'I wondered if your holistic wellness therapy might have ignited some faith.'

'Nah, the only things I've got faith in are cats and wine, and not necessarily in that order.'

'That's what I told the God-botherers.'

'The who?'

'There were a couple of Jehovah's Witnesses, a man and a woman, on your doorstep when I came back from the shops. They wanted to know whether you'd found Jesus.'

Chris couldn't remember the last time she'd been offered doorstep salvation. She'd assumed it had gone out of fashion with the rise of social media. 'What did you say?'

'I said you were an expert in finding people and if Jesus hadn't turned up by next week they should call back.'

'Thanks, Nick. I'll go and dig out my Devil fancy-dress outfit in case they return.'

Chris hadn't taken more than four steps down her hallway before she felt it – a strange atmosphere. Perhaps all that talk of Jesus and karmic auras was having an effect. In the kitchen, her attention was drawn by a low rattling sound that indicated that the fridge door was slightly ajar. Like most of her household appliances, it required a special knack and she could have been careless about closing it properly before leaving that morning. But still… Aitken and Waterman seemed especially skittish and it took a full five minutes of cuddles before they would settle down to eat.

She made herself a cup of tea and sat at the kitchen table staring at the wall. Was that what was making her feel uneasy? This whole Martin Livingstone mystery and the fact she couldn't get a handle on it, couldn't even figure out what the mystery was or even if there was a mystery at all?

'What do you reckon, Grayson?' He may have been an inanimate mannequin but he was an excellent sounding board. When Chris tried to discuss issues with Aitken or Waterman, they usually headed straight for the cat flap.

She took out the marker pens. There was instant therapy in a coloured pen. How about pink this time?

Chris drew a line connecting Martin's and Skye's names and wrote 'Will'. Writing 'Last Will and Testament' in full would have exceeded the wall's boundary and defaced the rear of the kitchen door.

'Should I have told Zeta that I found Martin's will?'

Grayson didn't answer. Fortunately.

On reflection, Chris had been keeping her friend in the dark. She hadn't told her about the visit to Pippa because… well, it had turned out to be irrelevant, a silly detour. And there was no one less in need of wellbeing therapy than Zeta.

But the will?

'We can guess how Zeta would have responded, can't we, Grayson?'

She would probably have made Skye her prime suspect and said it was her duty to report the findings. Skye had suffered enough with the disappearance of her father without having the full interrogative force of North Kent Constabulary land on her delicate shoulders.

'I know what you're thinking,' she said to Grayson. 'I'm being over-protective, aren't I?'

Grayson didn't seem to have an opinion one way or the other.

Chris did know why she hadn't told Skye that she'd found her father's handwritten will: because it would have been insensitive in the circumstances and, also, because it was none of her goddam business.

Pippa was connected to Skye with a firm blue line (naturally) and to Martin with a dotted green line. Chris's wellness session with Pippa hadn't elicited any reaction, but then was that odd in itself? She shook her head and switched on the espresso machine. A stronger injection of caffeine was needed to clear her head.

Next, in the bottom left corner, Chris wrote the names of Danny and Tony Figg and drew a cloud shape round them. As far as she knew there was nothing to connect Tony to Martin. As for Danny? The police may have tagged Martin as a dangerous developer-stalking eco-terrorist but Chris hadn't found anything that gave credence to this view. She reckoned the Figgs were just a red herring, a cul-de-sac that North Kent Constabulary were hurtling down. Using a red pen, she drew the shape of a fish next to their names. It was more of a flounder than a herring, but Chris was better with words than drawing.

Above the Figgs, Chris used a lime-green pen to replicate (to the best of her ability) the CrEW logo and connected it to Danny Figg's name with a downward arrow and to Martin with a dotted line.

Chris stood back and gulped down the coffee in one, scalding the inside of her mouth. 'What am I missing?' she asked Aitken, who had leapt onto the table with the express intention of knocking all the marker pens to the floor. Aitken was no more helpful than Grayson and managed to dispatch orange and yellow pens before Chris could scoop them up.

Finally, in the bottom right corner she drew a brown house with Chisellers' Cabin next to it. Now she was definitely crazy.

There was nothing that could connect a bunch of batty but genial woodworkers with the disappearance of one of their own. Was there?

Chris poured herself another coffee and paused to admire her handiwork. Her kitchen wall was a multicoloured mess of lines, doodles, names and childlike drawings. It might not get her any closer to finding out what had happened to Martin, but she would be a shoo-in for next year's Turner Prize.

'You know what, Grayson?' she said to her plastic buddy. 'I'm going to have to get the League back together.'

Twenty-Six

The Sea View Justice League were gathered around the kitchen table, or, rather, sixty per cent of them were. The previous year they had proven the power of collective thought in solving the case of the missing forensics professor.

This time round, Chris hadn't invited Barry because Zeta reasoned they had gleaned all his relevant intelligence already and, being retired, he no longer had the inside track on North Kent Constabulary's computer systems. Besides, Chris had only ordered two large thin-crust Vegetarian Hot pizzas, and if Barry had been there nobody else would have got a look in.

And Chloe? She was safe and sound in Melbourne, ten thousand miles away from the action. Technically, she could have joined them by video link, but that might have given the game away, that Chris had broken her half-promise to her daughter not to 'go off on another hare-brained escapade'. Still, they now had Grayson and, at times, one or both of Aitken and Waterman, so she reckoned that made them quorate.

Nick sat at the table and looked at the kitchen wall in despair. 'Jeez, Chris, what have you done? This is like one of those movies where they discover a serial killer's diary and it's full of weird drawings and cryptic quotes. It's going to take more than one tin of white-with-a-hint-of-apple emulsion to cover that lot when you're finished.'

Using a cloth, Chris wiped away one of the arrows and redrew it to demonstrate that the marker pen wasn't permanent. 'Thank you all for attending. The objective is to pull together information from our separate inquiries into the disappearance of Martin Livingstone. I have been assisting Martin's daughter, Skye, whilst Zeta has insight from the police investigation.'

Nick paused while taking a bite of pizza. 'What am I doing here, then?'

'I was about to ask the same question,' added Zeta.

'Nick is… how can I put this… our naif?'

'Our what?' asked Zeta and Nick in unison.

'Our innocent. Zeta and I both have knowledge about the case, but Nick knows nothing.'

'Harsh but fair,' agreed Nick.

'In any experiment you need a control, something neutral that doesn't add any stimulus.'

'Don't go overboard with your flattery, Chris,' said Nick. 'Can I still ask the occasional dumb question?'

'Yes, Nick, cos very occasionally they're not that dumb.'

Chris put a bottle of New Zealand Sauvignon Blanc in the centre of the table with three glasses. She had another cooling in the fridge – this could be a long session. 'Let's start with what we know about Martin's disappearance.'

'Can I stress that anything said this evening must be strictly between us?' said Zeta. 'I've already had bollockings from Sergeant Spurgeon and CID, and one more transgression will definitely tip them over the edge.'

Chris and Nick placed their hands over their hearts and nodded in a solemn vow.

'OK.' Zeta was convinced by this gesture. 'Martin Livingstone was last seen in the early hours of 21 March, carrying his handmade boat in the direction of Skinner's Beach.'

'So he drowned. Case closed,' observed Nick. 'Good. That was a quick solve. Shall we finish this pizza and go for a pint at the Duke?'

'Not necessarily. That's what we need to discuss. There are other possibilities,' said Chris, surprised at Nick's uncharacteristic callousness.

'Bloke goes to sea in a handmade boat and disappears? What other possibilities? "The most simple solution is usually the correct one" – that's what you're always telling me, Chris. Occam's Ladyshave or whatever it's called.'

Zeta grinned at Nick's joke. At least she hoped it was a joke. 'Misadventure's a possibility, though CID think he's faked his own death to avoid being investigated over the Danny Figg death threat. But we think that's a crap theory.'

Chris wrote 'Accidental Death? Absconded?' next to Martin's name with a black marker pen.

'And James suggested he might have just wandered off on account of being over fifty years old and therefore bewildered,' said Zeta.

'Who's James?' asked Nick. 'See, I've lost track already!'

'He's a fellow special constable and all-round good guy,' said Zeta.

'Can you tell "all-round good guy" James that the Over-Fifty Club appreciate his concern for their wellbeing.' But Chris added 'Lost?' to the wall anyway.

'What about suicide?' said Nick.

Chris couldn't add that word to the list though it had crossed everyone's minds. It was too bleak a thought and the impact on Skye would be too severe.

'Or kidnap?' suggested Nick.

'No ransom demand's been received,' Zeta replied.

'And he doesn't have a rich family,' said Chris.

'So what do you reckon then, Officer?' Nick asked Zeta.

'Murder. It's the only line of inquiry that hasn't been investigated yet.'

Chris selected a new pen, purple this time. 'All right, let's take murder as a theory. Who and why?'

'His alleged involvement in sabotage would be an obvious place to start,' said Zeta.

'But we don't know he was behind the death threat sent to Danny Figg. In fact, it's pretty unlikely it came from Martin,' said Chris.

'That's irrelevant. If Danny Figg thought Martin was responsible, that might be enough. And he's been a thorn in Figg's side going back nearly three decades.'

'Surely not if he was just making a legitimate protest about local environmental concerns,' said Nick.

'This is big business. The Hermon Village development is worth around £12 million. For Danny Figg it could be the difference between wealth and bankruptcy – more than enough motivation for murder.'

'But Skye told me that her dad gave up activism years ago,' said Chris.

'CID found footage of the Becketon City Council planning meeting that suggests otherwise.'

'I didn't realise they filmed those meetings,' said Nick.

Zeta nodded. 'And that's why Danny Figg's still my numero uno suspect.'

Chris noted that the wine bottle was nearly empty. Investigation was thirsty work. She drew a red asterisk next to Danny's name. 'Do we include brother Tony in this theory?'

'Danny Figg's got a brother?' said Nick.

Zeta nodded. 'A twin but estranged.'

'And I'm convinced that the fraternal animosity between the two is genuine, going back years,' said Chris.

'Is that fraternal animosity such that Tony would frame his brother for murder?'

Chris and Zeta paused and looked at each other. This was a possibility they hadn't even considered.

'Chris is right,' said Zeta, breaking the silence. 'Not all of your questions are dumb, Nick.'

Nick looked suitably proud.

'And Tony's gone AWOL. Departed in such a hurry that he left Daisy behind.'

'His wife?' said Nick, taking a fresh slice of pizza and topping up the Justice League's wine glasses.

'His pet dog.' Zeta pointed at the wall. 'So what's the significance of the whale?'

'What?'

'The pink whale?'

'It's a herring. A red herring – get it? I think the Figgs are leading us all up the garden path.'

'Jeez, Chris, I'd recommend art classes before you do any more missing persons investigations,' said Nick. 'I thought it was the cross-section of an onion.'

'Can we return to the matter at hand?' said Chris, annoyed at the spontaneous criticism of her artistic prowess.

'Yes, let's,' said Zeta. 'So who else is a suspect? How about CrEW?'

'Who?' asked Nick, who seemed to have adopted the role of the asker of simple questions.

'We think they're a small group of local environmental activists. They've daubed their logo all over the Hermon Village development, but we don't even know what "CrEW" means.'

'I reckon the "E" must be "eco" or "environmental". I haven't figured out what any of the other letters represent,' said Chris.

'Martin may have belonged to CrEW, but CID are getting nowhere with identifying any of the other members,' said Zeta.

'I see,' said Nick, opening the second bottle of wine. 'But surely an environmental group would be peaceful and caring.'

'It wouldn't be the first time that an internal disagreement spilled over into rivalry and bloodletting,' said Zeta.

Chris sat back in her chair and stroked an imaginary beard. 'This death threat to Danny Figg – have you seen it?'

'Yes, of course,' replied Zeta.

'Did it have the CrEW logo on it?'

Zeta thumped the table so hard that Nick had to act fast to avert a tragic Sauvignon Blanc spillage. 'No, it didn't!'

'And you said this… what d'ya call them… CrEW lot put their logo on everything,' said Nick, refastening the bottle's screw top.

'Exactly,' said Zeta excitedly. 'Chalk one up for the Sea View Justice League. Even CID didn't spot that!'

'That means you can take CrEW off your list of suspects, doesn't it?' asked Nick.

'It certainly warrants a double question mark pending removal,' agreed Chris, and she marked the kitchen wall accordingly.

*

They were already halfway through the second pizza. Chris had never seen Zeta eat so much, let alone something as unhealthy as pizza. Feeling starved of attention, as well as starved of pizza, Waterman leapt onto the table and stuck his nose into the box, dislodging a piece of green pepper. Neither Zeta nor Nick seemed to care about this flagrant breach of food hygiene standards.

'Good to see you've included the Chisellers' Cabin on the wall. They seemed like a very strange bunch when I visited,' said Zeta.

'Yeah, they're certainly strange, but none of them has any reason to wish Martin harm.'

'What about that head guy? What's his name… Eric?'

'Eric?' Chris scoffed at the idea. 'He might try and kill us with cake and cheap biscuits, but murder?'

Nick stood to stretch his legs or maybe channel a Columbo persona. 'Perhaps he didn't mean to. What if he sabotaged the cora-thingy out of envy? A couple of discreetly drilled holes and… glug, glug, glug.'

'If you're not going to make sensible suggestions…' said Chris.

'Hey, I thought we were meant to brainstorm? And you told me Martin and Eric were always at each other's throats.'

Chris paused to think about that. Eric was the only Chiseller who had not shown concern about Martin's disappearance. And then there was his 'if he comes back' comment. She shook her head. People didn't commit murder for control of a community woodworking group any more than they did because of a local environmental protest group.

The cat flap rattled as Aitken returned from his evening prowl around the neighbourhood.

'Why have you got Pippa Atlantis's name up there?' asked Zeta as she bent down to scratch Aitken's ear.

'We went to see her,' said Nick.

'I went to see her,' corrected Chris. 'Nick gave me a lift because Pippa lives in the middle of nowhere.'

'And this is the first I hear of it? This was supposed to be a collaborative investigation! Explain yourself, Heron.'

'I thought you were busy. We're not joined at the hip, you realise,' said Chris defensively. 'And I wasn't convinced about the backstory. Why Pippa was so anti Skye seeing Martin.'

'You think she killed her one-night stand twenty-five years after the event?'

'No. Not now I've met her. She's away with the fairies but not a psycho killer. I'll cross her off the wall.' And with her red pen, Chris did so.

'It looks like we've hit a brick wall,' observed Nick. 'Does anyone fancy a pint before closing?'

'What about the break-in at Martin's place? Any link?' asked Zeta. 'I could try and nudge Sergeant Spurgeon to get someone to attend.'

'Well...' The handwritten will made just a week before Martin's disappearance swam back into Chris's mind. It was accompanied by a mental image of Skye squinting under the harsh spotlight of an intensive CID interrogation. Chris shook her head. 'You were right, Zeta. It looked like opportunists, and Martin didn't have anything worth stealing.'

The pizza was now finished and the wine bottles empty. The three of them stared in silence at the kitchen wall for a full two minutes.

'So what do we reckon?' asked Chris.

'I'm still voting for a tragic accident,' said Nick.

'If that's the case, there's nothing we can do,' said Zeta. 'But if CID's right and Martin's done a runner? We've had no credible sightings, no bank or phone activity.'

'And murder? That was your number one theory, Zeta,' said Chris.

'We've exhausted our small list of suspects, so unless anyone's got any other ideas, I vote for Nick's proposal to catch last orders at the Duke.'

Nick stood. 'If this was like the movies, a letter would turn up out of the blue or a new witness would appear and suddenly crack the case open.'

'Deus ex machina,' said Chris.

'Took the words out of my mouth. Come on, let's hit the pub,' said Nick, heading for the door.

'You're on,' said Zeta, following him.

Part Two

Twenty-Seven

It was an ark.

Admittedly, it wasn't three hundred cubits in length – it was almost exactly the size of Nick's Fiat 500 – but it was very definitely an ark. It was wooden and boat-shaped and had a small cabin on the deck.

Felix's head appeared above the starboard side. 'What d'ya... think, Chris?'

Ah, that voice!

'I think it's beautiful.'

And it was. A tribute to the power of community.

*

Barely a month had passed since the extraordinary meeting of the Sea View Justice League. A month during which progress on the case had amounted to precisely nothing. Chris continued to send regular text updates to Skye that consisted of the message: *Sorry, no news. Chris x*

Zeta had come up against a similar impasse. No ransom notes had been received, no unexpected breakthroughs made and, fortunately, no bodies had washed up on the beach. Wilf had even given up on the coracle-spotting and had just a single rescue to his name, a Portuguese water dog that had turned out to be scared of the sea. It was still early summer, but if it continued this way, Old Ted's record would be safe for another year.

*

Paulette and Libby's heads popped up either side of Felix so that the three of them resembled a human Whack-a-Mole game.

'Just got to build the steps, put a door in the cabin and apply the pitch,' said Libby. 'A week, tops.'

'Not forgetting fixing the figurehead,' added Paulette. 'How's Jethro getting on with that? He's refused to show us any work in progress.'

'Apparently, being his muse disqualifies me from having a prior peek. He said my nose is too long and my ears are in the wrong place. It doesn't bode well.'

'Perhaps you should consider plastic surgery so you match Jethro's carving,' suggested Libby with an evil grin.

'Ah, Christine! Just the woman I was looking for.' Eric appeared from around the bow end of the ark.

Since the Justice League meeting, Chris had taken to examining Eric for longer and treating all his interactions with caution. The idea that Eric could have engineered Martin's demise by sabotaging his coracle, however ridiculous, meant she couldn't help but view him as a suspect.

'Liz Fyffe-Hermon has agreed to loan us Andrew and Pepsi for Harbour Day. Two conditions: they have to stay on the harbourside and we will cross-promote her farm shop and Alpaca Experience.'

'Excellent,' said Eric in a sibilant tone which disturbingly resembled the love child of Hannibal Lecter and Mr Burns from *The Simpsons*. 'Could I ask one more favour of you? That you invite Mr Figg to the launch as our guest of honour?'

'No problem. I've got his email address if you want to draft something for me to send.'

'Oh no, in person. Mr Figg has been such a generous benefactor and we wouldn't have this magnificent vessel without his contribution. An impersonal email would be inappropriate.'

The last thing in the world that Chris wanted to do was step inside the Hermon Village building site and encounter Danny Figg again. On balance, she'd rather take a non-stop flight to Melbourne with a planeload of teething babies. 'You're the Cabin chair, Eric. I think the invitation would be better coming from you.'

'But you've got the charm, Christine,' replied Eric in a manner so oily that Chris felt the urge to cycle home and leap into a lava-hot shower for a carbolic soap scrub-down.

'Sorry, Eric, I'm not the woman for the job. You'll have to find another volunteer. There is not a force on this earth that could make me deliver the invitation to Danny Figg in person.'

*

'So you agreed to give the invitation to Danny Figg in person?' asked Zeta, fishing a camomile and hibiscus teabag out of her mug and placing it on the saucer next to an open packet of biscuits.

Chris joined her at the table in the furthest corner of the Wavecrest Cafe.

'I couldn't say no. They all looked so, um, pathetic and needy.' She helped herself to a biscuit, took a bite and wrinkled her nose. 'Acquired taste, these biccies. Anyway, the Chisellers have done so much graft whilst I've been swanning around pursuing improbable theories about a missing woodworker that I felt I owed them. How are things at the station?'

'It's weird,' said Zeta. 'It's like the whole "Figg death threat and daring coracle escape" never happened. The hotline's now straight to voicemail and no one can recall when they last saw Turing and Beech lurking. It's as though the whole station's being gaslit.'

'Any intel on CrEW?'

'Not a veggie sausage. On the plus side, there's been no more environmental graffiti. Are you enjoying those biscuits?'

'They're surprisingly moreish,' Chris said, dunking the second half of her biscuit in her tea.

'And how is Skye?' asked Zeta.

'She's not going to let it go.'

'You'll be pleased to know that Skye Livingstone is who she claims to be.'

'You checked her out?' Chris was outraged.

'Not me personally. I persuaded DS Beech to do it. We're not idiots, Chris. You don't have someone turning up out of the blue claiming to be a long-lost daughter without doing some verification.'

'You don't trust anyone, do you?'

'It goes with the uniform,' said Zeta. 'Still, that's one more name you can wipe off your kitchen wall.'

'I suppose so,' said Chris. 'What flavour are these biscuits?

'Liver.'

'Hah! Very funny, Zeta. I can't stick around too long; I've got to deliver that invitation. Do you fancy chaperoning me or is Sergeant Spurgeon's exclusion order still in place?'

'Harrumph!'

'Sorry?'

'I didn't say anything.'

'I distinctly heard you harrumphing me.'

'That was Daisy,' said Zeta.

It was only then that Chris noticed a dog lead tied to the arm of Zeta's chair, the other end disappearing beneath the tabletop. 'Daisy? As in Tony Figg's dog?'

Zeta made a clucking sound with her tongue and Daisy, the mastiff and ex-company secretary, wandered out from behind Zeta's chair and looked up at the tabletop longingly. 'Yep. And she's not happy that you're scoffing all her snacks.'

Chris stared at Daisy and then grabbed the biscuit packet. A cartoon dog grinned broadly beneath the tagline 'Chompalot – Savoury Treats for Good Dogs'.

'For frick's sake, Zeta, why didn't you tell me I was eating dog biscuits?'

'I was going to, but you said they were "surprisingly moreish".'

Chris swilled down her tea and waved at the barista to order two double espressos. 'What are you doing with Tony Figg's dog?'

'She'd been abandoned.'

'Abandoned? Where's her owner then?'

'Apparently on a very long holiday, which, all things considered, is probably a sensible decision. Atherton couldn't bear to let Daisy go to a dogs' home. He thought he could train her up as a North Kent Constabulary sniffer dog.'

'And how's that going, being a sniffer dog?' Chris bent down to address Daisy directly.

'Well, she certainly smells. Daisy's not made herself too popular, particularly with Sergeant Spurgeon. I've never seen a grown man cry over the loss of two bacon sandwiches before. So before there's a case of dogicide to investigate, I thought I'd better take her for walkies and figure out where she'd be happiest.'

'I wish I could take her, but with Aitken and Waterman, I'm outvoted two to one.'

'And my lifestyle is definitely not dog-friendly,' said Zeta sadly, 'so I'm afraid it's the Dog's Trust for you, my darling.'

Daisy gave a little moan, inducing guilt as only a pet can.

'Hang about,' said Chris. 'I've got an idea.'

*

It wasn't easy to ride an e-bike while escorting a dog. If Daisy had been a greyhound or a Labrador, she'd have had no difficulty keeping up a decent pace. However, a mastiff handicapped by too little exercise and too many stolen bacon sandwiches was another matter. Once they were safely off-road, Chris managed to get Daisy to stand with her hind legs on Chris's thighs and her front paws on the crossbar. This arrangement suited them both well for the journey to Hermon Hill Farm, where Liz was awaiting their arrival.

'Daisy, meet Ernie.'

The two dogs circled each other on a thorough sniff and then, seemingly having reached mutual approval, scampered (as much as a geriatric collie and an overweight mastiff could scamper) off in the direction of the farmhouse.

'Thanks for taking her in,' said Chris. 'Her owner's gone AWOL and we don't know if and when he'll be returning.'

'I'm happy to keep her for as long as needed. Ernie could do with the company. He can't keep up with the farm dogs and I'm a poor substitute,' said Liz.

'I should warn you, though, that you might see a musclebound police officer hanging around. A Constable Atherton. He's grown quite attached to Daisy.'

Liz laughed. 'You can tell Constable Atherton that he's welcome to come round and visit whenever he likes. It's always handy to have a bit of visible police presence. Are you coming in for a cuppa?'

Chris shook her head. 'No, I'm afraid I've got to visit your least favourite person, Danny Figg.'

'I'm learning to let bygones be bygones. Besides, it's been strangely quiet on that side of the wall in the last month.'

As Chris approached the front gates of the Hermon Village development, she could see what Liz meant. The silence was deafening. She looked through the observation slot, but nothing seemed to have changed or even moved since her previous visit. The gates were slightly open. She stuck her head around the opening, but the site was apparently deserted.

'Hello? Anyone at home?'

As she entered, her feet caught on something heavy, nearly tripping her. It was the padlock and chain that usually secured the door. She bent down to examine it. The padlock's shackle had been cleanly severed.

Twenty-Eight

Chris pushed Rod through the gates and propped him up on his stand ready for a quick getaway.

'Hello? Mr Figg? It's Chris Heron from Chisellers' Cabin.' Her voice sounded echoey in the stillness. Certain locations were particularly spooky when deserted: schools, shopping centres, sports stadiums – and now she could add building sites to that category.

She tried to visualise what had changed since her previous visit. The graffiti that had decorated the Portakabin office had been painted over and the CrEW tag and the words 'Hands Off Our Trees' were just a ghostly apparition through white emulsion. A rusty paint tin and brush sat on the steps leading to the office door. The drips down the side of the tin suggested that the paint inside was dark green. Chris stepped over the paint tin and rapped on the office door.

'Mr Figg? It's only me, Chris Heron. I've got an invitation for you.'

'*Chris.*'

She thought she heard her name whispered, so she knocked again and pressed her ear against the door, but there were no sounds of movement from inside.

'Hello? Anyone around?'

The cement mixer had been moved closer to the hole that Danny Figg had previously either pushed her into or rescued her from. Unable to resist the temptation, Chris checked that the coast was clear and climbed the steps again to peer into the hole.

The hole had been filled to about two-thirds of its depth with concrete. It was rough-surfaced but dry and solid-looking, not that she was going to test it. It looked ready for a final top-up and the hole would be no more. At the current concrete level the word 'TRIP' had been written in block capitals on a wooden support panel. Chris assumed that the word 'HAZARD' lay just below the surface, a handwritten warning serving as Danny Figg's nod to health and safety.

The edge of the wooden surround wobbled under her grip, so she hastily stepped back from the hole and descended to firm ground. To nearly fall into a hole once would be unfortunate, but twice?

'*Chris.*'

There it was again. Was it the wind rustling through the trees of Hermon Copse? She left the hole and walked towards the treeline.

'CHRIS!'

There was no mistaking it this time. She spun around, looking for the source.

'Up here!'

She recognised that voice; muffled yet distinctive.

To her right was a large yellow digger, its bucket raised to maximum height.

'Nick?'

Above the toothed rim of the digger's excavation bucket a head emerged. The head of a giant red squirrel.

'Nick?'

'Thank God you've turned up. I was getting desperate.'

'What are you doing up there? Looking for your nuts?'

'It's not funny, Chris. They've left me up here and I can't get this outfit off. I can't reach the bloody zip!'

Chris took a few seconds to process the situation. Being stood on a deserted building site talking to a giant squirrel trapped in the bucket of a JCB rivalled any of her cheese dreams for bizarreness.

'First question, Nick: how did you climb up there?'

'I didn't. I just got in the bucket and they used the lever to raise it.'

'Second question: why?'

'It was supposed to be a photo op that'd get loads of publicity about the destruction of Hermon Copse.'

'Dressed as a goofy squirrel with googly eyes, buck teeth and a sticking-out tongue?'

'It was the only outfit the fancy-dress shop had. It was either this or a comedy beaver.'

'OK, that's logical. Stupid, but logical. Third question: who are "they"?'

'I can't tell you.'

'Thought as much. Fourth and, hopefully, final question: where are "they"?

'We heard a police siren, so they told me to stay hidden and they'd come back and rescue me, but that was hours ago.'

The cut padlock, the green paint, the squirrel costume – it was so obvious that Chris was embarrassed by how slow she'd been. 'You're CrEW? You're an eco-terrorist?' she said with a hint of admiration.

Nick clutched his paws to his head in despair, his giant eyeballs rolling, his tongue lolling. 'We're eco-activists – we don't terrorise anyone. Just push the lever and get me down. I'm desperate for a pee. If I wet myself, I'll never get the deposit on this costume back.'

Chris stepped up into the cab of the digger, which smelt of cigarettes, diesel and maleness. It was more complicated than she had imagined. The large steering wheel? That was self-explanatory. But what did all those levers and switches do? There were no helpful labels or instructions to inform the novice. She searched the cab for a user manual, but all she could find were some snapshots of the driver's family and a leaflet for a hair transplant clinic.

She leant out of the cab. 'There's no way I'm going to be able to operate this. Can you call your mysterious collaborators and ask them which lever they pulled?'

'Call them? Where do you think I'm storing my phone in this costume?'

'So give me their number and I'll call them.'

'I can't do that,' yelled Nick. 'The first rule of CrEW...'

'... is "you do not talk about CrEW"?'

'Exactly.'

'In that case, you're stuffed, as it appears they've taken the digger's keys with them too.'

Nick howled, and Chris could see the tops of his ears flapping over the bucket edge as he shook his head in anguish. 'You can't leave me here, Chris. If I'm caught, I'll... I'll be ruined.'

Chris considered their options. In truth, they weren't spoiled for choice. 'I'm going to see if there's a spare key somewhere,' she shouted up to the panic-stricken giant squirrel.

She recalled her first visit to Danny Figg's Portakabin office and the open key cabinet on the wall. Security in the Hermon Village development was surprisingly lax, so it wasn't beyond the bounds of possibility that spare keys to the plant machinery were kept there. The door was locked, but a small window on the far side of the office was slightly ajar. Chris delved into her backpack for the bicycle maintenance kit that she had never used. She inserted the bicycle spanner into the gap between the window and the frame and, with a sharp push, dislodged the latch. The opening was head height. An athlete could have pulled themselves up and in, but for Chris a handy wheelbarrow, upturned, made a high enough platform to enable her to wiggle through. Did this count as breaking and entering? Technically, she hadn't broken anything – yet.

Thankfully there was a sofa on the other side of the window, which meant that when Chris inelegantly tumbled through head first, she had a soft landing. The blinds were drawn and so it took thirty seconds of fumbling before she could find the light switch.

She went straight to the key cabinet. It was open; in fact, it couldn't be closed as the lock had been left with the lever sticking out. Apparently, Danny had lost the key to his key cabinet – perhaps

Alanis Morissette could write a song about that? Inside, the keys were helpfully labelled, including one that matched the JCB's number plate. This was easy, too easy. Danny Figg Homes's insurance company would have had a fit. He may as well have hung a sign on the gate that said 'Thieves Welcome'. Perhaps that was the idea?

As she prepared to switch the light off and exit the way she had entered, Chris stopped to browse the framed photographs that lined the wall. There were Danny and his brother T in the boxing ring, friends before it all fell apart. Was Danny already planning how to cheat his brother? And there was the clipping from the *Becketon Weekly Bugle*, a yellowing article with the headline 'Nutkin Nabbed!' and the sub-headline 'Police Capture Wycken Woods Protestor'. Chris took it off the wall and placed it under the desk lamp to study the accompanying photograph. It showed a young, barely recognisable Martin Livingstone being handcuffed by two police officers. Behind him stood a small group of activists and supporters holding a banner: 'Save Wycken Woods!'

She took a photo with her phone and replaced the newspaper article on the wall, adjusting it to make sure it was perfectly straight.

*

'You took your bloody time,' shouted the giant squirrel.

'Do you want rescuing or not?' shouted Chris in response.

She clambered into the digger's cab, inserted the key into the ignition and the engine roared into life. There were no instructions anywhere, why would there be? Only a reckless fool would attempt to operate an industrial digger without extensive training.

Chris looked at the controls. Beside the steering wheel were two levers, like dual gear sticks. To her right was another lever. They looked identical. To her left was an illuminated display with incomprehensible symbols that flickered in turn.

'Just do something!' shouted the squirrel.

Chris tentatively touched the right lever and, with a metallic groan, the digger's bucket tipped forward. The squirrel screamed.

If she got this wrong, Nick would fall five metres and Danny Figg would find another dead squirrel deposited on his doorstep.

She stuck her head out of the cabin. 'Sorry, Nick, I daren't. If I kill you, who'll take the bins in? I'm phoning the fire brigade.'

'Don't, Chris! They'll arrest me for sabotage and you for trespass, and then who will look after Aitken and Waterman? From up here I can see a huge pile of sand fifty metres in that direction.' Nick pointed his paw towards the treeline. 'Just drive the digger there and I'll jump.'

Chris gripped the steering wheel and stepped on the accelerator. The digger lurched backwards and a *Crash!* followed as the back end hit the nearest temporary toilet. She looked in the rearview mirror as the green toilet rocked, fell backwards and, like a domino, took the two other toilets with it.

'You're in reverse gear!' shouted Nick.

'Yeah, I've just figured that out, thanks!' Chris shouted back. 'Hang on.'

She checked out the lever on her right. Helpfully, it was recognisable as a gearstick. If only she'd taken another two minutes to study all the controls thoroughly. With a sickening crunch, she moved the gearstick into first and gently eased on the accelerator. The digger lurched again, forward this time, and at a snail's pace it chugged across the site before coming to rest against a bank of sand.

Nick clambered out of the bucket, hung from the edge for a couple of seconds and then dropped into the sand below, unharmed.

'Quick, let's get out of here!' shouted Chris, leaping from the cab, and the squirrel and the cyclist ran for the exit.

*

'You idiot.'

Nick nodded and took another sip of the double brandy. He was still shaking. If he looked rather out of place in the public bar of the Cooper's Arms dressed only in a T-shirt, boxer shorts and socks, it was less attention-grabbing than the full squirrel outfit.

'What the hell were you doing? You could have been caught. Do you want an enraged gangster property developer after you?'

'It was a good bet that the site would be deserted. It's been dormant for the past month – we've been keeping watch.'

'Mucking around with heavy machinery? You could have been killed. Or arrested. Or both. Why take such a stupid risk?'

'It's the planet. It's *our* planet. And if we don't make a stand now, what's going to be left for future generations?'

'So wave a few banners, share a few memes. But vandalism? That's going too far.'

'Oh come on, Chris. A bit of green paint never hurt anyone.'

'And we were right about CrEW not being responsible for the death threat, I hope?'

Nick looked shocked. If he'd still been wearing the squirrel head, his eyes would have rotated in different directions. 'We'd never do anything like that. We're pacifists – that's the second rule of CrEW.'

Chris was not without empathy. As a student, she'd been involved in many sit-in and sit-down protests, at least until pub-opening time. That was then. But now, approaching the bus-pass stage of life? And she'd never dressed up as wildlife – well, once, as a sexy badger, but that wasn't a relationship she remembered with fondness.

'It's the other members of your gang I'm angry with. Abandoning my mate to his fate in a high-rise bucket. If I could get my hands on them…'

'It's no good, Chris. You can threaten all you like, but there is not a force on earth that can make me reveal CrEW's identities.'

'Is that what happened to Martin? Did they abandon him too? Is he chained to a tree somewhere?'

'Martin?'

'Martin Livingstone, the missing coracle mariner.'

'Not a member of CrEW and never has been. Trust me, I would know.'

'So if Martin's not CrEW, who is?'

Nick sat back and made a mouth-zipping gesture.

Chris leant forward, grabbed his brandy glass and downed the contents.

You don't need to tell me, thought Chris. I've just figured it out.

Twenty-Nine

'There you go, Grayson. That keeps us in wine, cat food and plastic polish for another week,' said Chris, pressing 'send' to dispatch the proofed copy of *More Love Up the Aisle* to the author. This speedily written sequel promised another helping of steamy supermarket romance, with the action having moved to the fresh fish counter, or rather under it. And as it paid the bills, who was she to criticise its artistic merit?

To avoid having to stare at her now empty work in-box, Chris connected her phone to the laptop and transferred the photo of Martin Livingstone's arrest. The original newsprint had faded and her phone capture had made the image even less clear. She experimented with various filters and image-sharpening tools, but if the article hadn't identified the handcuffed man as Martin, she wasn't certain she would have been able to do so. She attached the photo to a WhatsApp message to Skye: *Not sure if you've seen this before? Chris x*

Within five minutes there was a phone call from Skye.

'Is that the best-quality photo you've got?'

'Yes, I'm afraid so. Unfortunately, I wasn't in a position to get a better shot and the newspaper was a pretty old edition.'

'Do you think there'll be a copy of the paper in some archives somewhere?'

'Good thinking,' said Chris. 'Leave it with me.'

The *Becketon Weekly Bugle*. It certainly rang a bell, but from a long time ago. A time when not only were there competing local papers but you were prepared to pay for the pleasure of reading them.

A Google search threw up a Wikipedia page. Who were the selfless souls who wrote these pages for the common good? According to Wikipedia, the *Bugle* had closed down twenty years previously, shortly after being taken over by Niven Media Group.

A further five minutes of research and Chris was on the phone, navigating her way through Niven Media's automated call routing. After she'd wasted twenty minutes on button pressing, going back to square one and hurling abuse at a recorded message, not only was the phone answered but there was a human being on the other end of the line.

'Archives.' The voice was terse and the absence of any 'How may I help you?' follow-up was notable.

'Hi, I'm after a copy of the *Becketon Weekly Bugle*. I'm not sure of the exact date, but at least twenty-five years—'

'Are you a historian?'

'Um… of sorts.' Chris had seen *The Crown* and had *I Claudius* on DVD, so she reckoned that qualified her.

'An accredited historian?'

Could historians be accredited? Did they have lapel badges they flashed at each other during secret historian meetings? Chris thought carefully about her answer. 'Of course I'm accredited.'

'In that case, send your request in writing and we'll arrange a viewing appointment in due course.'

'In due course? What does that mean?'

'We're quiet at the moment, so you should hear back in a couple of months.'

'A couple of months? Look, this is life and death, literally. I have to find—'

The line went dead. Unsurprisingly, archivists weren't people people.

Where else to look? In the olden days she'd have gone to her local library and viewed the past editions on microfiche, but the library was now little more than a pick-up-and-drop box staffed by volunteers. Any local archive had gone the way of government cuts, as had the professional librarians. The Niven Media website did provide one more pathway: they also produced Kent's favourite TV news magazine programme, *Look Lively*, and Chris reckoned that ace reporter Alice Buttler owed her a favour.

*

At Chisellers' Cabin there was virtually a full contingent. Woodworkers scurried round the ark applying finishing touches, sanding and varnishing. All except Eric, who was standing under the awning studying a letter.

'Hi, Eric. Sorry, I didn't get the chance to visit Hermon Village to invite Danny Figg.' It was prudent to get an alibi established, just in case. 'I'll send an email instead, OK?'

'Whatever,' said Eric, apparently too absorbed by the contents of the letter to take in Chris's news.

The rest of the Cabineers were more enthusiastic about Chris's arrival – suspiciously so.

'Ah, here she is,' said Felix. 'Just in time for the... unveiling.'

'The unwhatting?' said Chris.

'The ark's figurehead. Your likeness lovingly created in balsa wood by our own Auguste Rodin,' said Libby, pointing to a large object covered by a sheet.

The artist gave a bow in recognition, as far as the fused discs in his lower back would allow. 'I think I've captured something,' said Jethro, throwing off the sheet.

The audience gasped collectively. If Picasso in his most abstract mood had decided to craft an ark's figurehead, he would have been proud of this effort. However, as a faithful representation intended for public display, it fell a little short in Chris's critical eyes. And as for those critical eyes, one was the size and shape of a tangerine, the other a half-sucked Mint Imperial. Jethro had certainly been taken by Chris's long, straight nose, which here resembled a toucan's beak. Her hair looked like Brian May had suffered an electric shock whilst tuning his guitar.

'For frick's sake!'

'Good, isn't it?' said Jethro proudly. 'I think I've captured something.'

'"Something" is the word. Why am I playing dominos?'

'Those are your teeth.'

'I for one think it's fabulous,' said Paulette, acting as peacemaker.

'Yes, it's very… creative,' added Felix after a pause. Even his sonorous voice couldn't soothe Chris's troubled brow, which, according to Jethro's handiwork, resembled a relief map of the Himalayas.

'And let's face it, nobody will know it's supposed to be you,' said Libby quietly.

'I'll know it's me,' hissed Chris. Vanity wasn't one of her many shortcomings, but that didn't mean she didn't care how others saw her.

'And it'll look even better after I've painted it,' said Jethro cheerfully.

Eric saved Jethro from being bodily thrown into the pile of wood shavings (followed shortly by the figurehead) by wandering in, head down, still clutching the letter.

'No… no… It's terrible,' he muttered.

The assembled members of Chisellers' Cabin stopped dead in their tracks. In the last few weeks, Martin's disappearance had scarcely been mentioned, as though to do so would be tempting fate. And in Martin's case, that fate was all too clear and didn't bear contemplation.

'What's terrible, Eric?' asked Libby, breaking the silence.

'The news. It's the worst thing.'

'No…' Tears welled up in Paulette's eyes.

'The… the… the… complete… bounders,' said Eric. Which, for him, was positively foul-mouthed.

'Who are?' asked Felix.

'The Harbour Day organisers. They've banned the ark. They claim that there's no guarantee it's seaworthy, that it lacks certification.'

There was the sound of collectively held breaths being simultaneously expelled.

'You twat, Eric,' said Libby angrily. 'That's not the worst news.'

'It's health and safety gone mad, that's what it is,' said Eric defensively. 'All those wasted man-hours. All those materials. All that expense. And now for nothing. I can't think of anything worse.'

Libby and Paulette stomped off to the far side of the workshop. Chris gave them a full five minutes to calm down and then followed.

'Hi, I've got a couple of things. First, can your god-daughter, Alice, help me get access to the press archives at Niven Media? I'm presuming that as she works there she can say the magic words.'

'She'll need to know why,' said Libby.

'It's for Martin's daughter. She wants a copy of a photo of her dad from an ancient edition of the *Becketon Weekly Bugle*.' Which was the truth, if not the whole truth.

'In that case, consider it done. She owes me for that scoop, inadvertent as it was on my part.'

'And she owes me for broadcasting my backside to half a million *Look Lively* viewers,' added Chris.

'What's the second thing?' asked Paulette.

Before Chris could answer, Eric bundled into the workshop as excited as a rutting stag. Felix trailed apologetically in his wake.

'Listen up, I've got it!'

'I don't doubt that for a minute, Eric,' said Paulette drily.

'The Harbour Day organisers want proof that the ark is safe, that it's watertight, right?'

'If you say so.'

'In that case, we show them it is. We launch it in the sea off Skinner's Beach.'

'I'm not going to sea in this… thing,' said Felix doubtfully. 'And I'm certainly not… rowing.'

Eric's enthusiasm was gathering pace. 'We don't have to go anywhere. Just prove that it's buoyant and then those Harbour Day Marxists will have to concede.'

'It'll be our word against theirs,' said Libby.

'Like a tree falling in a forest,' said Chris. The others looked at her in confusion. 'If nobody is there to see the ark, how will they know it floats?'

'So we'll get Alice Whatshername from *Look Lively* to cover it. That's a scoop for her, and once the Harbour Day committee see it on TV – on the local news, no less…' Eric had reached optimum jabber-point.

Chris, Paulette, Libby and Felix all looked at each other, willing each other to intervene, but that moment had passed.

'Ladies, affix the figurehead. Felix, secure the trailer. This coming Wednesday, we launch!' announced Eric.

Thirty

Chris wiped 'CrEW' off the kitchen wall, consigning them to history. The search for Martin had been simplified yet felt more unachievable than ever.

It was probably just as well that Eric had bowled up with his fruitcake idea of launching the ark when he did, as Chris had been about to confront Libby and Paulette with her revelation that they were the other members of CrEW. It had seemed insignificant at the time, Nick exchanging words with them in passing during the Cliffstaple Fun Run. But it hadn't been a greeting, mere pleasantries between casual acquaintances; it had been an exchange of information, the Lycra equivalent of a dead-letter drop. Like in a crooked arcade game on Heybourne Pier, the penny had finally dropped.

And if she had confronted them? She might have lost her cool about the way they'd abandoned her neighbour and Rioja buddy, leaving him trapped in a JCB claw bucket dressed as a screwy squirrel. She might have said things she'd have gone on to regret. And that wasn't Chris; she didn't issue threats – at least not to people she hadn't been married to. Paulette and Libby weren't to know how their well-meaning protest to protect endangered foliage had become conflated with the Danny Figg death threat; that the police had wasted time on that rather than on the search for Martin.

Besides, Nick was an adult and didn't need her to start acting like an over-protective sister or enraged… enraged girlfriend? No, Nick could fight his own battles. As long as he took his lucky escape as a sign that CrEW should cease hostile activities.

There was a knock on the kitchen window, but Chris did not leap up in surprise for she was expecting this. Her mother would have said that was due to her daughter's psychic powers, but it was just an understanding of human nature. She anticipated Zeta's behaviour in the way that a long-married couple might finish each other's sentences.

'Hi, Zeta. The door's unlocked,' she said without looking round. 'To what do I owe the honour of this visit? Trouble at t'station?'

'No, I'm not due back in till next week. I did get a call from Athers though.'

'Oh?' said Chris, putting the kettle on and spooning cat food into two bowls. 'Constable Atherton? On your private line?'

'Yep. It surprised me too. I've certainly never given him my number. He wanted an update on Daisy.'

'Daisy's living the life of Riley on the farm. She and Ernie are bestest buddies, but I think Ernie's a bit too old to get beyond first base – unless someone invents doggie Viagra. Liz sent me a couple of photos. I'll send them to you so you can forward them on.'

'Thanks. Hopefully that'll stop him brooding. And, hot news, there's been a break-in at the Hermon Village building site.'

'Oh, really?' Chris switched on her best deadpan expression.

'Yes. Nothing stolen, but three temporary toilets have been destroyed. Danny Figg's furious.'

'Because he's got nothing to go on? Any clues?'

'That's why Athers and PC Passwater were there, to look at the CCTV.'

'CCTV?' Chris froze, her hand clutching the spoon laden with unspecified fish pâté. She hadn't even considered CCTV. Of course a building site with tens of thousands of pounds' worth of equipment would have cameras. 'And?'

'Not working.'

'None of the cameras?'

'No. The system had been down for a couple of months according to Figg.'

Chris unfroze and put the food bowls down for Aitken and Waterman. 'Oh, that's a shame.'

'I mean, what sort of building developer lets his site go unmonitored?'

One who doesn't want any recorded evidence of his nefarious activities, thought Chris. 'Tea?'

'Thanks. There was an eyewitness though.'

Chris stood stock still once again, her hand gripping the kettle.

'An eyewitness? That's fortunate. Who?'

'Some zonked-out homeless druggy, according to Athers. Claimed the perpetrator was a giant squirrel who made its getaway on an electric bicycle.'

Chris allowed herself to breathe again and placed two mugs of tea on the table. 'That's drugs nowadays. Having a puff of something to make you mellow, enjoy a bit of prog rock and empty the fridge at one in the morning isn't enough any more – you have to experience full-on hallucinations.'

'I'll take your word for that,' said Zeta, swallowing a gulp of tea and studying the wall. 'Your evidence board is looking a bit sparse. Running out of murder suspects?'

'They're not suspects, they're leads. Why is everyone so keen to assume Martin's dead?'

'In fairness, it is over two months now, Chris. It's not so much "if" but "how" or "who". Any biscuits?'

Chris took the Charles and Diana tin from the cupboard and slid it across the table. 'You eat a surprising number of my biscuits for a food faddist.'

'No custard creams?' said Zeta, selecting a Bourbon as compensation. She studied the leads diagram on the wall. 'I see you've rubbed CrEW off.'

'Yeah, they were the red herring. Had nothing to do with Martin's disappearance.'

'Surely my news about the Portaloo Massacre puts them back in the frame?'

Chris shook her head. 'No. Martin wasn't a member of CrEW and they weren't responsible for the Danny Figg death threat. I'm sure of it.'

Zeta just nodded. She didn't ask Chris how she was so sure about CrEW's membership list. One of Zeta's most admirable qualities was she was only curious when it mattered.

'Can't see where else we can go then. Who's Will?' Zeta said, pointing at the top right corner of the wall. 'Is that Skye's boyfriend? Do we know if he'd met his future father-in-law?'

Chris took a deep breath. She'd been avoiding bringing this up as she could guess what Zeta's reaction would be. Why had she written that word up on the wall at all? A subliminal cry for help? 'Just something I found at Martin's place. A handwritten will in the back of a book on woodworking.'

Zeta stopped in the process of eating her Bourbon. 'When was this will written?'

'This year. Fourteenth of March.'

'A week before he disappeared?'

'I guess so.'

'And you've only mentioned this because I asked whether Will was Skye's boyfriend?'

'It's been up there in plain sight, in black and white – or rather in pink marker. It was just something that Martin had scribbled down, probably not even legal.'

'Witnessed?'

'By the next-door neighbours.'

'Then it probably is legal. Who are the beneficiaries of Martin's estate?' asked Zeta.

Chris paused. 'Um, Skye.'

'The sole beneficiary?'

'Yes.'

Zeta grabbed a pen from the table drawer and drew a red circle round Skye's name. 'There's your motive.'

'I knew you'd react like this.' Chris angrily grabbed the red pen from her friend.

'Like what?'

'Like Skye's now the prime suspect. That's why I didn't tell you before about the will. What's the plan now? Haul her in for questioning and rubber-hose a confession out of her?'

Zeta gave a bemused smile. 'Steady on, Chris. I'm just looking at the evidence in front of us, and you must admit that financial gain is as strong a motive as any.'

'But Martin doesn't have anything worth inheriting.' Chris was in mother-hen mode. 'And if your lot had shown any interest in catching whoever broke in and ransacked his house, they'd have confirmed that too.'

'Remind me of the address.'

'29, Gable Terrace. But it's tiny, a fisherman's cottage.'

Zeta tapped away at her phone. 'A tiny fisherman's cottage that is apparently worth… get this… £450,000. Nearly half a million motives.'

'You don't seriously think that Skye could have hunted down her long-lost father, won his confidence, got him to make a will in her favour and then, what, sabotaged his coracle?' What had started out as a sentence to point out how ludicrous it was to even consider Skye as a suspect ended in forming a fairly convincing plotline. 'You've met her. She's not capable of anything like that.'

Zeta shrugged. 'What do I know? Psychologically, it must be easier to murder a stranger for money, and until last year Skye wasn't even aware that her father existed.'

Chris grabbed the biscuit tin and rammed the lid back on firmly to express her distaste at her friend's reasoning.

'Skye came to me for help, remember? She followed me halfway across Kent to beg me to look for her father. She went to the police and she agreed to be questioned by you, a police officer. Why would she have done all that if she'd murdered her long-lost father for his charming fisherman's cottage?'

Zeta thought for a minute. 'Because without a body it takes seven years for someone to be declared deceased. If you'd murdered someone for their legacy, you'd want to chivvy up the process, make sure the body was found. The more search parties the better.'

'Zeta, you seem to spend your life thinking the worst of everyone. Skye's twenty-five and you've got her marked down as some Machiavellian criminal genius.'

'Look, Chris, I know it's improbable, but I wouldn't be doing my duty if I didn't at least look into it. What's Skye's full name?'

'She changed her surname to Livingstone. So before that she'd have been Skye Atlantis.'

'Sounds like a—'

'Yes, an airline. I've already made that joke. Go ahead if you must, but you're wasting your time. I know Skye's genuine.'

'It's nothing personal,' said Zeta, 'but if you found out about the will, there's the chance that CID could too. What if those neighbours reported that they'd witnessed it? It's best if we're the ones to do the first sweep.'

'Do what you gotta do,' said Chris grudgingly, 'but be discreet. Skye's gone through enough as it is.'

She had intended to tell Zeta about Eric's mad plan to test-launch the ark and to ask her whether, in her capacity as a trained lifeguard, she'd attend as their water safety consultant. But now that Zeta had pointed the finger of suspicion at Skye, everything else seemed trivial by comparison.

Thirty-One

The sky was light blue, and puffy clouds dawdled across it, propelled by a gentle summer breeze. Above, a jet contrailed its way towards… Melbourne, perhaps. The weather forecast suggested it was set fair for the day, with highs of 24°C and a westerly wind of 6mph.

'Bugger,' said Chris, closing the weather app on her phone.

Some sort of freak summer storm had been her last chance of avoiding the inevitable – the ark photoshoot. Even now, she was tempted to chuck a sickie, but that would have gone against her principles. Only two days off in a lifetime of work was a record she was keen to maintain.

At Skinner's Beach quite a crowd had gathered. One of Eric's modest array of talents was his ability to marshal the troops. Chris imagined that in a past age he'd have been in the trenches with a whistle, sending young lads over the top to their doom. As she looked at the ark, rocking on the gentle swell, the analogy felt disturbingly apt.

Most of the Chisellers were there, including two out of the three Daves. An elderly couple were unpacking a picnic, laying out sandwiches, sausage rolls and mini quiches, determined to make a day of it. Another couple had brought folding chairs and a thermos and seemed to be discussing the figurehead.

'I reckon it's a gargoyle.'

'Or it's that hunchback of the opera.'

'What would he have to do with an ark?'

'It's an ark? Perhaps it's Noah then.'

'Or Mrs Noah.'

'If that's what she looked like, I'm not surprised God decided to flood the earth.'

Chris moved swiftly on in case the couple happened to see the likeness. At the shoreline, Alice from *Look Lively* was interviewing Jethro, who was resplendent in naval uniform, complete with an impressive row of medals.

'I didn't realise that Jethro had been in the service,' said Chris to Paulette.

'Two years in the Sea Scouts. And before you ask, no, I don't know where he got that uniform.'

'But Captain Jethro the salty seadog's a good story,' added Libby. 'I had to come up with something to get the camera crew along. Alice!'

Alice concluded her filming and strode over to the group.

'This is Chris. You've already met?' said Libby.

'In a way,' replied Chris.

'I understand you want to roam our vaults?' said Alice. 'Let me know the day and I'll put your name on the door.'

'How about tomorrow at eleven?'

'Fine. I'll tell the dungeon keeper to expect you.'

'Thanks,' said Chris as she fired off a quick text to Skye. 'I think I must have spoken to him on the phone. He wasn't terribly welcoming.'

'He's not used to human interaction, but he does know his way round the archives, so you'll be in safe hands. Are you guys ready to board, only we're due at the Heybourne Canine Beauty Pageant?'

*

Eric was in an ebullient mood. He'd had his hair cut especially and was wearing a yacht club blazer, cravat and nautical cap ensemble. 'I'll go fore with Felix. Paulette and Libby will take the stern. And Christine, you're midships. Don't forget your lifejackets.'

'Look, Eric,' said Chris with a last desperate throw of the dice, 'why doesn't one of the Daves take my place? After all, I've got my figurehead. I don't want to hog all of the glory.'

'Nonsense,' said Eric. 'Besides, the weight distribution has been carefully calculated to ensure optimum stability.'

Chris was on the verge of inquiring how Eric had assessed her weight, but she decided that, on reflection, she'd rather not know. Time to bite the bullet. If she stood facing out to sea on the far side of the ark's cabin, she would be hidden from the camera and the chances of her social-trending in Melbourne would be minimised. Ten minutes and then she'd be back on Rod and heading for home as fast as her battery-assisted pedals could whirl.

As they clambered over the side and took their appointed positions, the ark rocked, demonstrating both its ability to float clear of the seabed and its tenuous stability.

'Everyone ready? Alice, is the camera rolling? Good. I have a short speech.' Eric took three sheets of A4 paper from an inside pocket and cleared his throat.

The first few sentences suggested that Eric's oration would be part self-congratulation and part vilification of the officiousness of the Harbour Day Committee. Chris tried to block out his drone and kept her gaze firmly on the horizon and the golden strip of sand on the edge of the Isle of Lepus. The island was only about three kilometres distant from Skinner's Beach as the seagull flew, or ten times that by road or rail over the girder bridge that connected Lepus to the mainland. In all her years living in this part of North Kent she'd only visited the island three or four times. It was a curious place: a mix of isolated communities, deserted beaches, unspoilt wilderness and three medium-security prisons. She should pay it another visit, make a day of it with Zeta. They could take their bikes on the train, try to circumnavigate the island.

'So, as we have ably demonstrated, our ark is safe and our message for the Harbour Day Committee is: "If the boat floats, you must give us your vote!"'

As Eric finished his lengthy speech, Chris gave an audible groan at his attempt at a rhyming couplet. At least now they could disembark. On balance, she'd rather be walking barefoot along that sandy Lepus beach, which, strangely, seemed to be closer now than when the speech had started.

'Crew, haul us in!' commanded Eric.

Chris turned to see, with alarm, that they were no longer nestling cosily in the shallows off Skinner's Beach but had drifted on the tide.

'Who has charge of the mooring rope?' barked Eric.

'I have, Skipper!' answered Libby and Paulette simultaneously.

'You can't both have an end. One must be tethered on shore.'

Libby and Paulette both presented their rope ends to Eric.

'Oh, f… f… fiddlesticks!'

'We're adrift?' said Chris.

'Perhaps we should abandon…' Despite the rising feeling of panic, everyone patiently waited for Felix to conclude his sentence. '… ship.'

'Abandon the ark?' Eric was outraged by the suggestion. 'There's a thousand man-hours of work in her, there's craftsmanship, there's… community.'

*

Back on shore, the *Look Lively* team were packing up their kit. Alice Buttler sighed. A bunch of delusional geriatrics re-creating a scene from the Old Testament followed by a provincial beauty contest for dogs? This wasn't what she'd dreamt of when she chose TV journalism as a career. Life wasn't fair. If she'd been one of those nepo-babies with family connections in the industry, she'd have had her own primetime series by now and an Emmy within five years. As for Cliffstaple, this place was dead. Nowheresville. Nothing exciting ever happened here.

'Alice, next time your godmother asks for a favour,' said cameraman Connor as he affixed the lens cap to his camera, 'include me out. OK? And what's with that loon who thinks he's the reincarnation of Nelson?' He glanced across at Jethro, who paused in the act of eating a sausage roll to click his heels and present a salute, rendering his sausage roll an irresistible target for a dive-bombing seagull.

'Never again, I promise you. We both deserve better,' said Alice.

Her attention was drawn by the spectators on the beach, who were excitedly pointing out to sea.

'Hang on, Connor. Get the camera back on. Something's happening out there.'

*

What was happening out there was five members of Chisellers' Cabin having a heated debate on board a handmade scale model of Noah's Ark that was becoming ever more distant from the safety of the shore.

'Should we jump?' said Libby, peering over the edge to assess the depth. 'We're wearing lifejackets so we shouldn't drown.'

'And drift who knows where?' replied Paulette. 'Expert advice would be to stay on board.'

'Why don't we just steer the ark back towards Skinner's Beach?' Chris asked the obvious question.

'Steer it? What… with?' said Felix.

'The… whatdyacallit? The tiller?'

'There's no… tiller.'

'You've built a boat without a tiller?' said Chris, horrified.

'No. *We've* built a boat without a tiller,' corrected Eric.

'So what does everyone think? Stay put or jump?' asked Libby.

Chris looked forlornly back towards Skinner's Beach, where people were waving in either concern or encouragement. Occasionally the shouts of 'Jump!' or 'Don't Jump!' carried across the water as if those on board the ark were contestants in a gameshow.

'I think we should put it to a vote,' said Eric.

Chris took out her phone. Zeta would know what to do. She was a trained lifeguard, so this lot would have to take her advice. Zeta didn't pick up the call. Chris tried again. Still no answer. Damn. 'I'm calling the coastguard.'

*

Alice shielded her eyes from the sun. The ark was becoming a speck in the distance. The wind had picked up, defying the weather forecast, and the ark kept appearing and then disappearing on the swell of the sea.

'What are they doing?'

Connor had the benefit of his camera's zoom function. 'Arguing, by the looks of it.'

*

'Coastguard's alerted the Cliffstaple lifeboat. They should be with us within the hour,' announced Chris.

'If we last that long,' said Paulette. 'Look.'

On the starboard side of the ark's hull, water was gushing between the wooden slats. The extra weight was causing the craft to list.

'That's not possible!' wailed Eric. 'Felix applied pitch to the starboard side. It's supposed to be waterproof.'

'No,' replied Felix, who, despite the current crisis, was maintaining his laconic air. 'I pitched the... port side.'

'So who was supposed to pitch the starboard?' demanded Eric.

The four other mariners looked at each other and shrugged.

'Does anyone have another plan?' asked Chris.

*

'Keep filming, Connor. I can smell a Pulitzer,' said Alice. 'Quick piece to camera,' she added.

'Here at Skinner's Beach in Cliffstaple, a tragedy is unfolding. Five intrepid community woodworkers are battling the waves in their homemade ark. Will the lifeboat reach them in time? We can only watch and hope. Thoughts and prayers, ladies and gentlemen, thoughts and prayers. This is Alice Buttler for *Look Lively*.'

She turned to Connor. 'What are they doing now?'

'Trying to bail out,' he said from behind the camera. 'With their shoes.'

*

'This isn't working!' shrieked Paulette. 'It's getting deeper!'

'Of course it's not working,' replied her life-partner. 'You can't bail out with Crocs. I told you to wear wellies.'

A wave lifted the ark and dumped it back down. There was a sickening creak and the wooden planks seemed to shift underfoot. The ark lurched further to the starboard side and Chris had to grasp the rail for balance. She found herself staring into the dark water. Ahead, the sandy shore of Lepus seemed temptingly close.

'Do you think we can swim from here?'

'I don't think we're going to have much… choice,' said Felix. 'She's… breaking… up.'

As if hearing Felix's observation, the ark's groaning boards started to splinter and separate.

'Eric!' shouted Libby. 'You're the skipper, you need to give the order.'

'Order?' said Eric. He was bewildered, frozen into torpidity, like a toddler lost in a shopping centre.

'I'll give the order then,' said Paulette. 'Abandon ship! Women and children… women first!'

Paulette and Libby leapt over the side, into the water. Felix chivalrously waited ten seconds before joining them. Chris paused, looking back at Eric.

'Come on, Eric, we've got to go.'

'I can't leave her,' said Eric sadly. 'It's the law of the sea. The captain can never abandon his post.'

Chris moved towards the prow of the ark. She'd grab Eric and drag his sorry ass overboard if she had to.

There was a thud and the whole ark shuddered, flinging Chris into the air, over the ark's side and into the sea.

*

'She's going down,' said Connor, commentating on the action to the concerned crowd on Skinner's Beach. 'They've abandoned ship. All of them except that busybody fella.'

'Eric? Why, what's he doing?' asked Alice.

'Singing, by the look of it.'

'Piece to camera, Connor.'

Standing with her back to the sea, Alice Buttler smoothed her hair and moistened her lips.

'Oh, the humanity!'

Thirty-Two

Zeta wasn't available to offer her lifesaving skills to the beleaguered ark crew. She was at North Kent Police Station, even though not officially on duty. No one would have queried why she was there in her free time – they would have been too grateful for any assistance – but as it was, the station was eerily quiet. The competing demands of policing both the Heybourne Canine Beauty Pageant and the Bottisham Beer Festival had almost evacuated the building. The likelihood of anyone wandering up to the sole unused office on the seventh floor was minimal. Therefore, the chances of anyone stumbling upon a special constable surreptitiously (and possibly illegally) searching the database for information on Skye Livingstone/Atlantis were equally remote.

Due to budget cuts (and the political expedience of maintaining a visible police presence), efficiencies had been made in backroom staffing. After all, crime-fighting didn't require bureaucrats, box-tickers or paper-pushers. And they certainly couldn't afford internal IT security expertise – which was why the automatic monthly password update system had been turned off and usernames and passwords had remained unchanged for the past two years. Even staff who had long since left the building lived on in the IT system. At some stage someone would notice – probably after a disaster or a data-protection inquiry – and money would be diverted from another budget to bring in some outlandishly expensive consultants at ten times the cost of the station's single, now redundant, cyber-security officer.

Zeta rested a chair against the door. This was not barricading the entrance, which would have been a giveaway that she was up to no good, but was intended to buy her precious seconds. If caught, she'd pretend to be in the middle of an embarrassing and intimate telephone argument with a lover.

She opened her black notebook and found the relevant entry about ten pages from the back. When he had retired the previous year, PC Barry Conway had left his protégée a precious gift – a list of a dozen access codes and corresponding passwords. North Kent Police hadn't merely allowed backdoor access to their most confidential data, they'd left the front door wide open.

She selected a username and suddenly DI Dunn was no longer on a stakeout, investigating cigarette smuggling in Dover, but had (according to the system) just logged on thirty kilometres north, in his former posting, Becketon. Zeta had always fancied being a hacker, sitting in a dark room with a dozen monitors, typing furiously, figuring out the passwords to top-secret sites within three guesses. This was not quite that fantasy made flesh, but it still got the adrenaline pumping.

'Be discreet,' Chris had urged, and Zeta would be. Not just because what she was doing in Room 701 broke all the rules, but also because she was not without empathy for Skye. After all, they were both members of the 'Disappeared Daddy' club, weren't they?

She started with the usual official routes. Ideally she would have Skye's full name and date of birth to focus the search, but she was confident that the country was not heavily populated with Skye Livingstones or Skye Atlantises. It turned out that not only was Skye cute, she was as pure as volcanic mineral water. No criminal record, clean driving licence, no outstanding court orders. Her credit rating was top drawer, her TV licence up to date and council tax paid. Zeta couldn't check her bank account, but there was nothing to suggest financial difficulties or unpaid debts. Even her social media accounts, Instagram and TikTok being the most used, were annoyingly wholesome, full of arty photographs of buildings and playful puppy videos.

Of course, none of this proved that she hadn't plotted to murder her birth father for his legacy, but despicable criminals rarely came out of nowhere. They always had some backstory, even if it was only a police warning for shoplifting a tube of Smarties or appropriating a traffic cone on a drunken night out.

There was just one anomaly. The school records of Skye Estella Atlantis (all the records confirmed her suitably starry middle name) started at age thirteen. Before that, nothing. And, crucially, no birth certificate. Zeta made a note in her black book.

Perhaps that missing information could be cross-referenced from her mother's records. 'Pippa Atlantis' was as unique a name as her daughter's. Her Facebook feed was full of bland motivational memes, and LinkedIn was little used – surprisingly for a one-woman business. As with her daughter, everything seemed in order: self-assessment deadlines met, DVLA record up to date, no bankruptcies, no sign of any shell companies. Boring. But, then again, everything was from the past twenty years. Before that, nothing – no council tax records, no presence on the electoral roll.

Zeta sat back in her chair and fished a tub of homemade salad and a carton of orange juice from her bag. Atlantis. Pippa Atlantis. Nobody was really called that. It must be a stage name, a nom de plume or whatever the appropriate term was for a holistic wellbeing coach. Therefore both Pippa and Skye must have had a previous identity, but what? Perhaps Chris knew.

Her phone showed a notification of two missed calls from Chris. Zeta hadn't noticed it as her ringer was on mute and had merely vibrated in the bottom of her bag. She had figured that her ringtone, the rousing chorus of Katy Perry's 'I Kissed a Girl', would have drawn unwanted attention. The message left on Zeta's voicemail seemed to be an incoherent melange of bird cries, crashing waves, raised voices, and then a single identifiable word: 'Frick!'

Zeta tried to call again, but there was nothing – no ringtone, no straight to voicemail, just a steady high-pitched tone. She decided she'd pop round to Chris's after she'd finished at the station, just to double-check that all was well.

If she couldn't ask Chris, she'd have to ask Skye herself.

'Hi, Skye, it's Zeta.'

'Is there any—'

'No. No news. Sorry. I'm logging an official missing persons report as I understand the police weren't terribly helpful when you tried to do that.' In the Pantone of lies, this was a white one, or rather white with a hint of peach, but she could hardly tell Skye the true purpose of her query.

'Oh, OK.'

Zeta wasn't sure if Skye sounded relieved or disappointed. 'Am I right in thinking that Atlantis isn't your birth name?'

'Um, is this relevant?'

'I wouldn't ask if it wasn't, Skye. It's just for the paperwork.'

'If you're sure?'

'I'm sure.'

'No, it's not my birth name.'

'Which is?'

There was a pause as Skye gathered her breath. 'It's Boggs. B-O-G-G-S.'

Zeta was thankful that Barry had retired. She could imagine him slapping her on the back and guffawing. 'Skye Boggs? Sounds like a khazi on an aeroplane!'

Fortunately, she wasn't afflicted with such a childish sense of humour. 'Thanks, Skye, that's really helpful.'

And it was. Within seconds Zeta pulled up an Isle of Skye birth certificate for Skye Estella Boggs: 'Mother's Name: Penelope Boggs; Father's Name: Unknown.'

There was little else of interest about young Skye. She appeared to have been home-schooled and there were no records of any serious incidents or illnesses. She double-checked on the DBS – no juvenile criminal record. Time to wrap up this session and call in on Chris, thought Zeta. But first, to be thorough, she would just check Skye's mother.

About Penelope 'Pippa' Boggs there was a little more information. Birth certificate registered in Bristol; electoral roll records for the Isle of Skye and, before that, south-east London. Council tax bills, credit history and a now-dissolved company, Pippa's Perfect Gardens, with her as the sole director. Six points on her driving licence for two speeding offences.

What about any criminal record? Was Pippa less than perfect?

Zeta accessed the DBS database again, typed 'Penelope Boggs' into the 'Name' section and 'Pippa' into the 'Also Known As' section and pressed return.

'Shit.'

A red bar flashed up on screen: 'Restricted FG/09/L8R.'

Zeta didn't know what that code meant, but she wasn't going to stop and wonder. It was the kind of code that didn't go unnoticed when someone casually bumped into it. Zeta logged out, removed the plug from the wall socket and, using a wet wipe, cleaned every surface she'd touched.

She exited Room 701, unsure whether she'd ever be able to visit it again.

Thirty-Three

According to local legend, in ancient times the Isle of Lepus was populated by a band of powerful druids who resisted all intruders, inflicting terrible curses upon them. As a consequence, the island was the only part of Kent to remain unconquered by either Roman or Viking invaders. And the legend may have been true; nobody had ever discovered Roman or Viking remains.

In terms of size, it was relatively insignificant: fifteen kilometres long by seven wide. The clay that underpinned London stretched as far as the Isle of Lepus and brought with it a curse of a different kind. The soil was poor for crops, suitable only for sheep farming and wildlife, including, naturally, the hares. The uncultivated land was covered in dense woodland. Nor was the Isle of Lepus any use as a port or even a stopping-off harbour on the route between the continent and the Thames Estuary, as it was surrounded by a shelf which meant that, within a kilometre of the shore, the water was too shallow to accommodate any cargo or trading vessel. It was upon this shelf, no more than a metre and a half deep, that the ark rested.

The Arkonauts stood chest-deep in seawater, looking at each other in bemusement. Behind them, on the prow of the ark and apparently unaware that they had run aground rather than sunk, Eric stood, chest proud, hand thrust against the peak of his cap, singing 'Nearer My God to Thee'.

'Come on, Eric, you're not going down with your ship, we can wade to the shore.'

Eric looked positively crestfallen that his heroic appointment with Davy Jones's locker was the dampest of damp squibs. 'We're all safe then? Let us join hands and offer a prayer of thanks.'

Chris could have offered plenty of silent prayers, but none of them would have been considered Christian. She strode towards the shore, determined not to look back either literally or figuratively.

Her trainers were heavy with water, so she slipped them off and carried them, carefully feeling out the smoothest of the pebbles with the soles of her feet until the seabed became sandy. Seabirds swooped and shrieked above her head. A plan was forming in her mind. Find a train station or, even better, an Uber. Go Directly to Sea View, Do Not Pass Go, Do Not Return to Chisellers' Cabin. Repress this whole hideous incident with wine and self-loathing.

The beach appeared deserted apart from an abstract sculpture fashioned from driftwood. She stopped by a wooden sign planted in the dunes to catch her breath and squelch her sandy feet back into her trainers.

'Hi zere! Are you all right? Ve saw your boat run aground.'

Of all the accents that Chris might have expected, German was low down on the list. The owner of the voice was in his sixties, fit, friendly-looking, and stark-bollock naked. In embarrassment, Chris looked away and up at the sign, which read: 'Lepus Naturist Beach'. She had lived in this area for thirty years and this was the first she'd heard of a naturist beach. It didn't seem proper, not in North Kent.

'Vould you like coffee? Ve haff a Thermos.'

Chris looked back at the speaker, which was a mistake. Why did men embrace naturism at the stage of life when their testicles started to hang low and swing like the weights on a grandfather clock?

'Coffee? No, thank you.'

The man was joined by a woman of a similar age and in a similar state of undress. Clothed, the two would have passed for an attractive, dignified, even handsome couple, but... If God had intended us to be naked, thought Chris, he or she wouldn't have invented Marks and Sparks underwear.

'We have doughnuts too,' said the woman in a rural accent – Norfolk, at a guess. Perhaps the pair were on a naked exchange visit.

'And you are soaking. Ve must get you out of zose vet clothes.'

'Thanks, but I need to escape, I mean, catch a train to… somewhere else.'

'Can ve offer you a lift?' said the man. 'My wife has a vulva.'

'Sorry?'

'Safest cars you can buy,' said the woman. 'She's parked just up top there. We can run you into town and drop you at the station?'

The man and woman were being joined by other naturists rising out of the dunes like a graveyard disgorging a plague of zombies. They might well have been all shapes and sizes, but Chris was doing her damnedest not to look. She would have to act fast. It wasn't just the danger of being engulfed by naked flesh; the *Look Lively* team would be haring round to the Isle of Lepus, the shipwreck being the scoop of the year. Then there were the coastguard and police to consider. Chris had had more than her fair share of fame; she wasn't going to hang around for another helping and she certainly wasn't getting into a Volvo with doughnut-wielding nudists.

'That's very kind, but I'd prefer to… Um, is there a bus stop nearby?'

The Norfolk woman pointed to a path between the dunes. 'Follow that track, take the second left and after ten minutes you'll reach the main road. The bus will stop if you smile and wave, but they're only once an hour, mind.'

Chris took one last glance behind her. Half of the naturists were flocking towards Paulette, Libby, Felix and Eric, who were wading ashore; the other half were staring in fascination at the ark as it started to disintegrate under the force of the waves. She gave a silent cheer as the figurehead detached and floated off; hopefully, next stop Norway.

‘Second left, ten minutes, bus stop. Thank you,’ said Chris, nodding to the couple but avoiding eye contact before she made her escape.

*

Chris was not good with directions even when she was concentrating, but the combination of a near-death experience, two mouthfuls of seawater and exposure to overexposure meant that she somehow missed the second left turning. The path she was following was heading towards the woods and becoming more overgrown, with only a set of tyre tracks distinguishing it from the surrounding scrub. She sought guidance from Google Maps, but her phone was dead. Drowned. Chris cursed. It was an expensive new smartphone, but ‘water-resistant’ obviously didn’t mean resistance to the North Sea. Her insurance covered her for loss, fire and theft – but shipwreck? There was bound to be something in the small print to invalidate any claim.

She turned back, but the path split into three, giving her a sixty-six per cent chance of becoming hopelessly lost. Ahead there was an opening and some kind of building. Chris pressed forwards.

In the clearing was the creator of the tyre tracks, an ancient Land Rover with an attached trailer that was carrying all manner of rubbish from an old fridge-freezer to a broken Ikea wardrobe. The building was a tiny cottage-cum-shack with masking tape covering cracks in the windowpanes and a tree branch growing out of the crumbling chimney stack.

In the front yard stood half a dozen sculptures, similar to the one Chris had seen on the beach when she’d waded ashore. They were made from reclaimed materials but were more eerie than the one outside the artist’s studio in Blekeness. Iron rods had been twisted and deformed into branches or perhaps outstretched arms. Copper wire, green with oxidisation, clutched a yellow flip-flop and a chunk of broken surfboard. Another artwork was a discarded mattress disgorging electrical cables like pampas grass, making Tracey Emin’s bed look positively homely by comparison. Most people would have scoffed or muttered about the sculptures 'not being proper art', but somehow, in those natural surroundings, they spoke to Chris. Understanding what they were saying was another matter.

'Amphitrite!'

Chris spun round to face a man emerging from the shack. At least, she assumed it was a man. He was as wiry as the twisted green copper, had long grey hair and was wearing a tattered and paint-spattered pair of brown overalls. He was probably average height, but the way he bobbed up and down on the toes of his bare feet made it difficult to judge.

'Sorry?'

The man approached, not in a straight line but jigging from side to side, his green eyes wide and unblinking.

'Have you come to reclaim your wares?' he gabbled excitedly.

'I'm a bit lost,' admitted Chris. 'I was looking for a bus stop. My name's Chris. Chris Heron.' She offered a handshake.

The man danced round her outstretched arm and reached for her head. She flinched as he extracted a piece of seaweed from her hair, cradled it lovingly and then threaded it onto a copper wire adjacent to the flip-flop.

'You see, my boat's run aground and my phone's broken and I need to catch a bus to the nearest town,' Chris explained.

The man stared at Chris eye to eye for a full ten seconds. 'For a moment I thought you were... she.'

'She? Who?'

'Amphitrite. The Goddess of the Sea. She brings me gifts and I, in my clumsy human way, try to create meaning from them.'

Oh great, thought Chris. Of all of the woodlands in all the world, I have to stumble into this geezer's. He was clearly a screwdriver short of a toolkit, but the question was whether he was of the 'engagingly eccentric' or the 'raving psycho' variety. In such situations, Chris reverted to her rarely used charm offensive.

'I was admiring your sculptures. They're... remarkable.'

'They are meagre offerings, yet we are bonded by a common enemy.' Once again, the man stared directly into her eyes. 'Have you been sent by them to spy on me again?'

'By who?'

'The monsters who poison our seas and rivers, who lay concrete over our meadows, who destroy our forests.'

'Oh, *them*. No, definitely not. I'm firmly on the side of the rivers and the forests and... all of that lot. I must say it's been lovely meeting you, but I must dash, bus to catch. If you see, um, Amphitrite, do send my love.'

Chris turned to leave, but the man grabbed her wrist tightly. 'Come! Come!'

The man led her into the trees, following a barely visible track, one that had been made by animals rather than ramblers or off-road vehicles. The tree canopy effectively blocked out the sunlight except for the odd shaft.

Of all the dumb things I've done in my life, thought Chris, allowing myself to be at the mercy of the Wildman of the Isle of Lepus has to be in my top five, just behind that three-year gym membership contract.

'These are Wycken Woods, aren't they?' she said, trying to prove that she wasn't really hopelessly lost and vulnerable.

'They are an ancient source of magic and earth power,' said the man, leading them into a clearing. 'Behold!'

'Oh my goodness!' exclaimed Chris.

Thirty-Four

In the clearing stood a soldier.

A four-metre-tall First World War Tommy.

He was in mid-stride, rifle at the ready, staring into the trees. The arms were made from entwined briars and steel cables. His head, complete with determined facial expression, seemed to have been fashioned from dog rose and barbed wire. His uniform, which included a distinctive domed helmet, comprised a patchwork of found materials: a discarded tent, a battered tarpaulin, a torn yacht sail. His rifle had once been a drainpipe, a wooden barrel and part of a propeller from an outboard engine.

'The Wycken Giant,' said Chris in awe. 'He's magnificent!'

'He is nearly finished,' said the man in a hushed, reverential tone, 'my soldier. And when he is ready, he will help me repel the Invaders. Those who seek to destroy these woods.'

'You made this all by yourself?'

'And he must remain a secret. Until he's ready.'

'I promise I won't tell anyone, not even Amphitrite.' Chris bit her lip. More than once, her flippant sense of humour had got her into trouble and this was not the time or the place and, especially, not the audience.

Thankfully, the man laughed, displaying surprisingly white and healthy-looking teeth. 'You can't keep any secrets from Amphitrite – she knows everything!'

Chris no longer felt as scared; cautious rather than terrified. Perhaps this was in recognition of the man's artistic sensitivity or maybe the sentinel soldier was working his magic. 'I know where you can get more wood for your sculpture. Loads of it. A whole ark's worth, in fact.'

*

The drive back down the path took no more than five minutes, but Chris felt sure she'd have still taken many a wrong turn if she'd tried it on foot. The coughing, rattling and clunking of the old Land Rover made conversation impossible, which was just as well. Chris didn't dare say anything that might jeopardise their tenuously amicable relationship. She didn't even ask the man his name. They wouldn't see each other again and she was hardly likely to add him to her embarrassingly short Christmas card list.

They stopped at the crossroads where, an hour before, Chris should have turned left, and got out of the Land Rover. Below, they could see the beach, which was alive with both naked and clothed figures. Alice and Connor were filming interviews, which made Chris thankful she had made her escape.

'Over there.' She pointed to the remains of the ark, still clearly visible above the waves. 'It's not deep. Perhaps you could go salvaging when the people have left.'

The man smiled and was about to respond when there came the shrill sound of a police siren. He ducked down beside the Land Rover and Chris followed suit. The police car sped past and off into the distance, no doubt searching for a path down to the beach.

'I'm not in the mood to answer questions either,' joked Chris, but she noticed that the man was physically quaking, his eyes wide with fear. 'Are you all right?'

The man said a single word – 'Invaders' – got back into his Land Rover and disappeared down the track towards his home, his sculptures and his giant soldier.

*

It took four and a half hours and £18.75 of the sodden emergency £20 note that Chris kept in her phone case to get back home. The 'once an hour' bus never arrived and didn't pass her on her four-mile walk to Lepus Halt train station. By the time she boarded a train to Cliffstaple, (changing at Bottisham), her clothes had dried, or at least had stopped dripping. The happy sight of 15, Sea View had never been more welcome.

Chris fell asleep in the bath. Even the screaming of the washing machine downstairs was not enough to keep her awake. It took the combination of the chill of the water and a hungry Aitken clawing at her most accessible breast to rouse her.

In the kitchen she plugged in her phone to charge it, but it made a disturbing fizzing sound, so she quickly unplugged it and turned to her laptop. An online tip suggested that a waterlogged phone could be rescued by burying it in rice to absorb the moisture. Chris followed the advice and hoped she wouldn't forget it – an iPhone would be an unappetising addition to a seafood paella.

There were three emails from Zeta:

Sorry. Missed your call. Tried to leave message. Will call you later. Zx

Is your phone broken (again)? Made a discovery, can't say any more. Can we meet tonight? Zx

Chris. Saw news report. Are you OK? Please call. Zx

Chris didn't feel up to one of Zeta's interrogations, so she responded with: *I'm fine. My phone's knackered and so am I. Perhaps tomorrow evening? Chris xx*

The only other email of note was from Skye confirming her attendance at the Niven Media Group offices for 11 a.m. the next day. It would be good to have a bit of company for the trip down to the vaults.

By the time Chris had finished her luxury supper of a peanut butter and cucumber sandwich accompanied by two packets of pickled onion Monster Munch, it had gone ten, so the choice was between a bad movie, an early night or a Zoom call with Chloe together with a large vodka and tonic. The latter won – easily.

'Hi, Mum, how's things?'

Chloe was the polar opposite of her mother and was impressively chirpy in the mornings. It usually took a hot shower, three mugs of strong tea and two solid hours of swearing before Chris was prepared to say as much as 'Good morning' to another human being.

'Not bad. Phone's broken, so it may be a few days until I get it fixed or buy a replacement.'

'What is it with you and technology?'

'I know. My laptop hates me as well. Where are my favourite boys?'

'Um, at school, I hope. It's gone nine here. And I'm supposedly working on a sales report and not having a chat with my old mother back in Britain.'

'Agh, sorry. I've lost track of the time and the day of the week again. That's the danger with self-employment, it all melds into one.'

'So what've you been up to today?'

'I visited an al fresco art exhibition.' Which was, technically, true.

'Cool. You've seen the news, I presume?'

Chris took a deep breath. She had deliberately avoided switching on the TV, and with her phone out of action, she was shielded from any pop-up news alerts. 'News?'

'About the Cliffstaple Chisellers' Cabin. It came up on my Kent News feed. Hang on, I'll send you a link.'

With a creeping dread, Chris opened the link in the email and watched the clip from that evening's *Look Lively.* There was coverage from the launch and then, from a distance, the foundering and sinking of the ark. Alice looked suitably ashen-faced in her piece to camera, suggesting that this was a tragedy of epic proportions and only 'thoughts and prayers' could save the intrepid mariners. This was followed by cheerier footage of the plucky survivors being fed coffee and doughnuts on Lepus beach. Certain features of the suppliers of the coffee and doughnuts had been pixelated to avoid offending a teatime TV audience. Finally, there was an 'exclusive' interview with Eric in which he reassured any 'kiddies' watching that there had been no animals on board and then proudly extolled the workmanship and community-spiritedness that had created the ark. Chris couldn't figure out how a leaky boat with no steering which sank on its maiden voyage was an example of expertise, but Eric sounded almost heroic. Perhaps he was angling for Leonardo DiCaprio to portray him in *Cliffstaple Ark – The Movie*.

Crucially, at no point in the five-minute feature was there any indication that she had been present, let alone forming twenty per cent of the ark's crew. Her hiding-from-the-camera technique had triumphed. Chris stifled her sigh of relief lest it be spotted by her ever-observant daughter.

'I owe you an apology,' said Chloe.

'Whatever for?'

'As soon as I saw it was about that ark and those weird woodworkers, I assumed you were involved. Called you all sorts of names.'

'That's understandable. After all, I do have a track record for stupid adventures.'

'And I rather bullied you into getting involved with them in the first place. I thought it was a gentle pastime that would get you out of the house and meeting people.'

'Which it did. No reason to apologise, Chlo.'

'But that Eric chap.'

'What about him?'

'You told me he was an arse. And now I see he is,' said Chloe.

'Since the ark is sunk and my shelf is finished, I have no need to return. There's a new art class starting up at the Parasol Centre next month. I'll sign up for that instead.'

'Good idea, Mum. That sounds like a much safer option. Must dash – work call incoming.'

'Speak soon. Love to all the boys.'

*

In bed, with Aitken on the pillow beside her and Waterman lying across her legs and pinning her to the mattress, Chris opened her laptop and took a last look at the photo from the *Becketon Weekly Bugle*. Without the captions, she would never have recognised

Martin, the infamous Wycken Woods protestor. If tomorrow they were able to track down the original article, would that make any difference? A memento for Skye, perhaps, but Chris doubted it would bring them any closer to their real objective: locating her missing father.

Thirty-Five

Niven Media Group's offices were a stiff cycle uphill, but the view from the top of Cliffstaple Hill was worth the effort. Before her stretched an unbroken panorama of the bay as far as the outskirts of Bottisham to the west and Heybourne-on-Sea to the east. In the near distance lay the Isle of Lepus and beyond that, on the distant horizon, the Essex coast. The view seawards was certainly preferable to that of the offices – a sterile 1990s office block with ample parking space but little character. A building designed for efficiency and cost-effectiveness rather than joy. It wasn't as offensive as Heybourne Shopping Centre; it was just, well, dull.

Skye seemed to disagree. She was patrolling the outside of the building armed with an old-fashioned SLR camera, taking photos from every angle. Perhaps to someone of her tender years, 1990 was vintage-chic. In that case, thought Chris, Skye must regard her as prehistoric.

The reception area was vast, with a long desk that was staffed by a solitary, smiley woman whose name-badge read 'Wilma'.

'Hi, we're expected. Chris Heron and Skye Livingstone to see, um, someone from Archives?'

'That'll be Dessie,' said Wilma, handing over two security passes attached to lanyards.

Chris made a mental note to remember to return the pass. At home she had a drawer full of expired passes attached to an array of lanyards entwined like multicoloured spaghetti. 'Is someone coming to collect us?'

'From Archives?' Wilma gave a snort. 'That'd mean Dessie seeing the daylight! It's against regs, but you'd better find your own way there. Take the lift to the basement and there are some stairs on your left that'll take you down to the sub-basement.'

As Chris and Skye headed for the lifts, Wilma shouted after them, 'And don't worry! Despite appearances, Dessie's mainly harmless!'

*

The basement itself seemed to attract little footfall, being no more than a stark corridor populated by cardboard boxes and abandoned flipcharts. There was movement from behind a disused drinking-water dispenser, but Chris was not in the mood to go rat hunting. As they descended the stairs to the sub-basement, the only illumination was from a red bulb.

'It's like entering a darkroom,' said Skye excitedly, who seemed to be enjoying the experience more than Chris.

The staircase ended in an anonymous door. Chris knocked twice.

'Bugger off!' said a voice from beyond the door.

Chris didn't heed the instruction and opened the door. Skye followed her in. The room was vast and dark, lit by a single desk lamp and the glow from a computer screen. Chris was reminded of the last scene of *Raiders of the Lost Ark* – there were storage racks and filing cabinets that stretched into infinity.

'Which part of "Bugger off!" didn't you understand?' The owner of the voice appeared from out of the gloom. He was short and wide, with thick square glasses, a dark beard and thinning hair, like a fifty-year-old human mole.

'You must be Dessie. Alice Buttler arranged our visit? We want to search for an old copy of the *Becketon Weekly Bugle*.'

'Just cos the upstairs talent says something, doesn't make it so. I've got enough to do without babysitting tourists.'

Dessie shuffled forward and squinted at them both. His magnified eyes lit up when he saw Skye. Chris sighed to herself. Why were men of all ages so easily swayed by unattainable beauty?

'Lovely,' said Dessie, staring at Skye's chest.

'We'd better go,' said Chris to Skye.

'That's a Leica R6.2 if I'm not mistaken. Do you mind if I…'

'Not at all,' said Skye, taking her camera from around her neck and handing it to Dessie, who cradled it as if it were a baby mole.

'Classic. Proper workmanship. Great to see a young woman with such good taste.' He gently handed the camera back to Skye. 'The *Becketon Weekly Bugle*, you say? Got a date?'

'No, sorry,' said Chris. That piece of information had been cut from the photo in Danny Figg's office. 'It'll be from twenty-six or twenty-seven years ago.'

'OK, take a seat at the table there and I'll stick the kettle on. None of the *Bugle*'s been digitised, so you're going to have to wade through the originals.'

Dessie's attitude had been transformed, not by Skye's youthful looks but by the beauty of her comparatively ancient camera.

*

Equipped with two mugs of tea, Chris and Skye methodically searched through copies of the *Bugle*. At five-minute intervals, Dessie returned from the darkest recesses of the vault with more box files to add to the growing pile. Chris had to force herself to focus on finding the article and not get sidetracked by articles on 'new' cycle paths, council elections or the 'Births, Deaths and Marriages' column.

After an hour, Skye shouted 'Got it!' and laid the newspaper across the table to display the double-page 'exclusive' on the capture of the elusive Wycken Woods protestor.

Though the newsprint was aged, the temperature-controlled environment in the sub-basement had kept it in remarkably good condition. The key photo of Martin's arrest was clearer than the framed version in Danny Figg's office. On the left, two male police officers stood either side of the apprehended Martin Livingstone. Behind them, a dozen of Martin's supporters had unfurled a banner.

Skye traced her finger over the photo. 'It's a fabulous shot.'

'Is it?' Chris didn't have that many photos of her own father, but at least they didn't feature him in handcuffs.

'Look, it's a Fibonacci spiral. A perfect composition.' Skye could see that Chris was still baffled. 'I'm an illustrator, so I'm a bit of a geek.'

Her finger traced from her father, in an arc over the group of protestors, before resting on a long-coated figure leaving the frame on the right.

Chris realised that she had never asked Skye what her occupation was. She avoided that question in social situations as some people used it as a shortcut way of categorising others, to ascertain whether they were worth talking to or not. Besides, she was fed up of seeing people's eyes glaze over when she told them she was a freelance proofreader.

'Whoever the photographer was, he knew his stuff,' continued Skye.

'Thank you,' said Dessie, wandering over to the table. 'I'm particularly proud of that one myself.'

'You were the photographer?'

'Twenty years, man and boy, for the *Bugle*. Till they hid me down here.'

'So you knew the reporter?' asked Chris.

'John Dorset. Yeah, top man. I worked with him loads. Old-school reporter, in the days when they went out to find a story rather than sat on their arses and trawled social media posts. The capture of Nutkin was his last scoop before retirement.'

'Do you know how I could get in touch with him?'

'Through a medium, I guess.'

'You mean…?'

'Yep. Last year. Silly sod was trying to fix a leaky gutter and fell off the ladder. Good turnout at his funeral though.'

'That's a shame,' said Chris to Skye. 'This was the first run-in between your father and Danny Figg. That John Dorset may have had some information, perhaps some more photos.'

'Why would you ask a hack for photos?' scoffed Dessie. 'Give me five minutes.'

Within four minutes Dessie had returned with a manila envelope. 'These are from my personal archive. But you're welcome to them, as you have such impeccable judgement,' he said to Skye.

Skye spread the black and white photos across the table. There were a couple of closer shots of Martin and the police officers. Martin looked exhausted, bedraggled and resigned to defeat, his face etched with dirt and despair.

Another shot was of the buoyant protestors holding their 'Save Wycken Woods!' banner – a group of clean-cut young men and women who weren't facing the same prospect of imprisonment and humiliation that awaited their hero. They were probably all bank managers or estate agents by now.

Skye lingered over the final photograph from the envelope. It was almost identical to the photo that had appeared in the *Bugle* but had been taken a few seconds earlier. She placed her finger on the long-coated figure, a slim, upright woman captured just prior to her exit stage left.

'She lied. She lied,' muttered Skye, before turning to look at Chris.

'That's Mum.'

*

The cats had already been fed and the tea was already brewing when, at six o'clock sharp, Zeta knocked on the kitchen door. She took a seat at the table next to Grayson.

'So you survived?' said Zeta.

'Just about. No thanks to those woodworking idiots.'

'If only you had a friend who was a trained lifeguard who could have offered you advice – advice such as "Don't ever put to sea in a homemade boat, you bloody idiot!"'

'If you've just popped in to tell me stuff I already know, this could be a long evening,' said Chris.

'Ticking-off over. I've got a bombshell.'

'So have I.'

'It's about Pippa,' they said simultaneously.

'You first,' said Zeta.

'I did some research into the archives of the *Becketon Weekly Bugle* about the arrest of Martin at Wycken Woods. To cut a long story short, I obtained a previously unpublished photo of the event.'

Zeta nodded her approval of her friend's investigative technique.

'And who else do you reckon was in the photo?' said Chris.

'Pippa Atlantis, I assume. You did say your bombshell was about her.'

'Yeah, that was a bit of a spoiler, wasn't it? Pippa had told Skye that Skye was the result of a drunken one-night stand, that she didn't even know the name of Skye's biological father.'

'So the question is,' said Zeta thoughtfully, 'not only why did she lie, but why has she maintained that lie for more than twenty-five years?'

'That's what I've been trying to figure out all afternoon.' Chris pointed to the evidence chart on the kitchen wall. She had drawn a green circle around Pippa's name and embellished it with four red question marks. 'Was she ashamed of her past? Of being an environmental activist?'

'Maybe she feared being tracked down and arrested?' suggested Zeta.

'But why still keep it a secret? Her daughter would think her a hero, and nobody's interested in a local protest from decades ago. And that doesn't answer why Pippa was so against Skye reuniting with her father.'

'Survivor's guilt?'

Chris pondered this. It was a motive she hadn't considered. 'Because she abandoned Martin? After all, he got prison and she, we assume, got off scot-free?'

'Which brings us to my bombshell.'

Zeta hadn't wanted to drag Chris in, but she had no one else she could share the information with. She trusted James and Barry, but they were connected to the force, and all it would take was one slip, one overheard conversation, one drunken boast.

'You know I was checking out Skye?'

'Yeah?' Chris's hackles rose. She felt almost maternally protective towards Skye.

'Turns out she's clean – annoyingly so.'

Chris's hackles lowered. 'Told you.'

'So while I was in the system, I checked out Pippa Atlantis.'

'And she's not clean?'

'For a start, her real name's Penelope Boggs.'

'Penny Boggs?' Chris laughed. 'Fair's fair. I'd want to keep that secret too.'

'It's worse than that. There's some sort of high-level security block on her records.'

'What does that mean?'

'That someone somewhere wants to keep something secret.'

'What kind of secret?' asked Chris.

'Your guess is as good as mine,' answered Zeta, not strictly truthfully. She had an idea, a theory, but it was not anything shareable without more evidence.

Chris was tempted to open a bottle of wine but felt she needed a clear head to mull over all the possibilities. Instead, she made them a second cup of tea and added a fifth red question mark to Pippa's name on the wall.

'Questions, questions, questions. So what now, Officer?'

Zeta leant so far back in her chair that she nearly tipped over. 'There's only one way we're going to get answers – by confronting Pippa Atlantis ourselves. Fancy going undercover again?'

'The opportunity for more yogic breathing and disgusting tea? How can I say no?'

Zeta got up to leave. 'Before we do anything stupid, are we one hundred per cent sure that it was Pippa in that photo?'

Chris opened her laptop and accessed her email folder. 'Skye sent me scans of the photos. I've only met Pippa once, but it's clearly her, albeit a younger version.'

Zeta looked over her friend's shoulder at the photo. 'Can you zoom in on that section?'

'On Martin Livingstone? You know what he looks like, surely?'

'No, on that group of supporters. Namely the woman front left in the dungarees and the square glasses.'

Chris zoomed in as far as she could whilst still maintaining a reasonable resolution.

The photograph may have been from another era, but that face and those glasses had hardly changed. The current version had accompanied DI Turing and DS Beech in that first CID briefing.

'I've seen her before,' said Zeta, 'and it's not good news.'

Thirty-Six

'So where's the first stop? The lighthouse or the bird sanctuary?' asked Nick as the Fiat 500 cruised into Blekeness at 23mph.

'Um.'

'Yeah, I know, it's that wellbeing freak again, isn't it? What's it this time – is she doing a two-for-one offer?'

'When we can tell you, Nick, you'll be the first to know. I promise.'

'I spend enough of my life worrying about you as it is. You could find danger at a church fete, let alone whatever you and Special Constable Jama have cooked up together this time.'

'I do appreciate you,' said Chris, giving Nick's arm a squeeze and causing him to veer onto the wrong side of the road.

'You appreciate I'm the only one with a car. It'd be nice to be more than a handy lift for once.'

'You are,' said Zeta from the rear seat. 'You're our back-up.'

Nick pulled over to the side of the road, directly opposite the house with the 'Varuna' nameplate. 'Take care.'

'Don't worry,' said Chris, climbing out of the car. 'I'll text you if we need help.'

'Text me? What with?'

Nick had a point. Her phone was still nestling in a Tupperware tub of paella rice, where it would be staying for at least the next forty-eight hours.

'OK, Zeta will text you.'

Chris and Zeta held a council of war on the grass verge.

'What's the plan?' said Chris. 'There is a plan, isn't there?'

'You're going back for another dose of therapy. I'm your friend Lena, who has come along for the ride. Once inside, we tell Pippa that we're investigating Martin's disappearance.'

'And she's going to say, "It's a fair cop, you've got me bang to rights. He's tied up in the attic"?'

'No, she'll deny knowing him, at which point you whip out the incriminating photo from Wycken Woods.'

Chris scratched her chin. 'This plan of yours, Zeta. It sounds an awful lot like the tactic you used with Tony Figg. You remember that one, don't you? The one that nearly got us mauled to death by a mastiff named Daisy?'

'But this time we've got hard evidence – the photo.'

'A photo from twenty-six years ago. I'm not sure how this is going to help us find Martin.'

'We know Pippa is not all she seems. When we prove she's been lying, it'll crack that facade and then who knows what will come flooding out. Besides, have you got a better idea?'

Chris was forced to admit that she hadn't and, apart from having to drink another cup of an undrinkable infusion, what did they have to lose?

*

Pippa opened the door. She wasn't wearing her Japanese pyjamas but a pair of blue jeans and a T-shirt with an Indian floral design. Seeing her for the second time in the flesh, Chris was certain that it was indeed her in the long trench coat at the edge of the photograph. To her credit, she certainly didn't look twenty-six years older; perhaps that tea did have rejuvenating properties after all.

'Chris! Lovely to see you again! And you've brought a friend with you.'

'Yes, this is Lena. I told her all about your wellbeing programme and she wanted to experience it first-hand.'

Pippa ushered them into the sitting room. Apart from an open laptop sitting on the side table, nothing seemed to have been changed from Chris's previous visit.

'Do make yourselves comfortable while I rustle up some tea. Kabusecha was your favourite, if I remember correctly?'

'Oh no, we're fine for tea, thank you,' said Chris hastily. 'We stopped off at Starbucks on the way over and had macchiatos with caramel shots.'

Pippa's head popped back round the door and she smiled broadly. 'Tea's not just for refreshment; it opens our hearts and minds. We can't possibly start a conversation without tea.'

Once Pippa had disappeared, Zeta sprang up from the sofa as though she were a burglar casing the joint. She quickly examined the bookshelves, the ornaments and the pictures, and she even (quietly) opened a couple of drawers.

'What are you looking for?' whispered Chris.

'I don't know. Anything that connects her with Martin,' replied Zeta. She returned to her place on the sofa just before Pippa entered with a tray bearing an ornate teapot and two small handleless cups.

Pippa knelt primly, resting her buttocks on her heels, poured the steaming green liquid into the cups and handed them in turn to Chris and Zeta.

'Are you not having one?' asked Chris, noting that Pippa had not brought a cup for herself.

'Once a month I practise Detarame – twenty-four hours in which the only thing that is allowed to pass my lips is pure water from the Kitaguchi Spring in Fukushima Province. Please, drink.'

Chris decided to forego etiquette and, metaphorically holding her nose, downed the green tea in one. She coughed, willing herself not to involuntarily spray the tea across the room. She glanced across at Zeta and was impressed by her friend's ability to sip the tea without showing any sign of revulsion.

Pippa rose, effortlessly, creaklessly. 'So, Chris, have you been keeping up your breathing exercises? Have you embraced your inner spirit? Is your chi balanced?'

'Well, I certainly feel more enlightened than last time.'

Pippa smiled and lit an incense stick at the feet of the Ganesha statue. The familiar scent of cinnamon, sandalwood and stale alcohol filled the room. 'Do you wish to book the full course or would you prefer to do something together with, um… Lena, wasn't it? I've been told my Tantric Sexual Togetherness course for couples is life-changing.'

'C-c-couples?' stuttered Chris. 'No, we're just—'

'Friends. Just friends,' interrupted Zeta.

'Completely platonic,' said Chris.

'And she's not my type anyway,' added Zeta, rather hurtfully.

'OK, there's Primal Screaming for Beginners? That's usually for groups of six or more – very popular for corporate team-building awaydays – but I'm sure we could adapt it.'

Chris and Zeta shook their heads.

'How can I help you then?' said Pippa as she lit a pair of candles. 'I'm getting a sense that you are both here for another reason.'

'We know your daughter,' said Chris.

'You're friends of Skye's? How lovely. You should have said before! You must tell her to give me a call more often, but you know what young women are like, eh? Such busy lives.'

'You told her that you didn't know who her father was, that she was the result of a one-night stand,' said Zeta.

'I'm not sure what this has to do with my Spiritual Enlightenment programme. Maybe I should give Skye a call to ask whether she's aware that you're here today.' Pippa took a smartphone out of her pocket.

Zeta gestured at Chris and mouthed 'The first photo.'

Chris extracted the photograph of Martin with the police officers and laid it face-up on the carpet at Pippa's feet.

'This picture was taken by the *Becketon Weekly Bugle*'s photographer. That is Skye's biological father, Martin Livingstone,' said Zeta.

Pippa leant forward as though she was touching her toes, picked up the photograph and examined it, frowning. 'He looks vaguely familiar, but it was a long time ago and we were both very drunk.'

Zeta mouthed 'Second photo' at Chris, who handed the group photograph to Pippa.

'And that, on the far right of the picture, is you,' said Zeta.

'Isn't it amazing what they can do nowadays!'

Chris and Zeta looked at each other quizzically.

'With deepfakes,' Pippa said. 'You just can't trust your eyes. I saw one the other day of Prince William using a pair of dolphins as water-skis! If you didn't know better, you'd swear it was genuine.'

'It's not a fake,' said Chris. 'It's the property of the photographer. He will verify its authenticity and he still has the negatives.'

Pippa threw her head back and laughed. 'There's no fooling you, is there, Chris? You're as sharp as a tack. All right, yes, I was there.'

'And so you knew Martin Livingstone.'

'Very briefly, and, as I said, it was a long time ago.'

'So you admit you lied to Skye.'

'A white lie. You're a mother, Chris. Have you never told Chloe a little white lie?'

Chris shifted uneasily. Not just because she'd told Chloe many a white lie (and some Day-Glo technicolour ones as well), but also because she was sure she'd told Pippa her daughter was named Zoe.

'It's not a white lie,' said Zeta sternly. 'This is just the tip of the iceberg, isn't it?'

'Oh dear,' said Pippa, looking disappointed. 'Are you sure I can't interest you in spiritual guidance, Lena? You're transmitting some very negative karma.'

'No. We're looking for the truth and we're not leaving until we get it,' said Zeta, folding her arms in defiance.

Pippa handed the photos back. 'That's a shame. I must say, I thought better of you, Christine Heron.'

She pressed a button on her phone and there was a cacophony of locks clunking and bolts slamming shut. Metal blinds dropped down to cover the windows, plunging the room into semi-darkness, with the only light coming from Pippa's phone screen and the flickering candles.

'And you, Zeta Jama.'

Thirty-Seven

'You've locked us in!' said Zeta.

'With such powers of perception, I can see why they think so highly of you in North Kent Constabulary. Don't you approve of my advanced home security?'

Pippa switched on a desk lamp and directed it at Chris and Zeta's faces, as if they were under interrogation.

'I can get armed assistance within thirty minutes,' said Zeta, reaching into her bag.

'Thirty minutes!' Pippa chuckled. 'I don't think your authority extends that far, *Special* Constable. A pretend police officer calling out a tactical firearms unit to apprehend an unarmed spiritual lifestyle coach? It's a moot point anyway. My home security includes a Faraday cage.'

Chris looked quizzically at Zeta.

'It blocks out radio waves and phone signals,' Zeta explained, withdrawing her empty hand.

'We've brought back-up with us. If we don't check in, they'll spring into action,' warned Chris, squinting into the light.

Pippa pressed a couple of keys on her laptop and turned the screen to face them. On screen was the Fiat 500 on the far side of the road. Pippa zoomed the camera in on Nick in the driving seat. The three women watched as Nick, blissfully unaware that he was being scrutinised, proceeded to pick his nose and examine the contents.

'Spring into action? Looks like he's already been sprung,' remarked Pippa.

Chris felt a tremor of fear shudder through her. I hope Aitken and Waterman are prepared to lend me a few more of their lives, she thought. Zeta was certainly the calmer of the two, or at least that was the impression she was giving.

'What do you want from us?'

'What I want,' said Pippa, 'is for us all to have an open and honest chat. One that doesn't result in either of you two doing anything rash.'

She opened a cabinet and withdrew a bottle and three crystal tumblers. 'Suntory twelve-year-old single malt,' she said, pouring three generous measures. 'One of my many weaknesses.' She pulled up a chair, said 'Chin-chin!' and took a sip.

Chris sniffed the contents of her glass and followed suit, cautiously. The whisky was excellent – smooth, slightly smoky and warming. She nodded to Zeta to indicate it was safe to drink.

'OK, you've got me. I was at that demo, but so what? What are you both – journalists of some sort, I assume?'

'Journalists? No, I'm a proofreader and Lena—'

'I think we can drop the "Lena" pretence now,' said Pippa.

'And Zeta's an online solutions consultant.'

Pippa took another sip. 'And special constable. And you, Chris, are also a blogger.'

'I wouldn't say that. I have a blog, but I haven't updated it for two months,' Chris protested.

'Did you both target my daughter for some kind of scoop?'

That whisky was too good. Before Chris had realised it, she had drained her glass. Pippa topped it up immediately.

'Skye approached us – well, me, actually – to help her find her father.'

'Why you?'

'Because I happen to vaguely know Martin and I've got an accidental reputation for finding people.'

Pippa looked genuinely perplexed. Either that or she was excellent at playing the part. She poured herself another whisky. 'That's your business – finding people?'

'It's not a business. It's something we do for free.'

'It's more of a hobby,' said Zeta, proffering her empty glass.

'And that's what all this is about? You're looking for Skye's father out of the goodness of your hearts?'

'Your daughter is very persuasive,' said Chris.

Pippa picked up the Wycken Woods photo from the floor. 'Has Skye seen this?'

'She's the one who found it,' said Chris. She detected a slight change in Pippa's expression, a slight fracture in her impenetrable self-confidence.

'And you think I know where her father is?'

'Do you?' asked Zeta.

Pippa shook her head slowly. 'I don't know anything about this Martin. I haven't seen or spoken to him for twenty-six years and I certainly don't know where he is now. Have you tried looking up a tree for him?'

There was a pause that felt significant but probably lasted less than a minute. The silence was broken by Zeta placing her glass on a side table with a clunk.

'My turn,' said Zeta. Chris had heard this tone of voice before. Zeta had switched into her 'cop interrogation' mode.

'For a start, you're not Pippa Atlantis. Your real name is Penelope Boggs.'

'It's not a crime to change your name. How would you fancy going through life being named Boggs?' said Pippa defiantly.

'You were part of the group of activists protesting about the Figg development in Wycken Woods.'

'EnviroKent,' Chris interjected, remembering the faded newsletter from Martin's filing cabinet.

'When Martin was arrested, you were already pregnant and you fled to the Isle of Skye. At some point after that you changed your identity and Penelope Boggs effectively disappeared, to be replaced by Pippa Atlantis.'

Pippa nodded. 'Not bad, so far.'

'And all was fine until Skye tracked her father down. You tried to stop her from seeing him, and when that didn't work, you had someone intimidate him. But Martin wouldn't back down, so you framed him and murdered him!'

Chris nearly spat her Japanese single-malt whisky across the batik carpet. This was not part of their agreed playbook.

'Murdered?' said Pippa, back to her calm, smiling self. 'Why would I murder Martin? I mean, he probably owes me a small fortune in child support, but still…'

'It's the Wycken Woods protest. That's the key to all this, isn't it? You weren't just a member of EnviroKent; you'd infiltrated the group, even going as far as nurturing a sexual relationship with one of its leaders.'

'Infiltrated? That's a new one. Who for?' Pippa sounded chirpy, but Chris noted that she'd poured herself a third whisky.

'Special Branch,' said Zeta. 'No! It's not the police, is it? You're MI5!'

'Your friend has quite an imagination,' said Pippa to Chris.

'You're telling me!' agreed Chris.

'Your job was to gather intelligence about the group – how they operated, what sites they were planning to target, how they were financed.' Zeta's attack was gathering pace.

Pippa flinched slightly, which didn't escape either Zeta or Chris's notice.

'That's it, isn't it?' continued Zeta. 'Someone thought EnviroKent were being funded by a hostile power.'

'You could have shared this with me,' Chris whispered in her friend's ear.

'It was only a theory until now,' Zeta whispered back.

'But just as the hammer was brought down on the operation with Martin's arrest, you discovered you were pregnant by him. That wasn't part of the plan, was it? So you and your unborn child got hidden – a new identity, a new life. Martin would never learn who you really were, would never find you and wouldn't ever know he had a daughter. And that worked until your intelligent, inquisitive daughter found him. So you had to do something. You had to get rid of him.'

Zeta sat back and took a sip of whisky, trying to look more self-assured than she felt.

'That sounds like a jolly exciting movie. Probably needs a couple of car chases though. Best of luck with your screenplay, Zeta.'

'It's the truth.'

'I'd suggest that you gather some evidence before you make slanderous accusations.'

'You're on the system, Penelope. I can't access it because, as you say, I'm a pretend police officer. All it needs is for the right questions to be asked by the right people. It was a long time ago. Times change. Those who ordered your infiltration have probably moved on. Perhaps they've retired on a juicy pension or they're now so high up, they're untouchable. I reckon you're probably expendable by now.'

Pippa looked as though she was about to counter Zeta's argument, but instead her shoulders slumped slightly.

Zeta picked up the Wycken Woods group photograph and pointed to the woman with the square glasses. 'Or shall I ask her – she's your handler now, isn't she?'

'You know I can't answer that,' said Pippa.

'But I'm not wrong, am I?'

Chris gulped. Things had taken an unexpected turn. She was locked in a house with a super-spy. I've read enough le Carré to know that this won't turn out well, she thought.

Pippa stood, switched on the main light and paced the room. 'You think you've uncovered a scandal, don't you? What's your motive? To create havoc at the Home Office? Force a few resignations? Maybe you two fantasise about bringing down the government, is that it?'

Chris's head was starting to swim due to the alcohol and the multiple revelations. 'We are just looking for Martin on behalf of Skye. That's all. There's no hidden agenda, no desire to bring anything down.'

Pippa looked at them both in silence.

'Martin was harmless,' Chris continued. 'All he cared about was woodworking and his daughter. Why have him killed?'

Pippa poured them all another whisky. 'We don't assassinate people nowadays – it's surprisingly expensive. And all that paperwork? It'd never get signed off.'

'If you tell us the whole truth, maybe we can piece together what happened to him,' said Zeta.

'OK,' said Pippa, retaking her seat, 'full disclosure, but if a word of this gets out, it won't just be my neck that's on the block.'

Chris and Zeta looked at each other and nodded their agreement.

'Yes, I reported that Skye was in contact with Martin Livingstone. That's my duty. You never fully retire from the service. So they put a couple of field operatives on the case – job experience types from the sound of it – purely to gather intelligence.'

'The Jehovah's Witnesses,' said Chris. 'They followed me as well, didn't they?' She recalled the snogging couple in the Range Rover, blocking the path as she left the Cabin, and Aitken and Waterman acting skittish on her return home. Oh God, they'd even looked in her fridge!

'Yes. That suspects board on your kitchen wall was very useful intelligence, apparently. Filled a few gaps in our knowledge.'

'And the burglary at Martin's house?'

'They went a bit off-piste there. They thought it'd put the shits up Martin if and when he returned home.'

'That's how you knew who we were?' said Zeta.

'Of course. Standard background checks. And then Chris here turned up on my doorstep pretending to want holistic therapy. Sorry, I couldn't resist having a bit of fun with that disgusting tea and those daft breathing exercises.'

'And what about the Figgs?' asked Zeta.

'Who?' said Pippa.

'Danny and Tony. Are they part of the operation?'

'I have honestly no idea who you're talking about,' said Pippa. 'It's really quite simple: Skye tracked down Martin, I reported it, as was my duty, and they put a couple of ops on the case to check the cover story was still watertight. I'm guessing that Martin spotted our agents and scarpered.'

Pippa picked up the empty glasses and returned the half-empty bottle of whisky to the cabinet. 'You see, I'm a nobody, an old bit-player who is stuck out in the desert flogging phoney wellbeing schemes to the gullible. If the powers that be want to cover it up, they will, and if necessary they'll throw me to the lions. I'm as much a victim as anyone.'

'A victim?' said Chris. 'You haven't been so scared that you took to the North Sea in a coracle.'

'Metaphorically, perhaps I did. I had no choice in the matter. They told me where to go, what to do. All my friends and relationships surreptitiously vetted. I haven't had a secret in nearly thirty years. Can you imagine that?'

'It appears we're in something of a Mexican stand-off. You can't keep us here forever,' observed Zeta.

Pippa laughed ruefully. 'No. And I hate houseguests – all that extra laundry. Go on, report it if you must. Skye will have to get used to being without a mother as well as a father.'

'We are here solely for Skye's benefit. If what you are saying is true – that you had nothing to do with Martin's disappearance – then we've no interest in any of the backstory,' said Chris.

'What does my daughter know?'

'Apart from the photo, nothing. She knows that you were at

that protest and she knows Martin's her biological father, that's all.'

'What can I tell her? She'll never forgive me.' And suddenly, shockingly, Pippa's calm facade dissolved into tears.

Chris put her arm around Pippa's shoulders in a gesture of human empathy that surprised Zeta as much as it surprised Chris herself. 'Tell her that you were scared. That you ran away. That your instinct was to protect your daughter and that you've kept it a secret all these years because you were ashamed.'

Pippa looked embarrassed by her outpouring of real emotion and wiped her eyes on her sleeve. 'I really hope Martin is safe. And I really hope you find him. He was a good guy, so passionate about those damned woods. Perhaps if things had been different...'

'Will you unlock the doors and let us go, then,' said Zeta.

'Oh, they're not locked. The departmental budget would only stretch as far as the window blinds, so I had to make do with sound effects.' Pippa gave a weak smile. 'And that Faraday cage stuff – that was a bluff too. You could have phoned out at any time. Ninety per cent of surviving undercover is knowing how to bullshit unashamedly. It's why MI5 recruit from the public school system.'

'And you'll stand down the agents?' asked Chris.

'I'll feed back that there's no longer the threat of exposure,' replied Pippa. 'It doesn't sound like those agents were ready for fieldwork anyway.'

*

Outside, Nick was asleep in the car. Chris tapped on the driver's window to wake him.

'How did it go?' he asked, rubbing the sleep from his eyes. 'Have you both achieved inner serenity?'

'The truth is very liberating, Nick. That's right, isn't it, Zeta?'

'It is.'

'Home?' suggested Nick, switching on the ignition.

'Yes. And a takeaway curry – my treat,' Chris replied.

Thirty-Eight

According to estate agents and home-improvement experts, coffee, fresh flowers and baking bread are the most appealing domestic aromas. Chris reckoned you couldn't beat the smell of a prawn jalfrezi and mutter paneer from the Curry Favour Indian restaurant on Cliffstaple High Street.

Zeta and Nick were sat around the kitchen table feasting on aloo gobi, tarka dhal, bhindi bhaji, chicken tikka masala, Peshwari naan and, naturally, a huge pile of poppadoms. Even Grayson had a plate of his own, together with the lukewarm polythene-wrapped onion salad that usually went straight in the composting bin.

'So what do we think?' said Zeta, ladling dhal onto a hunk of naan bread. 'About Pippa's story?'

'Don't ask me,' said Nick, a tad grumpily. 'You won't even tell me what went on in there.'

'That's for your own safety, Nick. What you don't know can't hurt you,' said Chris. 'And to answer your question, Zeta, I believe her, and not just because she got me half pissed on premium whisky. It's a credible version of events which fits with all the facts we've gathered.'

'And what about Skye?' asked Zeta.

'We leave it to her to sort things out with her mother. I don't see there's any benefit in us wrecking their relationship.'

'So can we...?' Zeta gestured towards the kitchen wall.

Chris nodded, wetted a cloth under the tap and, on tiptoe, rubbed out Pippa's name, question marks and all.

'I'm pleased to see you've finally erased CrEW,' said Nick. 'I assume you've told Zeta my guilty secret?'

Zeta grinned and nodded.

'But before you ask, no, I'm not telling you who the other members are – you'll have to torture me first. And you'll never guess.'

'Paulette and Libby.'

'You're a witch. How could you possibly know?'

'Chris has got supernatural powers, Nick. I'd have thought you'd have realised that by now,' said Zeta. 'Can you settle an argument and tell us what the letters represent?'

'We figured out that "C" must be "Cliffstaple",' said Chris.

'"E" is either "Environmental" or "Ecological",' added Zeta.

'But we're a bit stumped on the "W". "Wise" or "Wellbeing" were our best guesses.'

Nick looked down at his tarka dhal, somewhat embarrassed. '"Warriors",' he muttered. '"Eco-Warriors".'

Chris laughed so loudly that Waterman shot out from under the table in fright. '"Warriors"? You, Libby and Paulette?'

'Wasn't my idea,' said Nick.

'So what about the lowercase "r"? "Recycling"? "Responsibility"?'

'"Retirees"?' suggested Zeta rather unkindly.

'It doesn't stand for anything – like the "S" in Harry S Truman or the "K" in JK Rowling. It was either "CrEW" or "ChEW" and I was outvoted, two to one.'

'OK,' said Zeta, drinking from her bottle of lager, 'CrEW and Pippa Atlantis have been wiped off the evidence wall, so who's left?'

'We've still got the Figgs, Danny and T,' said Chris. 'Did the police ever get anywhere with that death threat? After all, isn't that where all this started?'

Zeta shook her head. 'No, it fell off everyone's priority list. One moment it was "emergency CID briefing", the next it was "move on – doesn't matter". I suspect Danny decided he didn't like the attention after all. That squirrel died in vain.'

'Squirrel?' said Nick, and Waterman stuck his head back round the kitchen door to check one hadn't muscled in on his territory.

'I don't suppose it will hurt to share this with a couple of civilians now,' said Zeta, pulling up the relevant images on her phone.

The first image was of the squashed squirrel. Chris couldn't help but think it looked familiar with that patch of red on its tail, but surely all squirrels were identical, weren't they?

'A squirrel, eh?' she said, pointedly looking at Nick. 'Who'd've thought?'

Nick blushed and concentrated on the contents of his plate.

The next image was of the note: 'You're Next!'

'Bit clichéd, isn't it? Cutting the letters out of a magazine?' said Nick.

'Mind you,' said Chris, 'I may not approve of the sentiment, but ten out of ten for punctuation.'

The final image was of the envelope with the handwritten script: 'To Danny Figg'.

'That's a woman's handwriting,' said Nick, mid-poppadom.

'Are you sure?' asked Zeta.

'I've marked enough sociology exam papers to be able to tell the difference.'

'I agree with Nick,' said Chris. 'We can disregard the death threat. It sent everyone off track but had nothing to do with Martin's disappearance.'

'It was all a pink whale?' said Zeta, having another dig at Chris's artistic ability.

'Absolutely,' said Chris. And now I know who wrote it, she thought, as she wiped the words 'Death Threat' from the wall.

'While we're on the subject, what about the Figgs?' said Nick. 'Chris, you told me they were... what was the phrase? "Nasty pieces of work".'

'According to Sergeant Spurgeon, Danny Figg's got an alibi for the time of Martin's disappearance,' said Zeta, referring to the relevant entry in her little black notebook. 'He was attending a Chopin recital at the Royal Albert Hall.'

'Danny Figg at a Chopin recital?' scoffed Chris. Recalling her encounters with the halitosis-bearing, hard-hat-wearing, dodgy property developer, she found it hard to imagine him appreciating anything more cultural than Chas and Dave.

'He's got the booking form to prove it – apparently.'

'What about his brother then, Tony "Big T" Figg?'

'He seems to have done a runner. Premises vacated, dog abandoned, no sighting since our visit.'

'That sounds suspicious,' said Nick, pushing his empty plate away.

'There's absolutely nothing that ties him to Martin Livingstone. No indication that they so much as met,' said Zeta.

'Rub out the Figgs?' asked Chris.

'Rub 'em out!' said Zeta in a mockney accent.

'The Figg brothers sent the whole investigation down a blind alley.'

'Barking up the wrong tree,' agreed Zeta.

'There's not much left,' noted Nick. 'Just Chisellers' Cabin. Remind me, what was the thinking there?'

'Chris thought that Eric might have sabotaged Martin's coracle in order to assume total control of the woodworking group.'

'I was just covering all the bases,' protested Chris, gathering plates.

'It turns out Eric couldn't even build a seaworthy ark, so I reckon we can rule out him bumping off a woodworking rival.' Zeta used the cloth to wipe 'Chisellers' Cabin' off the wall.

Nick yawned and belched simultaneously, which was quite a neat trick. 'That's it. Everyone's wiped off the wall. Shall we say case closed? I'd better crash. I'm invigilating in Brighton tomorrow.'

Chris sighed and started to load the dishwasher. 'I can't see what else we can do. If someone's done away with Martin, they've covered their tracks too well.'

Zeta stacked the empty food trays and as she deposited them in the bin whispered to Chris, 'And I can't be involved. If I did set off alarm bells with that computer search on Penelope Boggs, I'm going to have to keep a very low profile.'

Nick got up to leave. 'What about the police themselves? When it's a TV drama, it's always a dodgy cop what does it.'

'Ash and Beech?' Zeta smiled. 'Pains in the arse perhaps, but they're too by-the-book to be secret assassins. At least now there's a missing persons report.'

'So we can but hope?' said Chris.

'People can't just disappear off the face of the earth,' said Nick, putting on his coat.

'They can and do, in their thousands,' said Zeta sorrowfully.

'So Martin's just a statistic?' said Nick.

'Not to Skye,' said Chris. 'And not to us.'

*

Nick had left, the curry had been demolished and the tepid onion salad had been consigned to the food-composting bin.

'I think Nick's probably right,' said Chris as the dishwasher chugged into life. 'We've all been chasing mad theories when the sad reality is that Martin accidentally drowned. If he was safe and well, he'd have let Skye know.'

'There are still two suspects we haven't discussed.'

'The Jehovah's Witnesses?' Chris opened the drawer and selected a black pen.

'No, don't write them up. They've already studied your wall once – we don't want to stir that pot again.'

'Means, motive and opportunity?'

'Pippa said they just had a watching brief and I believe her.' Zeta seemed to be having an internal debate, the logical side of her brain fighting her gut instinct. 'But then again, if they were inexperienced agents, they could have got carried away or simply made a mistake.'

I believed Pippa, thought Chris, but she had me wheezing like an asthmatic hamster with those damned nostril-breathing exercises. She looked at Grayson, as though he could help marshal her thoughts. 'Let's say those agents killed Martin, either deliberately or accidentally. Why did they then stage that burglary? Why put the frighteners on someone who's already dead?'

'Good point,' said Zeta. 'I'm happy to discount the Gruesome Twosome. And now, my duvet is calling me.'

'There's one thing I still don't get. What's the connection between the police investigation and MI5?'

'That's easy. CID and uniform have been played – they provided a handy smokescreen. When Martin became CID's prime suspect for the Danny Figg death threat, that would have raised a flag on the system and alerted MI5.'

'The police and MI5 were both interested in Martin but for different reasons?'

'Precisely. And it suited MI5 to get DI Turing and DS Beech to do all the donkeywork on their behalf.'

Chris and Zeta stood shoulder to shoulder and gazed at the kitchen wall. All that was left was Martin Livingstone's name.

'If you want to wipe Martin's name off the wall, I'll help you hang the poster back up,' said Zeta.

'No worries. It's late, I'll do it tomorrow.'

'Sweet dreams.'

'And you, Zeta.'

Thirty-Nine

Sometime in the early hours of the following morning, the combination of premium Japanese whisky, bhindi bhaji and mortal terror had the predictable effect: Chris had a vivid nightmare.

The shopping centre was completely empty. It was closed for the day, staff and shoppers had departed, but Chris couldn't leave until she'd found Chloe. Chloe, a toddler again, had crawled off between the never-ending racks of clothes. Chris was frantically searching, separating the red and black dresses, shouting her daughter's name.

Then she heard his footsteps. He was looking for her. The security cameras all turned and blinked in her direction, revealing her hiding place. She ran for the escalator, but as fast as she climbed, the escalator took her back down. She could hear his footsteps getting closer, boots thumping on the shop floor. The soldier.

She climbed again, but the escalator kept extending, getting higher and higher until she finally reached the top, exhausted, unable to speak, unable to run. The soldier was on the escalator, getting closer. Chris leant back against a shop mannequin that morphed into Grayson and then collapsed, burying her in arms, legs, wigs, sunglasses and brown nylon Y-fronts. As she looked on, paralysed, not able to shout for help, the soldier's head appeared above the top of the escalator. First his helmet, then his barbed-wire hair, then his dog-rose eyes gleaming a fierce red…

Chris half woke in a tangle of bedsheet and cat, stumbled to the loo and then downstairs for a glass of water before staggering back upstairs again to bed and sleep.

She woke again at half eight to the dull thump of a hangover. Just desserts for yesterday's transgressions.

By the bed was an upturned glass. The water had formed a damp patch on the carpet, which she had apparently tried to mop up with her discarded knickers. She half remembered getting up in the night and something about a bad dream, but it was lost in the fog of over-indulgence. Urged on by Aitken and Waterman's empty stomachs, and their tendency to use Chris's own stomach as a trampoline, she threw on her dressing gown.

She was relieved to find that the kitchen was not the scene of carnage she had expected and then recalled that she and Zeta had at least managed to load the dishwasher and seal the rubbish bags. On the table was Zeta's little black book, so Chris tucked it into the drawer and switched the kettle on. Of the many hangover cures Chris had tried over the years, by far the most effective was three consecutive mugs of builder's tea, white, no sugar.

On the kitchen wall only Martin's name remained. During the night another word had appeared below it in Chris's somnambulant handwriting: 'Wycken'. Fragments of that dream resurfaced: the empty shopping centre, the racks of dresses, the escalator, the soldier's relentless approach, his helmet – dirt brown, battered and shaped like… a giant's soup bowl… like an… upturned coracle!

*

The bus from Lepus Halt trundled merrily along the rural road, the branches from the overhanging trees playing percussion on its roof. It was a double-decker, which seemed to Chris to be an extravagance, considering she was one of only five passengers. The other four, a group of pensioners who seemed to be enjoying one of their regular circumnavigations of the Isle of Lepus, were all on the lower deck and kitted out in cagoules. This left the top deck completely vacant for Chris, who took her favourite spot, front right, so she could play at being driver.

Her first thought on deciding that she needed to check out the soldier statue had been to call on the services of her next-door neighbour. The Fiat 500 was not in the drive. Probably just as well, as she'd been exploiting Nick's kindness too frequently of late. Chris recalled him saying he would be invigilating in Brighton. At his usual driving speed, he'd probably arrive there round teatime.

She had briefly considered contacting Zeta, but this was a one-woman job. Any strangers would put the wind up the already skittish sculptor. If that was Martin's coracle doubling as a First World War helmet, she'd need all her soft-diplomacy skills to coax out information regarding how and when it had come into his possession. He'd already fled at the sound of a siren, so if he detected Zeta's inner police officer, it would surely cause him to disappear into the undergrowth.

It was an enjoyable ride, but Chris couldn't get too carried away with the humps and swooping turns of the road as she had to judge when to alight, and from on high the countryside looked very different from just a few days previously. Google Maps would have been useful, but her phone was on the final day of its organic, rice-based drying-out treatment.

Twenty-five minutes into the journey, a familiar strip of white sand hove into view. The beach seemed to be empty, but Chris assumed that all the naturists were hunkered down in the dunes, concealed from upper-deck gawkers. There was no sign of the wreck of the ark; it had either been salvaged or, hopefully, swept far out to sea. She rang the bell, but, contrary to what the naked Norfolk woman had said about the responsiveness of the Lepus bus drivers, this one kept going for a further quarter mile. She thanked the driver anyway, as was the etiquette in this part of the world.

Chris nearly walked past the path as some angry clouds had conspired to block out the sun and the foliage had merged into a dull green. She hadn't looked at the weather forecast before leaving, whereas those cagoule-clad OAPs on the bus clearly had.

She followed the tyre tracks to the clearing with the shack and the sculptures.

‘Hello?’ She certainly didn’t want to creep up on the man unannounced. ‘I hope you don’t mind, I just want to have another look at your fabulous soldier sculpture.’

There was no answer, but in the clearing where there had previously stood six abstract sculptures, there were now seven. The new addition was a Medusa. A banshee with hair made from red rope and discarded fishing net screamed red-lipped at the world. Most horrifying was the head of the monster – Jethro’s hand-crafted likeness of Chris herself. That’s the trouble with balsa wood, she thought. It’s unsinkable. Still, if it couldn’t rest on the bottom of the ocean, here, far away from humanity, was the next best resting place for that figurehead.

‘Hello?’

Still no answer, and no movement from the shack either. Chris wished she’d asked the man’s name – that would be friendlier than ‘Hey, Wildman.’

It was steadily getting darker and Chris thought she heard the distant rumble of thunder. She desperately tried to remember whether it was a good or bad thing to be caught in a wood during a thunderstorm. A solitary tree was bad, and standing on a golf course holding a metal club aloft was simply asking for trouble, but she remembered reading somewhere that a whole forest of trees was OK because the canopy diffused lightning strikes.

She found the narrow path by the side of the shack and picked her way through the brambles until it opened into another clearing. There stood the Wycken Giant with his back to her, slightly stooped, rifle at the ready as though about to advance into the trees. In the gloom he seemed more colossal, more sinister. She shivered, partly from the drop in temperature but also recalling that dream, of being pursued through an empty shopping mall. A spot of rain hit her shoulder. What she wouldn’t have given for one of those cagoules now, rather than the knee-length shorts and T-shirt she had chosen.

As Chris looked up at the soldier’s head, it was silhouetted against the grey clouds. Then, with a *Crack!*, a bolt of lightning provided a flash of illumination. She tried to get a clearer sight of the helmet by listening for the thunder claps and anticipating the arrival of the accompanying lightning. *Flash!...* a glimpse of brown tarpaulin stretched over a frame of... *Flash!...* interwoven branches... *Flash!...* willow branches. She'd been right. There on the soldier's head sat Martin's coracle. There could be no doubt.

She cursed herself for being without a working phone, for not being able to take a picture and instantly send it to Zeta. She should head back to Cliffstaple and gather Zeta and Skye, and perhaps also the whole of North Kent Constabulary. Having found the only solid piece of evidence into Martin's disappearance, there'd be no need for subtlety.

Another rumble of thunder and then the sky opened and emptied its contents in a biblical torrent that would have floated the ark if it hadn't already been broken and adrift on the North Sea. A lightning bolt cracked the sky and then, above the thunder, there came a howl, half human, half beast. From the direction of the shack the foliage started to thrash from side to side as though someone or something was approaching.

Chris looked around in panic. She didn't want to run blindly into the trees, not in this semi-darkness with a tempest raging above her head, but she didn't want to face whatever was closing in. The soldier's left leg was clad in an olive-green tarpaulin, tied loosely with twine. Chris eased herself through a gap in the material and hugged the inner frame of the statue, hoping she would be effectively concealed. The tarpaulin stank of oil and rotten fish, but at least it kept the rain from battering her head.

Through an eyelet, Chris had a partial view of the clearing. After a few seconds, the Wildman appeared. The lightning strobed, giving his movement the effect of stop-frame animation. If on that previous occasion his appearance had been eccentric, the theatre of the storm had dialled it up to deranged. His hair hung lank and wet, and one strap of his overalls had fallen off his shoulder. Another flash of lightning picked out the glint of his green eyes. In his left hand he held a stick – no, a spear, hand-crafted to a fine point, with a jagged barb. He threw his head back and, as the rain blasted his face, he let out a howl, guttural and primal.

He disappeared from view, but above the sound of the rain drumming on the tarpaulin Chris could hear him muttering. Gibberish or an unknown language? Chris couldn't tell. He was circling the sculpture, speaking in tongues. Chris prayed that he wouldn't notice that his soldier was now very generously endowed in the trouser department and dressed to the left.

Wildman reappeared in Chris's sightline, standing with his back to the soldier, arms raised to the heavens. A terrible thought crossed her mind. What if this wasn't an art installation but an effigy, a totem? What if the plan was to set it alight to appease the Wycken gods?

Wildman gave a final howl and headed back through the undergrowth towards his shack. Rather than wait for him to return with a flaming torch that would turn her into a human doner kebab, the most prudent course of action was to get the hell out of there. Chris removed herself from the soldier's trouser leg and took a rough path that went into the woods but, crucially, in the opposite direction to Wildman's clearing.

From under the canopy of the trees, it seemed as though the storm was abating. Or perhaps she was just better sheltered. At least she could finally hear herself think. Chris leant against a tree to catch her breath, recover her senses and consider her options.

Wycken Woods were not big; she'd checked them out on a map of the Isle of Lepus that morning. At an estimate, they weren't much more than three or four kilometres across. In an hour or so she could cut through the woods and exit the other side, find a road and a bus stop and be back at home in time for supper and gin.

*

That was the theory. What had looked straightforward on Google Maps was anything but in practice. Paths petered out, fierce bramble thickets forced detours and, at one point, a brook swollen by the storm caused Chris to make a complete about-turn.

Is that the same tree stump I passed twenty minutes ago? Which side of a tree does moss grow on? What kind of animal made those tracks? Are wolves native to Kent? Time became as muddled as direction. With no watch or phone or even sight of the sun to give her guidance, an hour's stroll became two, three, maybe four? Chris wished she had been given something useful to proofread like *Wilderness Survival for Dummies* rather than a semi-literate potboiler about sex in a high street retail environment.

She sat on a tree stump (the same one she had already passed four times) to rethink her tactics and drink from her flask. Although it was midsummer, the light would not last forever and stumbling around a wood in complete darkness would be irresponsible, even for her.

Head back to the soldier, Chris, she said to herself. Our guy will have calmed down by now – that storm probably sent him a bit doolally. Maybe he'll tell me where he sourced that helmet.

That helmet – the coracle. Martin's coracle. Chris hadn't considered how it could have come into Wildman's possession. Had he found it on the beach? Had Martin made it across from Cliffstaple and abandoned his craft? If so, where was he now?

Chris's clothes were still damp and clung to her body. The sun was setting and the temperature was dropping. A terrible thought struck her as she sat there shivering. What if Martin had made it safely ashore and then, exhausted, had stumbled upon the Wildman's shack. Could Wildman have mistaken Martin for an 'Invader'?

Had Chris unwittingly also become the hunted?

Forty

'It must be in here,' Zeta muttered as she tipped the contents of her rucksack onto the floor of her bedroom and rechecked every one of the now empty pockets.

It was only an ordinary notebook, bound in black leather. In monetary terms it had no value, but in sentimental terms it was priceless. It had been her father's, the one thing she owned that had once belonged to him. It never left her person and she'd never mislaid it before.

'Calm down, Zeta. Think. When did you last use it?' Thankfully, the answer came to her. She'd referred to the notebook the previous evening, in Chris's kitchen, to check Danny Figg's alibi. She grabbed her keys and headed for Sea View.

As a novelty, she tried the front door first, but there was no answer. The door to Chris's back garden was locked, so she pulled herself up onto the brick wall and sat atop it. From this vantage point she could see into the kitchen, but there was no sign of Chris. A scrabble announced the arrival of Aitken on the wall beside her and she spent a minute playfully scratching his ears.

It was late for Chris, who normally fed her cats at six o'clock sharp. Zeta tried Chris's phone again. It rang, which was an improvement, but then went to voicemail.

She returned to the front of the house just as the Fiat 500 was just pulling into next door's drive.

'Looking for Chris?' asked Nick. 'Anything important?'

'No. I think I left my notebook there last night. I'll call back tomorrow.'

'I've got a spare key. I'm sure she wouldn't mind me letting you in to fetch it.'

Zeta shook her head. That sounded like an invasion of Chris's privacy. 'It'll wait.'

'She probably got caught up in that storm. I had to pull off the motorway, the rain was so heavy. Knowing her, she's probably found somewhere warm that serves wine to dry off.'

*

It wasn't warm where Chris was and there was certainly nowhere in the middle of Wycken Woods that dispensed wine.

The evening was closing in, and as the light faded, the woods came alive. Birds frantically twittered, cawed and pecked, a fox barked, and something unidentified chirruped. As with the light, the chances of Chris finding a path out that didn't run slap bang into a raving lunatic with a pointy stick were also fading.

One last go. She left the stump that had been her base for the past few hours and headed north-east-ish (assuming the soldier lay due south of the stump) until she met the brook. Water must flow somewhere, she said to herself. I'll follow the stream and see where it takes me.

She didn't want to get her shoes wet again and risk trench foot, so she tried to follow the brook by sticking closely to its edge. But after only thirty steps, she slipped on a wet, mossy rock and fell backwards into the water. Her clothes had only just dried and getting soaked again was an inconvenience. What was more of an issue was her ankle. It had got wedged between two rocks and twisted at a strange angle. She reached down and felt it. 'Frick!' It hurt – a lot. She tried to stand, but the ankle would not bear her weight and the best she could manage was an inelegant hop.

Half hopping, half crawling and then assisted by a fallen branch that doubled as a makeshift walking stick, Chris returned to the stump. She leant back and, with gritted teeth, eased off her trainer and sock. The light wasn't good enough to see if it was swollen, but it felt swollen and – 'Frickin' frick!' – it really hurt. If she was lucky, it was a bad sprain. If not…

What to do? Calling for help wasn't an option; that would only summon Wildman and his barbed spear. She couldn't expect to be rescued. Nobody knew where she was and she hadn't shared her experiences in Wycken Woods with anyone. Not Chloe, because that would have prompted awkward questions about how exactly she'd got to the Isle of Lepus in the first place, putting her firmly in the frame for that ark misadventure. And not Zeta, because – and this now seemed so stupid – she'd made a promise to keep the soldier statue a secret. Chris took her promises seriously, even if they were with deranged woodsmen.

The woods had become eerily silent. The birds had flown or nested down for the night, the foxes had ceased their mating calls and even the things that chirruped had stop chirruping.

What was that?

Between the trunks of the trees, in the deepening darkness, something had moved. Whatever it was hadn't scampered or scurried; it had stepped so that twigs had cracked and branches rustled. There weren't bears in Britain – were there? There were badgers, but no human had ever been stalked and killed by a badger – had they?

There it was again, now to the left of her position.

Chris recalled a news item about the reintroduction of bison to Kent. They wouldn't let them loose in Wycken Woods to trample unwary hikers or foragers – would they? It hadn't sounded like a bison, but then again, what did bison sound like? Probably like cows with attitude, she concluded.

Crack! There was definitely something moving out there. It seemed to be circling.

Chris crawled as far as a bush. In the dark she couldn't tell what type, but it was thick and thorny. She lay flat on the ground and wriggled, wormlike, the thorns catching and tearing the back of her shirt and shorts, drawing long scratches across her bare flesh. At the centre there was a relatively dry and prickle-free space, by the main stem. Chris sat there with her knees clutched to her chest, her ankle throbbing, and listened and waited.

Wycken Woods. Zeta had suggested that they were the key, the place where all of this had started. Chris shook her head. The pain from her ankle and the thorns sticking into the back of her neck made logical thought impossible. If Wycken Woods were the key, she didn't know who held it, what it unlocked or even where the keyhole was. Had Zeta been there, perhaps she could have worked it out. Mind you, if Zeta had been there, she wouldn't be crouched in the middle of a bush with a busted ankle debating with herself about Kentish bison.

Rustle. Something was close now and moving about the tree stump.

Chris manoeuvred herself carefully to find a gap in the foliage to peer through. She tried to control her breathing, tried not to gasp as another thorn met the inside of her thigh.

Legs. Legs crept past her bush. Human legs, barefooted and trailing a spear behind them. They stopped, and Chris could have reached out to touch the back of that knee. Then, with just the faintest snap of a broken twig, the legs disappeared from view.

Is this what Martin had experienced in his last hours, she wondered? Did he try to run? Did he try to hide? Did he try to use reason or beg for mercy? This was *Lord of the Flies* in real life, with adults instead of schoolboys, and, spoiler alert, no naval officer was coming to rescue her in the end. Was there, somewhere in the depths of Wycken Woods, a clearing with another spear rammed into the ground? A sacrifice to Amphitrite and the ancient woodland gods – Martin Livingstone's head on a stick?

Think positive, Chris. I'm trying, she countered soundlessly. I'm really trying. I've been in worse situations than this and survived, haven't I? She began listing 'Chris Heron's Top Ten Perilous Situations', but that didn't help lighten her mood. This was definitely in the top three.

In her head she sought advice – from Zeta and Chloe; from Nick and Barry; from Aitken, Waterman and Grayson; and, yes, even from Simon and Jan. All was silent. This time she was on her own.

*

Zeta switched on the bedside light and reached for her phone. Nothing in reply to the two voice messages and three texts she'd sent. Chris's phone must still be out of action. Mislaying her precious black notebook troubled Zeta, but not as much as not being able to contact her friend. It was only a day since their meeting, hardly a long time, but, still, a nagging feeling made sleep impossible.

Nick was probably right. Chris was late home because she had stopped somewhere to shelter from the storm. Nobody would want to cycle through that.

Zeta put her phone down and switched off the light.

*

An owl hooted, on its own nocturnal hunt. An animal scampered along a tree branch overhead; a squirrel, most likely. In the darkness, something ran across her foot, a beetle or a spider. That was all right. She could handle insects and arachnids. There it was again, brushing her ankle. What was it? A shrew? A mouse? A rat? Chris prayed that the unidentified creature wouldn't be tempted to take a right turn up the leg of her hiking shorts.

She shifted her position, trying to deter inquisitive beasts and find some respite from the thorns that managed to locate every area of exposed flesh. The thick stem of the bush dug into the small of her back. He must sleep, she reasoned. Even Wildmen must sleep sometime.

She'd wait until first light; her ankle might be better by then. She'd find the road or an early-morning dog walker. That was a plan. All she had to do was survive the night.

*

Zeta tossed and turned in her bed. She tried to summon up happy images to help her drift off to sleep. Happy images like her sitting on the wall scratching Aitken's ear. Looking down at the garden, Chris's kitchen and the bicycle storage bay.

A storage bay that contained Rod, Chris's orange e-bike with its distinctive red-trim wheels.

Zeta sat bolt upright in bed.

Forty-One

It was light enough for Chris to see her feet. Somehow, despite all the discomfort and pain and visits from the local fauna, she'd managed to catch some sleep, her head resting on her knees. She had no idea whether it was just a few minutes or a couple of hours, but she had survived the night and dawn was approaching.

She listened. The dawn chorus was in full voice, an orchestra of blackbirds, thrushes and chaffinches. Did that mean that the danger had passed? Birds didn't hang around singing where there was danger.

Chris slithered out of the bramble, now identifiable as a blackberry bush. As she emerged, she saw, right beside her nose, a footprint, the heel and toes distinct in the fresh mud. He'd come that close to finding her hiding place.

An almost horizontal shaft of sunlight pierced the trees. She dragged herself across to where the sunray met a tree trunk, creating a band of bright yellow, and raised her foot to inspect it. It wasn't pretty. Her ankle was swollen to twice its normal size and was the colour of an expensive full-bodied Burgundy.

By the base of the tree was a branch, probably dislodged by that frisky squirrel the previous night. It was longer than the makeshift walking stick and forked into two at one end, forming a near-perfect crutch. She hobbled over to the tree stump to get her bearings again. In the direction she was facing, perhaps only two hundred metres distant, was the giant soldier statue. Just beyond that lay the cottage and, beyond that, the road. It was worth a try.

Easing herself up onto her makeshift crutch, she set off. After five minutes she could see the effigy of the soldier through the trees. Chris lumbered forward, freezing at every snap of a twig, every squawk of a surprised bird. She peered round a tree at the edge of the clearing. All seemed quiet.

She shuffled over and leant against the soldier's leg that had concealed her the previous day. A droplet of rain that had collected on his coracle helmet fell onto the back of her neck, causing her to start in alarm and land painfully on her dodgy ankle.

Chris listened, counted to one hundred, then left the sanctuary of the soldier's trousers and headed towards the Wildman's cottage. As she approached, the weird statues came into view, casting strange shadows in the early-morning sunlight, and then the cottage itself appeared.

Suddenly there was a shout, a cry, and Chris ducked into a bush to hide, which, as bad luck would have it, was another blackberry bramble. 'Frick!' she said as quietly as she could. From this new vantage point she could just make out the chimney of the cottage, out of which a coil of white smoke was spiralling. Damn. Apparently Wildmen were early risers – that was if they slept at all.

With one escape route now firmly closed, Chris shuffled back past the soldier. 'Shh!' she whispered as she passed him. 'Don't let him know which way I've headed.'

Her new plan, which was, coincidentally, her only plan, was to head north-east to that brook, follow it and hope it led her safely out of Wycken Woods.

*

Zeta leant her bicycle by the front door of 15, Sea View and knocked twice. Thirty seconds later, she shouted through the letterbox. 'Chris! It's Zeta!'

Hardly waiting for an answer, she scooted down the alley, climbed the wall and dropped into the garden. The back door was locked and through the window she could see two cats standing on the table. They yowled at her appearance.

Zeta was knocking on the front door again when the door to Number 17 opened.

'What the f— Oh, it's you, Zeta. Do you know what time it is?' said Nick, dressed in T-shirt and boxer shorts, his bed-hair awry.

'I can't get hold of Chris.'

'It's half-six, you'll wake the neighbourhood. If I'd known that notebook was that important, I'd have looked for it myself.'

'It's not just that. I don't think she made it home last night.'

Nick disappeared, then reappeared a minute later with a set of keys and opened Chris's front door.

'Hello?' Zeta and Nick shouted in unison.

'I'll look upstairs. You check down here,' instructed Zeta.

Upstairs, all the rooms were empty and Chris's bed still had the duvet pulled over it and the pillow plumped. She returned downstairs to find Nick in the kitchen feeding Aitken and Waterman.

'They're starving, poor loves. Chris would never leave them with empty bowls.'

'Her bed's untouched. She obviously didn't come home last night and her bike's in the garden, so she wasn't out on that. Any ideas?'

Nick shook his head. 'I was in Brighton all day yesterday. Didn't see her at all. Should we phone the police?'

'Fat lot of good that'll do. I'll try and get hold of Sergeant Spurgeon when he clocks on at the station. That'll be better than calling 999.'

'On the bright side, I found this in the drawer.' Nick brandished Zeta's notebook, which she took gratefully.

'I assume you've tried calling her.'

'Her phone was kaput, but I'll try it again.'

Zeta called Chris's number and a dull ringing sound emanated from a Tupperware box of rice by the kettle. Nick dug his hand into the rice and, like winning a lucky-dip prize, extracted a smartphone.

'Impressive. It still has some charge left.'

'It's locked, I assume?' said Zeta.

'Yes, but I'm guessing Chris's passcode is her birthday. Bingo!'

'Anything in her calendar?'

'No. And the only missed calls are from you and me.'

'What about her browser history?'

Zeta grabbed the phone so she could look for herself. Chris's last internet search had been the question 'Can donkeys be gay?' Nothing that gave a clue to her current whereabouts.

Zeta sat down at the table. 'Where are you, Chris? And why haven't you hung that picture back up like you said you would?'

She looked up at the kitchen wall, which was blank except for 'The Hunt for Martin Livingstone' written in green ink and underlined in red. Underneath that, written untidily in Chris's handwriting was a new addition: the word 'Wycken'.

'Nick, go get the car keys.'

*

Progress was slow. Slower than a post office queue the week before Christmas. The disadvantage of following the course of the brook was that the ground was uneven and the banks difficult to negotiate with only one good leg and a wobbly tree branch for a crutch. A couple of times Chris had tried a shortcut only to hit one impenetrable barrier or another – a thicket on one occasion, a steep muddy incline on the next. On the third attempt she nearly lost the brook itself.

She counted her steps, promising herself a reward each time she hit her target. One hundred steps: takeaway pizza. Three hundred steps: duvet day. One thousand steps: vodka frenzy. Each fifty steps she had to stop to catch her breath and block out the pain from first her ankle and latterly her armpit, which had been rubbing against the crutch as it supported her weight.

At step four hundred and seventy-three she fancied she heard a dog barking. Then, on the wind, possibly a whistle and human voices. She was tempted to shout out in response, but that would likely have attracted the attention of You Know Who, and to head towards the barking was to risk getting hopelessly lost again. No, she had a plan and was going to stick to it.

*

The Fiat 500 raced over the girder bridge from the mainland and onto the Isle of Lepus. Such was the urgency that at one point on the motorway the speedometer had touched 73mph. In the passenger seat, Zeta studied an Ordnance Survey map that Nick had grabbed before leaving the house.

'It's pretty featureless. I can't see where Chris might have gone, or why.'

Zeta looked at the scanned photos of the Wycken Woods protest on her phone. There was nothing on them to indicate where the arrest of Martin Livingstone had taken place, if indeed that was the location Chris had been seeking.

'Take the next left and there's a car park on the right in a couple of kilometres.'

Zeta phoned the station and left a message for Sgt Spurgeon to phone her back. That was all she could do without any concrete information about where, when or indeed if her friend had gone missing.

There were two other cars in the car park. Fifty metres into the woods, Zeta and Nick encountered the owners, returning from walking their Labradors. Neither of them had seen anyone matching Chris's description or in fact any other human being. It was early, even for the local dog-walking community.

Zeta and Nick walked along the designated path, calling Chris's name continuously. After half an hour the path looped round and they found themselves back at the car park.

'There's another car park on the east side of the woods,' suggested Nick.

'We'll try that,' agreed Zeta, 'and after that, the beach. Someone must have seen her. Chris, you idiot, what have you got yourself into this time?'

*

Chris plodded on. Describing her speed as snail's pace would have insulted the athleticism of molluscs. Her stomach growled with hunger pains, her armpit ached and her left ankle was starting to imitate the right in its ability to inflict teeth-gritting agony on its owner.

The vodka frenzy reward had long been passed and she was approaching the improbable target of two weeks in the Maldives in only five hundred steps' time. Still the brook babbled on, unrestricted by road, railway or any sign of human habitation. Chris loved nature – the rolling hills of the Downs, the formidable peaks of the Scottish Highlands, the desolate landscape and tarns of Cumbria – but in her current frame of mind she'd have tarmacked over the whole fricking lot of them. In future, the only way she would experience the wonders of nature would be American-style – from a golf cart.

The other thing she hated about nature, Chris had decided in the previous two hours, was that it was indistinguishable. Every tree looked like every other, all bushes were identical and don't get her started on grassy knolls. When I rule the world, Chris vowed, flora will be strictly numbered and colour-coded.

Such was Chris's ill-tempered muttering that she nearly missed the fact that, to her left through a gap in the trees, a splash of sunlight seemed to indicate a clearing no more than fifty metres away. A road, perhaps. Or, better still, a car park?

Chris hobbled towards the light, tripped over a tree root and fell head first into the clearing. Hands clawing at the earth, she looked up.

'Oh, no. Oh my God!'

There, towering above her, stood the Wycken Giant. The brook she had followed had taken her in a long circuit back to the very place from which she was trying to escape.

Her eyes scanned the Wycken Giant, from his coracle helmet to his dog-rose-and-barbed-wire head, his yacht-sail tunic, his drainpipe rifle and, finally, his tarpaulin trousers. The trouser legs started to flap in the breeze – except there wasn't so much as a breath of wind.

From behind the giant, the Wildman appeared. Naked to the waist, hair woven with leafy twigs, his face and torso smeared with stripes of blue and green dye. War paint. He advanced, brandishing a barbed spear above his head.

Chris tried to stand, but her arms were too weak to grip the crutch. Her energy was spent. She shuffled backwards on her behind until she could go no further, her back resting against the gnarled bark of a large tree.

The Wildman's eyes glinted green through the face paint and his lips parted in a grin. Chris closed her eyes and felt the kiss of a fallen leaf as it brushed her cheek. She hoped Chloe would forgive her for her ignominious death, her mother ending her days as a trophy on a stick.

There was movement in the branches overhead. A rustling and then more disturbed leaves and twigs dropped onto Chris's face. She opened her eyes in time to see a figure leaping down from above and landing between her and the Wildman of Wycken Woods.

The figure turned. As they stood side by side, it was difficult to tell the leaping man and the Wildman apart: same build, same hair, same age. The new arrival had different eyes though. Brown, sad, kind.

Chris stretched out her right hand towards the man and smiled.

'Martin Livingstone, I presume.'

Forty-Two

'It's not broken, but it's a bad twist. Maybe some ligament damage too.'

Chris winced as Martin's fingers delicately examined her ankle. He was evidently as skilled at dealing with busted joints as he was with saw-cut hands. He gently dabbed iodine on her bramble scratches, which made her wince even more.

Behind them, in the cottage-cum-shack, the Wildman (now identified as Rupert) was making tea.

'What are you doing here, Chris?' Martin seemed bewildered. Understandably so, as, other than Rupert, she was the first human he'd had contact with in three months. Bumping into a casual woodworking acquaintance in an inaccessible part of a remote woodland was strange to say the least.

'I've been looking for you.'

'Why?'

'For your daughter, Skye. She asked me to.'

Martin stiffened, his eyes flitting about, alert to possible danger. 'It's not safe,' he whispered.

Chris patted him on the arm. 'It's OK. You're safe now. Nobody's after you, not any more. I promise.'

Martin's shoulders started to heave and he wept.

Rupert came out of the cottage bearing two mugs of tea and put his arm around his friend to console him.

'They were watching me,' Martin stuttered between sobs. 'They said my past had caught up with me… that now I was putting Skye in danger too.'

'I'm guessing "they" were a young couple wearing dark suits?'

Martin just nodded in response and blew his nose into a dirty cotton handkerchief.

'Some wires got crossed,' said Chris, with another small white lie. 'A misunderstanding that's been sorted.'

'So I can go home?'

'Absolutely.'

Martin shook his head in confusion. 'I still don't understand why…'

'The police thought you'd sent a death threat to Danny Figg.'

'A death threat?' Martin looked horrified. 'Figg is a nature-destroying capitalist pig, but, no, I'd never do anything like that.'

'And you weren't an active member of CrEW?'

'Who?'

'Just confirming what I already knew,' said Chris. 'You don't need to worry about the past; there's a whole new future waiting for you.'

The Wildman of Wycken Woods, wearing an incongruous flowery apron, presented them with a tray of freshly made campfire blackberry muffins. Even if Chris had not been at the point of starvation, these were a work of culinary genius.

Chris nodded in the Wildman's direction as he busied himself augmenting the sculpture featuring her figurehead with her now discarded makeshift crutch. 'You know,' she said to Martin between mouthfuls of delicious muffin, 'I thought he wanted my head on a stick.'

'Rupert? He's harmless. He cares about all living things and that includes humans – even the bad ones.'

'He's pretty scary with his spear and all that chanting and night-time prowling.'

'That's what living out here for years with too little human contact does. You create your own alternate reality.'

Without the veils of fear and suspicion, Martin had become loquacious. Chris had never heard him utter more than a mumbled sentence at the Cabin.

'Anyway,' he added, 'it's not paranoia when they really are out to get you, is it?'

Chris sat with her bandaged ankle propped up on a wooden stool whilst Martin lovingly whittled away, fashioning a pair of crutches from birch branches.

'I assume Rupert campaigned against the development of Wycken Woods with you.'

'More than that,' said Martin. 'He *was* the protest.'

Chris recalled the *Becketon Weekly Bugle* headline. 'He was Nutkin?'

'*We* were Nutkin. It drove the authorities crazy. They never realised there were two of us – we gave them the runaround for months. When the time came to give it up, we agreed that I'd surrender to the police and Rupert would stay behind to look after the woods, in secret.'

'But you got the raw end of the deal. You were sent to prison.'

'A small price to pay. Look at all these beautiful trees. We saved them, Chris. We won.'

And, twenty-five years later, Martin felt he had won again when Skye discovered him. 'It was like a ray of spring sunlight lighting up my life.' Not only did he have a daughter that he never knew existed, but that she was brilliant, kind and, like him, cared about the planet was beyond his wildest dreams.

Another tear appeared in Martin's eye. 'Chris, I never thought I could unconditionally love another human being until I met my daughter.'

'But then the Jehovah's Witnesses appeared?'

'Who?'

'The dark-suited couple?'

Martin nodded. 'I was sure I was being watched. When you've been an activist, you never lose that feeling. Then they confronted me one night, dragged me into their car and told me that I was endangering Skye. That's when I knew I had to leave, to keep her safe.'

'You drew up a new will, making Skye your sole heir.'

'She's all I've got, so why shouldn't she have everything I have? And I thought they'd get me in the end, however far I ran.'

Rather than running, Martin had paddled. In his coracle he had headed for the Isle of Lepus, for Wycken Woods and for Rupert, the only human being apart from his daughter that he truly trusted.

'So Skye's been looking for me? You said that's why you're here.'

'Everyone assumed you were dead, but she never gave up hope.'

'I've put her through hell, haven't I?'

'It's been tough for her,' conceded Chris.

'I couldn't get in touch to let her know I was safe. That would have put her in danger. At least, that's what I thought. At some stage I was planning to send her a message via Rupert.'

The idea that the Wildman of Wycken Woods appearing on the doorstep would reassure anyone made Chris smile.

'There you are. Try these for size.' Martin handed Chris a beautifully crafted pair of crutches.

She tried them out. They were more stylish and sustainable than the ones she'd been issued by Kent Coast Hospital when she'd had that hip replacement. She made a couple of circuits of the clearing and even Rupert applauded and cheered her progress.

'Are you ready to go home?' Chris asked Martin.

'If you're sure Skye's safe and still wants her father in her life.'

There was a rumbling, clunking sound and the three people in the woodland clearing turned their heads towards the track. A white Fiat 500 cautiously navigated the Land Rover ruts and stopped at the entrance. The passenger door flew open and Zeta sprinted across the clearing.

*

It was late afternoon by the time the Fiat 500 trundled down the hill and back into Cliffstaple, now with two additional passengers.

Nick and Zeta had been late to the party. They had explored the woodland paths from the other car park and then walked down to the beach. Nobody there had seen Chris the previous day. Zeta suspected that, as they also seemed to have forgotten their swimming costumes, the beach dwellers were not the most reliable of witnesses. It was on their journey back from the beach that Nick had spotted the narrow rutted track.

On their arrival, Rupert, having been assured that the newcomers were not more 'Invaders', put the kettle on for another brew-up. Zeta called her sergeant with the news that not only had Chris been found safe and well but so had Martin Livingstone. Furthermore, she could prove him innocent of all charges.

While Martin and Chris filled Zeta in on the full story, Rupert gave Nick a guided tour of his sculptures. From the sound of their conversation about symbolism in nature, Nick and Rupert struck up an instant, albeit strangely matched, friendship.

After Martin had gathered his worldly belongings (which amounted to one small backpack), he'd hugged his best and oldest friend for a long time. From that point on, the Wildman of Wycken Woods would have as much of a social network as he desired.

'You know the whole town's been looking for you?' said Nick over his shoulder as they stopped at the traffic lights at the bottom of Cliffstaple Hill.

Martin shrank back into himself and stared out of the window as if bewildered by the sight of buildings, cars and people.

'We'll drop you back at home first,' said Chris from the front seat.

'If they'll have me back there,' muttered Martin.

'Why wouldn't they?' asked Zeta.

'They're all lovely people. Such good neighbours, and I've let them all down,' said Martin. 'They're probably ashamed to know me.'

'I wouldn't be so sure about that,' said Chris as they turned into Gable Terrace.

The road was lined with people who all cheered at the sight of the Fiat 500. Neighbours leant precariously out of their upstairs windows to wave. A police car was parked across the road and beside it stood Sgt Spurgeon, PC Atherton and SC James, all of whom were beaming broadly. On a pair of step ladders were perched Alice and Connor from *Look Lively*, ready to secure another scoop. Outside Number 31 stood Martin's next-door neighbours Glenys and Ken with a pot of tea and a plate of biscuits on a tray.

'How did all these people get to hear about Martin's return so quickly?' asked Chris.

'I'd put my money on PC "Tannoy" Passwater having been in the station when I called Sergeant Spurgeon,' replied Zeta.

Nick pulled up as near to Number 29 as he could manage. Chris got out, aided by her hand-crafted crutches, and moved the seat forward for Zeta to follow. Martin didn't move, dumbfounded by the crowd and frozen by the noise and the attention.

'Come on, Martin,' said Chris gently. 'They're friends. They're here for you.'

She took his hand and helped him from the car. The cheers intensified and were now accompanied by the clamour of pots and pans being rattled by neighbours who had nipped back indoors to raid their kitchen cupboards.

Suddenly the crowd parted and there stood Skye. She ran across the pavement and flung herself on her father as though she would never, ever let go of him again.

Part Three

Forty-Three

Hermon Village was no more.

Over the previous two months the tall, forbidding hoardings had been removed. The sign by the gate had been taken down. The vision of idyllic family life in modular surroundings – a kite-flying, baby-buggy-pushing utopia – had been consigned to the bin. In its place something new had sprung up: 'Figg Eco-Retreats' in green and brown lettering. This promised the 'Ultimate Treetop Getaway Experience' and, to assuage any doubters, it was accompanied by a photograph of a hygienically attractive young couple enjoying a glass of champagne amongst the foliage.

Even with Zeta and Nick as her wingmen, Chris still felt trepidatious as she passed through the security gates. Where previously there had been the Portakabin, temporary toilets and excavators, there was now a picnic area, fire pit and barbecue. The uneven sandy ground littered with bricks had become a bed of bark chippings with paths marked out by tree stumps. And the hole that had nearly swallowed her was no longer visible, replaced by a reception comprising a small cafe and adjoining toilets, all weatherboarded in green to blend in with the surroundings.

A substantial crowd had gathered for the official opening and Chris calculated that she knew twenty-three per cent of them.

'There's the Vice Squad,' said Chris as she waved at Eric and Felix.

Paulette and Libby had also been invited but, understandably, they didn't want to support Danny Figg's latest business venture. Chris had returned to the Cabin as a regular attendee. This was not just to keep her promise to Chloe, though her daughter was pleased that she'd committed to spending more time out of the house and in the company of others. Chris had also concluded that these oddballs, if not exactly friends, were actually decent folk and quite good company to boot. Adversity brought together strange shed-fellows. And she had a project: building a throne for Grayson to seal his head-of-the-table status. That would really piss off Simon.

Somehow, Wilf, Cliffstaple's numero uno lifeguard, had wangled an invite and was busy preening himself before two young waitresses. Laughing, one of the waitresses broke away from Wilf's charisma forcefield and approached Chris's party with a tray bearing flutes of sparkling wine. It was good stuff, delicious, in fact; proper local English domestic champagne that retailed at thirty-five quid a bottle. Their host was pushing the boat out.

Next to the picnic area was a crowd of excited children. The object of their attention was a pair of alpacas. Liz Fyffe-Hermon beckoned Chris over.

'I didn't expect to see you here, of all people,' said Chris.

'A holiday venue next door to my Alpaca Experience? The cross-marketing potential is too good to resist. I do want a discreet word with you, though, Chris.'

'And I, you.'

'Tomorrow at, say, eleven?'

Chris nodded and returned to Zeta and Nick, the latter having already started on his second glass of bubbly.

The local media were well represented, headed up by *Look Lively*, which had sent a young camera crew. Not Alice and Connor; their ground-breaking scoops on 'The Wreck of the Ark' and 'The Search for Martin Livingstone' had catapulted them to the heights of national journalism.

To Chris's surprise, both Skye and Pippa were in attendance, arms linked. Skye spotted her and blew her a kiss and whispered in her mother's ear, presumably explaining who the object of her affection was. Pippa showed no sign of recognising Chris or Zeta, save for an almost indiscernible nod.

Over by a makeshift stage stood the local MP, numerous councillors, a couple of Walruses (though thankfully not Simon or Jan) and the Lord Mayor of Becketon, bedecked in his golden chain like a pink septuagenarian gangsta rapper. Standing among them, laughing uproariously at some doubtlessly feeble joke, was Danny Figg, clad in a Lincoln green suit.

Danny Figg and the lord mayor mounted the stage in front of a vast curtain backdrop that shrouded the copse itself. A hush descended on the audience, punctuated only by an alpaca sneeze and a child's delighted squeal.

The mayor tapped the microphone and cleared his throat. 'It is with great pleasure that I introduce our esteemed host and, if the rumours are to be believed, impending knight of the realm, Mr Daniel Figg.'

Danny Figg bowed to the applause, took the microphone and gestured to the mayor, MP, Walruses and councillors.

'I'm not a politician. I'm a businessman with a sense of history. And I'm also a Man of Kent. Today is an important day for me and my family because today is the day Danny Figg embraces the future.'

At this point, Danny Figg paused and scanned his audience, who obediently applauded. To Chris, it sounded as though Danny had been taking elocution lessons. His aitches were no longer aggressively dropped.

'The future is the leisure industry, with its opportunities for profitable progress. The past is our beautiful Kent countryside, which we must protect at all costs. So how do we remain faithful to both our loves?'

Figg gave a creepy wink that Chris supposed was meant to be cheeky and saucy.

'With eco-tourism. And that's why I'm delighted that you, my friends, are here to endorse this venture. My friends from the council, who have been so accommodating; my friends from the police service, who keep us safe.'

Chris turned in the direction of Danny's gaze. On the outer fringes of the crowd, previously unnoticed, stood DI Turing and DS Beech.

'All of you – loyal friends who have supported me every step of the way. And new friends, here to endorse this ambitious venture. Ladies and gentleman, I give you: Figg Eco-Retreats!'

The curtain fell, revealing the trees. In them, like huge green baubles or, as Nick suggested later, giant gobstoppers, canvas globes hung from the branches on cables. Around each globe, wooden decking housed additional seating and, according to the brochure, a hot tub.

The crowd burst into applause and cheers.

'Wow! They went up quick,' remarked Zeta. 'Pretty impressive.'

Chris felt torn. The trees were all there, present and correct, but their natural beauty had been compromised, like a dog wearing a novelty outfit for social media likes. Still, better than a four-bedroom des res with a double garage, she supposed.

Danny Figg waited for the acclamation to subside. 'But who can I trust to look after this precious area? Who will ensure that our heavy footprints do not harm our flora and fauna? Who will see to it that modern life and the natural world co-exist in harmony? May I present Figg Eco-Retreats' chief ranger, Martin Livingstone!'

The door of the office opened and Martin, in brown park-ranger gear, appeared and waved sheepishly at the crowd.

'Poacher turned gamekeeper,' muttered Nick disapprovingly.

Chris looked towards Skye and Pippa, who were both clapping enthusiastically. Chris didn't know what tale Pippa had spun about the past, nor would she ever ask. Pippa's secret would remain exactly that. The joy on Skye's face at having both a mother and a father made that worthwhile.

*

When the crowd had thinned a little, Chris sidled up to Danny Figg.

'Chris! So good of you to come.'

'I wouldn't have missed it for the world. Surprised to see Martin, though. I'd have put you two down as mortal enemies.'

'Enemies? No, that's all in the past. Green is the future and, after all, I owe him a big favour.'

'A favour? How so?'

'The Wycken Woods protest.'

'But he prevented your development. You lost, he won.'

Danny grinned. 'Couldn't build on them woods. Too near the sea. Flood defences alone would've bankrupted me. When the council bought 'em back off me, they paid three times what I'd paid for 'em in the first place. That set me 'ole business up.'

'I hope you've extended the hand of friendship to Tony as well.'

''Oo?'

'You've not forgotten your twin brother, I hope?'

'T? Of course not! Blood's thicker than water, ain't it?'

Chris looked around. 'I thought he might be here today. I'd like to meet him.'

'T's otherwise occupied. I 'ear 'e's in property now,' said Danny with a wink, before returning to chink glasses with the group of councillors.

*

Chris, Zeta and Nick were sitting on the terrace of one of the eco-pods. The sun was getting lower, bathing them in a delicious warm yellow glow. From this vantage point they had a view over the lush Kent countryside. To the right, Chris could see into Hermon Farm. Liz was leading her alpacas back across the field.

From his backpack Nick produced an unopened bottle of sparkling wine and three glasses.

'I snaffled this from down there. Loads going spare and I reckon Danny Figg owes us a few drinks.'

Chris scoffed at the mention of Danny's name.

'Why did you come here today?' asked Zeta. 'You don't seem to be enjoying it.'

'I don't know,' said Chris, accepting a glass of fizz from Nick. 'Curiosity, I guess. Or closure.'

'I'd like to propose a toast,' said Nick. 'To a happy ending.'

'Is it a happy ending?' asked Chris.

'I reckon so,' said Zeta. 'Martin found and reunited with his daughter, and Hermon Copse saved. I reckon that's a win double.'

Perhaps Danny Figg is a reformed character, thought Chris. A property developer who has learnt to champion the preservation of the environment. If Liz and Martin could work with him, should she bury the hatchet as well?

'Yep,' she said out loud, toasting her friends. 'I guess just because a guy's a businessman, it doesn't necessarily mean he's a gangster as well. After all, trees are better than houses.'

'Hermon Village was a nonstarter anyway,' said Nick casually.

'What?' said Chris and Zeta together.

'That's what I've been told. The whole place is littered with pits and mineshafts, some of them dating back to Roman times and none of them mapped or documented. That's why the development ground to a halt. Figg couldn't build here without the risk of someone's eco-bungalow disappearing down a forgotten iron-ore excavation.'

'So that hole I nearly fell into twice?'

'The same. Light, semi-temporary structures like that reception are OK here, but that's the limit.'

'So Danny Figg's eco-evangelism is just opportunism?' said Chris.

'It's still a happy ending though,' insisted Nick, 'and this time no dead bodies.'

'That's true,' agreed Zeta. 'Apart from the squirrel. You were right and we were wrong, Chris. I thought Martin had been murdered and Nick thought he'd drowned. You were the only one of us who got it right, and you found him and brought him home. That's definitely a happy ending, eh, Chris? Chris...?'

Chris was miles away. She was back at the Hermon Village building site, peering over the edge of that hole at the fresh concrete. That handwritten warning on the side, 'TRIP HAZARD', but with only the first word visible: 'TRIP'... 'TRIP'.

'Are you still with us?' Zeta's voice seemed distant.

'She's gone again,' said Nick. 'She's always doing this.'

Chris opened her eyes. 'I'm an idiot.'

'We were just saying how you got it right.'

'I'm a disgrace to my profession.'

'Sorry?' said Zeta, confused.

'I'm a proofreader who ignores standard punctuation. That message written at the side of the hole. It wasn't "TRIP" as in "TRIP HAZARD". There was a full stop and I missed it.'

'How many glasses of bubbly have you had?' asked Nick.

'Not "TRIP" but "T.RIP".'

'Nope, still not getting you,' said Nick.

'As in "T. Rest In Peace".'

Zeta raised her eyebrows. 'You mean Tony Figg is...'

'... under the Figg Eco-Resort's office, encased in concrete.'

'But... Who?' said Nick, not following this at all.

'When Zeta and I met Tony Figg, he was vowing revenge on his brother, saying he'd got some sort of damning evidence.'

'And Tony Figg's not been seen since,' said Zeta. 'He's even abandoned Daisy.'

'Who?' asked Nick yet again.

'His mastiff,' said Chris. 'It appears that Danny couldn't risk whatever evidence his brother had coming to light, so he had Tony bumped off and, handily, already had a hole available for his unofficial burial.'

Zeta looked doubtful. 'And he wrote a little memorial inscription halfway through interment?'

'That's Danny's style. Couldn't resist a last little joke at the expense of his brother, a final sucker punch. And he wouldn't have anticipated me revisiting the hole before he'd finished the job.'

Zeta nodded, recalling the way in which Tony had brandished that memory stick and offered up dire threats against his brother. 'And all the CCTV so conveniently out of action.'

'When I first met Danny Figg, he told me "I sort out my own problems".'

'And Tony had become a problem,' suggested Zeta.

Chris almost dropped her glass. 'Oh my God!'

'What?'

'Today, I asked Danny about his brother.'

'And?'

'He said T was now "in property".'

The three friends paused, glasses in hand, unwilling to touch another drop of Danny Figg's wine.

'You're police, Zeta. Can't you just get him dug up?' said Nick.

'We can't just excavate on a whim. We need hard evidence. Tony Figg isn't even officially missing, let alone classified as a potential victim of fratricide,' replied Zeta.

'Danny Figg's got away with it again,' said Chris gloomily.

'Maybe he has, maybe he hasn't,' said Zeta, 'but don't start going off on one of your vendettas.'

Below them, businessman, prospective knight of the realm and now probable murderer Danny Figg was posing for photos with the local dignitaries.

Nick shook his head. 'Look at him. He's untouchable.'

'Nobody's untouchable,' Chris replied.

Forty-Four

A warm late summer's morning, a fully charged e-bike battery and the Kent countryside beckoning – could life be any better?

Chris wasn't feeling much joie de vivre as she scooted along the narrow path at the rear of Hermon Hill farm. The previous day's epiphany about Danny Figg had left her in a sour mood. She hadn't slept well, wrestling with this new theory – was it another example of her imagination running wild? – and wondering exactly how far Danny would go to protect his business and reputation.

First thing that morning, she'd cycled over to Heybourne-on-Sea, to Tony Figg's office, in the vain hope that he'd reappeared, back from a world cruise or an extended stay at an anger-management clinic. The office door was still secured with police tape and the explanatory note left by PC Atherton was unopened and unread.

Zeta believed her, didn't she? Then again, Zeta knew there wasn't anything they could do about it even if her theory was correct.

As she cycled round to the front entrance of the farm, there was a steady stream of cars queuing to enter Figg Eco-Retreats, horns hooting, fumes billowing from exhausts. All potential customers adding stock to Danny Figg's gravy train.

Chris tried to block all this from her mind as she pedalled down the long path to the farmhouse and swung round to the kitchen door, where Liz Fyffe-Hermon was waiting with Ernie and Daisy.

'Morning, Chris!' chirped Liz. 'Lovely day for it.'

'Is it?' Chris replied grumpily.

'There's an old friend here who wants to say hello.'

Liz left the dogs and disappeared into a barn at the side of the building. Chris played with Ernie and Daisy until Liz reappeared holding a pair of reins.

'Tiny Barney!' Chris was delighted. 'Oh, sorry, should I call him Lance?'

'No, he's Tiny Barney from now on.'

'You bought him back from the stud?'

'At half the price. He wasn't, how shall I put it, performing. We were all missing him terribly – after all, he's one of the family. It's like he's never been away.'

Chris stroked Tiny Barney's nose and he nuzzled her midriff in response. Cats were best, but miniature donkeys came a close second.

Liz put the kettle on and, somehow, Ernie and Daisy shared the dog bed, though not without considerable sniffling and grunting.

'Who goes first?' asked Liz, putting two mugs of tea and a plate of homemade flapjacks on the table.

'How did yesterday go?'

'Really well. I took three bookings for the Alpaca Experience and the farm shop leaflets went like warm flapjacks. Business is finally looking up, Chris.'

'I'm pleased to hear it. You've made peace with Danny Figg then?'

'Absolutely. You know, he's not so bad once you get to know him.'

Oh, he is, thought Chris. If only you knew.

'So you haven't sent him any more death threats then?'

'Death threats?' Liz furrowed her brow unconvincingly.

'With a complimentary dead squirrel?'

Liz paused, mug in one hand, flapjack in the other. 'How did you know it was me?'

'Blame shoddy education standards. Very few people have such lovely handwriting nowadays. I proofread your farm shop leaflet, remember? So when a friend showed me the envelope that contained the death threat I recognised the handwriting immediately.'

'It was just a silly prank. I was in a fearful bate about being tricked about the planning permission for Hermon Copse.'

'And the squirrel?'

'You don't think I killed it especially? It was roadkill. You haven't told anyone, have you? I can't imagine Mr Figg would see the funny side.'

'As long as you can promise me that no wildlife was harmed.'

'I promise. I only added it at the last minute. Thought it would add a dramatic touch to the note.' Liz gave an embarrassed laugh.

If only Liz knew what a huge amount of precious time and police resources she had wasted with her silly prank. Chris was tempted to say as much, but Liz wasn't to know about the Martin connection and the mistaken conclusions drawn. Now that it was water under the bridge, there was no point in crying over squished rodents.

Chris had ticked the last item off her list of unanswered questions.

'So you wanted to see me?'

Liz slapped a chunky red dog collar on the table.

'It's a dog collar,' observed Chris.

'It's Daisy's dog collar.'

Chris looked across to the dog bed to confirm that Daisy was, indeed, collarless.

'Do you know how it came into her possession?'

Chris thought for a few seconds. 'From her owner, Tony Figg, I guess. When we first met Daisy she was wearing a fetching orange bandana. This collar was a later addition. Why?'

'I took it off to give Daisy a bath and found this hidden in a pocket.' Liz put a small plastic rectangle on the table. 'It's a GPS tracker.'

Chris picked it up and examined it. 'Presumably that tracks Daisy's location, but I don't need to resort to clever tech to tell you she's on the dog bed in your kitchen.'

'But that wasn't all,' said Liz, placing a blue USB alongside the tracker.

Chris couldn't have sworn in court that it was the same one, but it did look identical to the USB that had been brandished at her and Zeta by an angry Tony Figg.

'What's on it?'

'I haven't dared look,' said Liz. 'That's why I wanted to see you, so we could open it together. I needed a witness in case it contains anything, you know, dodgy.'

'Me rather than, say, the police?'

'I trust you more than them, Chris. Plus, to be honest, I am kind of curious about the contents,' said Liz, passing across her laptop.

Chris plugged the USB into the side. A red light glowed on the tip of the stick and there was a brief whirring sound before a text box appeared.

'It's encrypted,' said Chris.

'Oh, shucks!' said Liz, disappointed. 'I didn't think of that.'

'But if it is what I hope it is, Tony wanted it to be found and accessed, so it'll be an easy-to-guess password.'

'Password123?' suggested Liz.

'Even easier than that,' replied Chris, typing 'D a i s y' into the text box.

The USB glowed again and whirred into life. The screen filled with icons of folders.

Chris clicked on one titled 'Accounts' and twenty years of spreadsheets, balance sheets and end-of-year accounts appeared, all under various company names: Danny Figg Homes, Danny Figg Holdings, DF Funds Inc., DF Investments (Cayman) and many, many more. Chris could not tell one end of a balance sheet from another, but she was pretty sure that HMRC and the Serious Fraud Office could.

Another folder titled 'Audio' contained dozens of recorded conversations. Chris and Liz listened to two minutes of one that seemed to be a phone conversation between Danny Figg and someone referred to as Councillor Ridley about accelerating planning permission and whether said councillor was enjoying his new Lexus. Chris couldn't imagine that Tony had the guile to tap his brother's phone; presumably Danny had wanted some insurance and recorded them himself. Somehow they had come into Tony's possession.

A folder simply named 'Video' had footage of clandestine meetings at motorway service stations. Another named 'Texts' had thousands of private texts and WhatsApp messages.

'Deus ex machina,' muttered Chris to herself.

'What did you say?' asked Liz.

'Have you got a spare memory stick?'

It took Chris an hour to copy the contents onto the laptop and then back onto a spare USB, just in case the precious contents should go missing.

'Do you know what we should do with it?' asked Liz nervously.

'I know a special constable who will,' Chris replied.

'All those files – what are they?'

'Daisy, old girl?' called Chris, and Daisy rose from her bed and plodded over to sit at her feet. Chris patted her flank. 'Come and have a look at your daddy's handiwork.'

With no little effort, she lifted the mastiff onto her lap so that Daisy's nose was almost touching the screen.

'This, my darling, is payback.'

Printed in Dunstable, United Kingdom

66787356R00180